The characters in this novel are based on real persons and events surrounding the culmination of George Armstrong Custer's controversial career. Pictured in happier times, the flamboyant and enigmatic Custer was ever the center of attention. A Major General of Volunteers at the age of 23, he was a daring and reckless combat commander—the "beau ideal" of the U.S. Cavalry and the nation. Eleven years after this picture was taken, Custer, sometimes called "Son of the Morning Star," would achieve his permanent niche in history on a river the Sioux called Greasy Grass but which is known to this day as the Little Bighorn. Photograph by Matthew Brady.

A ROAD WE DO NOT KNOW

*A Novel of Custer
at the
Little Bighorn*

Frederick J. Chiaventone

Simon & Schuster

Simon & Schuster
Rockefeller Center
1230 Avenue of the Americas
New York, NY 10020

Simon & Schuster and colophon are registered trademarks
of Simon & Schuster, Inc.

Designed by Edith Fowler

Manufactured in the United States of America

10 9 8 7 6 5 4 3 2 1

Library of Congress Cataloging-In-Publication Data
Chiaventone, Frederick J., date.
        A road we do not know : a novel of Custer at the
Little Bighorn / Frederick J. Chiaventone.
        p.   cm.
        1. Little Bighorn, Battle of the, Mont., 1876—
Fiction.   2. Indians of North America—Wars—
1866-1895—Fiction.   3. Custer, George
Armstrong, 1839-1876—Fiction.   4. Dakota
Indians—Wars, 1876—Fiction.   I. Title.
PS3553.H472R6   1996
813'.54—dc20   96-26015   CIP
ISBN 0-7432-4179-7

For information regarding the special discounts for bulk purchases, please contact Simon &
Schuster Special Sales at 1-800-456-6798 or business@simonandschuster.com

ACKNOWLEDGMENTS

I don't believe that any work of fiction is properly the result of solitary labor. Thus there are a great many people to whom I am greatly indebted. First and foremost, I wish to thank my wife, Sharon Reeber, artist, linguist, companion, and a beautiful woman to boot. Even though she was great with child while this book was in progress, she was an insightful first reader and ruthless editor and critic. I could not have done it without her.

Thanks also to my close friends in Weston and environs who encouraged me throughout, of whom special mention must be given the lovely and talented Celtic chanteuse, Connie Dover, who read my material, edited and critiqued it, and made invaluable suggestions in return for which I got to listen to her try out songs for her new album—I think I got the better end of the deal; Mr. George Nelson, mule skinner, packer, trail guide, and one hell of a horseman; Roger Landes, for provision of some great reference works; and Mr. Kirk Lynch, America's foremost crafter of the enchanting Irish Uilleann pipes (and a brilliant player), who drank coffee with me every morning as I puzzled over the next scene or agonized over the previous. Thanks also to M. R. Peck, avid reader and insightful critic. And to Dr. Linda Faris, D.V.M., and Dr. Jim McCrea, D.V.M., for their assistance on the behavior of horses and mules.

At Fort Leavenworth, my last duty station and alma mater, a special "hats off" to "the Lost Boys," who encouraged me in my work and convened regularly at the High Noon Saloon to discuss history, politics, and literature. They include: Dr. Roger Spiller, George C. Marshall Professor at the U.S. Army's Command and General Staff College and associate editor of *American Heritage* magazine, mentor and friend; Lieutenant Colonel Jeff Prater, USAF, close friend and a fine historian, and to his wife Dana, a superb historian in her own right; and Dr. Sam Lewis, friend and confidant. Also, Dr. Jerry Brown, friend, and originator of the Sioux Wars Staff Ride program and my editor in chief for the *Historical Dictionary of the United States Army*; and, of course Lieutenant Colonel D. K. Clark

(U.S. Army, retired), my bunky at the BOQ when we were still second lieutenants, and a tireless researcher of the Indian Wars period. D.K.'s work on the Seventh Cavalry's command and control is some of the best ever done. Thanks also to "the girls" at the Combined Arms Research Library—Pat, Diane, and Carol, who let me run amuck in the stacks and original records. Thanks also to George, Steve, and Rich—the staff of the Frontier Army Museum at Fort Leavenworth, Kansas.

A special thanks also to Harry Coyle, old colleague and friend from our Staff College days who took the time to read my stuff and yak over lunch while still struggling with his own book on the battle of Petersburg. Harry encouraged me to keep writing and then slipped a copy of my stuff to Simon & Schuster. Without his aid, counsel, and encouragement, it would never have gotten this far. Other invaluable assistance came from: Dr. Douglas Scott of the National Park Service, who led the forensic team at the Little Bighorn, listened patiently to my theories, and provided invaluable insight into the physical evidence of the fight; Arthur Shortbull, great-great-grandson of the Oglala *wicasa wakan* Short Bull, for insights into the Lakota lifestyle and language; Howard Boggess (Little-Old-White-Man), great-nephew of Crow scout Curley, for sharing his wealth of information on Plains Indian culture; to Kelly Johnson for her help with Lakota cooking, beadwork, and language resources; to Rhett Johnson for access to his collection of Native American artifacts; and to Jackie Ahlstrom for her assistance with clothing. Not to be forgotten are my brilliant and talented editors at Simon & Schuster, Paul McCarthy and Michael Korda, who took a special interest in this work and allowed me remarkable license. Any errors of fact that remain despite their best efforts are entirely my own responsibility.

Thanks also to my mom who, when my brother Mike and I were kids, allowed us to stay up late once to watch Errol Flynn play George Custer in *They Died with Their Boots On.* And finally, a special nod to my great-great-grandfather, Private Barney Townley, Company D, Fiftieth Wisconsin Volunteer Infantry, who signed up to fight in the Civil War but instead wound up in a fight with the Sioux at Fort Rice, Dakota Territory, in September of 1865. Ultimately luckier than George Custer, Barney Townley eventually mustered out and returned to his home and family.

FREDERICK J. CHIAVENTONE
Weston, Missouri
1996

For
Sean, Owen, and Dad
(Alfredo Luigi Chiaventone, Conte di Castel Vecchia)—
your American Dreams came true.

CONTENTS

PART THREE

"A GOOD DAY TO DIE!"
Collision

PART FOUR

"THE DARKNESS OF THEIR EYES"
Abeyance

AFTERWARD
"WALKING THE BLACK ROAD"
Recessional

AUTHOR'S NOTE

In the past 120 years there has been so much written about the battle of the Little Bighorn that it might seem that all has been said that can or needs to be said. Yet every year more material appears in the form of articles, paintings, books, film, and television. Despite the plethora of words written and spoken about the drama that unfolded on those barren Montana hills in 1876, the saga of the Little Bighorn continues to exert a horrible fascination on the imagination of the public.

Like many Americans, I was first exposed to the myth of the Last Stand as rendered by Hollywood. For me it was a dashing Errol Flynn playing the ill-fated George Armstrong Custer. Custer and his men "died with their boots on," much to my fascination and that of my younger brother Mike. Our Mom had allowed us to stay up late one night to watch the legend unfold and it took immediate hold on our imaginations. Many years later, after a full career as a cavalry officer, I found myself, like so many others, still fascinated by the myth. I had even, while traveling cross-country between assignments, plotted my route to take me through the Crow Agency, where I could stand on Last Stand Hill and listen to the mournful sound of the wind in the buffalo grass.

A few years ago, while teaching at the Army's Command and General Staff College, I was fortunate enough to be afforded a chance to revisit the site of the battle along with a number of senior military officers for a more in-depth look at the campaign. The colonels and generals on this Staff Ride, all veterans of Vietnam or the Gulf War, were given only that information which was available to Custer and his officers on 25 June 1876 and asked to explain what they would have done in Custer's place. Much to my surprise, and theirs, all of these combat veterans made precisely the same tactical decisions as had the ill-fated commander of the Seventh Cavalry. As we walked over the terrain and discussed the events that had transpired on that distant summer, I found myself looking at those events from a different perspective.

With renewed interest I embarked on a project to research the battle, and its participants, more thoroughly. This book is the result of that research. In addition to the usual secondary sources, I have consulted the official records of the campaign, the journals, letters, and reminiscences of the Army participants as well as transcripts of interviews with many of the Native Americans who witnessed or took part in the fight. In reconstructing the battle I also tried to recognize the fragile and tenuous nature of memory. I have thus tried to balance the testimony of the participants against the most recent forensic analysis of physical evidence and temper all with my own experience of command and of soldiers under stress.

A Road We Do Not Know is rather a different approach to the battle of the Little Bighorn. The characters who usually assume so much prominence in most of the literature—George Custer, Sitting Bull, and Crazy Horse—are in this work almost secondary. Instead, the real focus of this book is the experience of battle as seen from the perspective of ordinary men (and women) drawn into circumstances beyond their control. I have also tried to give the reader some sense of the various motivations that drew men into the frontier Army or, in the case of Native Americans, led them to resist the seemingly irresistible advance of white civilization. If the reader is looking for glowing accounts of glorious charges and counterattacks, he will be disappointed. There is, in truth, nothing glorious about combat. It is dirty, heartbreaking work. Those who experience it and survive are seldom the same afterward. Thus this is more a story of uncertainty, fear, desperation, and individual survival. Where I have taken some license with a few of the characters, it is solely to convey to the reader a more intimate feel for the environment. I trust that my more informed readers will forgive these few alterations to history. While this is, first and foremost, a work of fiction, I have tried to make it as accurate as possible. Finally I should note that, whatever else it might be, this book is not a morality play. The reader will find no heroes or villains here. The characters in this book are only human beings, each doing what he feels he must do in the frightening and dangerous environment that results when cultures clash. Like them, we are all traveling down a road we do not know.

PART ONE
"Look for Worms . . ."

APPROACH

Q: State your name, rank, regiment and where serving.

A: Charles A. Varnum, First Lieutenant and Quartermaster, 7th Cavalry, serving at Fort Abraham Lincoln, Dakota Territory.

Q: On what duty were you on the 25th and 26th of June 1876 and with what command?

A: I was Second Lieutenant, 7th Cavalry at that time in command of a detachment of Indian scouts, with the 7th Cavalry under General Custer. . . .

Q: At that time what were the indications if any of the proximity of hostile Indians?

A: I was not on the trail exactly on the morning of the 25th, but was detached scouting. The indications were the statements of our Indians that they could see the village.

Statement of Lieutenant Charles Varnum, 7th U.S. Cavalry
(Extract from Official Records, Court of Inquiry
Convened 13 January 1879 at Chicago, Illinois)

Several of us boys watched our horses until the sun was straight above and it was getting very hot. Then we thought we would go swimming, and my cousin said he would stay with our horses 'til we got back. When I was greasing myself, I did not feel well; I felt queer. It seemed that something terrible was going to happen.

Statement of Black Elk, Oglala Sioux

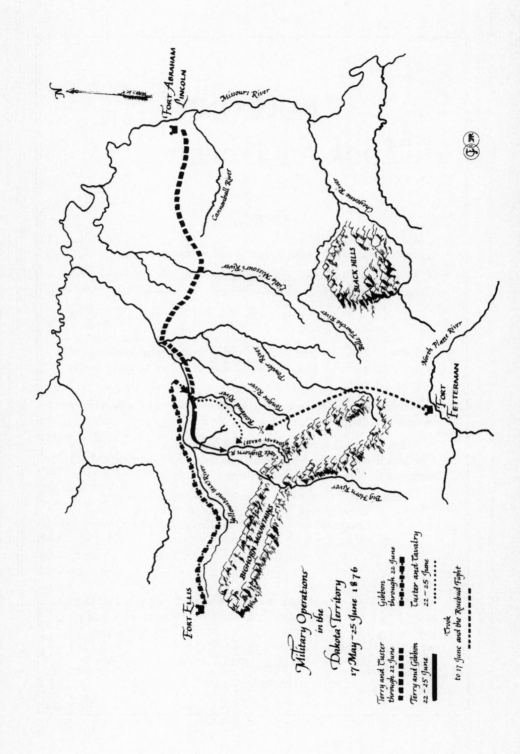

Military Operations in the Dakota Territory 17 May – 25 June 1876

Terry and Custer through 22 June

Terry and Gibbon 22 – 25 June

Gibbon through 22 June

Custer and Cavalry 22 – 25 June

Crook to 17 June and the Rosebud Fight

Sunday, 25 June 1876, 0200 Hours
Somewhere in the Dakota Territory

The slow, arrhythmic clicking of the horses' hooves was the only sound that registered in Lieutenant Charles Varnum's groggy mind as his small detachment worked its way slowly down the rock-strewn defile. They had been moving forward steadily since nine o'clock the night before, and it was now nearly 2 A.M. The scouts had put in a hard fifty miles yesterday and had hardly stopped since. The brief rest of the previous evening had been just that, brief, and the young cavalry officer was now close to exhaustion.

Ahead and behind him stretched a narrow file of Indian scouts, most of them Arikaras, also called Rees, the rest a small party of Crows. Lieutenant Varnum found the Rees to be somewhat flighty and excitable, with a tendency to exaggerate their reports. The first sign of trouble and he felt sure they'd as soon disappear as not. The Crows, with their strange, pompadoured hair and jovial demeanor, were recent additions to the regiment and an unknown quantity. Varnum imagined that they were probably as bad as the Rees. The interpreters, Mitch Bouyer and Charley Reynolds, would probably stand by him in a fight, for all the good they would do. He hoped like hell they wouldn't run into the Sioux out here in the dark. There were an awful lot of them out there somewhere, and three men would hardly do well against them. Best not to think about it. Best not to think about much of anything at all. Varnum glanced anxiously around him.

"What the hell am I doing out here?" he thought bitterly. He found it ironic, his being named chief of scouts. That was a laugh. He felt as if he hardly ever knew where the hell he was going. He just kept moving forward, searching desperately for the thing which he least wanted to find. At least out here alone in the dark. Lately he had come to hate the dark. Whatever fears a man had, however bad they might seem in the daylight, they were a thousand times worse in the dark. At night a man's fears were his own. There was no sharing them out. That was probably the worst thing you could say about being a scout. There was so much time to spend with your own thoughts, your own fears. So many empty miles alone.

The scouts always put in more miles than the rest of the command, but it beat hell out of straggling along in the rear with those damned pack mules. At least they weren't eating the rest of the outfit's dust and trying to keep the cantankerous, long-eared beasts moving under their hated loads of rations and ammunition. The general had insisted on moving light for this march. He wasn't going to be held up by the bulky, slow-moving Army wagons. The problem was that no one had yet got the knack of loading the creatures, with the result that the packs were forever slipping off, scattering hardtack and cartridges all over the countryside. The troops didn't like fishing the debris out of the sagebrush, which seemed to be alive with rattlesnakes coiled in the sparse shade. The snakes were seldom happy with the outcome of these encounters either. Only Lieutenant De-Rudio seemed to enjoy the experience.

Although the rest of the unit had left their heavy cavalry sabers behind, DeRudio had brought his along. He employed it solely, and with obvious relish, on every snake that happened to cross his path, much to the amusement of his fellow officers. Varnum thought him an odd little fellow with his swarthy looks and Italian accent, always full of wild tales about campaigning with Garibaldi and narrow escapes from the Italian authorities. DeRudio's tales grew more elaborate with each telling and elicited broad winks among the listeners. With his talent for exaggeration it was obvious why DeRudio hadn't been offered the job that had brought Charles Varnum out into the middle of nowhere tonight. The brass apparently felt that Varnum's dour, matter-of-fact, brook-no-nonsense Yankee nature was better suited for the task at hand. So, as the rest of the regiment's officers took turns minding the packtrain, a decidedly unpopular extra duty, Lieutenant Varnum was excused.

Varnum's position as chief of scouts, while it was a hell of a lot of work, did have its advantages. Besides exempting him from the onerous extra duty as a muleteer, scouting gave him a great sense of freedom. It was a chance to be out ahead of the van, to drink in the fresh emptiness of the country before a thousand ironshod hooves churned up the dust in blinding, choking clouds. There was, thankfully little dust now, almost as if the earth itself hugged every mote and particle close, an immense sandy blanket to keep off the damp chill of the evening. As hot as it had been the day before, it was hard to believe it could get this cold at night, and the lieutenant shuddered in his thick Army greatcoat of blue wool. The gentle movement of his horse and the warmth of the animal between his thighs was having a somnolent effect on him, and his neck ached from the weight of his head's spastic jerks as he nodded in and out of consciousness. Just a few more miles.

" 'Tenant! Wake up, sir!" Mitch Bouyer's thick voice was dragging him insistently out of the arms of sleep. A gloved hand had reached up out of the darkness and was gently shaking his arm. "Come on, Lo'tenant. We're stoppin' here. Got to walk up, anyway. We'll hole up, get us some shut-eye and go up top just before sun's up."

Varnum shook his head to clear the cobwebs and saw Bouyer's rough face peering up at him, the inevitable pipe clenched in his jaw.

"Are we there, Mitch?"

"Yeah," Bouyer grunted. "Nearabouts as we can get, Lo'tenant." He waved at the massive shape that rose out of the darkness before them.

"There she be, Lo'tenant," Bouyer explained. "Dat damn bump dere, she's the Crow Nest. Lookout spot that dem Crow use for huntin' an' horse stealin'."

It had taken the young officer weeks to get used to the half-breed scout's strange patois, part English, part French-Canadian, part Sioux, part Crow. And that damned pipe didn't help a bit. Two Bodies, the Sioux called him, but Varnum thought something like Four Tongues would be more descriptive. The lieutenant swung slowly out of the saddle, his legs starting to buckle under him as he hit the ground. They felt like rubber, and he crouched for a moment trying to rub some circulation back into them, his spurs grating on the small rocks that lay in a sandy carpet underfoot.

"Where's Reynolds?" he asked as he straightened up, rubbing the back of his neck and yawning.

"He'll be wanderin' about here sniffing 'round, eh. Say he be back direct."

Bouyer jerked his head toward the surrounding darkness and spat out of the corner of his mouth, the pipe never moving.

"White-Man-Runs-Him gone up ahead already. Figgers we'll be kicking dem rocks down the hill, wakin' up ever damn Sioux for miles." Bouyer snorted in amusement, then paused for a moment and dropped his voice, "And they's a heap of 'em out there, damn sure."

The lieutenant squinted up at the looming mass of the hill, hoping to catch a glimpse of the Crow scout Bouyer referred to but couldn't see a thing. When he looked back for Bouyer, the man had already moved off, so Varnum slipped the reins over his horse's head and passed them to the young Ree brave who stood quietly nearby. The Ree merely grunted at the officer and moved off into a stand of small pines, the lieutenant's large American horse dwarfing the three ponies the Indian led away.

"Bouyer's right, Mr. Varnum." A soft voice from the dark startled the groggy officer. It was Charley Reynolds, another scout and the only other "white man" with this small party.

"About what, Mr. Reynolds?" The lieutenant turned in the direction of the disembodied voice.

"It'll be fairly dark for a while yet, so there's no sense in hurrying up to look at nothing. We ought to get some rest while we can."

Varnum nodded silently. "You think he's right about that other bit, Charley? Think there's as many as he says?"

Reynolds rubbed a bandaged right hand over his drooping mustache —one of his fingers was infected and the pain made him wince.

"It's hard to say for sure, Lieutenant. I will say this though—the Crows are awful jumpy of late and these are their stomping grounds. When they get nervous, I'd say it's a pretty reasonable man who sits up and takes note. We've been following one hell of a big trail the last couple o' days, and it seems to me the folks who are leaving it ain't all too concerned with us finding it. That ain't good medicine, if you ask me. *Citius venit periculum cum contemnitur!** as the Latins used to say."

Varnum bristled at the scout's implied warning. "I should think it will be bad medicine for them if we catch up with 'em, Mr. Reynolds. There's not a tribe out here that's a match for the Seventh!"

The words came out easily enough. Such bravado was all too natural for a young lieutenant just four years out of West Point and not yet confronted by his own mortality. But even as he uttered it, he could feel a certain hollowness in the boast, as if he sensed that all was not right. He could feel a chill in his body that was not entirely the result of the night air, and was immediately glad that Reynolds was along. There was at least one man he could depend on if something went wrong.

Stocky, gray-eyed, and with an exceedingly mild manner, Reynolds was a bit of an anomaly as a scout. Obviously well educated, he tended to keep to himself and was unusually quiet and soft-spoken for a plainsman —hence the sobriquet "Lonesome Charley." Chameleonlike, Reynolds could shift easily between the cultured tones of northern Virginia and the gruff, nasal twang of the frontier. Varnum had noticed this tendency among some of his soldiers as well and supposed that it was some form of protective coloration. A man trying to run from his past would do well to blend into the surrounding speech patterns, and Varnum found it interesting to speculate on what Reynolds might be running from. Camp rumors about an unhappy love affair added a tinge of romance to the aloof and

* *"When you underestimate danger, it comes more quickly!"*

mysterious figure. Reynolds was unnaturally talkative tonight. It was out of character, and Varnum wondered if the scout was worried about something.

"No offense meant, Lieutenant. The Seventh's a good outfit and no doubt, but I'm just too old of a dog to take much of anything for granted —pride's a dog that just won't hunt. Get too sassy with Mr. Lo* and he'll surely have your hair in his lodge. I do not care to finish up like the late Mr. Fetterman."

Varnum frowned but felt the chill sweep over him again. He thought back to his plebe year at the Point when Captain William Fetterman was a name to conjure with.† He had indeed been a heroic figure. A brevet lieutenant colonel in the Civil War and much decorated for bravery under fire, Fetterman's lot had changed after Appomattox. Like so many of his brother officers, he was chafing over the dual indignity of being reduced to his permanent rank of captain and posted to Fort Phil Kearny, deep in the mountains of the Dakota Territory and as remote a backwater as there was. The garrison was supposed to protect traffic along the Bozeman Trail —mostly emigrants headed for Oregon, but also a lot of prospectors hoping to hit it rich in the gold and silver deposits up toward Virginia City. The problem was that the trail passed right through the Black Hills, sacred ground to the Sioux. The Sioux didn't like it and tried to drive the Army and the whites out. Under their war chief Red Cloud they'd managed to make Phil Kearny the most dangerous post in the country.

Having faced Lee's Army of Northern Virginia, Fetterman was not impressed by the ragtag Sioux.‡ The savages wouldn't stand and fight but preferred to work from ambush, raiding small parties of woodcutters and stealing cattle. Colonel Carrington, the post commander, had sat out the Civil War in comfort as a recruiting officer, and Fetterman despised the man. Carrington was a bookish, cautious officer who preferred a passive

---

* "Mr. Lo" was the frontier Army's nickname for the Indians. It was a cynical reference to French philosopher Jean Jacques Rousseau's romantic view of natural man epitomized in his descriptive line, "Lo, the noble savage!"
† Charles Varnum entered West Point in August 1868, a full two years after the Fetterman massacre, thus he probably first heard the story from members of his father's unit. Despite the fact that Fetterman and his men died as a result of his arrogance and stupidity, he was long accorded heroic status. In this way the nineteenth century was much like today, in that foolhardy or self-destructive behavior was hardly considered a disqualification for celebrity status.
‡ Fetterman's dismissal of the Sioux was not at all unusual in the post–Civil War era. The Army was officered almost entirely by men such as George Custer and Nelson Miles who shared both Fetterman's experiences and attitudes. After the horrors of the Wilderness, Cold Harbor, Antietam, Shiloh, and Gettysburg, campaigns against the Indians were considered little more than a nuisance.

defense against the Sioux assaults. Fetterman loudly denounced Carrington's tactics as timid and boasted, "Give me eighty men and I'll ride through the Sioux nation!" A sudden raid on a woodcutting party in December 1866 gave the impetuous captain his chance at glory, and he dashed off with his command to fulfill his boast. Just out of sight of the post, he found the Sioux—thousands of them lying in ambush. Within minutes Fetterman and his entire command lay dead—hacked to pieces in a paroxysm of fury and hatred.*

A lot of the Sioux up ahead had been in that fight, and Varnum found himself wondering: What are they thinking tonight? Do they know we're out here? Have they been watching us trying to find them? Have they found us already? The questions whirred like feathered shafts through the lieutenant's anxious brain, doubts mounting on doubts until he felt his head would explode with the horror of it all. Off in the blackness of the surrounding pines, an owl hooted softly and Varnum felt himself cringing unconsciously. Somehow, Captain William Fetterman did not seem quite so romantic a hero just now.

"Not scared of a fight, Mr. Varnum." Reynold's voice broke into the cacophony of the lieutenant's thoughts. "I just tend to be fairly particular about being on the side that wins. Out here you don't generally lose and get another chance. Guess there'll be time enough to worry about that later." He went on, "Still a good hour before daybreak, Lieutenant. You might as well try to grab some sleep before then. Figure we've got a fairly busy day ahead yet. I'll wake you when it's time."

Varnum nodded silently. The sky was beginning, almost imperceptibly, to lighten with the false dawn. Must be near to 3 A.M., he thought. He cast about for a soft spot but settled for a cleft in a set of large boulders that would break the chill wind now rising again. Removing the large wool greatcoat, he wrapped it cloaklike around his shoulders and snuggled down into the stony declivity. He adjusted the slouch hat over his eyes, now more accustomed to the darkness. Glancing out from under the brim, he could now pick out the forms of the Crow and Arikara scouts—"wolves," they called themselves—vague, blanket-shrouded shapes shifting in the gloom. They appeared to him as a ragged and feathered night watch in an

---

* In an ironic twist, the burial parties sent out from Fort Phil Kearney the next day found, along with Fetterman's corpse, seventy-eight soldiers and two civilian employees (who had gone along as a lark to try out their new Henry repeating rifles) for a total of exactly eighty men in the captain's doomed command. Fetterman had taken eighty men and ridden through the Sioux nation—he had just not come back. One of the braves who acted as a decoy to lure Fetterman into the ambush was a young Oglala named Curly. After the fight he would receive the name he has since been known by—Crazy Horse.

aboriginal version of *Hamlet*. The scouts seemed on edge, and Varnum found himself wondering idly if they had already seen their ghost. He listened to them murmuring quietly among themselves, a soft, burbling sound, like a brook rolling over tangles of driftwood. And there was the occasional rasp of Two Bodies Bouyer, like a black bear rooting through the berry bushes along the banks. It was a pleasant image, and when he closed his eyes, he could almost see a sleek trout lazing in a pool of his imagined stream.

Yes, he thought, they look like they're staging *Hamlet* in the rough. His mind drifted back to the stream, and it was with the vision of the undulating trout swimming before him that Lieutenant Varnum sank into a fitful sleep where other visions soon nudged the trout from view. In the fevered dreams that followed, the rocky outcroppings of the Crow's Nest assumed the shape of Castle Elsinore, the glow from iron braziers casting long shadows. An apparition that resembled White-Man-Runs-Him was speaking.

"I could a tale unfold," the taciturn Crow was saying, *"whose lightest word would harrow up thy soul; freeze thy young blood; make thy two eyes, like stars start from their spheres. . . ."* and Varnum found himself observing that Bouyer could learn a thing or two about the English language from White-Man-Runs-Him. Then Bouyer was there urging him to sleep in his strange patois.

"To sleep," the scout growled huskily, *"To sleep! perchance to dream; —ay, there's the rub; for in that sleep of death what dreams may come. . . ."*

Damn Bouyer. Always a gloomy sort. It gave one the shudders just to be around him.

0430 Hours
At the Base of the Crow's Nest

"Mr. Varnum! Lieutenant! It's time." Varnum's eyes fluttered open to see Reynolds stooping over him, the scout's good left hand tugging insistently at the soldier's greatcoat, his injured hand now supported by a large bandanna, which he had knotted into a sling around his neck.

"Sun'll be up in a few minutes, and White-Man-Runs-Him says he's found the camp."

The young chief of scouts was instantly awake and scrambling to his feet, his muscles cramped and aching from contact with the cold ground. He stretched, stifled a yawn, and blinked his eyes rapidly to clear the sleep from them.

"How long've I been asleep?" he asked.

" 'Bout forty-five minutes, give or take." The scout turned his head and yawned too, glancing up the hill as he did so. "I guess it'll have to do for today. We may have a bit of work ahead of us."

Varnum nodded as he stuffed his arms back into the sleeves of the greatcoat and buttoned it up against the morning chill. At least the wind had fallen off. Probably be another scorcher today, soon as the sun started to warm things up. He pulled on heavily soiled calfskin gauntlets.

"White-Man-Runs-Him—that's the big Crow, right?" Reynolds nodded curtly. "Says he's sighted the hostile camp, huh? How many does he figure? You been up there yet?"

Reynolds shook his head. "Don't know for sure, Lieutenant. Figured I'd best roust you first. Plenty of ground haze out there. Sun'll have to burn it off some before we'll see much." Varnum glanced over his shoulder to the eastern horizon. It was just beginning to redden with the coming dawn.

"Well, we'd better get on up there," Varnum said.

He adjusted his slouch hat and started moving up the hill. Reynolds fell in alongside of him, and the two scrambled up the rocky slope in the dim gray light, Varnum's heavy cavalry boots slipping and scuffing along

the rough and increasingly steep trail. A few minutes of climbing left him
breathing hard, the chilly air searing his lungs and his leg muscles aching
anew. A few minutes more and he dropped onto a flat boulder gasping,
sweat rolling into his eyes and welling into his uniform under his arms.
This was one hell of a climb. Better be a damn good view from the top.

The lieutenant looked up at Reynolds, now above him on the slope
and leaning casually against a tree. The man wasn't even breathing hard.
He was a tough old bird. Varnum found himself wondering just how old
Reynolds really was. How old was Bouyer for that matter?

Although only in their late thirties, the two scouts looked to be
ancient and Varnum felt somewhat embarrassed whenever they stopped
to wait while he caught his breath. Well, Varnum told himself, life is hard
on a man out here. Ages a man quickly. Maybe they're younger than they
look. The young officer used his teeth to tug off the gauntlets, now warm
and sweaty, and stuffed them into a pocket of his greatcoat, the chill air on
his wrists already helping to cool down his body. Standing up slowly, he
shucked off the heavy wool coat, dropped it on the ground, and took off
his hat to run his fingers through the damp hair now plastered to his head.
He'd leave the coat here, pick it up on the way back down. He looked up
at the scout again.

"How far up is this Crow's Nest place?"

"Not far. Another fifty yards or so."

"Say, Charley . . ."

"Yes, sir?"

"Nothing really, I just thought, well"—the lieutenant paused and
looked off up the hill—"well, you know. I'm just glad to have you along.
Another white man, I mean."

The scout was momentarily taken aback.

"Well, you are too kind, sir. To be truthful, I hadn't much else planned
for the evening and thought you might prove pleasant company." Reynolds showed a slight grin. "Besides, as you'll soon learn, the Sioux and
Cheyenne don't like to be out at night, so it's somewhat safer out here
when it's dark. If you stay in camp, one of our valiant youngsters might
accidentally set off his piece and blow you to Hades."

The lieutenant managed an awkward smile. He hoped his nervousness
was not too apparent, and he appreciated the offhanded nature of Reynolds's remark. The scout was obviously trying to put him at ease. He
glanced at Reynolds and then nodded toward the hilltop.

"I notice that our Crow and Ree friends were not too circumspect
about moving through the night."

Reynolds cocked his head. "Mmm? Ah, yes, I see what you're getting at, sir. Well, they are an unusual case, Mr. Varnum. Your exception that proves the rule, as it were." The scout paused, then went on. "These tribes are not especially superstitious about being out and about in the gloom, not like the Sioux and Cheyenne. The Sioux and Cheyenne don't like to fight at night. Figure that if they get killed their spirits won't be able to find their way into the next world. The Crow and Ree don't believe that rot. Plus they are a highly motivated group."

Reynolds's comment set Varnum to thinking again. Despite his years on the plains, he still had some difficulty in sorting out the motivations of the natives.

"Why should that be, Charley? Hell, I know they are not overly fond of the Sioux, but well, they are Indians after all, you know. That's one thing I never could figure out—why venture this deep into Sioux territory just 'cause maybe some Oglala buck once stole a bunch of their ponies or some such thing. It just doesn't figure."

He looked at the scout, who was playing absently with his grimy bandage. The man appeared not to have been listening as he tugged at the knotted rag with his teeth and adjusted the large bandanna he had rigged to do service as a sling. Reynolds continued to fuss with the arrangement as he considered the question. When he spoke, there was a distracted, almost sad quality in his soft voice.

"Well, Lieutenant, I think I see where your concerns lie, but you may put your mind at rest on that account. For one thing, this is not as far afield for the Crows as you may imagine. You know their name for this country, right?"

"Absaraka, or some such thing, isn't it?"

"Yes, exact to the dot. In their tongue that translates literally to 'home of the Crow.' This is their land. That's why we're headed for this so-called Crow's Nest." He pointed up the hill. "This is home to those fellows. Always has been, always will be. As far as they are concerned, the Sioux are the interlopers, the despoilers. Used to be that the Sioux were afraid to set foot in this country. The Crows are ferocious damn warriors, you know. Sioux mothers used to tell Crow stories to frighten unruly papooses." Reynolds grinned at the lieutenant. "Sort of like our boogeyman. Well, over the last few years, we've been pushing the Sioux west in greater numbers—Oglala, Hunkpapa, Brulé, Miniconjou—a whole heap of Sioux. Numbers tell, Mr. Varnum. You're an educated man. Who was it said that quantity has a quality all of its own? Napoleon, wasn't it?"

The lieutenant nodded.

"Well, while we've been pushing the Sioux out this way, the Sioux have been steadily pushin' the Crows and Rees too." He nodded toward the scouts. "These fellows are none too pleased. So when Colonel Gibbon sent out word that there was a soldier war party forming up, he had no trouble signing up the Crows to come along for the fun. Again, it's a case of simple mathematics. We win, they win."

"A *quid pro quo,* eh, Mr. Reynolds?"

The scout shook his head.

"Well, a *quid* anyway. I wouldn't bet on the *pro quo.* I know you don't trust 'em, Lieutenant, but I believe your doubts are misplaced on that account. Trust is not a consideration here. This is a matter of self-interest —and honor—on the part of the Crows anyway. They'll do what we asked 'em to do, and we'll have the better part of the bargain no matter how it comes out. Now, you'll notice the general is comfortable with the Rees— Bloody Knife and his crew—but they've been together for years. He knows their limitations, makes allowances for 'em. Now, these Crow gentlemen are new acquaintances, but the general doesn't worry about whether the Crows'll fight—nor do I. In fact, just the opposite. If we come across the Sioux, these Crows are just as apt to jump the gun as not. It's the prime reason why the general sent you and me along on this little soiree. He'll expect us to stir a little sober judgment into the stew. Oh, yes, they'll fight all right and they know that old Long Hair'll do as well. He's a fighter and they respect that. More's the pity, they trust him."

Varnum shot the scout a quizzical look, which Reynolds quickly picked up.

"Oh, if it were just up to Custer, they'd have no worry on that account. The man is a straight shooter. They know it, as do you and I. But he doesn't make policy, does he?"

The lieutenant, whose eyes had sparked defiance as if he were about to leap to the defense of his commander, said nothing. Varnum could see where Reynolds was going with his argument. The Indian scouts would see Custer as the representative of the U.S. government and figure that he would not make promises he couldn't keep. Even Varnum knew that this was a false hope at best, as the people who pulled the strings in Washington were little inclined to heed the advice, or keep the promises, of their own soldiers. It seemed odd to him that the Indians could be so naive in this respect since they themselves seldom felt obligated to adhere to the treaties signed by their own chiefs. Varnum shook his head slowly as Reynolds went on.

"Oh, it's a good thing our dusky friends are unfamiliar with Greek tragedy, Mr. Varnum, for they're livin' one as we watch. There's a line in

Antigone, I believe it is, 'What can wound more deeply than a false friend,' or something to that effect. Even you will agree that there's hardly a falser friend than Uncle Sam. Yes, we'll certainly have the better end of this bargain. God help 'em!"

Lieutenant Varnum nodded and gazed up the hill one more time. "Well, Mr. Reynolds, I'll just have to reserve judgment on that, though I'll admit what you say has the ring of truth to it. I guess everybody's out for what they think they can get and the devil take the hindmost. That sort of thing is way above my pay grade, but I can't say that it doesn't leave me with a bad taste in my mouth." The lieutenant stood up. The conversation was ended. "Guess we'd best get on up there."

"Yes, sir. I expect we ought to get back into this stew."

Varnum and Reynolds were up and moving again. The lieutenant struggled to keep up, gulping in the thin air and slipping on the loose rock covering the ground, his heavy brass spurs pinging and flaking off small bits of flint from the chips littered around in profusion. Centuries of idle hunters and warriors had obviously passed the long hours of watching by shaping new arrow or spear points on these slopes. With the coming of the white man it was a skill that was fading rapidly as flint was replaced by iron, which made a better point. Now even the iron was being replaced by rifles and revolvers. Things were changing quickly out here.

Varnum at least understood that change was coming to this country. You adapted to the changing times or you went extinct. That was the way it was. The Sioux hadn't figured that out yet. They kept fighting it, taking what suited 'em, like rifles, and trying to run away from everything that went with it. Well, it didn't work that way. The lieutenant didn't see why the Indians couldn't seem to grasp the simple truth of the matter. No matter what Reynolds said, Varnum thought the Crows and Rees had made a good bargain. They might have made a bargain with the devil, but it was the only reasonable choice they had. Who could blame them for that? He glanced up to see Reynolds striding along easily in moccasined feet, not seeming to breathe hard or miss a step. The man could quote Virgil and Milton and yet looked as comfortable out here in the rough country as a cat in a warm parlor. What a remarkable fellow. Varnum reached out and tugged at the scout's fringed sleeve.

"Damn it, Charley, why'd you have to mention stew? Now my gut's really startin' to grumble."

The scout grinned at him. "Napoleon, sir."

"How's that?"

"Well, I hear tell the old gentleman used to say that an Army moves on its stomach. So I figured that if I got your stomach operating we'd get a-movin' up this damn hill. Sooner we're done here, sooner we get some breakfast."

Varnum grinned despite himself. "Charley," he said, "you're becoming a damned fine strategist!"

0445 Hours
Atop the Crow's Nest

As they approached the crest of the hill, Varnum could see why the Crows had come to this particular spot. Stopping to catch his breath, he took in the surroundings and quickly concluded that this was probably the best natural vantage point in the area. From the top they should be able to see for miles across the expanse of undulating plain, across the Rosebud and Little Bighorn Rivers and as far as the Bighorn Mountains. They said this country was teeming with wildlife—buffalo, elk, deer, and antelope. The savvy hunter could shelter his horses at the base of the hill, then move to the top to watch for the herds of game. It would also be a good place to watch for the approach of the enemy. Varnum wondered if the Crows had finally found the "game" they were looking for. Well, he'd know soon enough. He saw them now, gathered at the crest of the hill with some of the Rees. They were obviously agitated about something. Some of them were pointing off to the northwest, others gesticulating emphatically in sign language with the Rees and Bouyer.

Varnum, with Reynolds alongside, strode up over the last few yards.

"What've we got here, Mr. Bouyer?"

A large Crow, whom the lieutenant recognized as White-Man-Runs-Him, uttered a few words in his own tongue and swept his arm over the landscape to point toward a spot off to the northwest. The other Crows were nodding in assent and grunting.

"What's he saying, Bouyer?"

Bouyer, half-turned toward the group of Indians, was squinting off into the distance, his thick lower lip stuck out and the ever-present pipe rigid between his tightly clenched teeth. He turned back to the chief of scouts, his jaw set, eyes hooded and fierce. Varnum thought that some of the color had drained from the man's face.

"He says to tell soldier chief it's a big goddamn camp down there!"

The chief of scouts glanced at Reynolds, whose brow was furrowed, upper lip pushing his mustache out in a bristly arc. The scout looked from

Varnum back to Bouyer and moved farther up the ridge, pushing his way through the knot of Crow and Ree scouts, whose collective attention was now riveted by something off in the far distance.

The sun was coming up behind them, and the lieutenant could now see his small detachment clearly, bright splashes of color against the gray boulders. What a motley collection. If his old neighbors back in Dracut, Massachussetts,* could only see the company he now kept. How different these people were from what Easterners imagined. Damn little spit and polish out here. He looked down at his own uniform. God, what a mess. He was caked with dust, and smelled of woodsmoke and soured sweat. Large white salt rings radiated from under his armpits, and his canvas-lined trousers were blackened from contact with saddle leather and sweating horseflesh. He rubbed a filthy hand over his face, unshaven for three days now. He'd spent nearly all of the past seventy-two hours in the saddle and smelled like a horse himself. Maybe that's why he hardly noticed the smell of his companions anymore. God knew they could all use a good bath.

The Indians that Lieutenant Varnum now found himself working with were nothing like those Mr. Fenimore Cooper or Mr. Hawthorne had described. Varnum had quickly decided that there was nothing very noble about these savages. Out here Mr. Rousseau's natural man was draped in filthy buckskins and tattered blankets, festooned with bits of fur, dangling feathers and animal bones, some wearing white men's vests and gunbelts. They looked more like something out of Dante's *Inferno* than characters from the *Leatherstocking Tales*.

Each of the warriors wore a strip of bright red cloth tied above the elbow of his left arm. This was so that the less sophisticated troopers would be able to recognize them as "friendlies" and not start shooting them up indiscriminately. In all, there was a curious, barbaric artistry to their appearance, but more a subject for Hieronymus Bosch than McNeil Whistler,† to be sure. Their thin, sinewy limbs and weather-crinkled faces

---

* *Born in Troy, New York, in 1849, Varnum moved with his family to Dracut, Massachussetts, where he attended school. After the Civil War the family joined Charles's father in Pensacola, Florida, where he was a captain in the Eighty-second U.S. Colored Infantry assigned to occupation duty during Reconstruction.*

† *James McNeil Whistler, the famous and somewhat eccentric American artist, was just coming into prominence and was no stranger to the officers of the Seventh Cavalry. A former West Point cadet, Whistler had been expelled after failing a chemistry examination. His best friend at the Military Academy had been fellow cadet Marcus Reno (Class of '57), later Custer's second-in-command. Years after the Little Bighorn, Whistler ran into Reno at a social gathering and was alleged to have remarked to him, "If silicon had been a gas I would probably be an Army officer today." To which Reno, it is said, replied, "Perhaps, and no one would have heard of your mother." This was obviously a reference to the painting entitled* Symphony in Gray and Black, *but more commonly referred to as Whistler's Mother.*

were more brown than red. And there were no shaved scalps or bristling crests of hair here, just heavily greased braids and thick black tresses, some tied back loosely with bits of rawhide sinew or colored ribbons from the sutlers' stores. The Crows had teased their hair up into distinctive pompadour shapes, or gathered a small tuft of hair into a tight bundle, which they then bound with a strand of rawhide to stand straight up from the top of the head. No, real Indians were not at all like the ones portrayed in the popular literature. Not at all like what he had been led to expect.

And yet there was something in their demeanor that grew on him. Over the weeks of campaigning Varnum had found himself strangely drawn to these fantastic creatures. At first it was no more than a horrible fascination, like being left to wander among the lions in the zoo, expecting at any moment to be mauled and devoured, ever surprised to find oneself still breathing and walking amid the hypnotic grace of pacing savagery. But his fears had quickly been supplanted, almost imperceptibly, by a feeling of camaraderie, even fondness, for his aboriginal companions. Their casual familiarity with the land was a constant source of wonder for the city-bred officer, and he had come to admire and respect their skills. There were times when he found it almost painful to return to the formerly comforting order of camp and trumpet. It was at times like this that Varnum felt a numbing sense of guilt—as if he were personally responsible for bringing change and ultimate destruction to a culture that had accepted him as an equal.

Unknown to him, Charles Varnum had made a subtle but telling discovery. The men he was with were exactly that—men—they were not pasteboard characters from some novel or mythical creatures from another world. The Westerners who demonized them and the Easterners who eulogized them were equally wrong. Each faction had cast them as players in some peculiar morality play, ascribing to the Indians the sins or saintliness that best supported their own point of view. But neither group knew them as they really were—as human beings—no more noble or savage than the whites themselves. Swayed by the arguments of both sides, Varnum did not know how to deal with the turmoil this stirred in his brain. For all his education and intellect, it was something the young lieutenant didn't like to think about.

The half-breed Bouyer too was less picturesque than he would have liked for a plainsman and scout. The squat body and square face seemed right, but his ragged black hat and checkered shirt, and the heavy wool trousers stuffed into old cavalry boots, did not. He should have been dressed all in buckskin and fur, with quilled moccasins and a raccoon cap with the head and tail still attached. Instead, the closest thing to fur that he wore was that ridiculous calfskin vest covered with white and brown splotches. Maybe Two Bodies was a good name for him—as if the inner man was Indian and he tried to use clothes to make the outer man look more white. The result was that he looked as if he wasn't comfortable in either world. In many ways he seemed more lonely than "Lonesome Charley" Reynolds.

Reynolds. Now there was a strange fellow. He dressed soberly, looking more like a farmer or merchant than a scout—no flamboyance here. Not at all like that dandy Hickock, or that posturing braggart Cody.* In fact, the only concession Reynolds made to his chosen vocation seemed to be the beaded moccasins that he favored. What could have brought him to this strange country? His speech was quiet and articulate; he was obviously well read—which was more than Varnum could say for most of the regiment. Why would he prefer the company of rough soldiers and mud-daubed savages to the genteel parlors of St. Louis or Chicago? Varnum thought again of the camp rumors that laid the cause at the feet of a woman—some dark and mysterious Mexican beauty. No one really knew, but the hint of intrigue made for wondrous speculations around the evening campfires.

Women. What better subject for lonely soldiers in the vast emptiness of the frontier than women—fair and fickle, dark and demure, with their whispered endearments, their graceful movements, eyes that promised, lips that denied. And their scents, of powder and lilac, roses and cloves. No wonder they were always the most favored of all topics of conversation, discussed in hushed and reverent tones, and frequently inspiring a round of song. Old tunes of melancholy and separation, of love unrequited, dreams of bliss or memories of dead children, themes all too familiar at every Army post. There had been no time for that last night, but perhaps tonight—perhaps there would be time after today's work. He knew the old man planned to rest the outfit for a day before moving into action, and he was as fond of the old songs as anyone. On more than one occasion he had noticed the general moved to tears by a soulful rendition of the popular ballad "Little Footsteps."

It was yet another of Custer's eccentricities. He was a remarkable

* James Butler "Wild Bill" Hickcock and William F. "Buffalo Bill" Cody had both spent considerable time employed as scouts for the U.S. Army and had served with Custer on numerous occasions. At the time of this campaign Cody was serving with the Fifth Cavalry, having abruptly abandoned his successful New York City stage show, Scouts of the Prairie. Hickock had tried his hand on stage with Cody but developed a debilitating case of stage fright and had moved to Deadwood in the Dakota Territory. Hickock would not survive the year.

man, Varnum thought, and a Gordian knot of a personality. He was vain and arrogant and yet solicitous to his officers and men. No matter how a man might infuriate him, he would never utter a foul word or berate the man in public. He was a fanatic hunter and yet he loved animals. Varnum had known him to sit up all night tenderly nursing a sick puppy. The general's temper was electric, and yet he never, as far as the lieutenant could tell, nursed a grudge. All were welcome at his quarters, where many an evening was passed in parlor games and gossip. The general would take his seat at the piano and stumble energetically through some popular tune with the junior officers needling him mercilessly—much to the delight of the ladies. Custer would just blush and grin sheepishly as he attacked the keys as if they were a regiment of Reb cavalry. Gales of laughter would greet his valiant efforts as he began to croak, "I'm Captain Jinks of the Horse Marines! I feed my horse on corn and beans . . ." before the whole company would join in.

As Varnum now considered his odd companions, a rush of sadness flooded over him. This moment will never come again, he thought, and all this, and all these men, will be lost in time . . . and I'll have helped to destroy them. The thought surprised and disturbed him. He had never considered himself much of a philosopher and preferred to dismiss such thoughts rather than to turn them over endlessly in his mind.

"Lieutenant!" Reynolds's voice was calling him back from his uncomfortable thoughts. "You'd better have a good look out there. I think we've got a problem."

Varnum glanced at the small, excited party gathered around White-Man-Runs-Him. He could now remember some of their names. There were a couple of the other Crows—Hairy Moccasin, Goes Ahead, and Curley, and the Rees—Crooked Horn, with his young nephew Red Star, and that youngster's friend Bull. The boys were beside themselves with excitement. It was a feeling obviously not shared by the older braves. White-Man-Runs-Him was talking with Bouyer and signing rapidly to Reynolds.

"What's going on, Bouyer?" Varnum asked. "Why is he so agitated?"

The scout was nodding curtly to the large Crow and glancing furtively to the northwest and then back to Reynolds.

"White-Man-Runs-Him says for me to tell the soldier chief and the 'Lucky Man,' that's Reynolds here, that we got more Sioux down dere than we've got bullets!" Bouyer jerked his head toward the valley that stretched out below them, much of it still shrouded in darkness. With his mention of the Sioux the young Rees started jumping about and pointing into the valley and exclaiming, *"Ota Sioux! Ota Sioux!"*

"Now, what're they saying, Charley?" The lieutenant turned to the other scout.

"It means, 'many Sioux,' Lieutenant." Reynolds muttered distractedly. He too was looking off toward the valley floor. "And it's as pretty an understatement as you are likely to hear this day." Without changing his position, he pulled a battered brass telescope from a leather case dangling at his side and handed it absently to the officer.

"Best take a look so you can tell the old man."

Varnum took the glass and, lifting it to his eye, began to scan the scene that lay before him. The vastness of the countryside was stunning. For as far as he could see, the prairie stretched, rolling and pitching, into infinity. Below him he could easily make out the course of two small creeks as they approached the Little Bighorn. Somewhere out of sight they must join before emptying into the river. There it was, twisting and bowing as it snaked a lazy course through the valley. It seemed almost to skulk through the cottonwoods and slip furtively down ravines, with only an occasional flash of silver to confirm its watery presence before disappearing behind a line of bluffs far off to the northwest.

Still no sign of hostiles. What did they see that he couldn't? Varnum swept the glass to the right, following a ridge of chalky cliffs. There! A smear of white. He focused more closely on the image. It was a tipi. No, two tipis, one of them apparently in a state of collapse. Where were all of these "ota Sioux" they were yelping about?

"Mr. Reynolds, I don't see but two old lodges down there. One of them seems hardly habitable. And I see no other signs of hostiles whatsoever!"

"You're looking in the wrong spot, Mr. Varnum. Move that glass off to the left following that ridge line." Reynolds's stiffened left arm swept like a compass needle across the landscape. "Off beyond where the river goes behind those bluffs, there's your pony herd."

Varnum strained to follow the guide's instructions. Damn! It must be twenty miles out to where the man was pointing. He still couldn't make out a damn thing. He rubbed his eyes and looked again. Nothing. He lowered the spyglass and shook his head, his lips thin, eyes narrowed to slits and straining to pick out the slightest sign of movement. White-Man-Runs-Him was speaking to Bouyer again. His voice was low but urgent and his gestures insistent. Bouyer turned to the lieutenant to relate the Crow's message.

"He says, 'Don't look for horses—look for worms,' eh!"

Worms? What in God's name were they talking about?

"Charley, do you see what they're seeing? I confess I see no ponies and certainly no worms!" The lieutenant handed the glass to Reynolds, who slipped it back into its case.

"You maybe can't see them, sir," Reynolds tossed his head back toward the Indians. "But they can. And Mitch and I can see 'em well enough. The ponies are so far off that all you can make out is a gentle rolling motion—that's the worms they're talking about. Imagine the way a large tangle of maggots squirms about on a buffalo carcass. Kind of a faint, wiggly mass. That's what the herd looks like from here. And it's one hell of a big herd. Hell, it's the biggest damn herd I've ever seen."

The scout turned toward the officer, and as he did, his face clouded with a look of dismay. Varnum followed his gaze back in the direction from which they had ridden the night before. The valley behind them was now flooded with light, and they could distinctly make out small wisps of smoke curling up from the ground. The regiment's night bivouac. The damned fools were making coffee!

"Goddamn them!" Reynolds blurted. "Sorry, Mr. Varnum. My apologies, sir." The officer brushed it off. Bouyer had moved over to the two white men and was shaking his head.

"Big goddamn herd, Lo'tenant." Bouyer was muttering. "By God, that's one hell of a lot of injuns. Goddamn." Bouyer's eyes grew wide as he noticed the wisps of smoke down below.

"Sacre . . . by God!" Bouyer exploded. "What are they, goddamned crazy down there? What they think? The damn Sioux don't have no eyes? Goddamn! They'll see us for sure now, you bet."

The half-breed was livid with rage and spat vigorously in the direction of the regiment's cookfires. Behind them, the Crows and Rees had also noticed the cookfires and grown more excited. Hairy Moccasin was muttering angrily. Bouyer shook his head in sympathy and turned to Reynolds.

"Hairy Moccasin wants to know if Long Hair thinks the Sioux all have eyes like Grumpy Bear?" He jerked a thumb toward the lieutenant.

Varnum started when he realized that the Crow was talking about him. He hadn't considered that they had their own name for him. He guessed maybe he needed a good night's rest worse than he had thought. Grumpy Bear. Hell of a name. He looked back at Reynolds, who had pulled out a small notebook and was painfully scribbling something,* the pencil gripped gingerly in his bandaged fingers.

---

* There is still some doubt as to who actually wrote the note to Custer. Varnum claims to have done so, which one would expect, but several of the Indian scouts remembered Reynolds having written the "talking paper."

"That for the general, Charley?"

The scout nodded briefly, his teeth chewing his lower lip as he concentrated on finishing the message. He glanced up and barked at the two young Rees in their own tongue. The anxious braves dashed over to him.

"Bull, Red Star, you take the talking paper to Long Hair. Ride quickly! Give it only to Long Hair. Tell him we have found many Sioux!"

The youngsters nodded, repeating, *"Ota Sioux!"* They snatched the note and scrambled down the back side of the slope to where the horses were tethered. Reynolds looked back at the lieutenant.

"What time have you, sir?"

Varnum reached into a vest pocket and snapped open a small brass hunter.

"Just five o'clock, Charley. The general'll be up and about by now. He'll likely want to come up and take a look for himself." Varnum turned suddenly at the sound of the Crows and Rees talking urgently again. Reynolds was already moving back to the lookout point. Now what? thought Varnum. He hurried over to join the excited Indians. In an instant he could make out the cause of their consternation. Down in the valley between them and the elusive pony herd were two riders. They must have come from the camp, which still lay hidden from sight. The riders moved rapidly across the rolling, grass-covered slopes below. Maybe the scouts had indeed seen something. Maybe the village was down there as they had said. Damn. The riders were headed east, toward the regiment's position. The campfires. Damn it. Had they already seen the smoke? The lieutenant caught the eyes of the two civilian scouts and could see the same question forming in their minds.

"Let's go!" he barked, but they were already moving. The trio turned and scrambled back down the hill with a pair of Ree braves close on their heels, all of them skidding, sliding, and tripping as they raced toward the horses. They had to stop those riders. They'd have to move quickly, cut them off, and kill them.

0500 Hours
Along Davis Creek

Lieutenant Colonel* George Armstrong Custer snapped open the lid of his gold watch. It was just after five o'clock. He thumbed the lid down until it closed with a quiet click and felt the satisfying heft of the heavy timepiece in his slender fingers. At thirty-six his figure was still lean and trim from years in the saddle, and he sat his horse with a lithe grace. The long years in the field had been not quite so forgiving of his pale complexion, now lined and creased by wind and weather and burned to a ruddy red. His legendary blond locks, which had earned him the nicknames "Fanny" and "Curly" at the Academy, were beginning to recede from his temples and had thinned out on top of his skull. Knowing that he was in for a long, hot summer campaign, he'd had Lieutenant Varnum use his clippers to crop his mane short for comfort, but the Indian scouts still referred to him as Long Hair.

He turned the watch over in his palm to read the inscription: "ON, YOU WOLVERINES!" He smiled thinking of the boys in the Michigan Brigade who had presented it to him during the late rebellion. Ah, those had been great days! The thunder of hooves, the crash of guns roaring in their ears. Wind in their faces, sabers flashing in the sun. God, but they had never felt so alive as when they had stared death in the face and plunged forward screaming "On, you Wolverines!" As he sat absorbed in his thoughts, the approach of another rider captured his attention. He looked up to see his brother Boston trot up on a docile gelding. The youngster's narrow-brimmed, high-crowned hat was in marked contrast to the fringed buckskins and beaded moccasins he wore. George Custer thought it made the boy look somewhat silly.

* During the Civil War, Custer had attained the rank of major general of volunteers in command of the Third Cavalry Division. This brevet, or "temporary," rank was vacated once the war was over and the Army demobilized. When the Army reorganized in 1866, Custer received an appointment as a lieutenant colonel in the Regular Army but, by custom, was still entitled to be addressed as "General."

"Morning, Autie," Boston said, using George's family nickname. "How are you getting along?"

"Just fine, Bos. Better than I've felt in weeks. Capital day, isn't it?"

It was, in fact, a beautiful morning and promised a fine, clear day. George Custer breathed in deeply, inhaling the clean, cutting crispness of the morning air. He relished this time of day, the fresh, cool dampness of the dew, the comforting warmth of a good horse between his thighs. Vic, his large sorrel, was not yet saddled. George thought he'd allow him another few minutes of freedom before strapping on the cumbersome McClellan. A few more minutes of freedom for the rider too.

Everyone wanted a piece of George Armstrong Custer, and although he did not shy from his hard-earned notoriety, it could also be very tiresome. In a way, he resented Boston's impertinent presence. He was jealous of the few minutes of twilight before the sun and the sergeants roused the rest of the sleeping regiment. With all of the bustle and madness of an army on the move, this was the only time he really had to himself. For these very few moments he didn't belong to the regiment or the Army or the Sioux. He could be alone to sort out his thoughts, unburdened by the responsibilities that weighed like a cumbersome saddle on his own back—as a commander, an older brother, a son, a husband, a national hero. But now Boston was here and around them the night bivouac was just beginning to stir.

"Surprised to see you up this early, Bos," Custer said, a slight edge to his voice. "I thought sure you'd be sleeping in on this day of rest."

Boston shook his head. "Figured I'd leave that to Tom today. Besides, the great oaf was snoring so loud there was hardly a man in the staff could hope to sleep through the racket." A grin lit up his sunburned face. "Come on, Autie, what do you say we slip over there and toss a bucket of water into his 'pup'? I still owe him one for that last stunt he pulled."

George Custer laughed. "Patience, Bos, your time will come. You want to employ a subtler stratagem with brother Tom. Maybe we'll stick him with the mules for a couple of hours tomorrow and you can tag along to watch the fun."

Boston sighed his disappointment.

"Tomorrow, huh? Not moving today at all?"

George shook his head. "Nope. Day of rest, Bos. We'll probably come up on our Sioux friends in another day's ride. I want everyone to be rested up and ready for the fun. You don't want to go into an action with the horses and men all played out—makes for an awfully long day. No, I'll let 'em all sleep in a bit today. We might move up a couple of miles to see if we can fetch up a tastier source of water, but that should be about it for the day. Scouts should be in fairly soon and we'll see what they've scared up. Gibbon should be in position tomorrow, so we'll just run a reconnaissance and see the best way to drive the Sioux up and into 'em." He grinned and jabbed a fist playfully into his brother's arm. "But tomorrow will be a bit more sporting, I'll wager. We'll let the boys rest up while they can." He looked away, up the line of troops scattered about the rank grass in the small meadow.

As it was, many of the troopers were already starting the morning stables routine along the picket line, checking the condition of their mounts, looking for saddle sores, examining hock, quick, and hoof, plying currycombs and brushes, doling out grain. Others were busy rolling up blankets and ground cloths. Here and there, small fires of sage and mesquite had been kindled in shallow holes preparatory to brewing the soldiers' champagne—coffee. It would probably taste fairly rough this morning. The water here was so alkaline that even the horses wouldn't drink willingly but rather contented themselves with the rank grass, which was heavy with dew. Didn't matter. At least he was here with his regiment and far away from Washington. He still smarted from the memory of his last visit there—it had almost cost him his command. Even in the crisp beauty of this Dakota morning he could not keep his thoughts from drifting back to the near-disastrous events of the preceding months.

He had been seated in his study at Fort Abraham Lincoln working on yet another article for *Galaxy* when his orderly had come in with a telegram. Congress had ordered him back to Washington to testify before the Clymer Committee, which was investigating allegations of corruption within the Grant administration. Attention had focused on irregularities that had been discovered in the operation of sutler stores on Indian reservations and Army posts—all of which were controlled directly by the secretary of war. As Custer had been a frequent, and vocal, critic of what he felt were shady business practices by some Indian agents and post traders, it was only natural that his testimony would be sought. It was damned inconvenient. There was a campaign coming up and hundreds of details to be attended to. He had protested that there was simply too much to be done for him to leave his post at this critical time, but Congress was not to be dissuaded, and Custer found himself boarding an eastbound train with Libby handing him up a sack of sandwiches.

"Don't you complain to me, Beau," Libby had scolded. "If you'd just kept your mouth shut, you wouldn't be gallivanting off to Washington at Congress's beck and call." She hadn't said it, but there was a distinct note of "I told you so" in Libby's voice, and he hung his head in frustration.

When he glanced up again, she was smiling broadly. "Come on, Autie, cheer up. You'll be back before you know it, and you'd best be ready to give a full account of the latest fashions and what's playing at the theaters and who's the rage, and . . ." He had held up his hands in mock surrender.

"Quarter, dear! You win. Never fear, I'll be as good a reporter as any the *Herald* can field and return with all the latest gossip . . . and maybe even a rag or two."

Libby had blown him a chaste kiss as he scrambled up into the railcar for the seemingly interminable trip east. The Washington into which his train pulled was deceptively beautiful in the midst of a particularly glorious spring. Flowers bloomed in profusion, and everywhere the air was fresh with the scent of honeysuckle and newly mown lawns. Congressman Heister Clymer, who met Custer's train, was delighted to see the young officer newly arrived from the plains.

"Ahh, General, so good of you to come out on such short notice."

"I didn't know that I had any option, Congressman." Custer managed a wry smile as the portly Clymer pumped his hand vigorously.

"Yes, yes, of course, we were forced to be a bit abrupt with General Terry, but you know this is a very grave matter we have to resolve. Your commander thinks quite highly of your abilities, General. I can see why he was reluctant to lose your services, even for a short time, with this campaign against the hostiles coming up. Now, before you say anything, sir, let me assure you that I believe we will have you back at your post in plenty of time for the campaign. You know, of course, that the secretary has all but admitted the whole thing and resigned—"

"The devil, you say!" Custer was taken aback and wondered if the whole trip had been for nothing. But Clymer quickly reassured Custer that his presence was still required.

"No, no, all quite true, General. It's a sad business indeed." Clymer placed a pudgy hand on Custer's elbow and steered him expertly through the throng of alighting passengers as porters hurried to grab the general's bags and hustled them toward a waiting carriage. "I know General Belknap was a fine soldier during the late rebellion, but I am afraid he has drifted into the clutches of Mammon . . . although how much of that is the doing of his late wife and her sister, who is his new wife, you understand, is as yet somewhat unclear. Well, I don't expect you to be aware of all the details, but not to worry, we'll sort it all out in the end."

Custer was too dumbfounded to answer and found himself walking dazedly alongside the prattling congressman, trying to take in everything that was being poured into his ear. During the carriage ride to the hotel Clymer began to sketch out the details of the scandal that was rocking the

Washington establishment in this centennial year. Rumors of irregularities within the Grant administration had long run rampant, but it was only recently that a spate of investigations into the activities of some of the president's cabinet members had uncovered specific evidence of widespread corruption and influence peddling.

The resulting furor had divided the capital into warring political camps, and George Custer was about to find himself thrust into the midst of the mudslinging. Secretary of the Interior Columbus Delano had admitted to taking kickbacks from the sale of positions as Indian agents, and the allegations of irregularities at several agencies made by Lieutenant Colonel Custer, among others, had led to an investigation of Custer's superior, Secretary of War William Belknap.*

"But if Belknap has resigned, Congressman," Custer had protested, "I hardly see where my testimony can be of any use whatever. It never amounted to much more than what you would call hearsay anyway. A few letters from some honest traders, the complaints of some of my officers and men, and that one incident with the champagne during the secretary's tour of posts. It's hardly damning evidence."

"Yes, yes, of course," Clymer reassured him. "I understand your concern, son, but it's not so much hard evidence we really need at this point but rather to establish that a pattern of deceit and corruption pervades this administration. Your reputation for honesty and straightforwardness will help us immeasurably in demonstrating that these scoundrels have done more than simply line their pockets from the public trust. Why, their greed has actually endangered the lives and security of our citizens and soldiers on the frontier. Oh, yes, it's a much bigger issue than you suspect, my boy. Our new secretary of war, Mr. Taft, is thoroughly pleased that we were able to prevail upon you to make an appearance before the committee. He has the utmost confidence in your abilities and your honest nature and believes your statements can only help to ensure that he receives the authority to sweep the department clean." Custer was doubtful but nodded resignedly.

When Custer finally made his statements to the committee, he was not prepared for the circus atmosphere of the proceedings. He had expected

* William Worth Belknap was appointed to this position by President Grant, an old Army friend. In 1870, Belknap had gained complete control over the appointment of post sutlers, and with the connivance of his wife milked this authority for personal profit. A congressional investigation of irregularities in Secretary of the Interior Delano's office involving similar activities on the Indian reservations led back to Belknap, who quickly resigned to avoid impeachment proceedings.

merely to say his piece and be dismissed, but it was not to be. Instead, he faced an excruciating cross-examination by Secretary Belknap's partisans.

"And can you tell me, honestly, Colonel," one Congressman sneered, "that you personally witnessed this transaction in which you allege that Secretary Belknap, your superior officer, agreed that in return for certain guarantees that all subsistence purchases for your regiment be made at this establishment he would receive the equivalent of ten cents on the dollar? Is that correct, Colonel?"

"Well, sir, I did not say that nor could I have actually witnessed this transaction as—"

"Then you really do not know, do you, Colonel?" There were suppressed titters from the gallery.

"Well, sir," Custer stammered, "from th-th-the almost uniform practices of the p-post and reservation traders any reasonable man could d-deduce that—"

"Any reasonable man," the congressman bellowed, cutting Custer off, "could deduce that this is all hearsay and slander, Colonel! I think the committee has heard about all it needs to hear from you in this regard. You are dismissed, Colonel."

Flustered, blushing, and stuttering badly, an enraged George Custer had stalked from the hearing and headed back toward his hotel room, his head reeling with the appalling hypocrisy of it all. As he dodged a stagnant puddle on Connecticut Avenue, he felt a hand on his elbow.

"A bad business, Armstrong." Congressman Clymer had followed him out into the street. "We knew that there would be some strong opposition to this committee, but we had hoped that the secretary's admission of guilt and resignation would take some of the wind out of their sails."

"Hmmpf! Well, sir, it certainly didn't seem too calm a sea in there today. Have you read what some of the papers have been saying about me?"

"Yes, well, don't mind all that, son. You know for every one of those rags that attacks you there are three that applaud your courage in bearding the lion in his den. All decent men are fully aware of the stench of corruption that has risen over this city, and they are only too glad to have a breath of clean, prairie air to help get the smell out. Don't worry too much on that account, Armstrong. You have a fine reputation, and it will take more than the illiterate scribblings of a few feather-brained printer's monkeys to soil it. I will warn you, however, that President Grant is none too pleased with your presence here." Custer stopped and looked quizzically at the congressman.

"I'm not sure I understand your drift, sir."

Clymer waved a hand lightly in the air. "Oh, well, it's nothing to you really. You know Grant likes to stand behind his old friends and comrades, and he's made the mistake of backing Belknap throughout this whole affair. I'm afraid he can't see that the old scoundrel took advantage of the president's faith in him. It's a hard draught for the president to swallow, you know. So, it appears he may see you as a sort of Judas goat. As I said, I wouldn't worry overly much about this. Why don't you pay him a courtesy call? I'm sure you can straighten the whole thing out."

But Grant wouldn't see him. In the course of the investigations the president's brother Orvil had been implicated in the Indian Ring's kickback scheme. The president had somehow become convinced that this was partly of Custer's doing. An enraged Ulysses S. Grant had exploded and ordered Custer relieved of command of the upcoming summer campaign. For weeks Custer agonized in limbo as he imagined the regiment moving into the field while he was left behind, imprisoned in a gilded cage of dinner parties, whist games, and theater parties but forbidden to leave the city.

Thank God for General Sheridan * and General Terry. If it hadn't been for their intercession, and the stinging editorials in the press, he would still be cooling his heels in Washington. Oh, how he had begged them for their help. It had been humiliating, but never so bad as it would have been if he'd had to follow the regiment's progress from some stifling hotel room in Washington. Yes, thank God for them. They were true friends—they were soldiers. They knew what this command meant to him. He'd resolved that he'd prove worthy of their efforts. Thank goodness it was all over now. He breathed in the fresh scents of buffalo grass and boiling coffee and gave silent thanks for his deliverance from what they called the Great Barbecue.

"Autie!" Boston Custer was almost shouting at his brother, who had been lost in thought."Not brooding about Washington again, are you?"

* *Lieutenant General Philip H. Sheridan, Custer's commander and patron during the Civil War, had risen to command the Division of the Missouri, which included all territory between the Canadian and Mexican borders stretching from Chicago on the east to include New Mexico, Utah, Montana, and Wyoming in the West. A hard-bitten soldier himself, Sheridan took an active, even affectionate interest in the impulsive young cavalry officer whom he viewed as a kindred soul. When General Robert E. Lee surrendered at Appomattox to end the Civil War, Sheridan bought the table on which the document had been signed and presented it to Libby Custer with a note that said, ". . . I know of no person more instrumental in bringing about this most desirable event than your most gallant husband." In the years following, he frequently did his utmost to ameliorate his protégé's occasional lapses of judgment.*

Custer glanced over at his little brother and snorted. "I try not, Bos. It was a singularly unpleasant visit this time."

"I just can't believe that Grant would use you so badly."

"Well, I'm not so sure I believe it myself anymore. Somehow I think it wasn't Grant at all but those buzzards around him. Good generals do not necessarily make good presidents, and Ulysses S. Grant is proving this true in spades. That host of blackguards who've flocked in to join his administration are like flies and maggots on a buffalo carcass. Luckily there are still a few honest men in the nation's capital."

Boston Custer snorted. He thought his older brother was much too forgiving. It was a weakness he had always displayed—George would blow up at a moment's notice, but as soon as the fury was gone, the whole thing would be forgiven and forgotten. George Custer did not hold a grudge and could never comprehend malice in others. Bos thought it was a tragic flaw.

"They sure seem to be in the minority these days," Boston said, spitting carelessly at the ground. "Most of 'em are a pack of self-serving, swindling rascals. It galls me to think of them back there in their shiny black suits and starched shirtfronts, eating expensive dinners and stuffing their pockets with ill-gotten gain. Like that scoundrel Belknap and his crew."

"Yes, well . . ." Custer sighed. "He's replaced and I'm back with the outfit. All's well that ends well, you know. In the end, Sheridan and Terry were able to make him see reason. He was, after all, a soldier. The thing is, I never attacked him or his family directly. You know how I feel about Fred.* Orvil's another story, but I never said a word about the rake."

"Well, by George, you'd think a man could control his own brother!" Boston exclaimed. George Custer just looked at him for a moment, then burst out laughing.

"Oh, that's rich. You're a fine one to talk. Just look at the antics you and that scoundrel Tom have pulled this trip. Why, if Mother could see just half of what goes on, there'd be none of her pot pies for the pair of you for months. And just tell me, my upright young paragon of virtue, where'd you come by those handsome moccasins you're sporting? And how about that bow and arrows Autie Reed is toting about in his kit? The bunch of you are a regular pack of buccaneers."

"Aww, Autie." Boston was blushing and stuttering, a family trait. "For the love of Mike, they're just a few souvenirs. The fellow was long dead and sure didn't need 'em anymore. It's not like we've been out kidnapping

---

* *The president's son, Colonel Fred Grant, was a member of General Sherman's staff and a close personal friend of George Custer's.*

Indian princesses or anything." But his embarrassed protests only caused his brother to laugh even harder.

"Well, if you haven't, it's only because I promised Mother I'd keep a close eye on the lot of you and not let you stray too far from the fold. Heaven knows what mischief you'd have been into if I'd not been along to supervise your excursions. And don't be too hard on brothers, brother. The way I see it, you may well have Orvil Grant to thank for this little entertainment."

Boston looked nonplussed. "What the devil are you talking about?"

George Custer paused, an enigmatic smile crinkling his face. "Well, Bos, look at it this way. If Orvil and the Indian Ring, along with their confederates, had been playing fair with the tribes, they'd like as not be comfortably ensconced on the reservations. But they've been systematically swindling and looting 'em for years. Being forced to give up their hunting grounds for a bit of spoiled meat, lousy blankets, and a sprinkling of moldy flour does not sit well with Mr. Lo. Of course they're off on a spree! Wouldn't you be? I sure as the devil would if I were a Sioux."

"Autie, it sounds to me as if you're fonder of the Sioux than you are of politicians."

"No mystery there, little brother." The Sioux might be the enemy, but George Custer could understand them. He could in fact empathize with them. He gazed off up the line of troops, and urged Vic forward a few paces, putting a little distance between himself and Boston. He wanted to be alone with his thoughts. But his younger brother didn't pick up the hint and trailed doggedly along, wondering what had put George into such an odd mood. Custer studiously ignored the youngster and sucked the morning air deep into his lungs. This was fine country to be loose in. He was lucky to be here. Yes, thank God for Sheridan and Terry.

So far, he had more than justified their confidence. General Terry had already come to rely on him completely. Custer had done his best to make himself indispensable. His knowledge of the country, of the enemy, and his regiment's speed and efficiency had contributed immeasurably to the column's progress. Terry's faith in him had blossomed. Custer brushed the memory of Washington from his mind. Better to think of happier times. Such as his last meeting with General Terry and the staff.

Just days earlier they had all assembled on the *Far West* for a final conference. The steamboat had swung gently from its moorings as the swollen Yellowstone River, muddied from the recent rains, churned and bubbled alongside. Custer had already come on board and was chatting with Captain Marsh when the rest of the column's officers had come clambering up the gangway. It was a cheerful assemblage. Everyone was in such fine spirits. He recalled the jokes, the good-natured joshing and backslapping. Even the usually taciturn Marcus Reno was engaged in a bout of good-natured haggling with one of the sutlers on board. The round-faced major was trying his level best to get a fifty-cent straw hat for twenty-five cents. In the midst of the bustle, Terry's adjutant, Captain Smith, appeared on deck and summoned the senior commanders.

"Gentlemen, the commanding general presents his compliments and asks that you join him in the wardroom." The mature captain assumed a formal posture and ushered the small group through the door. Custer winked at the man as he passed him. What great fun! This was what they all lived for, to be out on campaign. The blood racing through their veins. The air smelling cleaner. The food tastier. Everything appearing sharper and in absolutely crystal clear focus. They felt truly alive. There was nothing quite like the feeling of comfort and contentment as they gathered, brother officers all, in the warm glow of the oil lamps of the steamer's cabin: the rich fragrance of brewing coffee, the pungent aroma of burning cigars, the smell of the warm, wool uniforms and leather, the sweet scent of oil on steel.

General Terry was in a buoyant mood. "Gentlemen, my compliments! Glad you're all here. I trust you've had a good campaign thus far? Capital! Capital! I say, John, your 'web feet' have certainly earned their names this time out. Damned hard marching with all that rain up your way." Colonel John Gibbon nodded.

"It has been hard on the men, General. But they are holding up remarkably well, considering."

"Well, that's fine, John, fine. Gentlemen, I suppose you know why we're all here today. Suppose we just get right down to it, hmmm?"

The officers crowded around a table covered with green felt on which Terry's adjutant unrolled a large map, weighting the corners with an inkstand and some heavy ironstone coffee mugs. As the afternoon wore on, they discussed the campaign in detail—poring over the maps of the area, reviewing the newest intelligence reports as a secretary quietly made notes in the background. Major Reno's reconnaissance of a few days before had turned up some promising leads. The enemy was close. Traces of campsites and fresh trails indicated that the Sioux were below them and heading down the Rosebud River. From what Reno had found, and from what the agencies were telling them about bands that had gone missing from the reservations, there were a large number of Sioux somewhere up ahead. Terry seemed inordinately pleased with the way things were turning out.

"Well, gentlemen, this is all just capital. Looks like we're on their trail for sure. They'll be hard-pressed to slip away this time. So, how many does that add up to? Jim, you've a good head for figures. What's the count?"

Major James Brisbin, whose nickname was "Grasshopper Jim," frowned for a moment, then snatched a scrap of foolscap off of the secretary's writing desk. Pulling a stubby length of pencil from his pocket, he leaned over the map and made a few notes, half-mumbling to himself.

"Well, there's the agency returns, hmm, and then the information that young Bradley brought in . . ." He stopped and scratched his head vigorously. "Then, of course there's Reno's report—course he's new to this so that might be a bit on the large size . . . sooo." Brisbin screwed up his lips and scribbled a few more lines. Finally he stood up straight and ticked off his estimate.

"Well, looks to be somewhere near four hundred lodges. Now, that would run to about three or four thousand people altogether. We figure that'll include maybe two warriors for every lodge, so that totals up at maybe eight hundred warriors altogether. Sound about right to you fellows?"

A few grunts answered him in the affirmative, and he looked over at General Terry, who was nodding solemnly and stroking his long beard.

"Well, that's just excellent," Terry said, turning to Custer. "Why, Armstrong, you've nearly seven hundred fifty in the Seventh Cavalry alone, don't you?"

Custer nodded his assent, "Well, General, it's nearer six hundred right now, but yes, that's about right. Then again, we're not burdened with women and children either."

The kindly Terry smiled, his eyes twinkling with mischief. "That's only because we've managed to persuade you to leave Libby behind this time out. Although I hear tell you have most of the Custer children along with you nonetheless!"

The puckish jibe produced a howl of laughter from the other officers, among whom the Custer family had a reputation for childish pranks. Custer himself flushed, secretly enjoying the good-natured ribbing that his colleagues were eager to dish out. When the laughter had settled into a few coughs and some eye-wiping, Terry brought the conversation back to the business at hand.

"Well, well, eight hundred young bucks. This should not be too much trouble, I shouldn't think. It should be a fairly easy task to pen 'em up and force 'em back to the reservation. Now that you've got your column up, John, the net is closing quickly. If I recall, you muster about seven hundred effectives, John. Am I right?" Gibbon nodded. "And General Crook, you know, has pushed out of Fort Fetterman with about nine hundred men and is even now coming up from the south. With a little luck we'll pin 'em in between us and should catch 'em somewhere about here." He traced a small circle over the map with his cigar and let the soggy butt come to rest in a small area alongside a curling black line labeled as the Little Bighorn River.

As the meeting drew to a close, Terry restated the outline of the overall campaign plan. Terry and Gibbon's columns would move to the south. Crook's column, as yet unheard from, should still be moving north. If the current rate of movement could be maintained, they should be able to trap the Sioux between them at the Little Bighorn sometime around the twenty-sixth of June. The one real concern was this: What if the hostiles slipped off to the south or east before Crook could come up the Rosebud? What if they broke up, scattered into small bands, and ran? The campaign could drag on for months. Rubbing his chin thoughtfully, Terry turned to Custer.

"What do you think, Armstrong? Can you use the Seventh to keep the birds from flying the net?"

Custer beamed broadly. "No fear, General, I rather think we can manage to urge them along."

In a few minutes they had worked out the details. The Seventh Cavalry would split off from the rest of the command and proceed south, up the Rosebud River before feeling their way west toward the Little Big Horn. Terry agreed that this should "preclude the possibility of the escape of the Indians to the south or southeast." Grasshopper Jim Brisbin of the Second Cavalry offered to add a company of his outfit and a Gatling gun detachment. Custer thought about it for a moment, then shook his head.

"No offense, Jim, but I'd rather not mix in a new outfit this late in the game. Besides, another sixty fellows can't make that big a difference." He turned back to Terry. "I think I'll decline on the Gatlings too, General. I intend we should move fairly rapidly over rough country. The carriages tend to upset too easily, and I'm afraid they would embarrass our progress. I intend we shall take no wheeled conveyances at all, but depend entirely upon pack mules." Brisbin shook his head, but Colonel Gibbon nodded his agreement.

"Armstrong's right on the Gatlings, General, they have been no end of a nuisance to us. They hang up on the rocks or sink into the mud or tip over every few miles. We had another man hurt only yesterday. Besides, I'm not confident that they will work very well. The cartridges tend to jam in the barrels. I doubt they'll be of much use to the cavalry. We're moving fairly slowly already, so they might as well stay with us."

General Terry shrugged. "Thank you, John, I hadn't considered that.

Very well, Armstrong. Then it's settled. I'll have Captain Smith draw up your instructions in the morning."

When Terry's written orders arrived the next day, they were brimming with confidence. How had he phrased it? Ah, yes: ". . . *the Department Commander places too much confidence in your zeal, energy, and ability to wish to impose upon you precise orders which might hamper your action when nearly in contact with the enemy.*" Custer could hardly contain his excitement. What a grand day that had been—the sun shining down brightly, massed trumpets blaring a fanfare, the regiment cantering along the river as they passed by Terry and his assembled staff. Everyone had been in such high spirits, Terry calling out with mock sternness, "Don't be greedy now, Custer. Wait for us." The staff had all chortled at that and then, when he'd turned and called back, "Don't worry, I won't!" they had all laughed. A glorious day.

Custer smiled as he recalled the moment. Now it promised to be another glorious day. The air was still and clear, and the sun would soon burn off the morning mist. He made a mental note to make sure that these fires were out before then. The Sioux were close. He could feel it in his bones. Should catch up with them sometime tomorrow, he thought. Today's Sunday and we'll make it a true day of rest. Rest the regiment, rest the horses. They'd been riding hard the past few days, and this country was hard on man and beast alike. No sense going into action with everyone fagged out.

He replayed his general plan in his head. Keep the scouts out poking about, get the enemy's location pinpointed, and hit 'em first thing in the morning. Get 'em just as the sun comes up. Perfect. They'll be groggy, sun'll be in their eyes. We'll hit 'em from two sides, put 'em into a panic. The Rees and Crows can run off the pony herd, and we'll corral the women and children. And, if they try to run to the north, they'll run straight into Gibbon and Terry. Shouldn't even be much of a fight at all. They won't want to risk it with the women and children right there. With any luck this whole expedition should be over before the Fourth of July. A perfect birthday gift to the nation. Custer's luck.

He nudged Vic lightly with his knee, and the large sorrel turned easily around to head back down the line of troops, with Boston trailing alongside. The coffee was just beginning to boil, and the aroma had drawn the last of the sluggards out of their warm bedrolls, tin cups in hand. At the far end of the bivouac he could see some hurried movement among the troopers. Carbines were being snatched up. Something was happening. He leaned forward and dug his heels into Vic's flanks, urging him into an easy canter.

"Riders comin' in!" someone shouted. "They're Injuns!" Breechblocks clicked shut as copper-cased rounds were slammed into carbines all up and down the line. Above the commotion Custer heard a barked command.

"Stand easy, there!"

He recognized his brother Tom's voice, still hoarse with sleep. As he came up alongside the staff, all standing around in their shirtsleeves, revolvers drawn, he could make out two riders tearing down the valley toward them, individual dust clouds marking their progress. The riders were turning their horses left and right in wide zigzag patterns, churning up the dust and sagebrush. Must be Varnum's scouts coming back.

"Couple of the Rees, Autie," Tom Custer stated quietly as he thumbed the hammer of his Colt down gently on an empty chamber. "Looks like they've got some news for us. Mornin', Bos."

Lieutenant Colonel George Custer leaned over the withers of his horse and tapped his brother Tom lightly on the shoulder.

"More delicacy, if you please, Captain Custer. Would you insult our esteemed representative of the Fourth Estate? I am sure Mr. Kellogg's employers would be dearly disappointed to find anyone had beaten him to a story on this campaign." Tom grinned wickedly and turned to the reporter who stood with his eyes riveted on the approaching Rees. Tom Custer removed his oversized Stetson and made a sweeping bow.

"I do beg your pardon, Mr. Kellogg," he said with false gravity, "but those fellows do look remarkably like a couple of mugs I know who scribble for the *New York World*." The small knot of soldiers laughed. Kellogg smiled.

"Ah, they do indeed, Captain," he responded, "but I suspect that these two gentlemen are considerably more articulate than the villains you mistake them for."

The officers around them screamed with delight. "Touché, Mr. Reporter," they called, hooting and slapping their thighs in glee. Tom looked sheepishly up at his older brother, who was wiping tears of laughter from sunburned cheeks.

"Never lock horns with the press, little brother," George Custer said, wagging a finger. "Even Napoleon knew they are 'more to be feared than a thousand bayonets.' "

The Ree scouts, now within hailing distance, urged their ponies into a final burst of speed, lashing their flanks with rawhide quirts. The young braves were yelling and whooping, one through firmly clenched teeth from which fluttered the small scrap of paper on which Charley Reynolds had scribbled his hasty report. Custer looked over at his staff and grinned. "Looks like we've found 'em, boys!"

(TRANSCRIPT OF GENERAL TERRY'S ORDERS)

Headquarters Department of Dakota

(In the Field)

Camp at Mouth of Rosebud River
Montana, June 22nd, 1876 *

Lieut. Col. G. A. Custer, 7th Cavalry
Colonel:

The Brigadier General Commanding directs that, as soon as your regiment can be made ready for the march, you will proceed up the Rosebud in pursuit of the Indians whose trail was discovered by Major Reno a few days since. It is, of course, impossible to give you any definite instructions in regard to this movement, and were it not impossible to do so, the Department Commander places too much confidence in your zeal, energy, and ability to wish to impose upon you precise orders which might hamper your action when nearly in contact with the enemy. He will however, indicate to you his own views of what your action should be, and he desires that you should conform to them unless you shall see sufficient reason for departing from them. He thinks that you should proceed up the Rosebud until you ascertain definitely the direction in which the trail above spoken of leads. Should it be found (as it appears almost certain that it will be found) to turn towards the Little Horn, he thinks that you should still proceed southward, perhaps as far as the headwaters of the Tongue, and then turn towards the Little Horn, feeling constantly, however, to your left, so as to preclude the possibility of the escape of the Indians to the south or southeast by passing around your left flank.

The column of Colonel Gibbon is now in motion for the mouth of the Big Horn. As soon it reaches that point it will cross the Yellowstone and move up at least as far as the forks of the Big and Little Horns. Of course its further movements must be controlled by circumstances as they arise, but it is hoped that the Indians, if upon the Little Horn, may be so nearly inclosed by the two columns that their escape will be impossible. The Department Commander desires that on your way up the Rosebud you should thoroughly examine the upper part of Tullock's

---

* *Following the conference on the* Far West, *General Terry dictated these orders for Custer and his command. The focus of controversy for years, it is left for the reader to determine how specific they really were. For clarity, it should be explained that the Little Horn is yet another name for the Little Bighorn (names of geographical features were not yet standardized). Also, it should be noted that the Rosebud and Little Bighorn run from south to north. Thus to proceed "up the Rosebud" is to move south.*

Creek, and that you should endeavor to send a scout through to Colonel Gibbon's Column, with information of the results of your examination. The lower part of the creek will be examined by a detachment from Colonel Gibbon's command.

The supply steamer will be pushed up the Big Horn as far as the forks if the river is found to be navigable for that distance, and the Department Commander, who will accompany the Column of Colonel Gibbon, desires you report to him there not later than the expiration of the time for which your troops are rationed, unless in the meantime you receive further orders.

Very Respectfully,
Your Obedient Servant,
Ed. W. Smith, Captain, 18th Infantry
Acting Assistant Adjutant General

Añpakableza (Dawn), Moon When the Ponies Are Fat (June), In the Valley of the Peji Slawakpa (Greasy Grass)

The dogs were barking outside of the lodge, snarling and snapping at each other over some scrap or a discarded bone. Gall had been resting fitfully, his sleep marred by images of bearded white men fighting over the carcass of a buffalo. In his dreams he approached them, thinking to stop their fighting by saying that Pte* provided enough for all. But instead of listening, the men started to attack him. As they jumped over the animal, they turned into dogs and began to tear at the sleeves of Gall's shirt. He awoke with a start and decided that he would probably not get any more sleep.

The dogs did behave remarkably like the *wasichus*. The whites were forever squabbling over everything—their cattle, the big wooden lodges they built, the patches of dirt they scratched to make things grow or to find the shiny stones. They would not see that there was enough for everyone, that no one ever really owned what the Wakan Tanka provided. He thought they were a foolish and greedy people, and he could not understand why the Great Spirit had plagued the land with these strange people. They were like the grasshoppers who ate everything in their path and were never satisfied.

He rolled quietly out of his robes so he would not disturb his sleeping wives and children, and ducked through the opening of his lodge to relieve himself. As he walked behind the lodge, he saw the dogs still quarreling over the thigh bone of a buffalo calf. Gall looked around for a small stone and hurled it into the pack, where it produced a yelp and sent the animals

* Pte, or Uncle, is the Lakota name for the buffalo.

scurrying off in different directions. Emptying his bladder into the already wet grass, he stared into the heavy fog that hung over the river. Already thousands of sparrows were flinging their light bodies through the moist air, bursting from the fog in black knots as they swooped up from the river. Behind him most of the camp still slept, many exhausted from the dancing and feasting of the previous night.

It had been a riotous evening, with much singing and boasting and overindulgence in many things. The young men were especially pleased with themselves after the fight with "Three Stars" a few days earlier,* and this had been their first opportunity to strut and show off for the young women. Gall, a mature thirty-five and tending toward heaviness, had little time or inclination for such foolishness, but he would not begrudge the young ones their celebration. He too had once been like them—until he found Brings-the-Rain and Sweet Grass. They were good wives and had presented him with a son and two beautiful daughters, whom he loved with a jealousy that surprised even him.

He was glad the girls were still so young that he would have many seasons before the young men would come mooning about his lodge with lovesick eyes. Someday he would have to put up with the fistfuls of prairie flowers, the awful poetry, flutes playing mournfully outside in the moonlight. He grimaced at the thought. Oh, well, someday he would have to suffer it all, but not today. He fought back the urge to look in at his sleeping family. The little ones had been worn out by all the excitement and it was well that they were still snuggled into their robes. They'd be up and chattering away soon enough, and he might as well enjoy the quiet of the morning while it lasted.

Quiet was a rare thing in a camp this large. He looked down the river where the rest of the people lay. It was still a thing of wonder. So many lodges. So many of the tribes all in this one place. No one had ever seen or even heard of a gathering so large. Two weeks ago it had only been the winter roamers out here, but over the past several days more and more of the people had been coming out from the agencies to join the camp. Now there were thousands here. Nobody knew why they had all gathered. No one had called for a gathering. It was if they had all felt themselves drawn to this place by some irresistible force.

---

* On 17 June 1876 a large force of warriors had clashed with General George Crook's column on the banks of the Rosebud River. In a fierce battle that raged for most of the day, the Sioux and their Cheyenne allies had fought the troops to a standstill. Although both sides claimed a victory, the Army withdrew from the field, and Crook's troops would spend the next few weeks nursing their wounds and fishing along Goose Creek. Oddly enough, Crook did not think to inform the other columns of his fight with the Sioux and their allies.

All of them together! His people, the Hunkpapa at this end, and as far as you could see downriver the others—first the Blackfeet and Miniconjou, then the Sans Arcs and Oglalas, Two Kettles and Brulés, and at the far end the Shyelas, the Northern Cheyennes, and their friends the Arapahos. You could not count all the lodges. And everywhere you looked were the wickiups, the little lodges of saplings and brush that the young warriors fashioned for themselves, thankful, no doubt, to be out from under the watchful eyes of their parents, if only for a few days.

Gall stretched and began to forage for something to eat. Sweet Grass must have guessed he would be up early, for he found she had cached some stew in a small hole under the fire. It would be safe from the roaming dogs there, and she must have known he would find it quickly as he stoked up the fire. He drew the kettle carefully out of the ashes, sat down in the grass, and began to dip out the savory mixture with his fingers. It was delicious. Years before, Sweet Grass had secretly approached his mother to find out exactly how to prepare venison stew in just this way. She knew how much he enjoyed it and was determined to get it right. Not many wives were quite so eager to cater to their husband's small whims. He inhaled the heady aroma, picking out the slight scents of sage and juniper berries that accented the tender meat, and thought again how lucky he had been in his choice of women.

Nearby, he could hear someone stumbling awkwardly out of another lodge and looked up to see young Black Elk stagger sleepily toward the pony herd. He was a sickly youngster, skinnier than usual for his age and prone to bouts of coughing. The boy dreamed of being a great warrior, but Gall did not think this would be very likely. The boy was rather too dreamy and given to visions. This was not necessarily a bad thing. Perhaps it meant that he was meant to become a shaman, a holy man. There was much honor for the one who followed this path.

"You look troubled, brother." Gall looked up to see his friend, Crow King, standing in front of him. The tall figure in buckskin was smiling down at him.

"Is your head still bad from last night's fun?" Crow King asked lightly. Gall just grunted and indicated that his friend should take a place by the fire. He nodded toward the kettle.

"Have some stew, brother. It's the best thing for a bad stomach, which I am sure you have this morning. I recall that it was not just I who was doing all the celebrating, and I at least got to bed before sunup." He grinned at his friend and thumped his hand on the grass next to him. "Come, sit down and we'll eat and talk."

Crow King shuffled around the fire and eased himself into a sitting position next to Gall while at the same time reaching into the kettle for a couple of chunks of steaming meat.

"I had hoped you would offer me a bit of this," Crow King said, smacking his lips. "The smell woke me up, and I knew that Sweet Grass had been working her magic again and thought you might need a little help in doing justice to her labor."

Gall nodded and took a large swallow.

"Have as much as you want. The less that is left, the better she will like it. To eat well is the best praise of the cook."

Crow King reached over and patted his friend's ample stomach.

"I can plainly see you have been lavishing praise on her."

Gall laughed. "Yes, well, it would not do to neglect one's family duties."

"It's good to see you smile again. It's something I have not seen lately. Has something been bothering you?" Crow phrased the question casually, hoping to elicit a more candid response. While Gall was generally known for his straightforward nature, he could sometimes be evasive about expressing his inner thoughts. It was as if the veteran warrior saw it as his duty to present an air of detachment as an example to the younger men.

Gall hesitated for a moment, casting a sidelong glance at his friend. "It's nothing really, just a feeling I have that something is going to happen. Everything has gone so well this summer that I am sure this will be a good thing, but someone keeps whispering in my dreams that even a good thing can be dangerous." He shoveled another chunk of meat into his mouth, then continued to talk while chewing slowly and waving a large, greasy hand at the huge encampment.

"Look around us, brother. Never have so many of the people come together in such a way in this place. It is truly a wondrous thing. Even the Shyelas have joined us, with their little brothers the Arapahos and the Big Bellies. Old feuds are forgotten, there is plenty to eat, we sing and dance and play games and watch our children play in the sunshine, and everyone is happy." He waved toward his lodge adorned with hundreds of pictographs depicting the achievements of a lifetime.

"Never have I seen a gathering of so many. When the time comes to make the winter count, I don't know how we will record these days and everything that has happened in so short a time. And yet"—Gall paused, distracted—"and yet I am uneasy. The air is different. It feels like it does when a thunderstorm is approaching. Something is not quite right."

Crow King nodded and dipped into the kettle for more meat. Gall watched his friend chewing and went on.

"You remember the old stories as well as I do," Gall said. "Can you remember ever hearing of when we were so many and so powerful as now?"

"It is surely so, brother," Crow King said. "But why should this trouble you? It is, as you say, a good summer." He shook a balled fist in the direction of the herds. "The ponies are fat and we are stronger than we have ever been. It is no time for sorrows. Be happy, watch your children, eat this good food, and don't worry so much. What tomorrow brings, it brings."

Gall shook his head. "I don't know. This fight with Three Stars is troubling. I think it means there will be more trouble." Crow King licked his fingers and nodded quickly.

"Yes, yes," he said. "It was a bad thing. But we did not want to fight them. Even that wild Oglala Crazy Horse did not go looking for a fight. He and our friend Sitting Bull have told the people to stay away from the *wasichus*, is it not so? It was that hothead Shyela Wooden Leg who stirred up the young men and drew them into the fight. And this he could not have done if Three Stars had stayed far away from us and left us alone. But we chased Three Stars away. We showed him that we are strong and will not run away from him. Perhaps they are so frightened they will leave us alone."

"Yes," Gall said finally, "I tell myself this same thing. If we stay away from them, we will not have to fight, but the *wasichus* are true to their name,* and where you find one, you will almost surely find many more following behind. Now even Sitting Bull is acting strangely. He has more visions and says that 'many soldiers will fall into our camp.' This is not prophecy. It is common sense. But I wish he would not say it in front of the young men. It makes their hearts bad, and they may go to find more trouble and it may follow them home, as the wolf follows the hunter when he has killed an elk."

Crow King thought about this for a minute and frowned. "You think that Sitting Bull has been careless with his talk. Spotted Tail says much the same thing, but then he has often spoken against Sitting Bull and few listen to him anymore. The people say that Sitting Bull's medicine is very strong, and truly everything he has said has come to pass. It is no surprise that he is so popular. Do you think that perhaps he is being influenced by what all the people are saying about his powers?"

Gall stopped chewing and looked up at Crow King, surprised to hear his own thoughts expressed so starkly. They had been friends since boy-

---

* Wasichu, *although frequently translated as "white-eyes," more literally means "cannot get rid of them" in the Hunkpapa Lakota dialect.*

hood, and yet Crow King had never before indicated that he thought of such things.

"It is a hard thing to say of an old friend," Gall said slowly. "But yes, I think about it. Maybe I should speak to him about this. He has become almost too proud. I have begun to wonder if perhaps not all of what Sitting Bull says that Wakan Tanka tells him is just that."

Crow King grinned impishly. "Are you saying that maybe there is less of Wakan Tanka and more of Sitting Bull in his talk lately?"

Gall looked down at his food, unwilling to meet his friend's gaze. "I don't want to think this," he said slowly, "but he is becoming a hard man to like."

"And yet everyone likes him."

Gall nodded in exasperated agreement.

"I know, I know. But something just does not seem right. He seems different to me in some ways." He stopped for a second, thinking how best to explain the problem. He looked closely at Crow King and posed a question: "Would you not say that Bull has always been a generous man?"

Crow King looked puzzled but quickly replied. "Truly it is so. But what has this to do with anything that you have told me?"

Gall held up a finger and smiled grimly. "Ah, but it has everything to do with it. He is a very generous man and has always had a reputation for that, but is it not how a thing is given that lends it value?"

Crow King looked even more puzzled. "Yes, of course, but still I don't see what you mean. If anything he has been more generous lately than before. He can deny no one and many come to him for help and advice."

"Yes, they do. But it is as if *that* is why he gives his possessions away —to bring more of the people under his influence." Gall leaned forward, warming to his subject. "It seems that he gives a little to get much and to open the ears of those he would have follow him. So that when he says Wakan Tanka says this and Wakan Tanka said that, I'm no longer sure that this is so, or if the truth is that he is just blown up with how important the people have made him out to be. And if this is true, is he not made drunk by what the young men do? He says it is his medicine that makes their success possible."

"Bah!" Crow King scoffed. "Now you are being foolish. If I did not know you so well, I would say that maybe you are a little jealous. Sitting Bull is seen to be as great a visionary as ever he was a warrior. And this just when we are getting to the point where we no longer go out with the war parties so often as we once did. So as Bull becomes a wise old man, we are just becoming old men. I think maybe you envy his popularity. I am sorry if you think I am being harsh."

Gall merely shook his head. "No, you are possibly right. And I did not say that these things are truly so, only that they are things that cause me to lay awake at night wondering. As things are, I should not worry for, as you say, everything is going well for us. But sometimes at night I hear a voice in my head that says there is danger in too much pride. You know that I am no lover of the *wasichus,* and you and I and Sitting Bull have stood together against them for many seasons. But just because we have been fortunate in this last fight, I do not think we should make too light of the situation. Again, I say, look at all of our people gathered here." Gall swept his arm in a broad arc across the camp. "Before the circles came together, this was the land of the Crows and the Corn Indians, and even the Hunkpapas were afraid because the Crows are fierce enemies. Now this is our land, and we are so many and so strong that they run to hide behind the whites."

Crow King grunted in agreement, and Gall paused and lifted his finger meaningfully.

"But, will the *wasichus* not do as we did?" Gall asked rhetorically. "Even the Heyokas* cannot say this will not happen. You have said that Spotted Tail is of the Peace Talkers and Sitting Bull has often called him an old woman, but you and I both know that Spotted Tail has been a brave warrior. But since he was taken to the white man's fort, he has not been anxious to fight them at every turn. He says they are like bees in a hive and will swarm over us and deliver so many little stings that we will have to run away or die. And what if they are angry after the beating we gave Three Stars? What if they come now with more soldiers and the guns that talk twice.† It is not good that all of our families are here in one place."

Crow King was nodding slowly at the logic of his friend's argument. He waited patiently until Gall had apparently said everything that was on his mind, then stretched and prepared to get up.

"Well, brother," Crow King said slowly, "it is clear to me that you have thought much of this and a lot of what you say has sense in it, but still I think you worry too much. Look around us. This cannot last too much longer. There is not enough game and grass for all of the people to stay here for another day or two. Already the buffalo are far away, and we will have to go our own ways soon to be able to feed our families and our

---

* A Heyoka—the word means "contrary," or "joker"—was a sort of buffoon who did everything backward, saying good-bye when he arrived and hello when he left, washing with dirt and sometimes even riding his horse backward. He was much the same as the medieval court jester.
† "Guns that talk twice" meant artillery, also called "wagon guns," usually small mountain howitzers that fired explosive shells.

ponies. We chased away Three Stars, and it will be a long time before the soldiers come again, and we will be gone when they come."

Crow King stood up slowly.

"Again, I tell you not to worry about what you cannot change. What tomorrow brings, it brings, and only the earth is forever. You should just enjoy this while it lasts." Crow King looked down at his friend, who was now staring into the fire apparently deep in thought. Around them the camp was beginning to stir.

Gall heard a commotion and looked up to see that young Black Elk had awakened his friend Dewy Beard and the two boys were weaving their way noisily through the lodges and generally taking their time as they headed toward the pony herd. As they moved through the camp, they were joined by several of their friends. Some of them were still wearing their hair knotted on their heads to resemble bear's ears, remnants, he supposed, of the previous night's festivities, bright paints now smeared and smudged on their wiry young bodies. Gall knew that once the day warmed up most of them would take the first chance to head for the river for a swim. The dogs he had chased off earlier had now attached themselves to the group of youngsters. Gall looked up at Crow King and smiled. "Well, many dreams are about to come to a noisy end."

Crow chuckled and shook his head.

"I should have slept while I could, but I could not pass up this wonderful meal and your good company. You should smile more, brother. Maybe it will do you good to go teach those boys how to swim."

"Hunh," Gall grunted without much enthusiasm. "Teach boys how to swim," he repeated thoughtfully. "Do you think we can teach them how to swim in the sea of whites that will come to drown us? We should be teaching them how to fight, how to take the *wasichus'* guns and turn them against them. We have not seen the end of these people. First they came to hunt and trap the beaver and there were very few of them, and we did not care so much because they were few and they took little. Wakan Tanka had enough for all, and we did not begrudge them a pelt here and some meat there. They gave us presents. They brought the iron things that make better arrowheads and guns that shoot farther than our bows, knives that make it easy to take the hides of Uncle Pte and the scalps of our enemies. We did not hate them then." Gall paused, his face clouded over and his eyes became hard as he thought about the changing times.

"Then there were more and more of them," Gall continued, "but these men came to dig up the hills for the shiny metal and to scratch our mother with sticks to grow things, and they do not go away again. They stay and they tear the ground and chase away the game. They bring their sicknesses that kill the Lakota with spots and fever. They kill Pte for sport and they kill us for sport. They bring the burning water that makes the young braves crazy. First they were like small raindrops and we brushed them away and went to our lodges to stay dry, but now they are like the storms that fill the rivers and make the floods that carry everything away. They are a flood and they will sweep our lodges and our people away before them. Can we teach those boys how to swim against such a flood?" Gall threw a piece of stew meat violently into the fire, where it hissed and sputtered in the flames.

Crow King just watched and shook his head slowly. There was no talking to Gall today; he was too moody and depressed. Crow thought about saying something to try to cheer him up but decided he was wasting his time. If Gall wanted to mope around and let this beautiful day pass him by, then let him. Crow was more interested in having a cool swim and then maybe a nap in the shade of the trees as the day grew hotter.

As Crow King turned and headed for the river, Gall watched the boisterous mob of youngsters prancing happily through the camp and thought that maybe his friend was right. Maybe he worried too much. This would probably be a day like many others. He should just try to enjoy it. A light breeze stirred the air, and for the first time he noticed the sweet scent of the wild cherry blossoms as it wafted over him. Maybe he would watch the girls gather berries and turnips with their mother today. It was as much as he wanted to do on a day that promised to be so hot.

0530 Hours
Along Davis Creek

Private Patrick Kelly, Company I, Seventh U.S. Cavalry, was squatting on his haunches, balancing precariously on the balls of his feet. The brass spurs on his boots dug into his rump, but Kelly was seemingly oblivious to their pricking, as his full attention was on a shallow hole in front of him. Into this hole he was gingerly pushing scraps of sagebrush to fuel the small but very hot fire that he had managed to kindle a few moments before. The trick was to break up the fuel into dry little bits that would bring the flame to its hottest without smothering it and without giving off a telltale plume of smoke. Kelly's hair was an unruly mass of sandy curls that tumbled over his sunburned forehead and all but obscured his soft gray eyes. An old-timer in the company, Kelly had once tried deserting, but his escapade had lasted a brief four days before he was picked up by the local authorities. As a result, he had been on the wrong side of Sergeant Bustard ever since. Bustard thus took exceptional pleasure in supervising Kelly's efforts.

Sergeant James Bustard had spent most of an hour explaining in excruciating detail the finer points of campfires and the proper method for stoking them to their optimum temperature. At the same time, he had managed to make it abundantly clear that he had no confidence whatever in Kelly's ability to get his boots on the right feet, let alone handle anything as complex as getting the breakfast fire going.

"Easy there, Kelly! Don't smother her. Ease off a little, don't give 'er too much at once, you'll spoil 'er sure. That's it, just a nibble now and again. Yer far too ham-handed a bumpkin to do 'er justice."

Bustard lay stretched out full-length on a saddle blanket spread in the damp grass, his head resting on the seat of his McClellan saddle, boots propped on Kelly's saddle, with his spurs slipped neatly into the slotted seat.

"Don't look at me, ye dim-witted potato brain! Watch the damn fire, fer Gawdsake. Good Lord, what the hell was the Army thinkin' when they put yer idiot self in the cavalry? Musta figgered the horse'd do just enough thinking fer the both of ye."

Kelly's eyes dropped furtively to the fire hole just in time to keep from sticking his fingers into the nearly invisible flames. He drew them back quickly and reached for a few more sage twigs.

"Make sure them things is dead dry, Paddy, or ye'll have the whole damn bivouac smoked up to beat all. The damn Sioux'll think sure yer sending 'em love notes."

Kelly's bunky,* Private Gustave Korn, emerged from a nearby stand of timber, where he'd gone off to answer the call of nature. He now approached the small group, a load of firewood balanced in his arms and a mass of canteens swinging ponderously from his crooked elbows. The staggering figure caught Bustard's eye and earned Korn a burst of encouragement.

"Come on, Gussy, ye square-headed clod. We're burning daylight and my damned guts are rumblin'. Did'ja make sure it was dry, ye Dutch oaf?"

"*Ja wohl*, Sergeant. It's good and dry, just like you say." Korn grinned sheepishly from behind the wood. "I'm filling up the canteens good too. *Verdammnt* mosquitoes down there big like vultures they is, you bet."

Bustard cocked his head and observed Korn's progress as the stocky German moved unsteadily toward him. "I'll be happy if ye've managed not to piss on the lot, Gussy. And I hope ye had sense enough to get that water upstream of the rest o' these yahoos. Did'ja 'member to soak the covers down good? Looks like she'll be another scorcher today."

"*Ja wohl*, Sergeant! But it helps the taste not vun little bit. Maybe we find some better water on up ahead, *ja?*"

"Never count on it, Gussy," Bustard opined solemnly. "That bilge might be the onliest stuff for miles and we best get it while we can. If'n we come across some sweet water, that's all well an' good an' we'll change 'er out. But don't ye go bettin' the farm we'll find 'er. I reckon that stuff'll taste sweet enough afore this day's out." Korn nodded solemnly and cast about for a place to drop his load of firewood.

"Here, Gus, lemme grab them canteens for ya." Private James McNally shifted up on his knees and grabbed the canvas straps while Korn shifted the wood against his chest to let McNally slip the canteens off his arms.

---

* "Bunky" or "bunkie" was the common term for a soldier's bunkmate, or buddy. Although not a formal system, all troopers would "buddy-up" with another soldier upon joining an active duty unit. A bunky was a soldier's closest friend and confidant. Bunkies looked out for one another's welfare, shared rations and frequently blankets, as the standard issue of one blanket per man was often insufficient to keep a soldier warm in the field.

"Thanks, Jimmy. Dat water she's pretty heavy, you bet." Korn dropped to his knees in the grass, tumbled the wood into a small pile, and began rubbing the circulation back into his arms. He peered anxiously at the mess tin balanced precariously over the lip of the fire pit. "We got us some coffee now? *Gott*, but I've got some hunger now, boys." Kelly glowered silently up at his friend.

"We'd have it sure by now if Kelly were half as good with a fire as he is with the ladies," Bustard said archly, alluding to the reason for Kelly's abortive attempt to duck out of his enlistment. The sergeant punctuated his comment by heaving a pebble at his fellow Irishman, who was directing his full attention to the small campfire and studiously ignoring Bustard's commentary.

"They're much of a piece, ya know," Bustard said casually. "Ladies and fires, that is."

The young troopers sensed that Bustard was about to deliver a homily on the fairer sex, and every ear within range was pricked to full attention.

"Now," Bustard went on, seemingly to himself, "if you know anything a'tall about the ladies, God bless 'em all, which most of ye sods surely do not as I can plainly see from yer dumb mugs, ye'll know they must be handled very much like a good campfire. Gussy, slap some damn mud on them skeeter bites and stop fussin' at 'em. Ye're distractin' me! Now, as I was sayin', if'n you're careless, you'll get yer fingers burned good like Private Kelly there. But, if you're an experienced and worldly gent, much like meself, she'll be a rare comfort and a joy to ye." Bustard paused, and quizzical looks were exchanged among the young cavalrymen. Korn grinned broadly at McNally and nudged him with an elbow.

"Uh, Sergeant Bustard," McNally ventured, "how's that work? With the ladies, I mean."

"Well, Jimmy, you're a bright lad, ye are. It's like this, the first thing ye got to know is ye can't be impatient. Ye got to go slowlike. Feed 'er little bits o' fuel, like candies and such, ever so careful and gentle like to get the fire stoked up. But, whatever ye do, don't pile it on so thick and fast that ye smother her." Bustard shot a glance at Kelly, who quickly looked back at the campfire.

"Now, if ye tickle and tease 'er just a bit," Bustard drawled easily, "blow in 'er ear gentle-like, why, before long she'll be white-hot and ready to cook yer breakfast and bile yer coffee. Yes, lads, ye jest have to know what ye're about." He looked sharply back at Kelly, who was now scowling as if he'd like nothing better than to land a punch right on Bustard's nose. The other young troopers grinned wickedly at Kelly's discomfort.

"Kelly, my lad, you'd best hope your soldiering skills improve a mite this trip, for you're gonna need to keep the Army as a home. If your courtin' is like your fire-making, you'll starve for sure—except in your dreams!" This brought a burst of laughter from the other troopers as Kelly turned beet red and gritted his teeth.

This only encouraged the group, who blew kisses in his direction and started up an impromptu chorus of "Mother, Kiss Me in My Dreams" to the obvious delight of Sergeant Bustard, who had nudged his hat down over his eyes and was pretending to nod off. The song went on for a few bars as the troopers went back to their chores, Kelly minding the fire, which was now burning fiercely, while Korn fished some green coffee beans out of his saddlebags. The beans were set to roasting in his mess tin as he waited for the water to boil. Nearby, Henry and Fred Lehman were rolling up their blankets and strapping them onto their saddles while Frank Jones laid strips of bacon into another mess tin into which Ed "Soapy" Lloyd was adding slices of wild onion he had managed to gather up from along the banks of Davis Creek.

When the coffee beans were done to a deep brown, Private Korn dumped them onto a bandanna spread over a flat rock. Then, carefully unloading his revolver, he used the butt of the weapon to mash them into a coarse, mealy texture. Lifting the ends of the bandanna, he gingerly dumped the crumbled beans into the water now boiling in Kelly's mess can.

"Ah, *ja*. Now dere we go. We got us some coffee pretty soon now, boys." So saying, Korn slipped a hunting knife from the sheath at his belt and began to stir the grounds gently into the water, releasing an aroma that soon had all their mouths watering. Wiping the blade on his trousers, Korn slipped it back into its sheath and reached behind him to fumble with the strap on his saddlebag. His fingers slipped into an inner pouch and came back out with a pinch of salt, which was sprinkled into the brew. Paddy Kelly watched him curiously.

"What're ye doin' that for, Gus?"

"It takes the bitter out, Paddy. If we have only got some cinnamon, we have us a damn fine good brew here, you bet."

"Well, never have I heard o' such a thing, I'm sure. And where would ye be learnin' such a trick?"

Sergeant Bustard, stirred to activity by the aroma of boiling coffee, was now keenly observing the steaming mess can from under the brim of his hat.

"It's an old trick, Paddy. Pay close attention to Gussy there. He apparently knows somethin' of what he's about. Now, we had an egg about, we'd toss 'er in to draw the grounds down to the bottom." Heaving himself into an upright position, Bustard began to root around in his haversack and conjured a small tin of condensed milk, which he tossed lightly over to Korn.

"Here ye go, Gussy. Poke a hole in 'er an' we'll have us a real treat this morning."

"*Ja wohl*, Sergeant." Korn beamed happily and caught the tin deftly in a large paw while at the same time reaching for his knife.

Privates Jones and Lloyd sauntered over with their mess tin of bacon and onions and were soon joined by Henry Lehman, who brought a handful of raisins along with him. A few minutes later the pooled resources had produced a savory repast, and the two "sets" * were digging in with abandon. Henry Lehman, who had been a confectioner in his native Switzerland, saved some of the condensed milk for the coffee, but the rest he mixed into a mush of crumbled hard tack, the raisins, and a couple of spoons of sugar. The result was a sort of pudding, which had become a favorite with his fellow troopers who wasted not a second in slurping it down. With breakfast fairly done, the troopers began to clean up the remains, wiping out mess tins with handfuls of grass and doling out the last few drops of coffee. Sergeant Bustard had resumed his attitude of repose and was lighting up his pipe.

"Hoooee, boys, I am plumb stuffed!"

"Plum duff?! Who's been holding out on me? Lemme at it, fellas!" Soapy Lloyd had dropped his saddlebags in a heap and was pushing his way through his buddies toward the campfire. Bustard cast a jaundiced eye at Lloyd.

"Ease back there, Soapy. I said I was plumb stuffed, ye great dope. Unplug yer damn ears. Where the hell d'ye think anyone'd get plums around here? Fer Gawdsakes, lookit them blossoms over there. The damn plums won't be out for a couple o' months at least." Bustard tossed a tin cup in Soapy's general direction and settled back under his hat.

Lloyd was addicted to the sweet cobbler known as plum duff that was sometimes prepared by the company cooks in garrison. It was well known in the outfit that Soapy's weakness had once landed him in the guardhouse. Slipping into the mess hall after hours, Lloyd was in the act of gorging himself with plum duff when the officer of the day walked in on him. According to the popular account of the incident, Soapy had been so stuffed that when Lieutenant Mathey hove in view the gluttonous private

---

* The "set of fours," consisting of two pairs of bunkies, was the lowest level of organization within the cavalry company. Although it referred to both men and horses for tactical and administrative formations and drill, the "set" frequently developed into a close-knit social group that worked, messed, and played together.

was unable to waddle away and had spent the next thirty-six hours in the pokey with a bellyache of legendary proportions. Even Dr. DeWolf's liberal prescription of cod-liver oil, which Soapy felt the doctor had administered with far too much pleasure, had apparently not dimmed Lloyd's enthusiasm for the sweet delicacy.

A disappointed Private Lloyd turned back to rummaging through his saddlebags as Gus Korn used a handful of rank grass to wipe the last coffee grounds out of the bottom of the communal mess can. In a moment Soapy had produced a travel-worn deck of cards and was shuffling them expertly, his eyebrows moving up and down silently, inviting his friends to join in. Within seconds Jimmy McNally had spread his blanket out on the grass, and Soapy was deftly dealing out hands to him and the Lehmans.

Paddy Kelly shook his head, insisting he needed to write a few lines home. He pulled a couple of sheets of foolscap out of a waterproof wallet and licked the point of a stubby pencil. Using the bottom of his mess tin as a makeshift field desk, he spread the paper out carefully and reread the lines he had already written. In the background, Soapy's running commentary on the campaign assumed the droning buzz of the ubiquitous horseflies.

"Yeah, I'll bet ya a month's pay that old Hard Ass'll have us moving again before supper. You just watch an' see if he don't! Yessir, dollars'll get you doughnuts we'll be eating dust for lunch."

"Oh, shut up and deal, Soapy, and don't be slippin' anything off the bottom of that deck," Fred Lehman was saying. "Besides, you spent most of your month's pay on that sweet tooth of yours before we ever cleared Lincoln."

"Yeah," added Henry with a grin, "spent all your dollars on doughnuts, ya glutton. So, give it up."

"Oh, yeah? Well, I'll say what I please, you damned ignorant Dutchmen. This is all just a big lark to you lunkheads. Damn sore-asses actually like chambermaidin' them mules. You two monkeys ain't got sense enough to know when you're bein' took advantage of. Ante up, boys!"

Soapy Lloyd was a city tough who had no intention of sticking with the Army for a moment longer than he had to. He had been a railroad engineer, and a damned good one. But that was before the Panic of 1873 had plunged the country into the worst and most prolonged depression it had ever experienced. Banks failed, fortunes were ruined, thousands lost their jobs. More than eighty railroads were thrown into receivership. Soapy's was one of them. So Lloyd found himself out of work and stranded in New York City. He managed to find a low-paying job as a paperhanger for Solomon & Hart at 363 Broadway. It was not a very good option, but at least good enough to allow him enough money to indulge his passions for billiards, beer, and sweets. With fewer homes needing or able to afford Solomon & Hart's services, Soapy was one of those who soon found themselves at the bottom of the economic heap. Within a year he was out of work again and, lacking a very strong work ethic, without prospects. With no savings to fall back on, it hadn't taken him very long to exhaust his meager funds. It wasn't much longer after that that Soapy had managed to wear out his welcome at his favorite hangout, Niblo's Saloon. Everett Dutton, Niblo's bouncer and one of Soapy's chums, had finally broken the news one chill evening in November.

"Sorry, Soapy, old man," Dutton had announced, "but ye're more of a deadbeat than the boss can tolerate. I'm afraid yer cut off."

"Aww, c'mon, Everett, ya know I'm just down on my luck a bit. Hell, what's a sandwich and a beer more or less to Old Man Niblo? You know I'm good for it."

"It ain't what I know anymore, Eddy, it's what the old man says. Times are hard, that's sure, and I'm not about to join you out on the street —so out you go, there's a good lad."

Everett had gently but firmly guided Lloyd out onto Broadway, handing him his flipper. Soapy took the battered straw hat with ill grace and jammed it onto his head. As Lloyd turned to go, Everett slipped him two bits that he produced surreptitiously from the pocket of his brown suit.

"No hard feelings, Soapy. But orders is orders."

"Yeah, right. Orders is orders." Soapy stuck the two bits into his pocket but kept them clutched tightly in his fist so they wouldn't slip out the hole that had been worn in his only pair of serviceable trousers. For weeks he wandered the wintry streets of New York, becoming more threadbare and downhearted by the day. There was no work to be found and precious little charity even in the season of good cheer.

New Year's Eve of 1875 found Soapy Lloyd huddled in a narrow alley in the Bowery, attempting to make a nest out of packing crates and old newspapers to ward off the frigid night air. Although not entirely satisfactory, it at least kept him from freezing to death that evening, and with the dawn of 1876, Soapy awoke numb but alive with a copy of the *New York Herald* spread over his face. Sitting up and stretching his stiffened limbs, Soapy saw a story in the *Herald* that caught his attention. Several weeks old, it recounted the results of an Army scientific expedition into the Black Hills of the Dakotas. General George Custer, the expedition leader, was quoted as having declared that "the Black Hills are filled with gold from the grass roots down." *

Damn! thought Soapy. How had he missed that news? In truth, there was little mystery to this, since during the past two years whatever happened outside of New York City had been of no concern to him. But Soapy's perspective had changed somewhat with his descent into poverty, and the article in the *Herald* now held profound interest for him.

Gold! That was the ticket. To become a gold prospector suddenly struck him as being a capital New Year's resolution! Soapy ripped the story out of the newspaper and after carefully folding it put it in his pocket for future reference. With a new sense of purpose Edward Lloyd brushed off his ragged clothes and set out to roust his old pals to see if he could get one of them to back him in his newfound vocation. His enthusiasm, however, was short-lived. Soapy soon found that most of his old friends had been so only while he was flush and now they no longer knew him. The few who were sympathetic wouldn't part with more than a dollar or two, times being what they were, and so, at the end of a week spent pounding the pavement Soapy found himself with four dollars and change in his pocket and no closer to the goldfields than he was before he started.

"Son of a bitch." Soapy reached into his pocket for the old newspaper clipping and was about to crumple it into a ball when a strange thought occurred to him. "Well, I'll be . . ." Soapy unfolded the article again and, smoothing out the yellowed newsprint, carefully reread the story.

"Well, I'll be damned," he whispered under his breath. "Why the hell didn't I think of this in the first place?" If the Army had found the gold, why then it only stood to reason that if he joined up he could get awfully close to it. He'd let Uncle Sam pay his passage out West, hand him a few dollars for a grubstake in the form of Army pay, scout out the lay of the land a bit, and then jump for the goldfields at the first opportunity. It was the perfect scheme.

The only real trick was to convince the recruiter that Edward Lloyd was a born cavalryman—well, he certainly didn't plan on walking to the goldfields, and he might need a good horse to carry all that gold back out. But, being an experienced confidence man, Soapy solved this problem by hanging around Pelton's stables for a few days, doing odd jobs, mucking out the stalls, pitching hay, and talking to the grooms to get a feel for the lingo. It was nasty, backbreaking work, and Soapy quickly figured out why

---

* *The Army expedition into the Black Hills had, in fact, occurred in 1874, thus the newspaper account that Lloyd read was more likely reporting the large gold strikes that had been made by prospectors who had flocked to the region in 1875. The references to Custer and the Army's role in the expedition were probably in the form of background information.*

he was able to get it even in hard times. But it served his purpose. When he felt he had acquired enough raw knowledge to get him by, he convinced an old colleague to let him bum a ride on a freight headed for Pittsburgh —better not to risk it with the local recruiters, who also frequented Niblo's and were wise to Soapy. Once in Pittsburgh, he made a beeline for the recruiting office and parlayed his few days of shovelling horse manure into what he felt was the most convincing performance of his life. By the time he was done, he had the lieutenant in charge of the place believing that Edward Lloyd was nothing less than the reincarnation of J. E. B. Stuart. Within a week Soapy was on a train headed for the cavalry training post at Jefferson Barracks, Missouri.

Army life was a great disappointment to Soapy. An indifferent soldier at best, he spent more than his share of free time on extra duties and punishments. When he wasn't stuck in stables duty or sitting in the guard-house, he made straight for the local bawdy houses to forget his troubles. The result was that he never managed to hang on to his pay long enough to put together the grubstake he needed. With his training over he was assigned with a replacement draft to Fort Abraham Lincoln in Nebraska which, although closer to the goldfields, was not much better than Jefferson Barracks. Once again, Soapy's luck had gone south on him and, by the time he joined Company I of the Seventh U.S. Cavalry, the Sioux had jumped the reservation and were off on a spree. Not a complete fool, Soapy had no intention of playing hide-and-seek with a bunch of savages in the Black Hills. No sense in heading out by yourself if you can have a bunch of your pals along as an insurance policy, he thought. The way Soapy figured it, as soon as they whipped the Sioux they were chasing, he'd be able to slip off in the confusion afterward. With any luck he'd be playing poker in Deadwood before old Bastard Bustard knew he was gone.*

"Oh, you're a sly one and that's a fact!"

"What the hell are you muttering about, Soapy?" Henry Lehman demanded crossly. "Are we playing cards here or ain't we?"

Lloyd spit into the grass and tossed two cards facedown on the blanket.

"Dealer takes two," Lloyd said casually. "You mark my words, boys, old Hard Ass'll have us raw to the bone before the day's through."

---

* Soapy's story is far from extraordinary. The depression resulting from the Panic of 1873 threw thousands out of work, and the Army was seen as a convenient refuge where a man could get three square meals a day while waiting for a better opportunity. The gold rush that followed Custer's Black Hills Expedition was often too tempting an opportunity for young recruits to pass up, and the Army's desertion rates during this period were exceptionally high. These men were sometimes referred to as "snowbirds" because they would spend the hard winter holed up at an Army post and then "fly" in the spring.

Fred Lehman leaned over and tossed a card on Soapy's discards. "Give me one o' them pasteboards, Soapy, and quit yer croakin'. The problem with you is you're a lazy bummer. The old man is just energetic. You don't never hear him bitchin' about how long a day it is, an' he's up afore reveille every day and still up writing God-knows-what in his pup after you're already half the night in your roll."

"Hell, that's his lookout, ain't it? All I know is my butt is sore as be-damned and I can't get comf'table no how my bones're aching so bad. Old Goldilocks can ride around this country as much as he wants just so's he leaves me out of it. And I can tell ya that I ain't the only one what feels that way."

"Well, they're all a bunch a' lazy croakers!" Henry Lehman stated flatly.

"Oh, yeah? How about Cap'n Benteen? You tellin' me he's a lazy croaker, sodbuster?"

Lehman folded his cards and glowered at Soapy. "I ain't said no such thing, ya dope. And we ain't sodbusters, we're ranchers, and there's a big difference, ya ignoramus!"

"Whaddya mean about Cap'n Benteen, Soapy?" McNally was puzzled by Lloyd's allegation that Captain Benteen was not entirely happy with Custer.

"You'd see for yourself, Beans, if you weren't such a babe in the woods," Soapy shot back derisively. "You may have noticed that the old fellow ain't exactly part of the royal family, ya know."

"What's the 'royal family,' Soapy?"

"Why the Custer clan, ya great ninny! You know, Tom, Bos, Calhoun, Keogh, and the rest of 'em. Thick as thieves they are and uppity to beat the band. Think they're God's own gift to the Army, so they do. The bunch of 'em make me sick."

"What's this got to do with Cap'n Benteen?"

Soapy rolled his eyes and shook his head with exasperation. "Oh, you innocent! Don't you see? Benteen ain't one of the high society. He's on the outs, y'see? He don't take with those almighty, holier-than-thou airs your precious boy general puts on. Get it?"

Beans McNally sat wide-eyed, appearing not to comprehend the drift of Soapy's tirade. He turned to look at Sergeant Bustard who, although apparently asleep, McNally suspected had overheard the entire conversation. Bustard had, in fact, been listening despite himself and was heartily tired of the whole thing. He was about to bring the whole discussion to an abrupt halt when Henry Lehman burst out.

"Well, I still say you're just a lazy bummer, Soapy! You're afraid of anything that smacks of work. I swear your brains are in your ass and it's them saddle sores're doing most of the talkin' for ya."

"Yeah, dry up, Soapy," said Fred Lehman. "If you're of such a tender disposition, you should've signed on with the shank's mare cavalry so's you could stroll about the Dakotas at your leisure pickin' flowers . . . and stuffin 'em up your ass." McNally and Henry Jones broke up at this remark, and even Bustard only barely managed to keep from bursting out laughing. Soapy was indignant.

"I got flat feet, ya ignorant cowboy. Gawd, the infantry. That'll be the day—when I hook up with the damn webfoots. You think we've got snooty officers. Besides, you know what they say—'Ain't never seen a dead cavalryman.' "

"That's sure to change around here with ye boring us to death wid yer dam' bellyachin', Lloyd," Sergeant Bustard cut in. "Now shut yer gassy trap an' let us get a bit o' rest around here."

0700 Hours
Along Davis Creek

Sergeant James Bustard snorted violently and brushed at the horsefly that slipped under the brim of his campaign hat and tried to walk up his nose. With his breakfast safely inside him Bustard decided that the wisest course of action now would be to take a nice long nap. He hated to admit it but thought that in this case Lloyd was probably right and the outfit would be moving again pretty soon. In addition to being a damned pain in the ass, Lloyd was also an Englishman by birth, which would have been enough to sour the Donegal-bred Bustard on him in any event. But lately Lloyd's dire predictions of hard riding had been all too true, and Bustard had begun to look at him as a sort of company Cassandra, an unwelcome and annoying prophet. As to Lloyd's bellyaching about officers, Bustard could honestly care less. As far as he was concerned, he wasn't being paid to second-guess 'em or worry about their private lives and eccentricities. Officers were officers and that was that. What they did was their business and none of his. Bustard considered himself a professional soldier and, as such, was paid to keep his boys in line and follow orders. He was very good at his job.

Although only twenty-nine Bustard had been soldiering just about as long as he could remember. After leaving Ireland he had arrived in this country at the height of the Civil War and immediately signed on with the Seventh Missouri Volunteer Cavalry in 1864. Following the war, he had mustered out in Weston, Missouri, where his old commander, Colonel Price, had gotten him a job as a driver for Ben Holladay's Overland Mail and Express Company. Bustard enjoyed the work but, after a few months, it somehow just didn't feel right anymore. Many was the evening he sat along the banks of the Missouri River listening to the boom of the evening gun from across the river at Fort Leavenworth and thought back to his days in the saddle.

Within six months of leaving the Army, Bustard had had his fill of civilian life and, on a cool October morning in 1866, caught a ride on the steamer *Post Boy* and hopped off at the quay in Leavenworth City. With his haversack over his shoulder and a faded blue kepi pushed down over his eyes, he hiked up to the headquarters building at Fort Leavenworth and signed up for a hitch in the Regular Army. Bustard's timing was perfect, for the Seventh Cavalry, then being activated out at Fort Riley, was in need of experienced noncommissioned officers. He was accepted in a trice and, with the exception of one other brief fling with civilian life, had been with the outfit ever since.

Sergeant Bustard was fairly comfortable with his lot in the Seventh. The general bellyaching that troops were wont to indulge in was not of much interest to him, and he found discussions about the commander's idiosyncrasies a crashing bore. He'd heard it all before, mostly from the recruits, and didn't place much credence in the noise. The Army was a hard life and you'd best know it before you signed the papers. As far as Bustard was concerned, if you kept your nose clean and did your job, you'd have no complaints of the old man, who was no worse than some and better than many he'd seen in his years in the service. He was an odd one, to be sure, but then so were so many of the officers he had known over the years. Major Reno was overly fond of the bottle. Benteen himself was a bitter and humorless sort. General Crook was disheveled, preferring to dress like an ordinary mule skinner rather than a general. Colonel Mackenzie was said to be genuinely insane. Even Generals Sheridan and Sherman, on the few occasions when he'd seen them, had had a kind of wild look about them.

No, considering his contemporaries, George Custer was not all that unusual a sort. You had to admit that the Seventh was as well organized and efficient an outfit as any, and that, Bustard felt, was due largely to the commander's demanding personality. The one thing he found particularly odd was Custer's attachment to the Ree scout Bloody Knife. The Indian was a notorious tippler, a vice which the teetotaling Custer would not condone in his officers but cheerfully overlooked in the Ree. Custer in fact seemed to dote on the man. They went everywhere together and were forever skipping out ahead of the column to hunt antelope or buffalo—although admittedly they had not done so on this campaign. The general had made a point of learning the Ree's language, and they were forever gassing about something or gesturing at each other in sign language. Custer even included Bloody Knife as a foil for his practical jokes, a practice usually reserved for the inner circle of family and friends. Oddly enough, the Ree would, as often as not, give as well as he got in these exchanges, earning nothing more than a good-natured guffaw from Custer. Bustard thought it was a curious sort of friendship.

Actually this whole outfit was a curious sort of thing. In addition to the general's brother Tom, who commanded Company C, there was a little brother, Boston, and a nephew, Autie Reed, both civilians and apparently out for a lark, and there was Lieutenant Calhoun, commanding Company L, who had married the general's little sister Maggie. It was almost as if the whole regiment had been dragged along on a Custer family picnic.

Despite the frantic pace and hard riding, most everyone was in a good, almost giddy mood. Even the unfortunates saddled with the pack mules for a day would come back to relate their experiences with tongue in cheek, each vying with the others to cook up the most outlandish and hilarious tale of woe. Most of the officers joined in the fun, with only a couple casting a jaundiced eye on the atmosphere of hijinks and hilarity. As Soapy had intimated, Captain Benteen, for one, was singularly unamused by anything that transpired. Stuffy and standoffish, the white-haired old cavalryman had gotten a burr under his saddle back at the Washita and it had been there ever since. Hell, thought Bustard, it's been damn near ten years since that fight.* You'd think he'd get over it.

The action at the Washita, it appeared, was the basis for virtually all of the personality conflicts within the unit which, although few, were quite bitter. Bustard, however, was not convinced. Benteen, the focal point of the anti-Custer faction, had joined the unit as a captain at Fort Riley in 1866, not long after Bustard arrived there himself. The post scuttlebutt had it that Benteen had been offered his own command as a lieutenant colonel of Colored Cavalry but had refused to serve again with black troops and so had wound up a mere captain in the Seventh. Bustard didn't know how much stock to put in this rumor, but the headquarters clerk had once showed him a copy of Benteen's service record, which indicated that he had once commanded the 138th Colored Infantry. That plus the fact that Benteen had arrived at the unit with a chip on his shoulder tended to reinforce Bustard's view that there was more to this personal feud than professional differences. The Washita was just an excuse to bring the feud out into the open. After all these years Sergeant Bustard could remember the fight as clearly as if it had happened yesterday. But the one thing that really stood out in his mind was how god-awful cold it had been. The mere thought of it could cause a shiver to run down his back.

●

* *In actuality, the battle of the Washita had occurred only seven and a half years earlier. On 27 November 1868 the Seventh Cavalry, under the command of Lieutenant Colonel George Custer, launched a dawn attack on a Cheyenne village under Black Kettle located on the banks of the Washita River in what is now western Oklahoma.*

Oh, God, the cold! They had dismounted with every fourth man leading the horses to the rear and moved into positions in the early hours of a frigid winter morning. For what seemed like hours they lay motionless in the snow awaiting the word to attack. In the darkness below him Bustard heard the frantic barking of the village dogs and the tinkling of a bell. Just as dawn approached, Captain Myers walked up and down the line instructing everyone to shuck off their blanket rolls and overcoats. The added weight and bulk would have slowed them up considerably in the attack, but Bustard wondered if it made any more sense than waiting around freezing their asses off.

No sooner had Bustard rolled everything into a neat pile when he heard a lone rifle shot from the direction of the village. Instantly the regimental band blasted out the first bars of "Garryowen." They couldn't play much more than that, for the spit froze solid in their instruments. With a roaring cheer the boys had dashed over the crest of the hill and swarmed toward the village, shooting and shouting to beat all. It had been one hell of a fight. The Cheyennes, taken by surprise, fought hard but finally turned tail and tried to flee across the icy river. Others scattered down the valley on their ponies. In the middle of the fight Bustard had looked up to see Major Joel Elliot canter by with a small group of mounted troopers.

Bustard was thinking it odd that he hadn't heard anything about mounting up for a pursuit when Elliot turned to another officer and shouted, "Well, here goes for a brevet or a coffin!" and galloped out of sight down a side ravine. Later, as the troops were in the process of destroying the village, he heard voices asking, "Where's Elliot?" and sensed that something had gone terribly wrong. By now it had begun to snow again, and the adrenaline pumped up by the attack was beginning to wear thin. Bustard was shivering mightily and tried to stay as close as possible to the bonfires, which were being fueled with blankets, buffalo robes, weapons, and lodgeskins. The troopers from the band were nearby trying to thaw out their instruments. Glancing over his shoulder, he had spotted an agitated Lieutenant Godfrey in conference with Lieutenant Colonel Custer—both were peering anxiously at the surrounding ridgelines. Following their gaze, Bustard saw the cause of their consternation. On the hills surrounding the now-burning village, hundreds of angry warriors were beginning to appear.

"How many did you see?" Custer was shouting to make himself heard over the roar of the fires.

"Can't say for sure, General. When I topped a ridgeline farther up the valley, all I saw were hundreds of lodges—looks like Arapahos and more Cheyennes. We had a running fight all the way back and were damned lucky to get out!"

"Good job, Mr. Godfrey."

The lieutenant saluted and seemed about to move off when he stopped. "Sir, there was a heavy burst of firing off to our right. Do you think Elliot's people might be engaged?"

Custer sat up in his saddle for a moment then shook his head slowly. "I rather doubt it. Captain Myers's company has been fighting in that area all morning, and I suppose he would have said something about it." Godrey nodded quickly and dug his spurs into the flank of his horse. Custer remained staring at the surrounding hills for a moment and then, catching Bustard's eye, motioned him over.

"Sergeant, my compliments to Captain Myers, and have him take a party down the valley a piece to see if there's any sign of Major Elliot's troop."

It proved to be a wild goose chase. There was no sign of Elliot,* and by the time Myers returned, the Indians had not only gotten hold of the troops' grounded overcoats, but shots could be heard coming from the direction of the supply train. With snow swirling heavily around them and darkness approaching, Sergeant Bustard realized they were in a real pickle. It was at that moment that Custer really surprised him. With the band playing loudly, the regiment mounted, formed into columns of four and headed down the valley *toward the enemy.*

Now, we're done for sure! Bustard thought. But, much to his surprise, the Indians scattered! Rather than swooping down on the outfit, they lit out down the valley toward the other villages, whooping and squeezing off shots over their shoulders as they galloped away. The regiment continued to move until just after sunset, when Lieutenant Colonel Custer called an abrupt halt. Commanding all to complete silence, Custer ordered the regiment to about-face, and the whole command slipped silently up the valley and out of harm's way.

When they were safely out of the trap, a halt was ordered and everyone did his level best to get warm and grab some sleep. Bustard, who was detailed to help guard the now-relieved supply train, curled up in the bed of one of the wagons and pulled several empty feed sacks over himself to

---

* *Major Joel Elliot, despite his rank, was one of the youngest and least experienced officers in the regiment. In the midst of the battle he noticed a party of warriors disappearing down a small ravine and called for volunteers to mount a pursuit. Sergeant Major Kennedy and sixteen troopers followed Elliot to chase after the Indians and were never again seen alive. Their mutilated bodies were discovered several days later.*

ward off the cold. Unable to sleep, he had just resolved to get up and check the perimeter when two shadowy figures loomed just near the wagon. Bustard, slouching back into the feed sacks, recognized the voices as those of Captains Myers and Benteen. From the angry tones it was apparent that they were arguing.

"He's a goddamn, cowardly swine, I tell you. No officer worth his salt would go off and leave part of his command at the mercy of those savages. A coward and a cur of the first water."

"See here, Benteen. I've had a bellyful of your sass. Why you're so goddamned stupid the others in your little clique notice. I'll tell you right here and now, I personally went down that goddamned valley looking for Elliot's people. The stupid bastard had no business running off on his own when he had his own command to look after. It was a dereliction of duty plain and simple. If you ask me, he got what he well deserved."

"No one deserves to be abandoned on the field, Myers. No one. This is all Custer's fault, and I'll see the son of a bitch in hell for it."

"Why, you stupid sod. Didn't ya see all them savages out there in the hills waiting for us to hang about mooning over Elliot's crowd? If the general hadn't played it like he did, the whole outfit'd be in hell by now and you with us! What kind of a fool would sacrifice the whole unit for one idiot glory hunter and his crew—besides you, that is."

"That, Captain Myers, is a gross insult and I demand satisfaction."

"Stick your satisfaction up your ass, Benteen. I'll have none of your guff."

With that Myers had turned to stalk off, and Bustard could hear the pinging of Myers's spurs as they crunched through the hard-crusted snow. Benteen had lingered but a few moments longer before he too wandered off.

Thinking about the affair now, Bustard could not recall Custer ever having said anything about Elliot being in dereliction of duty with his unauthorized raid. To the contrary, whenever the subject came up—and it had come up frequently over the years, the men always referred to Custer's official report of the action, which noted simply that Elliot was a fine officer who had died bravely while gallantly leading his men into action. Benteen's venom puzzled the old sergeant. The captain was a fighter and that was sure, but you could never be certain that he thought anything through. He was more like a bull buffalo who lowered his head and charged into anything without giving it a second thought. Brave but stupid. Well, maybe that's what it took to be a good soldier, but Bustard, for one, was glad Benteen was not in command of the regiment.

Bustard's hand snaked out and slapped his thigh, smashing a bothersome horsefly to a jellied pulp. He grimaced and wiped the mess off in the grass. The insects were a damned nuisance, but he was consoled by the fact that at least he wasn't freezing his ass off in some snowbank. James Bustard hated the cold. He had just about settled back down to rest when a flash of movement caught the corner of his eye. It was Sergeant Curtis of Company F with Privates Finnegan, Howard, and Hunter. The troopers seemed glumly resigned to the loss of their free time. As Curtis trotted up alongside, Bustard pushed his campaign hat back on his head and waved easily at his old friend.

"Mornin', Bill. Where ye off to this fine day?"

Curtis reined up his horse and motioned to the detail to halt. "Mornin', Jim. Hey! I said hold up there, Finnegan. Control that damned horse." Finnegan hauled back on his reins just as the animal dropped down on its forelegs and dipped its head. The result was that the young trooper was pulled forward out of the saddle, slid over his mount's head and landed with a plop in the dust. Curtis rolled his eyes while the other troopers snickered quietly.

"Damn recruits. I swear, Jim, it's like puttin' pumpkins on saddles. Oh, some dope didn't lash down proper an' we lost a box o' tack back on the trail last night. Cap'n Yates says we're to go back an police 'er up afore the Injuns find 'er." Bustard shook his head in sympathy as he watched the young trooper dust himself off and climb gingerly back into the saddle.

"Well, watch your hair, Bill!"

Curtis smiled and waved, motioning for the small detail to follow along as he urged his mount into a slow walk. Then, turning in the saddle, he called back to Sergeant Bustard, "My hair'll be just fine, Jim. I expect them Injuns is off the other way."

Bustard watched as Curtis and the three troopers moved slowly from view, then settled his hat back down over his eyes and let his thoughts drift. "Poor old Curtis," he thought. "Lovely day like today and he's off to chase mule droppings."

0735 Hours
Along Davis Creek

Mark Kellogg turned up the collar of his coat and shuddered involuntarily in the morning cool. He looked across the stretch of prairie to the galloping figures of the Ree scouts and wondered how the hell they could dress so lightly and not seem to feel the cold. In addition to his coat, the reporter had draped a saddle blanket around his shoulders but still couldn't warm up quickly enough. He coughed roughly and grimaced as he felt the sour taste of bile and stale tobacco rising in his throat. He was getting too old and set in his ways for this sort of nonsense. Kellogg placed his hands in the small of his back and pressed in hard while leaning backward in a vain attempt to ease the soreness that had settled there. God, but this was getting to be a painful exercise. There were no tents and nothing to sleep on but a rough saddle blanket. With nothing but his saddle to serve as a pillow, there was no way possible to get comfortable. He might as well have spent the last few nights sleeping on a bed of nails.

Kellogg stamped his feet to try to stimulate some feeling in them and shuffled a little closer to the small campfire that some of the officers had kindled in a hastily dug hole. It wasn't much, but at least it generated some measure of warmth. Kellogg noticed that once it had been established that the onrushing Indians were Rees, everyone had relaxed visibly and gone back about the business of getting their breakfasts. Only George Custer continued to watch the approaching Rees, his eyes riveted to the fluttering scrap of paper. Captain Tom Custer, who was squatting comfortably by the small blaze, grinned at the visibly uncomfortable reporter and handed a tin mug of steaming coffee up to the older man.

"Wrap your hands around this, Mark," Tom said cheerfully. "It'll take some of the chill off and get your heart pumping again."

Kellogg gave Tom a small smile and took the mug gratefully, his fingers interlaced tightly around the shiny cylinder. He held the mug up close to his face and allowed the heavenly scented steam to wash over his face, clouding his wire-rimmed spectacles and drifting up into his clogged sinuses. He heard Tom Custer chuckling.

"Easy, Mark," Tom chided. "You're supposed to drink that stuff, not take a bath in it."

A bath. Kellogg screwed up his lips. Why did Tom have to bring that up, the damned scamp. Oh, what luxury that would be. To soak in a warm tub, lean back in the suds with a fresh newspaper, a large mug of coffee, a neatly rolled cigarette.

"Damn your eyes, Tom," Kellogg retorted. "You torture a man with the image of the one thing he wants most and most certainly cannot have. You've a heart as black as Hades itself."

The other officers looked closely at the blanket-draped figure with the large steam-clouded spectacles and burst into laughter. Even Tom had to chuckle at the comic sight of the shivering, gray-haired reporter who looked as much out of place as a catfish in the desert. Kellogg heard the laughter and smiled grimly. That Tom was a card. Always cracking jokes and making light of the most desperate or uncomfortable situation. It was amazing how lightly he took this entire expedition. Well, this Indian fighting was certainly a young man's game.

Another shudder rippled down Kellogg's spine, and he silently damned the chill of these prairie mornings. He knew it wouldn't last much longer, as the sun would soon be up high enough to bake their brains again. Already the dull yellow ball had risen well above the eastern horizon, and looking down the line of troops, he could now make out individual figures moving in the rising mist and half-light. The sudden arrival of the Ree scouts promised a break in the monotony of the trail which, to Kellogg's mind, had thus far entailed nothing much more than saddle sores and choking dust clouds. Of course, he had spiced it up just a bit in his dispatches for the *Bismarck Tribune* and the *New York Herald*, both of which had "appointed" him a special correspondent for this campaign. Although he had been eager for the job, there were times when he seriously asked himself what the hell he could have been thinking when he accepted Lounsberry's offer. Clement Lounsberry, publisher of the *Bismarck Tribune*, and an old friend of General Custer's, had been invited along on the march but had begged off at the last minute when his wife had become ill.

"Damn it, Kellogg, I really envy you, old man," Lounsberry had exclaimed. "Why, this campaign will be a real brushup. Three columns closing in on the savages, and no one there to tell the story but you, with the whole damn country hanging on every word you write. Why, it's a newspaperman's dream come true."

Kellogg couldn't suppress a slight smile. "Yes, sir, it's a small miracle."

"Well, it's not much of a miracle as miracles go, but for this business it's the closest damn thing there is. Why, you've only got to put up a banner headline reading A GREAT VICTORY! SAVAGE FOES ROUTED IN DESPERATE BATTLE! and our damn circulation shoots up a thousand percent. Makes for exciting reading at the breakfast table. Peace and prosperity are damned dull affairs when you come right down to it."

Kellogg thought for a minute of the story he would write and pictured his byline under the headlines. It sure beat the hell out of what he was doing now. An ordinary-looking man with graying hair and weak eyes, Kellogg was fast approaching his fortieth birthday, working in a Bismarck law office and picking up a little extra money here and there filling in at the telegraph office on those evenings when Old Man Snyder was ill or "indisposed"—which condition was usually induced by a too liberal an application of "medicinal" whiskey for Snyder's chronic coughing fits. It wasn't much in the way of a profession, but at least it paid for his room and board at the widow Christopher's place.

While not an especially imaginative or ambitious man, there were times when Mark Kellogg grew temporarily dissatisfied with his lot. These times usually occurred on those evenings when he was sitting in for Snyder at the telegraph office. With the cicadas buzzing outside of the window and moths fluttering around the globe of his oil lamp, he would lean back in the heavy oak chair and roll himself a cigarette from the small pouch of Bull Durham fixings he kept in his pocket.

Sometimes, as the smoke curled upward, a light breeze would pass by the open window and waft the smoke along with it out over the endless prairies, and Kellogg's thoughts would drift along in the slipstream as he waited in the small office only half-listening for the clack-clack-click of the telegraph key. When it started to clatter, what news would it carry? Would it be an epidemic in New York? A shipwreck near the Tierra del Fuego? Perhaps it would be a king dying in Europe or a battle in Ashantiland in West Africa. Whatever it might be, it would be more exciting than he could ever expect here in Bismarck. Sometimes the key would clatter to alert him to pick up his pencil and then begin its staccato monologue of dots and dashes. His pencil would race along the rough gray paper translating dots to E's and dashes to T's as the small brass fulcrum jittered and jolted through its electrical seizure.

A few of these reports would inspire him to write an article or two himself. Staring at the gray sheets, he would put down his pencil, pick up a pen, and begin to scratch out a short piece either as a news item or an editorial. Not wanting to be accused of plagiarizing his sources and possibly jeopardizing his extra income, these he would invariably sign "Frontier," fold them carefully into a square, and seal them into an envelope which, early the following day, he would post to some distant city like St. Paul or Chicago. But most nights he would just sit quietly, waiting in vain for the wires to sing to him, smoking cigarettes and then tossing the butts out into the darkness beyond the open window, watching the sparks dance crazily as they skipped into the dusty street like the fragments of a tiny comet. Then, resting his head in his hands, he would stare out into the black night, watching absently as the orange glow of the discarded butts grew dimmer and finally died.

Oddly enough, it was not his writing skills but his passion for playing chess that had landed him this assignment. He had been delivering a telegram to the offices of the *Bismarck Tribune* one morning and arrived early enough that the only individual in the building was the publisher himself. Lounsberry motioned him into his office and took the telegram while Kellogg waited patiently to see if there would be a response. As he stood uncomfortably in front of Lounsberry's desk, he noticed an ornate chess set on a small side table. A game was apparently in progress and Kellogg studied the pieces' positions with interest.

"What do you make of that, Mr.—uhhh?"

"Kellogg, sir. Well, I certainly hope you're white, sir."

"How's that, you say?" Lounsberry got up from his chair and, frowning, walked around his desk, a cigar clenched firmly in his jaw.

"Well, there's but two moves left and black is in checkmate. It's virtually the Williams-Staunton* match all over again." Lounsberry looked at Kellogg in amazement. He reached out his hand and grasped Kellogg's in a firm grip, his eyes reassessing the younger man.

"What's your name again, sir? Kellogg, you say?"

"Yes, sir, Mark Kellogg."

"Well, I'm damned pleased to meet you, Mark Kellogg," Lounsberry exclaimed, pumping the man's hand vigorously. "Now sit your ass down and let's play us a game of chess." And so Kellogg began a long and curious association with Clement Lounsberry, with many a winter's evening passed in quiet conversation and slow games in which knights slaughtered pawns, queens vanquished rooks, and bishops toppled kings as the cruel Dakota winds howled in the darkness outside.

---

* *Howard Staunton (1810–1874) was one of England's most celebrated chess players. Shortly after losing the great tournament of London in 1851 to Adolf Anderssen, he challenged his archrival Elijah Williams to a grudge match. Staunton won a majority of the eleven games played but, having given Williams a three-game handicap, still lost the match.*

Over the weeks that followed their first meeting, Lounsberry had come to discover that Kellogg had been a telegrapher during the Civil War and was now quietly writing freelance articles and editorials. Lounsberry read some of these pieces and decided that while not a brilliant writer Kellogg was at least competent and steady. Plus he was a teetotaler—a rare bird among newspapermen. When the same bout of whooping cough that put his wife in bed also emptied several chairs at the *Tribune*, Lounsberry was in a quandary. Much as he wanted to, he couldn't leave either his wife or the paper to go traipsing around the countryside with George Custer. Then he thought of his old chess partner, Mark Kellogg. Competent, sober, and with some experience in war reporting, he seemed a logical choice and was easily lured away from the drudgery of clerking for that simpleton lawyer.

"Yes, sir, chance of a lifetime, old man. Why, you know old Henry Stanley* was with Custer back in 'sixty-eight, and look at him now. Damn near as famous as the people he writes about."

Kellogg had jumped at the opportunity, especially when he learned that Lounsberry had arranged for him to cover the campaign for the *New York Herald* as well—Stanley's old paper. In a moment Kellogg's entire life had changed. He saw himself in the saddle, bronzed and windburned, riding alongside the famous General Custer as they trotted boldly into the center of a Sioux village. He even heard himself uttering a bon mot of his own: "Mr. Sitting Bull, I presume. I believe this is checkmate."

"What's that, Mark?" Young Autie Reed had walked up alongside him.

"Huh? Oh, nothing, Autie. Just thinking out loud again."

Nearby, the Ree scouts skidded to a halt, slid out of their saddles, and began scrounging around for something to eat. Kellogg reached into his coat pockets for his pad and pencil, and realized he had left them in his haversack.

"Hey, keep an ear open to what's happening will ya', Autie. I'm gonna grab my notes. Don't want to miss anything, y'know." Autie Reed nodded quickly but was already moving toward the knot of officers who had risen from their campfires and were standing near his uncle George.

"What's the scuttlebutt, Bos?"

"Ssshhh! Be quiet, Autie," Boston Custer scolded. "I can't hear a damn thing with you flapping your mouth."

---

* *Henry Morton Stanley, the famous English reporter and adventurer, had indeed been with Custer's outfit in 1868. Reporting for the* New York Herald, *he would later go on to find Dr. Livingston ("Dr. Livingston, I presume") in Central Africa and report on the Ashanti War in 1874.*

Boston put a finger to his lips and then pointed silently toward the campfire where Red Star, a young Ree scout, was squatting in the dust, a tin cup of steaming coffee held close under his nose. George Custer had sat down in the dirt nearby and was using a mixture of Ree and sign language to pump the young scout for information. His brow deeply furrowed, he appeared to be in what Bos referred to as "a brown study." Bos didn't understand a word of what was being said, but judging from the looks on the faces of brother George and Fred Gerard, another scout and interpreter, something was clearly up. George Custer made some rapid movements with his hands and spoke quickly in English.

"Let me see the talking paper."

Red Star shifted slightly on his haunches and reached down into his breechclout to hand a grimy and folded slip of paper to the soldier chief. Custer unfolded the note and read it carefully, then fired several questions at Red Star, who replied with simple shakes of his head and grunts. Custer looked up at Gerard, who fired another question at Red Star. This time the Ree nodded quickly and began to point in the general direction from which he had come into camp. After a few moments Custer stood up slowly and looked off into the west, rubbing his chin thoughtfully. Finally he turned to his brother Tom.

"Tom, we're going to have an officers' call. We'll need to move the regiment forward a bit until we can find out what we've really got out there. Red Star here says there's some wooded areas up ahead a piece where we can get the outfit holed up out of sight for a while. I'll take Gerard and Bloody Knife with me to see what Varnum's turned up. Reno's the ranking officer present and he can handle the movement forward. Queen's Own* can handle the administrative details. Start passing the word. I want to be out of here within the next fifteen minutes. The rest of the outfit can take a bit longer to get themselves sorted out. Tell Reno to keep movement fairly slow, as we don't want to kick up too much dust. Off you go."

Tom saluted briskly and headed off to locate Major Reno and Lieutenant Cooke. As he turned toward the bivouac, he almost tripped over Kellogg, who had come up to the group with pad and pencil in hand.

"Whoa, beg your pardon, Mark. Damn near put you in the dust there. Bit of a hurry, I'm afraid." Kellogg just smiled crookedly as he adjusted his wire spectacles.

---

* Lieutenant W. W. Cooke was Custer's adjutant. A Canadian who had formerly served in Her Majesty's Forces, he was commonly referred to as "Queen's Own."

"No harm done, Tom. Say, what's the ruckus? Have the scouts found anything out?"

Tom Custer grinned broadly.

"Well, Mr. Kellogg, I think they just might have found you a story. Have you ever conducted an interview in Sioux?" And with a light punch to Kellogg's arm, the young officer winked and headed off on his errand.

Kellogg blinked rapidly and watched him move off. He thought back to his last brief message to Lounsberry. Well, the next one, he was sure, would be a hell of a lot longer than two short sentences. Yes, Mark Kellogg, he thought, your star is surely rising. Watch out, Mr. Stanley, here I come. Next stop, immortality. Kellogg took a deep breath, squared his shoulders, and headed over to join the general. As he came up to where George Custer stood talking with Gerard and Bloody Knife, he overheard the Ree speaking in broken English.

"We find enough Sioux, keep us fighting two days, maybe three, you bet." Custer looked over at Fred Gerard and back to Bloody Knife and laughed.

"Oh, I imagine we can manage to get through 'em in one day."

Kellogg stopped and began to scribble a few words in his notebook. This might be just the sort of statement that would make a great quote to start out his story. He thought back to the last telegram he had dashed off to Lounsberry. Had it been just three days before? Well, the next time he sent something to his publisher, it would be the story of the century.

TO: MR. CLEMENT LOUNSBERRY, ESQ.
PUBLISHER, THE BISMARCK TRIBUNE
BISMARCK, DAKOTA TERRITORY

JUNE 22, 1876
IN THE FIELD

SIR:
WE LEAVE THE ROSEBUD TOMORROW AND BY THE TIME THIS REACHES YOU WE WILL HAVE MET AND FOUGHT THE RED DEVILS—WITH WHAT RESULT REMAINS TO BE SEEN—STOP—I GO WITH CUSTER AND WILL BE AT THE DEATH—STOP—

KELLOGG

Wikawañkap'u *(0700 to 0800 hours)*
On the Greasy Grass

Looking about him, Black Bear, an Oglala, noted with satisfaction that just about all the necessary preparations had been completed. He and his small band were leaving today. He had quarreled with Drags-the-Rope a few days before, and their relations had since declined steadily. Last night he had wandered over to visit with Hairy Chin, the old prophet, seeking advice as to what he should do. They had smoked and talked late into the night while the village beyond still echoed with the sound of the revelers.

"What was this quarrel about, that leaves you still concerned?" the old man had asked.

"It is really nothing, Grandfather. I told him the game was almost gone and we should have to leave soon, and he said it was not the people but the white-eyes who made the game so scarce." Black Bear shook his head solemnly.

"You said to him that the white-eyes had not told us to gather all the people in one place—or told him to steal your ponies." The younger man looked up suddenly, his eyes wide, but the old man just smiled and waved a thin brown hand as if brushing away a fly.

"Don't look so, this is not magic. Just because I am old does not mean that I am deaf to the women's gossiping tongues. Everybody knows what really happened. But I see you got your ponies back. So why should you still want to leave just because Drags-the-Rope is too fond of other people's property?"

Black Bear thought for a moment and raised his hands in exasperation. "I do not know," he said deliberately. "That is why I have come to see you. You are wise in these things, and I don't know what is in my own heart to make it so bad."

Hairy Chin said nothing but sat puffing the pipe and staring dimly at the thin wisps of smoke that curled lazily in the still air of the evening, rising slowly toward the lodge's vent. Black Bear watched the old man intently through the diaphanous curtain of tobacco smoke, which softened the old man's features to a ghostly vagueness. The young man half-expected to see the wizened body blur and dissolve, to drift upward with the gray tendrils into the starry night above them.

"Sometimes," the old man whispered in a soft voice, "your heart does not tell you why it pushes you to do something. It just knows that you must do it and need not know the reason. It is a great mystery to me how this works. If your heart says to do such a thing, then do it. Later you will know why it was important to do this thing."

Black Bear sat quietly with his thoughts, his fingers picking absently at the quills on his moccasins. After a long time he said quietly, "I think I must go." Hairy Chin just nodded. "In the morning I will gather my people and return to the agency. Drags-the-Rope will say that we are fools."

"What does it matter what he says?" Hairy Chin asked casually. "He does not hunt for your family. He does not live in your lodge. Who is to say he is not the foolish one?"

"He says"—Black Bear grunted—"that we are fools to make ourselves slaves to a piece of bacon, some tobacco, and hardtack."

Hairy Chin smiled quietly. "No, he does not say that. He only repeats what the Hunkpapa Sitting Bull is forever saying. Bull is full of such nonsense. He says not to take anything that the whites have to offer, but you notice that he does not throw away his rifle or his pistols. Do you believe he has made these himself from what Wakan Tanka puts here for us to use? Bah! Such nonsense. Does Drags-the-Rope throw away his guns or his wife's iron pot? I do not think so. You must decide for yourself what is proper to do. If you must go, then you go. If Drags-the-Rope wanted to go to the agency, he would not concern himself for a minute about what you might say." Hairy Chin paused and drew slowly at his pipe, filling his lungs with the sweet smoke. He appeared to have closed his eyes but was observing his young guest with great interest.

"This Sitting Bull and his friends say they are great men," Hairy Chin said finally, his voice quiet and firm. "And they would have you believe that Wakan Tanka speaks only through that old man, but I tell you this is not so. Red Cloud has been to where the Great Father of the white men lives, and he says that they are more than the leaves on the trees and more powerful than we know. You do not see Red Cloud here with us. He knows that it is dangerous to anger such men. Perhaps Red Cloud is wiser than all of them together. Everyone is proud of what our warriors did in the battle with Three Stars, but what does it matter if you kill all the buffalo today and can't eat tomorrow. How great is a leader who wins one battle or two but angers the enemy so that he will not rest until all of his people are destroyed? No, I say that Wakan Tanka does not give the truth to one man alone but to every man in a different way. If he tells you that you must go, why should you worry about what another man should say to you. You must do not what other men tell you but what you know is right in your heart."

Black Bear nodded slowly and it appeared that he felt better about his decision.

"Thank you, Grandfather. What you say makes much sense. I will do what I must. We will be leaving tomorrow." He sat quietly for a while longer and then rose to go. As he was about to duck under the lodge skins, Hairy Chin spoke again.

"This may be a very good thing, Black Bear. The soldiers are coming."

Black Bear stopped and looked curiously at the old man, who merely sat there smoking calmly and looking into the distance. "How do you know this, Grandfather?"

"It is a mystery to me. I listen to my heart. It does not tell me how it knows. Perhaps Wakan Tanka talks to it when I sleep." Then he smiled broadly. "Or perhaps I hear the youngsters telling stories and gossiping outside my lodge while I try to sleep. It is hard to tell these days. My dreams are full of chattering, and this camp is not the quietest place I have known." Black Bear smiled at the old man and ducked out of the lodge. Hairy Chin was right. He should follow what was in his own heart. Maybe it was time to leave.

Now, looking about the traces of their campsite, Black Bear began to feel comfortable with his decision to move on. All around was the continuous buzz and bustle of the village—the Oglala circle alone was over three hundred lodges. It had become just too much noise and confusion for Black Bear. However, his wife had not been particularly happy about the decision to move.

Pretty Elk was enjoying visiting with her cousins and catching up on all the family gossip. The thought of returning to the Red Cloud Agency had put her in an ugly mood, and the work involved in breaking down the campsite did little to improve her disposition. All morning she had gone about her chores, efficiently if not cheerfully stuffing the family's belongings into parfleche boxes and rolling blankets and sleeping robes into compact bundles that she secured with strips of rawhide. If anything, she expended a little more energy than was required to get the job done, thus a bit more noise was added to the already noisy atmosphere as she slammed iron kettles about and thumped the lodgeskins loudly into shape for traveling. At one point Black Bear had reached up silently to help her undo a section of the lodge skin that had become hung up on a pole. Pretty

Elk turned on him with a glare that bespoke trouble and a willow-shoot pin clenched tightly in her fist. Black Bear decided, wisely, he thought, to back away and let her finish her work without his help.

Now everything was ready to go—the ponies saddled or hitched to travois, family belongings stacked neatly on hides stretched between the travois poles—and Pretty Elk stood nearby chatting sullenly with her cousins. Black Bear thought he would give her a few minutes more with her cousins before setting off. Just then his friend High Eagle strolled up and greeted him.

"Good day, brother! Are you leaving us?"

Black Bear continued to watch Pretty Elk as he answered. "Yes, we are going to the agency now. I am tired of all this noise."

High Eagle smiled and nodded toward the group of chattering women. "This sort of noise, or the kind of noise that Drags-the-Rope makes when he is breaking wind?"

Black Bear looked at his friend and couldn't help breaking into a grin. He rolled his eyes meaningfully. High Eagle looked at Pretty Elk, who had turned to glare at her husband.

"You may be leaving the camp," High Eagle whispered, "but I think there will still be much noise in your lodge anyway. I hope you slept well last night, for I do not think you will get much rest tonight." Black Bear now caught a glimpse of Pretty Elk's expression and decided that his friend was probably right.

"Well, brother," High Eagle sighed, "you had best go then."

Black Bear shrugged. "Perhaps," he said. He was already wondering if he had made the right decision. Pretty Elk would not be at all reluctant to display her displeasure with him on the trip. He didn't think he would enjoy the experience. High Eagle shook his head sympathetically and walked off to check the pony herd. Black Bear watched as his friend strolled toward the great herd on the rolling prairie on the other side of the camp. It was time to go. Black Bear turned and leapt lightly onto the back of his pony and started to move in the opposite direction. Pretty Elk hugged her cousins and moved to join the small party that was following Black Bear out of camp. A pack of children ran alongside as the littler ones bounced happily along, tethered to the travois or strapped tightly onto cradleboards suspended from the flanks of ponies.

As the party moved across the river and up into the hills, Black Bear thought of what Hairy Chin had said last night. "The soldiers are coming." The phrase echoed in his thoughts as he looked back at the huge village that stretched for miles across the valley floor. If the old man's dreams were true, it was a good thing they were leaving. He had no desire to fight right now. He had seen enough blood shed in the fight with Three Stars. He thought they had been lucky to chase the long knives away that time, but such good fortune could not last long. The soldier chief would not like having taken a beating like that—he would be back. Or there would be others.

Black Bear had grown uncomfortable in the large village. Surely they had much strength with so many warriors but also they were, like the huge buffalo herds, so much easier to find. And they had their families with them. There were so many gathered in one place that it would be hard to move them all quickly if they had to get away. And they were so many that there was always noise. There was so much noise that he felt it would be impossible for the "wolves" to do their jobs properly, especially when so many young ones were distracted by the singing and dancing and the young girls. It was likely that the wolves would be more interested in flirting than in scouting. Their enemies could come upon them quickly, and no one would know it until it was too late. It made him uneasy.

As he rode slowly along, he turned these things over and over in his mind, and the further he got from the camp, the better he felt about his decision. Pretty Elk, from the sour expression on her face, still did not seem to appreciate the wisdom of his actions, but the children had already found much to amuse them along the way and seemed already to have forgotten about the playmates they had left behind. In a few minutes the camp was out of sight, and Black Bear turned his full attention to the trail ahead. The sun was climbing higher into the sky, and the young warrior began to hum to himself. After a few moments he smiled to himself—it was an old Oglala courting song he had often sung to Pretty Elk when they first met. Angry or not, she was still a beautiful woman and, who knew, maybe if he sang it a little louder, it might soften her heart just a little bit.

As they moved out into the open and across the rolling prairie, Black Bear did not know that several pairs of eyes were watching his small party move lazily along. Once he stopped and stared at the Wolf Mountains, which lay several miles distant, but even if he had known where to look, he could not have seen the small figures stretched out on the rocks of the Crow's Nest. As he sat there gazing at the mountains from behind which the sun had just risen, his young son Weasel rode up leading a pony he had just started training.

"Father," the boy said, "the rest have gone ahead already."

Black Bear looked at the boy and smiled. "Well, we should catch up with them, don't you think, boy? How about a race?" The boy grinned

widely and the two turned their horses and galloped after their party—
and away from Lieutenant Varnum's scouts.

Unknown to Black Bear, or to Varnum's detail, several miles to the east a
small party of Cheyennes was making its way slowly toward the large
village. Several days earlier, Little Wolf had gathered seven lodges from
the Red Cloud Agency and set out to join their friends and relatives on
the Greasy Grass. Little Wolf had lingered at the agency longer than he
had intended. After more than fifty winters he no longer moved as quickly
as he once did and time had simply slipped by without his noticing. It was
not until some of the younger warriors came in fired with tales of the
great camp that was gathering near the Greasy Grass and of the fight with
Three Stars that Little Wolf realized that the season was already well
advanced.

"It is not right that we should remain here in this place," he had
announced one evening. "Tomorrow we will go to join our brothers for
the Sun Dance and to hunt." That was all he said, although inwardly he
reproached himself for having let so much of the summer slip away without his noticing. The younger braves had said nothing in his presence, but
he knew they were all chafing to get away from the agency, and it was due
only to his reputation for cunning and strategy that they had held back
for so long.

"Don't worry," they had assured each other. "Little Wolf is clever. We
have not left yet because he knows that the time is not yet right. We will
be going soon." But more and more, as the summer dragged on, and
especially since the arrival of news about the great fight with Three Stars,
some of the younger men were beginning to wonder if Little Wolf was
really as clever as some of their older friends thought. "Maybe Little Wolf
is getting too old," they had whispered among themselves. "He forgets
things and dreams too much about the old days." Thus his announcement
that they were finally leaving had thrown the small camp into a frenzy of
activity.

"See," said Big Crow to one of the younger men, "I told you we
would be going soon. Something big is going to happen. Little Wolf's
dreams are telling him that we must hurry." And hurry they did, crossing
mountains and slipping alongside streams with greater urgency than they
had experienced in many years. Big Crow rode ahead of the party, scouting
the trails and finding the best places to make camp each evening. Everything had gone without incident, and they were making wonderful progress until this morning.

The camp was in the process of breaking up and preparing for the day's travel when Big Crow galloped headlong into the center of the group uttering a high-pitched cry.

"Hiyupo! Hiyupo!"

Everyone stopped what they were doing to watch as Big Crow leapt from his roan and ran over to where Little Wolf was adjusting the saddle on his pony.

"Little Wolf!" Big Crow gasped. "They're here! The *wasichus* are here."

Little Wolf finished tightening his saddle and turned to look at his friend.

"Where are these *wasichus?* And how many are there?" he asked calmly.

Big Crow breathed deeply and pointed over a slight rise to the west. "I saw them on the small creek that leads to the Greasy Grass. We can be there before the sun is directly above us. It's not far at all."

"How many?" Little Wolf insisted.

Big Crow was excited. "Hundreds!" he called out loudly for the others to hear. "They are like the grasshoppers, so many that you can't walk through the grass without making them jump." The other warriors crowded around in great excitement, brandishing rifles and pistols and yelping with glee. "Brave up, friends!" they yelled. Now they could share in the glory of their brothers who had whipped Three Stars. It was exhilarating. But Little Wolf did not share in the general giddiness. He held up his hands above the roar.

"Silence!" he commanded. "Hundreds, you say? Like grasshoppers? Look around you. How many of us are here? A dozen warriors? Fifteen, maybe? And three times that many women and children? What are you thinking?" he scolded them.

"Where are your heads? Has the sun made you all fools? Have you drunk the stinking water and become stupid? How can you say we should attack them?" He paused and looked around him, his mouth set sternly, his gaze level and unflinching.

Most of the braves had grown silent and looked at each other in embarrassment. But Big Crow, Medicine Bull, Black Horse, and Two Birds still grimaced and shook their fists in the air. Even his son, Young Little Wolf, looked pleadingly at his father, his teeth clenched fiercely, urging him to lead them into battle.

"Enough, I say." Little Wolf snarled angrily at the young men. "There will be no fight now. There is an end to it." The youngsters subsided but were obviously unhappy with the decision.

"Now," Little Wolf went on, "here is what we will do. Kills Elk, you will stay with the lodges and take our families around these *wasichus*. Five of the younger braves will help you do this. Big Crow, you will take me to where you say these *wasichus* are and we will watch them carefully. The rest of you will come too. You will not attack any of them unless I say that it shall be so. You will not let them see you but will follow them and watch everything they do and where they go. We will send back word to Kills Elk so that he will keep our families well away from these people and get them to the big village safely. The big village is close. If you want to fight, be patient. These *wasichus* must be going toward the big village, so there will be plenty of fight for you soon enough. This is how it must be."

Little Wolf looked at his son and then at the others, who by now had regained their composure. Even the younger hot heads saw the wisdom in what Little Wolf proposed—it was the smart thing to do. They would watch and wait. There would be time enough for fighting before very long.

PART TWO
"A Road We Do Not Know"

CONTACT

Q: Before you left the line to go back into the woods as you have testified, how many Indians were engaging the line and at what distance from the line?

A: The number actually firing I can't say. It was very heavy fire coming from the Indians and up the valley, the whole valley seemed to be covered with them. How many Indians that dust covered is impossible to estimate. That dust more or less covered the main force of the Indians. As a rule they fire from their horses and they were scampering around, pumping their Winchester rifles into us.

Statement of Lieutenant Charles Varnum, 7th U.S. Cavalry
(Extract from Official Records, Court of Inquiry
Convened 13 January 1879 at Chicago, Illinois)

The dust was like a great cloud, and everywhere the Sioux went the dust rose like smoke. We circled all round them—swirling like water round a stone.

Statement of Two Moon, Northern Cheyenne

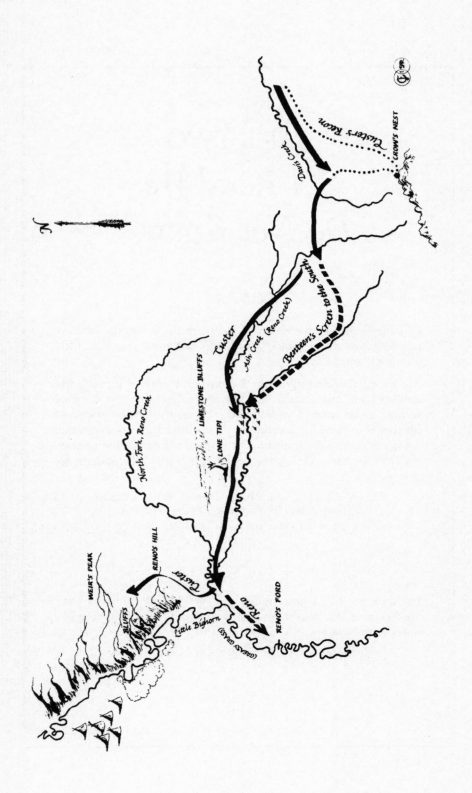

0845 Hours
At the Crow's Nest

Charley Reynolds reached over and tapped Lieutenant Varnum lightly on the shoulder. Varnum waved him off impatiently. The two men were stretched out full-length on the rocks, Varnum resting on his elbows, a pair of field glasses held up in front of his face.

"Just a second, Charley. I'm trying to see if I can make out that damned pony herd."

The attempt to cut off the Sioux they had spotted earlier had come to an abrupt halt when the Crows who had remained on the hill called out to them. Varnum would have ignored the curious "cawing" sounds, but Mitch Bouyer had immediately reined up and motioned for the officer and Reynolds to do likewise. Climbing back up the hill, they were met by White-Man-Runs-Him, who explained through Bouyer that the Sioux had galloped off out of sight and they would never catch them now. Frustrated, Varnum had taken out the field glasses, which he had snatched from his saddle before climbing back up, and thrown himself down on a rock ledge to peer anxiously out over the plains below. Nothing. He was still straining to make out details in the brown landscape when Reynolds shook him again, this time more insistently.

"I said, in a minute, Charley," the lieutenant growled at his companion.

"Sorry, Mr. Varnum. Just thought you ought to know there's a party of folks coming up behind us."

Varnum raised up and twisted around to look back down the hill, where he saw a small plume of dust rising from the valley behind them. Putting the field glasses to his eyes, he tried to focus on the source of the dust cloud.

"Damn!" he said under his breath. "Looks like the Old Man himself is coming up."

Reynolds grunted. "Can you make out who's with him, Lieutenant?"

Varnum studied the small party for a few seconds.

"Looks like Gerard, Bloody Knife, and Red Star. There're a couple others but I can't make 'em out through the dust." He lowered the glasses, then stuffed them back into their case and rose slowly to his feet.

"Well, Charley, I suppose we ought to go on down and meet 'em."

Reynolds nodded and dragged himself up painfully. His fingers were bothering him again, all the exercise having sent the blood throbbing through his extremities. Making his way down the hill behind the lieutenant, he could feel every jarring step send a searing heat shooting through his arm. When they got down to the horses, Reynolds found that climbing into the saddle was even more difficult than he had expected, and he winced visibly.

"You okay, Charley?"

"Sure, Lieutenant. Just this damn hand acting up again."

Reynolds forced a smile but thought longingly of the small flask he kept in one of his saddlebags. A shot of whiskey would certainly be welcome about now, but the Old Man would smell it a mile off and he thought he'd best be stone-cold sober for this meeting. He nodded to the lieutenant, and the two urged their horses into a walk as they headed back down the draw toward Custer's party. Before they had gone very far, Mitch Bouyer trotted up alongside and the three men rode together in silence.

A few minutes later they came upon Custer and a small group of scouts. In addition to Fred Gerard, Bloody Knife, and Red Star, they now recognized Bob-tailed Bull and Little Brave as rounding out the party. Varnum reined up and proffered a smart salute.

"Good morning, sir!"

Custer returned the salute, smiling broadly.

"Good morning Mr. Varnum, Mr. Reynolds. Hello there, Mitch. What've you gentlemen found for us, eh?"

Custer never stopped but motioned the scouts to fall in alongside as they continued toward the lookout point. Varnum did not waste any time but quickly filled in the commander on the events of the morning, culminating with the abortive chase after the hostiles.

"Did they spot you, Mr. Varnum?"

"No, sir, but the Crows think they must have spotted the smoke from the command's breakfast fires."

Custer looked at the young officer thoughtfully, turned to look back in the direction of the command, then shook his head slowly.

"Possible, I guess, but highly unlikely, Lieutenant. The outfit's still quite a ways off, and we've got this mountain between us and the hostiles, with the sun in their eyes to boot. Even if they had seen smoke, they wouldn't know who or what was making it. I think we're fine on that score. We'll know more once we get a look at your village."

Bouyer and Reynolds exchanged looks but said nothing as the small party approached the wooded area at the base of the Crow's Nest. Leaving the horses in the care of Bob-tailed Bull and Little Brave, the rest climbed toward the rocky promontory above, Reynolds lagging behind now in company with Bloody Knife.

"Your hand hurts you, Lucky Man. Maybe you stay with the horses for a time?"

"No, Bloody Knife," Reynolds said, "this is too important. There'll be time to rest a bit later."

Bloody Knife grunted, "You say it is so, Lucky Man, but I think many will not rest again this day or any other."

Reynolds looked over at the taciturn Ree, whose face remained impassive. If the Indian was worried about something, you couldn't tell by looking at him. And he had stated his opinion flatly, as if whatever happened there was nothing to be done about it. Charley shook his head and looked up the hill, where he could see that Custer and his party had already reached the top and were surrounded by the Crow and Ree scouts. When Reynolds and Bloody Knife had caught up with the group, Custer indicated that he wanted to address the scouts.

"You have done well, wolves," Custer said in English, using his hands to sign his meaning as Bouyer and Reynolds whispered additional translations to their respective groups of Crows and Rees.

"When we catch up with the Sioux, there will be much booty for you. If what you say is so, the Sioux have many ponies and you will have as many as you can take."

The scouts all nodded in agreement—except for Bloody Knife, who listened unmoved.

"The Great Father in Washington will be pleased with what you will do today and you will all be honored by him and receive medals like my friend Bloody Knife."

Lieutenant Varnum listened in rapt attention, wondering at the fluidity of his commander's hand movements as he expertly signed his thoughts in the universal language of the plains. The general is in his element, Varnum mused, and then the thought occurred that he had never seen Custer out of his element. He spoke to the scouts with the same ease that he played sentimental songs on an old piano—however well or badly he did either. And he seemed as comfortable with Mitch Bouyer or White-Man-Runs-Him as he was with General Terry or Captain Keogh. Everything he did he seemed to do with his entire being—there was nothing hesitant or lukewarm about the man. Varnum tried to think of a single word that he could use to describe the man. What occurred to him was "passionate." It seemed an odd sort of word to describe a soldier, and yet nothing else seemed to fit. Yes, Varnum decided, George Custer is a man of passion. The young lieutenant started as his commander turned and nodded to him.

"Alright, Mr. Varnum, let's see what we can see."

Varnum and Reynolds fell in alongside the general as he moved quickly to the rocky ledge and surveyed the countryside. The lieutenant began by pointing across the valley to the two tipis that sat at the base of a chalky outcropping, Custer listening with interest as the young officer described the stage upon which the morning's dramatic events had been played out.

"As you can see, sir, one of 'em's already collapsed, and White-Man-Runs-Him says that he thinks they're burial lodges,* so it's possible they got into a scrape with some of Colonel Gibbons' people up north. Several hundred yards to the right and closer in, you can see the ridgeline where those Sioux outriders disappeared. The Crows say they bet they circled back around to the village, which lays over that way." Varnum swung his arm to the left in a slow, level arc, one finger tracing back along the chalky cliffs and coming to rest pointing toward a gentle slope some fifteen miles distant. "The scouts say the pony herd looks like a mess of worms squirming about."

Custer peered off into the distance, one hand shading his eyes, which had narrowed to slits. He was shaking his head slowly. Varnum watched his commander intently, noting the crow's feet that crinkled at the corners of Custer's eyes above ruddy, sunburned cheeks. The lieutenant was surprised to find himself thinking that up close Custer looked much older than he was. He wondered what was going through Custer's mind. The general was a hard man to read, the mask of command always seeming to veil his inner thoughts and fears. Did he even have fears? Varnum wondered. Was the man ever afraid?

Custer was often edgy, brusque, even irritable, but it was hard to know if this was anxiety or just nervous energy. Varnum was often afraid and hated himself for it. He had been nearly terrified on the night march and yet even more afraid that others would see his fear. If Custer was

---

* This was in fact a burial lodge, believed to have contained the remains of Old She-Bear, a Sans Arc warrior who had been mortally wounded a few days before. Old She-Bear had not received his wounds from Gibbon's scouts, as Varnum inferred, but rather in the fight with General Crook's column on the Rosebud.

truly without fear, what a relief it would be to be like him. Fear complicated things. It made the days seem longer and the nights almost endless. Lieutenant Varnum didn't feel afraid now and asked himself if it was Custer's presence, his seeming fearlessness, that made others less fearful. Custer shook his head doubtfully as Mitch Bouyer came up and pointed down into the valley.

"General, if you don't find more damn' Injuns in that valley than you ever saw together in your life, you can hang me!"

Custer cast a sideways glance at Bouyer and grinned. "It'd do a damned sight of good to hang you, wouldn't it?" The general nudged Lieutenant Varnum with an elbow, and the young cavalryman broke into a broad smile.

"Well, Mitch," Custer said, "my eyes are as about as good as anyone's, and I can't see a village, Indians, or anything else." Charley Reynolds walked back a few yards to retrieve the lieutenant's field glasses and brought them over to Lieutenant Colonel Custer.

"Here you go, General. Take a look through these glasses."

Custer took the glasses and scanned the valley floor below, tracking slowly from right to left, pausing now and again to focus on some distant object. As he squinted through the field glasses at the spot where the scouts had indicated the pony herd lay, Reynolds came up alongside him and spoke quietly, indicating individual landmarks and waving an outstretched hand in a gentle, rolling motion. His fingers wiggled slightly as if to imitate the movement of worms that the Crows had described.

A few miles to their rear, the rest of the column had arrived at the wooded grove the boy Red Star had found earlier and described to scout George Herendeen, who had remained with the main body of troops. Once they had been admonished to keep quiet and out of sight, the troopers had been put at their ease to tend their horses or grab some more sleep. Leaving the sergeants in charge of the details, a small group of officers wandered casually down a nearby ravine. Herendeen, seeing the group move away, decided to follow to see what was up and soon caught up with Lieutenants Calhoun, Edgerly, and Cooke, who were trailing along behind Captains Custer and Moylan, a large, good-natured Easterner.

"Oh, hullo, George." Edgerly smiled at the scout as he fell in alongside. "Everything going satisfactory for you? We're gonna grab a quick cigarette. Care to tag along?"

"Don't mind if I do, Mr. Edgerly. Thought you were gonna have some sort of strategy powwow."

Tom Custer looked back over his shoulder and waved. "Well, hullo,

Herendeen," he called out lightly. "Nothing quite so serious. We'll leave the strategizing to the general."

"And the second-guessing to the colonel," put in Moylan, referring to Captain Benteen's brevet rank from the Civil War. The rest of the group laughed at this quip.

"He's a fair cranky sort, ain't he though," said Herendeen.

Moylan laughed again.

"Cranky's hardly the word for old Skull-and-Crossbones," he retorted. "The man's a trial. I swear he complains more'n any private in th' outfit. If he's called late to dinner, he's whining that the general hid his invitation so's to embarrass him in front of everybody."

Another titter rippled through the small group. Moylan stopped and cast his eyes about, quickly deciding that this was as good a spot as any, and the rest came to a stop, throwing themselves down easily in the rank grass.

"The other day," Edgerly piped up, "as we were going into camp, Colonel Keogh called him over and said he'd saved him a nice soft spot for his pup right next to him, and you know what he did?" Despite Benteen's touchy disposition, Myles Keogh, the dashing Irish adventurer, was known to be kindly disposed toward the man. It seemed to many to be a one-sided relationship.

"No," said Tom Custer, "but I'll bet it wasn't gracious. Fire away, Mr. Edgerly."

"Well," the boy went on, "old Skull and Crossbones just looked at Colonel Keogh, sort of slant-eyed–like, climbed off his mount, and started pokin' through the grass with a stick lookin' for snakes!" This brought another burst of laughter from the other officers.

"Jesus!" exclaimed Moylan. "I swear, if you gave the man cherries, he'd be spittin' the pits right in yer eye."

The officers guffawed as they lay about casually, some chewing on bits of grass while the others fished in their pockets for their cigarette fixings. Moylan deftly rolled a neat paper cylinder, licked it and popped one end into the corner of his mouth, and then tossed the small Bull Durham sack over to Herendeen, who nodded a silent thanks. In a few moments those who wanted them were puffing contentedly on their smokes and gazing up at the bright, clear sky, enjoying the quiet of their surroundings. It was a pleasant and relaxed atmosphere, but Herendeen noticed that Captains Custer and Moylan, although seemingly completely at ease, had casually loosened the flaps of their holsters, and their heavy Colts now lay handily in the grass by their sides, the hammers drawn back to half cock. Herendeen finished his cigarette and got slowly to his feet. Yawning and stretching his arms out wide, he said, "Well, gentlemen, I thank you for your hospitality, but I think I'll go find a wallow and snatch some shut-eye."

Tom Custer opened one eye and lifted a finger to the brim of his hat, which was pushed low over the bridge of his nose. "Sweet dreams, George," he said, and folded his hands lightly on his chest. The others mumbled their good-byes, and Lieutenant Edgerly, who had gotten up and was relieving himself in a small stand of ash trees, grinnned sheepishly over his shoulder. Herendeen gave a light wave of his hand and wandered back up the ravine toward the rest of the outfit. As the scout drifted out of sight, Edgerly plopped himself down on a nearby rock, quietly slid his pistol out of its holster, and allowed his eyes to wander casually about the area. Captain Myles Moylan, his voice musical with a faint Irish brogue, spoke quietly to the young officer: "Never ye fear, Win. If there's redskins around, we'll not spoil yer fun."

Edgerly smiled nervously and slid the large Colt back into its holster. A broad grin creased Tom Custer's face.

"Boys," Tom said, "I suspect that Frederick the Great would feel right at home here in this little camp, and I for one am without a care." Calhoun, puzzled by the remark, frowned.

"Tom, what the hell are you talking about?" he said, unsuspectingly taking the bait.

"Why, look about you, Calhoun, old man. It's Sans Sioux Ici!" *

Calhoun groaned loudly as his fellow officers roared with delight at the pun. Calhoun picked up a small rock and hurled it in Tom's direction. Tom Custer shifted slightly, dodging the small missile that bounced harmlessly into the grass beyond, then, closing his eyes, settled down for a short nap as insects hummed soothingly in the warm sunlight and every breath of a breeze set the ash trees rustling with their distinctive feathery rattle.

Big Crow was pointing at the narrow trail just where it passed by a rocky outcropping that jutted slightly, overhanging the dusty path. "See where they passed last night. Look at all their pony tracks in the dirt! It's as I told you—there must be hundreds of them to tear up the ground in this way."

Little Wolf nodded quietly and motioned for Big Crow and Black Horse to move out of their hiding spot toward the trail. The two younger

---

* Although not original to Tom Custer, "Sans Sioux Ici" (Without Sioux Here) was a popular pun with Army officers referring to Sans Souci (Without Care), the name of Frederick the Great's palatial summer retreat located near Potsdam, Germany.

braves urged their ponies forward onto the trail and disappeared around a slight bend. Almost immediately Little Wolf heard Black Horse cry out.

"Little Wolf, come and see! The *wasichus* have left something behind!"

Frowning, Little Wolf raced his pony around the bend to find Big Crow and Black Horse kneeling in the dust examining a large wooden box that lay broken open in the middle of the trail. The old warrior leapt down from his mount and examined the box closely.

"There must indeed be many *wasichus*—many soldiers. This box has the soldiers' markings on it." Little Wolf reached into the shattered crate and pulled out a small, square object wrapped in brown paper and held it in his hand. "And it is full of the hard crackers the soldiers eat. There must be very many because they only carry their crackers in these boxes when there are many to feed. This is not a good thing."

Big Crow and Black Horse looked at each other. They had done well to find the soldiers' trail and the box of crackers. They were so excited by their find that they had almost forgotten the danger that lurked ahead of them and were thoroughly surprised when the dust nearby erupted violently just as they heard the first shot. The three Cheyennes looked up in amazement to see a small group of soldiers galloping headlong toward them, their large pistols flashing with fire and smoke. The warriors did not lose another second as they leapt onto their crude saddles and fled into the underbrush, their quirts whipping their ponies' flanks as bullets whistled overhead or slapped into the dust behind them. They rode furiously through thickets and sagebrush until Little Wolf reined up suddenly and turned his pony to look behind them. The soldiers were not following. Something very strange was happening here, and Little Wolf was not sure what it was. He looked at the others.

"This is not good," he said finally. "These soldiers are much closer than we thought, or they would not send so few of their people for this box that they dropped. These few have not followed us—they must have gone back to tell the others. If they come again, we will not be able to keep our families far enough away from them." Big Crow thought they should go after the soldiers and kill them, but Little Wolf was firm.

"No! I say we must leave them alone for now and take our families far to the north of this place. Then we will turn and go to the village." Little Wolf turned his pony again and started north. It was better to give these *wasichus* a wide berth. If the time came to fight, they would need the help of many more warriors than were in his few lodges.

Not more than an arrow's flight away, Sergeant William Curtis peered anxiously in the direction the Cheyennes had fled. He had holstered his pistol and now held a Springfield carbine in his hands. He noticed that his palms were slick on the smooth stock of the weapon and that his uniform shirt was soaked under his armpits. His heart was racing, the blood pumping furiously through his veins. Damn! That had been a close call. Had they been following behind the outfit all this time? Now Curtis worried about the possibility of more warriors lurking nearby. The regiment had passed through only a few hours ago, and now there were hostiles all over the goddamned place. If he knew one thing for sure, it was that to run a blind chase after Indians was tantamount to suicide. No, they needed to get as far away from those bucks as possible, and quickly. Private Howard rode up alongside of him, a smoking revolver in his hand and his eyes bright with the excitement of the moment.

"Sergeant, shouldn't we follow 'em?"

Curtis shot the boy a fierce look. "Ain't too fond of yer hair are ye, boy? Cap'n Yates said nothing about chasin' any redskins we happened to come on, now did he, boy? We'll do what we've come for and no more." He turned to the others and barked out his orders.

"You lads police up that box pronto and let's get the hell out of here!" Curtis glanced quickly at the young troopers, who scrambled to gather up the remains of the box and lash it to one of the horses. He thought Captain Yates would not like this development at all. And the general, well, he'd be fit to be tied.

"Damn, Charley. The scouts may have it right," Custer said finally. "There's something not quite right down there. Though I'd be hard-pressed to swear that it's a large village." He paused, then addressed the whole contingent.

"Well, gentlemen, let's assume for the present that what we've got down there is that camp we're looking for. You scouts are in for a hard day, I'm afraid. I want you boys to do as full a recon as you can manage. It'll mean a lot of riding for you. Major Reno is moving the whole outfit into a concealed position now. We'll keep 'em hidden there today and move into position to surround the camp after nightfall. I intend we shall attack around dawn tomorrow. Is that clear?" He waited as Reynolds and Bouyer finished translating.

One of the Rees moved forward and said, "We are not going to attack them now?"

Custer replied in Ree, while signing so that the others could understand his answer.

"No. No attack today," Custer stated firmly. "Today we scout and stay hidden. Tomorrow at sunup we will attack."

White-Man-Runs-Him turned to Bouyer and spoke a few words while the half-breed listened, nodding solemnly, and then turned to Custer.

"White-Man-Runs-Him says, 'What do you think of this village down there? Do you think they will wait for your attack?' He thinks dey for sure saw us, General!" Bouyer looked dead into Custer's eyes and clenched his pipe even more firmly between his teeth.

Custer nodded that he understood the question and turned to all of the scouts, who had now sat down on the ground in a half-circle facing the officers.

"This camp has not seen our army; none of their scouts have seen us." He passed his hand over his eyes and waved away the question, as if by denying the possibility he could prevent its happening. Most of the Rees obviously agreed with his assessment and were nodding in assent, but several of the Crows looked back to White-Man-Runs-Him to see how he took the commander's pronouncement. The large Crow stood up. Nodding for Bouyer to translate for him, he pointed down into the valley.

"These Sioux we have seen at the foot of this hill," the Crow said, alluding to the Indians they had started to chase earlier that morning, "two going one way and four the other, are good scouts. They have seen the smoke of our camp."

Custer, who had always been a fairly quick learner of the tribes' tongues, apparently understood enough of what the Crow said to begin his answer even before Bouyer finished translating. Custer grew red in the face, and his voice was harsh when he spoke.

"I say again," he spat out, "we have *not* been seen! These Sioux have *not* seen us! I am going ahead to carry out what I think. We will wait until it is dark, and then we will march; we will place our army around the Sioux camp and then attack when the sun comes up and is in their eyes."

The Rees thought this was a good plan and nodded, vigorously grunting their approval, but the Crows grumbled and argued against it. Charley Reynolds leaned over to Lieutenant Varnum and whispered in his ear: "You see what I was telling you, Mr. Varnum. These Crows are anxious to get at the Sioux, and they'll for sure have us jumpin' the gun if they get their way."

The Crows, for their part, were convinced that Custer's plan was a mistake and did not hide their disapproval. "That plan is bad," said White-Man-Runs-Him. "It should not be carried out. These scouts have seen our smoke and they will tell the others of our coming and they will attack your army. We should go today, now! We should capture their horses so they cannot attack us and they cannot run away."

The other Crows sat there grunting in assent as White-Man-Runs-

Him shook his fist in the direction of the pony herd. Custer looked over quickly at the three civilian scouts, Reynolds, Bouyer, and Gerard, who stood looking at each other, and Lieutenant Varnum, who seemed to be waiting anxiously for a reply. The commander's ears had turned a bright red, as if he was trying hard to suppress his anger and frustration at the Crow's stubbornness. Finally he drew a deep breath and pronounced his decision.

"I have said what I propose to do; I will wait until dark and then go ahead with my plan. This is my final word." He stared coldly at the Crows and then turned on his heel and started to walk back down the side of the hill toward the waiting horses.

Ohiñhañni *(Forenoon)*
Along the Greasy Grass

Taschunka Witko,* the one they called Crazy Horse, ducked under the flap of Sitting Bull's lodge and dropped lightly onto a buffalo robe that had been spread in the grass. The old prophet and visionary said nothing but looked at the younger warrior as if taking his measure. This, he thought, was a truly strange young man. He was said to be brave to the point of being reckless and looked every inch the fighting chief that he had become. His body was lean and hardened, the muscles rippling easily under the smooth, light skin that was so unlike many of his Sioux brothers'. Even his hair was an unusual shade, not the dark tresses one would expect of a Lakota but a light brown—as if there were some white blood in his heritage.

While he knew the man was pure Oglala, somehow Sitting Bull couldn't shake the feeling that this man was not of any world that he knew. Neither white nor red, but a visitor from another race of fierce warriors. Perhaps there was something *Wakan*, something mystical, in the young warrior. Sitting Bull tried to look into the man's eyes to see if they held any clue to his inner nature, but the small, dark orbs were constantly averted to this side or that. The old man found it frustrating that this Oglala seldom, if ever, looked you right in the eye. It was as if he did not want to reveal what was in his heart.

And who could tell, really, what was in his heart. So much of him was a contradiction. He was a great warrior, but would take no scalps. He was a fighting chief, but he often evaded his responsibilities by disap-

---

* *Taschunka Witko, or Crazy Horse, (or more literally, His-Horse-Is-Crazy), an Oglala Sioux, was born sometime around 1842, although this cannot be confirmed. Orginally called Curly, his bravery in battle at about the age of fourteen earned him the name by which he is known to this day. Even among the mystical Sioux he was considered a bit odd: a loner, a fierce warrior who would not take scalps and retained no personal possessions except for his weapons and his ponies. As one of Red Cloud's clan known as "Bad Faces," Crazy Horse is said to have been one of the decoys that successfully lured Captain Fetterman's command to destruction on 21 December 1866.*

pearing for months at a time. He was married, but Black Shawl, his wife, was frequently left alone. He kept a lodge, but it was strangely empty. Beyond a few robes and weapons, he himself owned nothing but his war ponies. He seldom spoke, even to Black Shawl. It was hard to credit the stories of his passionate youth, and yet, there on his left cheek was the scar that spoke much of his past. It had been placed there by a jealous husband. No Water had made this scar with a bullet. This was from the fight over Black-Buffalo-Woman, who had been No Water's wife.

That had been an ugly and dangerous time, although now Sitting Bull remembered it only vaguely. Try as he might to recall the incident, he could grasp only fragments of the memory—Crazy Horse had been a moody young man and very full of himself. With his strange good looks and his prowess as a hunter and a warrior, he could easily have had any woman he wanted, but the one he wanted was already married. However people frowned on it, the young brave had gone out of his way to show up wherever Black-Buffalo-Woman might be found. Whether she was digging turnips, tanning hides, or picking berries, there was the strange young brave glancing furtively at the comely woman. This was particularly unwise, for her husband, No Water, was known to have a bad temper. Surly at the best of times, if provoked he could be vicious. And Crazy Horse had seemed to go out of his way to provoke him.

Black-Buffalo-Woman was not blameless in this affair, for she too would encourage the handsome young warrior's attentions—casting meaningful glances at him, letting the corner of her mouth lift into a sly smile. It seemed that she enjoyed playing with him like the young cougar plays with a rabbit as it learns how to hunt. Perhaps she too had cause, for it was known that No Water beat her often. It must have been so, for she finally left him one day, taking her few belongings and presenting herself at Crazy Horse's lodge. He took her in and they lived like man and wife, but everyone in the camp expected that this was not the end of the story. And they were right, for, a few days later, No Water burst into Crazy Horse's lodge. Crazy Horse and Black-Buffalo-Woman were sitting near the fire eating when her husband ripped back the lodge skins and ducked into their presence.

"I have come!" No Water announced and, before anyone could speak, he thrust a revolver into his rival's face and fired. Crazy Horse pitched forward into the campfire, his upper jaw smashed by the bullet. No Water grunted in satisfaction, cast a dark glance at Black-Buffalo-Woman, and stalked out. Crazy Horse was lucky that day, for No Water thought that he had killed him, as he surely intended to do. It was not long after this incident that Black-Buffalo-Woman returned to No Water's lodge and

Crazy Horse took Black Shawl for a wife, although without much enthusiasm. Sitting Bull shook his head. Nothing about this young man was quite normal. Not even his family life.

"Tatanka Iyotanka,* did you ask me to your lodge only to stare at me?" The young Oglala broke the silence between the two men. Crazy Horse was not the most patient of men. His eyes cast furtively about the interior of the lodge, seeming never to rest in one spot. Sitting Bull just smiled quietly and waved his hand carelessly as if brushing away flies.

"You did well in the fight with Three Stars," Sitting Bull said quietly. Crazy Horse grunted. "That fight was a mistake. I agreed with you in the council that we would not seek a fight with the long knives. But the young men had bad hearts." He shrugged. "Once they had started the fight, there was no choice."

"The young braves follow where you lead them in battle. This is a good thing."

"I am no chief," the Oglala said sullenly. "If people follow me into a battle, that is their concern. I do not tell them they should do this or they should do that. I did not choose that fight. I think it was a foolish thing to do, and now we will probably have to fight again. You want to talk to a chief, but I am just a warrior. I will go now." He began to rise, but Sitting Bull waved him back to the robe.

"You are a very touchy person, Crazy Horse. I understand what you say, and I have said it myself many times. We do not want to fight these men, but we will if we have to. I will not go back to their agency." Something in Sitting Bull's voice caught the younger man's attention, and he looked curiously at the holy man for the first time.

"Is this why you asked me to come? Did you think the Oglala were going to go back to the agency?"

Sitting Bull shrugged noncommittally. "I have heard that some of your Bad Faces have left this morning to go back to the white man's place." He looked down as if studying the progress of a horsefly that had landed on his knee and was skittering down his leggings.

"This is true," the young man admitted, "but this is a private matter.

---

* Tatanka Iyotanka, or Sitting Bull (Hunkpapa Sioux), was born sometime around 1830 along the banks of the upper Missouri River. Originally given the name Jumping Badger, most people referred to him as Hukesni, or Slow, because of his deliberate, or stubborn, nature. The name Sitting Bull seems to have fit his nature perfectly. After early successes in both the hunt and at war, he soon rose to a leadership position in the circle and with Gall and Crow King founded the warriors' Strong Heart Society. Considered generous and warmhearted by his people, he became widely respected among the various tribes for his wisdom as a holy man, or wicasa wakan, wielding great political power—a Sioux version of Cardinal Richelieu. He was adamantly opposed to white expansion into Sioux lands.

There was trouble over some ponies, and Black Bear has taken his family away from here. It is only a few lodges. As I said before, I am not a chief. I cannot say to Black Bear that he should stay, and even if I felt that way, I would not say so."

Sitting Bull nodded. "I see." The old man paused for a moment to swat the horsefly, then he went on, changing the subject abruptly. "Do you remember my dream?"

"The one about the soldiers, you mean?" * Crazy Horse sat upright, suddenly interested in what the old man had to say. When Sitting Bull talked about his dreams, it usually meant something important was going to happen. "Of course I remember. This was before the fight with Three Stars. We beat him just as you said we would. What about it?"

Sitting Bull shook his head. "No, that was not my dream. I did not see that fight. The people think that this was the fight I told them about, but they are wrong. I tell them this, but they believe what they want to believe."

Crazy Horse looked at the old man again, his narrow face creased by a frown. "What are you telling me, Tatanka Iyotanka, that we will have another fight with the long knives?"

"I think this is so. In my dream I saw many soldiers upside down, falling into camp like so many leaves. This tells me that they will come here to us. This was not the way of the fight with Three Stars."

The Oglala brave leaned forward as he thought about this. "Yes," he said slowly, "it was Wooden Leg who led the young men down to the Rosebud to find these soldiers. They did not come to us." He looked up at the holy man. "What else did your dream tell you?"

Sitting Bull shook his head slowly. "It is hard to say what the Wakan Tanka tells a man when he sleeps. There are pictures, but what the pictures mean . . ." He shrugged and let the sentence trail off. He thought for a moment and then went on. "I remember that the soldiers in my dream had no ears . . . perhaps they will not listen to warnings to stay away from us. I do not know for sure."

The holy man stopped for a moment and then looked up at Crazy Horse. "I think that if these soldiers come and we kill them, as the dream

* During the annual Sun Dance ceremony, which took place along the Rosebud River in early June, Sitting Bull claimed to have had a vision in which he saw soldiers and their horses falling upside down into camp. He interpreted this vision to mean that the U.S. government would launch an attack on the camp of the Sioux and their allies but that the Indians would be victorious. Shortly after Custer's column broke off from Terry to move south toward the Sioux, the Ree and Crow scouts found the site of this ceremony and read the signs that had been left describing a Sioux victory over the soldiers. The scouts thought this was powerful medicine.

tells me, we must leave their property alone. Wakan Tanka told me this. We must not take their scalps or their guns or their ponies. This is very powerful medicine and we should not touch it."

"I do not understand this, Uncle," Crazy Horse said, shaking his head. "Why should we not take their guns and their ponies? We have always done this, and, if the soldiers come again, we will need every gun and all the bullets we can get. Why should we not take the spoils from foolish soldiers who fall into our camp?"

The old holy man shook his head again, then looked straight into the younger man's eyes.

"This I do not know. Sometimes when the Everywhere Spirit tells you what is to be done, you do not ask 'Why must I do this?'—you simply do it. Perhaps there is a great plan of which we know nothing. But this much I do know—if the soldiers come, we must not take their things. This is very important. You must say this to your young men. One by one, I will gather the others and explain this medicine to them. I have spoken with you first because you have always supported me when I opposed the *wasichus,* and I know I can rely on you when I tell you this must be done." For once, he noticed, the young Oglala held his gaze, as if searching for confirmation of the truth of this pronouncement. Finally, Crazy Horse was satisfied that the holy man was in deadly earnest and nodded his assent.

"I will do this. For what it is worth, I will tell my people what the Wakan Tanka has said to you. But it will be difficult. If the soldiers do come, it will be hard to keep the young men from counting coup and taking their trophies."

Sitting Bull knew this was true; he too had been young and a warrior once himself. But he counted on men such as Crazy Horse to provide an example to the others. He knew that the strange young Oglala had little use for material things beyond weapons anyway. And he had always been one of the fiercest in battle. Maybe his example of restraint would be copied by his warriors.

The younger man got up without a word and slipped out of the lodge while the holy man was lost in his thoughts. Yes, maybe Crazy Horse would make a good example. Sitting Bull thought he would now have to send for some of the other warriors and chiefs to pass the word to their young men, but he was tired. When Crazy Horse had gone, Sitting Bull's aged mother, Her-Holy-Door, pushed under the flaps of the lodge, which had been rolled up for ventilation.

"Do you wish to eat now, son? You have been fasting the whole night and must be hungry. I have made a fine stew."

The *wicasa wakan* shook his head slowly. He had spent nearly the entire night on a nearby hill praying to the Everywhere Spirit and did not really have much of an appetite.

"No, Mother, there is much to be done yet. Perhaps I will have something when I go to visit with Gall or the others." He yawned loudly. "And I need to check on the ponies."

"Bah! You do not have to do any of this," Her-Holy-Door scolded. "Your nephew, One Bull, has taken the ponies off to graze long ago. And Gall"—the old woman snorted her distaste—"well, he can wait forever if you ask me. I know you are old friends, but he is a difficult man, and lately whenever you talk to him, you become so upset that your stomach gives you trouble. You should listen to me and stay away from him for a while. You were always such a stubborn child, and you have not changed the older you get. If you won't eat, you can at least get some sleep."

Sitting Bull smiled sheepishly at his mother. It did not matter that he was already an old man who had seen fifty winters. To her he was always a child. A stubborn, willful child at that. Well, he was very tired and really wanted to sleep. Perhaps his mother was right. There was time to talk to the others later. And he did not particularly want to talk to Gall right now anyway. He was annoyed with his old friend's behavior of late. It seemed that he and Gall now quarreled about the slightest thing. Sitting Bull was not eager to have another argument with Gall so soon. For now he would sleep.

He stretched out on the buffalo robes and stared at the camp from under the side of the lodge. A group of women were walking by headed toward the river and, as they were carrying hoes made of buffalo bones, he knew they were going off to dig for wild turnips. The lilt of their laughter as they gossiped floated happily through the warm air like sweet music, and he smiled contentedly, dust motes floating lazily across his closed eyes. It was such a delicious feeling as the warm waters of sleep flowed over him, washing his cares from his mind.

A few paces away Gall was just returning to his lodge. He had gone out with Brings-the-Rain and his daughter, Watches-Them-Closely, to help them pick berries but had found that he was too distracted to enjoy the outing. Brings-the-Rain had noticed, as she noticed everything, and told him to go back to the lodge.

"You're not paying attention," she'd said, snatching the berry basket from his hands, "and you're going to get bitten by a snake, although you're so sour the snake would probably die!"

He'd looked up puzzled, and she had broken into laughter and chased him away. Now, as he passed by Sitting Bull's lodge, he considered stopping to have a serious talk with him. He turned toward the lodge but then hesitated.

No, he thought. I am not ready to talk to him yet. We will probably argue and I do not want to fight today. Gall turned away and walked slowly toward his own lodge. There will be time later, he thought.

1020 Hours
At the Base of the Crow's Nest

Lieutenant Colonel George Armstrong Custer was not in a good mood as he slid down the trail leading from the Crow's Nest to the small grove where the horses were picketed. The Crows were being obstinate, insisting that the command had been discovered and they should attack immediately. Damn fools! All they saw was the pony herd and the prospect of stripping off as many of the Sioux's animals as they could get away with. They didn't know for sure that the Sioux were even down in that valley or, if they were, how many were in the village. And it was broad daylight. Knowing how the Sioux operated, this was the worst possible time to make an attack. If they hadn't already spotted the command, the dust the outfit would raise moving toward the village would alert them for sure. It was a recipe for disaster. No. They had to wait until dark. Get a good recon going and then move the outfit into position under cover of darkness. Then they could launch an attack at dawn while most of the warriors were still in their sleeping robes and with the sun in their eyes. Damn. He'd have to have a long talk with Varnum and Bouyer and make sure they kept the Crows on a short leash for the rest of the day. All it would take would be one reckless brave to spoil the whole plan.

He glanced back up the hill to see if Varnum and the others were following. The young chief of scouts was right on his heels, skipping and sliding down the narrow, dusty trail. Reynolds, Bouyer, and Gerard were close behind Varnum. Custer flipped the reins over Vic's neck and swung lightly into the saddle just as Varnum came up.

"Lieutenant Varnum," Custer barked. "Your people have done well, but I don't want any mistakes now." Varnum nodded. "I want you to detail two of the Rees to remain here. I suggest Bob-tailed Bull and Forked Horn. They're older and more experienced and less likely to do something foolish. Have 'em keep their eyes peeled but stay out of sight. I want the rest of the scouts to move back to the concealment halt with the rest of the regiment. I'll have further instructions for them later. Is all that clear?"

The lieutenant came to attention and fired off a smart salute. "Yes, sir."

Custer nodded and turned the large sorrel back toward the main command just as the three civilian scouts came off of the hill to join Varnum. The four stood and watched as Bloody Knife came down from the lookout, eased into his saddle, and followed Custer down the narrow track a hundred yards, where the two reined their horses to a stop.

"Well, gentlemen," Varnum said, "you heard the general. No attack today. Let's round up the scouts and head on into the bivouac. Bob-tailed Bull and Forked Horn will stay here and keep an eye on the valley. They're not to do anything but watch and report anything out of the ordinary. If anything happens, Bull is to send Forked Horn back with a report. Clear?"

Reynolds, who was interpreting for the Rees, nodded and went off to inform the two warriors of their assignment. Bouyer went with him to gather the rest of the detail while Gerard waited with the chief of scouts.

"Looks like the general isn't all that pleased with our Crow friends, Lieutenant." Gerard nodded toward the figures of Custer and Bloody Knife, who were apparently deep in conversation.

"Well, Mr. Gerard," Varnum observed, "I'm not so sure about that. They did what he wanted 'em to do—which was to find the Sioux—that is, of course, if they did find 'em, which we ain't all that sure of yet. I think he just doesn't want anyone to spook 'em before he can get a good look at the lay of the land and get the plan all thought through." Varnum's voice was low and calm. "Hell, you know as well as I do that if they give us the slip we'll be out here chasin' our tails all summer and never even see another Sioux."

Gerard nodded in agreement, "Yes, sir, haste does make waste. I will allow as that's a fact." He looked again at the two riders, the Ree Bloody Knife in a loose cotton shirt and black vest, and Custer in a fringed buckskin campaign jacket, as they sat conversing a hundred yards away. They were having a fairly heated discussion, if he was to judge by the emphatic gestures that punctuated their sign language.

"How do we even know there is a village down there?" Custer insisted. "I sure didn't see it!"

Bloody Knife's gaze was steady, unblinking. "There is a village," the Ree scout said quietly. "It is the biggest village I have ever seen. There are more Sioux there than we have bullets. Just because you did not see this does not make it not there. You have good eyes, Son-of-the-Morning-Star, but you are a white man and your world is little. You squint making the paper talk. You live in houses where the walls are close to you. In your forts and towns everything is right in front of your nose. You can see these stones well." Bloody Knife pointed at the ground and then jerked his head toward Varnum and the scouts. "You can even see those men over there and tell me who each one is and if he is carrying a knife or if his saddlebags are buckled. But your world is smaller than my world. You see what you expect to see and nothing else. You cannot see what you don't know to look for. Most white men cannot see what they do not want to see." The Ree shook his head slowly.

"When we look at a place, we do not see just what is there but what should not be there." Bloody Knife cast an arm in the direction of the Little Bighorn. "Where we looked, we could see the ground moving when it should not move. Your eyes tell you it was just the wind in the buffalo grass, but I know there is no wind to make the grass move. There is a big village there. This plan is not a good one, old friend."

"Don't tell me you're taking that Crow's side in this. White-Man-Runs-Him is wrong. We will not attack today." Custer's face was flushed with anger, but the scout continued to shake his head in defiance.

"I did not say that the Crow is right," Bloody Knife said calmly. "He is wrong too. He is too eager for a fight."

The cavalry officer was puzzled and frowned at the Ree curiously. "What the hell do you mean? White-Man-Runs-Him is wrong, but I am wrong too? So what's right, Bloody Knife? Can you answer me that?"

"These Crows are wrong when they say that the Sioux have seen us." Bloody Knife waved his hand in the air. "These Sioux are too full of themselves and will see only what they want to see. If a dust cloud rises, they will say it is a herd of buffalo. If they see smokes, they will say it is the camps of more of their friends coming to join them. No, they do not know you are here."

"But you are wrong too. All you soldier chiefs think about is that the Sioux will get away and you think always, 'How will we stop them before they scatter like so many seeds in the wind?' But the Sioux will not run away—not today. They are too many and they think their medicine is strong now. If you attack them, they will fight and they are too many for us." Custer looked at the Ree thoughtfully and was about to speak when the scout raised his hand to indicate that he had not finished.

"You think that the walk-a-heaps, the soldiers with the long guns and the guns that speak quickly, will be here tomorrow and you will catch them in between you"—Bloody Knife closed his two hands together—"like a bear catches fish. But you don't know that this is true. Where are their scouts? *You* now have the Crows who were with them before, and now No Hipbone and the walking soldiers are like blind men. Do they send the paper that talks? No! That is because they are still far away from here. You see how the creeks are high. There has been much rain, and they will be slower than you, Long Hair. The Crows tell me that there are many streams and hard country between them and us. Your butt is made of iron so that you can ride all day. We have come here quickly, but they are slower. They will not be here tomorrow and maybe not until the day after that." The Ree shook his head with finality. "No, you should not attack today—or tomorrow. We should wait until we know where the walking soldiers are so we can catch these Head-Cutters between us. If we do not wait, we will attack alone, and there are too many Sioux!"

George Custer sat silent for a moment, his eyes drifting back toward the Crow's Nest, behind which his scouts told him that a large village was located. The Sioux were so close. Was Bloody Knife right about Gibbon? Two days? Impossible. Gibbon's people must be closer than that. They had worked through the march times so carefully on the *Far West*, calculating every mile they had to cover. Even allowing for the slow rate of march imposed by the Gatling guns, Terry and Gibbon couldn't possibly be more than twenty, twenty-five miles off. Crook, of course, was off to the south somewhere. But he was new to this country, and Custer discounted Crook's ability to navigate the rugged terrain that was so different from the Arizona deserts he was used to.

No, it wasn't possible. Bloody Knife must be wrong. Gibbon would be coming into the lower end of the valley early tomorrow. His scouts might even now be watching the same Sioux camp. Bloody Knife was too pessimistic. And no matter what the Ree said, he might be able to keep the outfit out of sight for another day, but he'd never be able to keep it hidden for two days. With all the hunting parties wandering through this country, one of them was bound to stumble on the command, and then the element of surprise would truly be lost. Custer looked around at the countryside as he turned things over in his mind. Whatever happened, it would be his decision. His responsibility. Custer blew out a long breath.

"I hear what you are saying, Bloody Knife, but it's no good. Gibbon will be in position tomorrow, and if we wait longer, the Sioux will see us first and scatter. No, we have to go tomorrow. Don't worry, we'll do a good scout today and make sure we know where the Sioux are and how many of them are in this camp—then we'll attack and push them into Colonel Gibbon's walking soldiers, who will be waiting for them."

Custer looked back to the Crow's Nest where the rest of the scouts, with the exception of Bob-tailed Bull and Forked Horn, were now mounting up and preparing to join him and Bloody Knife. The Crows were talking heatedly among themselves, and he could almost imagine what they were saying. They were probably trying to think of how to slip off and into the Sioux herds at the earliest opportunity. He'd have to make sure they weren't left to go off pirating on their own hook.

The report rendered to Captain Yates by Sergeant Curtis had put the bivouac into an uproar. The cry "Indians to the rear!" was echoing up and down the company lines as Myles Keogh brought the word to Tom Custer, Moylan, and Calhoun, who were still enjoying their cigarettes in their secluded glade. Tom Custer and Jimmi Calhoun had immediately headed for their horses, intending to ride out to inform George Custer of the bad news.

Tom and Calhoun spurred their horses forward over the rough terrain, a plume of dust boiling in their wake. Behind them the outfit was in a chaos of frantic activity as horses were saddled, gear strapped hastily onto the cruppers, and carbines and ammunition checked hurriedly for serviceability. Officers and sergeants were shouting orders as the regiment was hastily formed into companies, and flankers were deployed, carbines at the ready, to right and left of the column. The last thing Tom had noticed before galloping off was the rotund Major Reno deep in conversation with Captain Benteen, who was gesticulating forcefully, obviously giving the inexperienced Reno advice on how best to organize the outfit for the move forward. Despite having done a fairly competent job during his independent recon several days earlier, Reno was still considered a "greenie," or greenhorn, by the acerbic Benteen. Tom Custer smiled. It was just like Benteen to put in his two cents worth. Nobody did his job well enough to suit the old fart.

The two young officers had not gotten more than five hundred yards from the outfit when Lieutenant Colonel Custer and his small entourage hove in sight and pulled up short just as Tom and Jimmi galloped up. Even before reining to a halt Tom could tell that his brother was in high dudgeon, his faced flushed with anger.

"Tom! What's the meaning of this? Mr. Calhoun, get back to your command. Who gave you permission to leave the outfit? Get back where you belong. By thunder, I've a mind to put the pair of you under arrest." Just then Colonel Custer's attention was diverted by the large column of dust being stirred up by the advance of the regiment several hundred yards distant.

"What in the name . . ." Custer sputtered. "Who the devil moved these troops forward? My orders were to remain in camp all day."

"Armstrong! Damn it," Tom shouted, "the game is up. They've tumbled us."

"The hell, you s-say. What are you talking about? This better not be one of your jokes. S-spit it out, man."

Tom Custer struggled to control his horse, which was dancing with nervous energy, the large sorrel-roan still eager for the run that had just been aborted. Tom knew from George's stutter that his older brother was thoroughly agitated now.

"No joke, Armstrong. Yates's people went back to pick up a box of tack the mules dropped last night. They ran straight into a Sioux war party* already poking through the box. Yates told Keogh, who told me, so Jimmi and I figured you'd best know soon as possible."

George Custer was thunderstruck. This couldn't be happening. Damn the luck. He had to think. If they'd been spotted, it wouldn't take long for the word to get back to the village and the whole camp would scatter in a thousand directions. It would be disastrous. Terry and Crook would be furious. Grant would hold him personally responsible for having busted the operation. They were all counting on him to keep the hostiles from slipping out of the net, and here he was about to flush the whole covey before anyone else was in position. Time, time. He must have time to think. Maybe he had a little time left. If that war party had been behind the outfit, they would want to give it a wide berth going back to the village.

He tried to work the calculations out in his head. If the village was maybe fifteen miles out, given the kind of terrain they'd already passed over, that might give him another three or four hours at the outside. But there wasn't any time left to lose. Something had to be done and done quickly. He'd have to work out a flexible plan of action, reorganize the outfit into fighting battalions that could shift rapidly to meet a changing situation. The Washita fight flashed through his mind. There he'd underestimated the enemy's strength, and it had almost been a disaster. Arapahos and Cheyennes had gotten around his flank and into the supply column. He'd have to beef up the pack train to protect the extra ammunition. What

---

* This was, in fact, Little Wolf's party of Cheyennes, who were not yet a part of the Sioux encampment but just arriving from the Red Cloud Agency.

if they slipped off to the south? Damn! He'd have to make sure that none of them were moving upriver and around his left flank.

Custer nudged Vic into a walk toward the advancing regiment, Tom and Calhoun completely forgotten now, his brain working feverishly, sorting through the few options that were left. Whatever he did, one thing was clear—the plan would have to change.

1105 Hours
Along Davis Creek

Orderly Trumpeter Private John Martin raised his instrument to his lips, took a deep breath, and sounded Officers' Call. Even before the last notes had died away, the regiment's officers were scrambling forward at a gallop and dust was swirling in a dense cloud around the slight Italian, adding yet another layer of the powdery soil to his uniform. He blinked his eyes rapidly and tried vainly to fan the billows away from his sunburned face. Glancing to his left, he caught sight of Lieutenant Cooke, the regimental adjutant. Cooke grimaced at the young man and motioned him forward.

"Si, Lootenante!" Martin called as he trotted over to Cooke and saluted smartly.

"Very good, Private Martin." Cooke's clipped accent fascinated the young immigrant. "That'll be all for now. Keep out of the way, but don't wander off too far. Clear? Off you go then. There's a good lad." With a slight nod of his head Cooke indicated that Martin's job was done and that he could retire.

Martin, born Giovanni Martini, had been in this country only three years and, with his imperfect English, was not completely sure of what was expected of him. He deduced that he was to remain handy in case the lieutenant needed him. The young Italian was especially eager to do well. The better he did—the better he understood and spoke the language—the sooner he would be a real American. He wanted so badly to become an American that he had even changed his name to the more Anglo-sounding John Martin. When he had first arrived in New York, a friend had urged him to join the Army. Martin had thought it a stupid idea but now had to admit that his friend had been right.

Now, three years later, Orderly Trumpeter Private John Martin was detailed from Company H to serve as the general's runner for the day. It was a job that he found particularly interesting, not least for the fact that he got to listen to the discussions among the officers. While he did not understand everything they said, he felt intuitively that they used language which was more educated and hence more valuable if he was to succeed in this country. Besides, it put him toward the head of the column, which meant that there was less dust for him to eat than while trailing along in Captain Benteen's command. Even more appealing was the fact that it got him away from Captain Benteen who, for some reason Martin could not fathom, seemed to dislike him intensely.* Benteen's directions to the young immigrant were laced liberally with expressions such as "You ignorant Dago!" and "You Eyetie idiot!" Working directly for Lieutenant Cooke, the very proper but easygoing Canadian, was much more enjoyable.

Cooke, "Queen's Own," was a true gentleman. Giovanni noticed that the lieutenant always looked him straight in the eye while addressing him and spoke slowly and clearly in his distinctive, clipped accent to explain exactly what he wanted him to do. He felt he could learn a lot from the odd-sounding officer with the even odder sideburns,† which seemed to tumble down the man's face to form a sort of fork-tailed beard that was forever flapping in the breeze behind him as he rode. Martin glanced at the lieutenant, who was now scribbling furiously in his little notebook as the general addressed the other officers who had dismounted to crowd around him in a small knot.

"Very well, gentlemen," the general was saying. "We have a dilemma facing us. Mr. Varnum and his scouts have located what appears to be a large village about fifteen miles to our front." He pointed in the direction of the Crow's Nest before continuing. "I had hoped that we would use today to rest up the outfit and do a thorough reconnaissance of the hostiles' positions, with the intention of striking the camp at first light tomorrow. I no longer believe that this is possible. As you know, Captain Keogh has informed me through Captain Custer that a war party has been discovered on our back trail and shots have been fired."

The officers all nodded silently while exchanging anxious glances. General Custer drew a breath and went on.

"Coupling this report with the comments of our Indian scouts, who have sighted a number of Sioux scouting parties this morning, it is possible that these parties may have observed the dust kicked up by the command

---

* Benteen's attitude toward Martin was hardly a secret. When later asked about the young private, Benteen described him as "a thick-headed, dull-witted Italian, just as much cut out for a cavalryman as he was for a king!"
† Cooke's whiskers, worn in a style called Dundreary, which featured a clean-shaven chin, were indeed unusual, even in the Seventh and attracted a number of comments. The Indian scouts were especially fascinated by this unusual style of facial hair.

during this last move." He looked sharply to where Major Reno and Captain Benteen were standing, the latter with his arms crossed over his chest and his lips pursed in distaste.

"We must assume," Custer said deliberately, "that the hostiles, if they do not know it already, will soon be aware of our presence. Therefore, we must alter our original plan. Any delay at this point will allow the village to scatter and escape—so we will move to the attack today." There was an audible intake of breath within the small circle of men. A few muttered comments were exchanged. Custer let the impact of his decision sink in before going on.

"All right then," Custer said quietly, "each company will detach six men under the direction of a noncommissioned officer to report to Captain McDougall with B Company and the pack train. This will ensure adequate protection for the ammunition reserves." McDougall nodded quickly and looked at Lieutenant Cooke, who was making a note of the order.

"I want a complete inspection in all companies of horses and equipment, and I want particular attention paid to the serviceability of all weapons and ammunition. The companies will move out in the order in which they report that this has been accomplished and that they are ready to move." He reached under his buckskin campaign jacket to pull out his gold hunter and thumbed the lid open. The other officers quickly reached for their own watches, and a series of dull clicks was heard as the lids popped open.

"I have it at ten minutes past eleven. I'd like the command to move out within the next thirty minutes." He looked around the circle of men all busily adjusting the hands of their watches. "Is everything clear? Are there any questions? Colonel Benteen?"

"No questions, *General*." Benteen seemed almost to spit out the last word. "I would just note that H Company is ready to move this instant." Tom Custer and Jimmi Calhoun shot sour looks at the white-haired cavalryman.

George Custer just blinked rapidly, his face flushing red. "Thank you, Colonel," he said softly. "Then you may have the honor of leading out— when the rest of the outfit is ready to move." Benteen forced a tight-lipped smile and nodded curtly, his hooded eyes darting quickly around the small group of officers and coming to rest on Calhoun and Tom Custer.

Calhoun whispered, "Damned show-off!" Tom Custer snorted and shook his head.

Lieutenant Colonel Custer glanced quickly at Cooke, who nodded to indicate that he had made note of the meeting, then nodded himself at the assembled cavalrymen. "Very well, gentlemen, thank you. You may see to your companies. Please inform Lieutenant Cooke as you complete your checks."

The dusty figures saluted raggedly and turned to rejoin their units, spurs jingling lightly and saddle leather creaking as they mounted their horses and moved away. Lieutenant Colonel Custer and Lieutenant Cooke chatted as Martin sat quietly in the saddle and watched the other officers returning to their units.

Martin sometimes had difficulty accepting the enormity of the change his life had undergone in just a few short years. He had come off the boat full of hope and brimming with expectations, only to have them dashed by his cousin Giuseppe. Giuseppe had already been in America for two years and was weighed down by the realities of a country suffering economic hard times.

"Giovanni," he had said. "It's a terrible time for you to have come here. This country's having a depression right now. There are no jobs for foreigners, and a foreigner who doesn't speak English doesn't have a prayer."

Giovanni had been stunned. He had saved months to book passage from the Old World, and now it looked as if the New World would reject him. He had pleaded with his cousin. He had used all of his money just for the trip over. He was broke. What could he do? Giuseppe had shrugged his shoulders helplessly and said that the best he could do was to let him stay with him in the tiny apartment he shared with a wife and four small children. There was nothing else for him to do. Everything he owned was in the small carpetbag he had dragged with him all the way from Italy, but even that seemed like too much to cram into the shabby little tenement.

Martini had accepted his cousin's generous offer but felt guilty about it. He couldn't help thinking that he was just one more mouth to feed in a household that already had too many mouths. In his depression every bite he took tasted bitter, flavored as it was with the knowledge that it was as much as stolen from the children. Giovanni loved his cousins, and even more for the fact that there was never a word of complaint from either Giuseppe or his consumptive wife, Loredonna. He could hardly bear to see the gaunt faces of the children or listen to the wracking wheeze of their dying mother, and so took to wandering the alien streets of New York late into the night. It was on one of these nocturnal wanderings that Giovanni had met another young immigrant who gave his name as Baldassare Spalletti. As they wandered the littered streets, Martini poured out his heart to his new companion, who listened with a mixture of interest and empathy to his tale of woe. Finally, Spalletti stopped him.

"You know, Giovanni," he said, "you cannot stay with them. I hear the pride in your voice, and I know it will not allow you to drag these good cousins deeper into their poverty."

Martini nodded, tears running freely down his face.

"Look," Spalletti went on, "as long as you don't speak the language, you will go nowhere. You must try to learn English. How do you think your cousin, and myself, for that matter, are able to work at all? Our English is not perfect, but we at least can get along."

"Yes, I know that. But how can I learn the language, Baldassare, if I can't get a job, and how can I get a job if I don't know the language? You see my dilemma?" He threw up his hands in frustration.

"That, my friend, is your great problem. You have to take a job that nobody else wants. One where they don't care if you can speak the language as long as you are willing to try, and have a strong back."

"Yes, yes, I know that," Giovanni protested. "Don't you think I have looked all over this city for such a job?"

"You think that this city is the only place in this country?" Spalletti scolded his young friend. "No wonder you can't find any work. You have to be smarter than that, my friend," he said, tapping Giovanni's head with his finger.

"This is a huge country," Spalletti exclaimed. "Beyond this stinking sewer there are thousands of miles out there where men are needed to work. If I were you I would start looking elsewhere and stop sobbing about your luck. In this country a man makes his own luck. He makes his own opportunities." He handed Giovanni a grimy handkerchief with which to dry his eyes, and the two walked on again in silence. As they turned the next corner, Baldassare spotted a broadside pasted on a crumbling brick wall. The sign announced in large letters MEN WANTED FOR THE ARMY! Spalletti pulled up short.

"There is your answer, my friend," he said, rapping the poster with his knuckles.

"What? What does it say?" Giovanni stared at the sign uncomprehendingly.

"It says that the American Army is looking for men like you."

"The Army?" Giovanni was baffled. "Why should I join up with the Army? I'm not a soldier. I'm a musician."

"Yes, of course you are! I can see how beautifully you play . . . what is it that you play?"

"The trumpet."

"Yes, your beautiful trumpet! It must be a wonderful profession. I can see how you've been able to do so well with your musical talents, *signore*. I must have been dreaming to insult you by mentioning such a thing. Can you ever forgive me, *maestro?*"

Spalletti's sarcasm was not wasted. Giovanni flushed with shame. He was immediately contrite, damning his own pride that had refused to acknowledge the desperate nature of his situation. As he thought about Spalletti's suggestion, it occurred that it might be a pretty good idea after all. He would at least no longer be a burden on his cousin. And soldiering was not entirely foreign to his nature. He had, in fact, served as a drummer boy for Garibaldi's army. The American Army could not be worse than that. If nothing else, the Americans were not at war now. How bad could it be to be a soldier in peacetime? And what better way, really, to learn the language?

The next day, Giovanni packed up his few belongings in his carpetbag and bid a tearful farewell to his cousins, thanking them profusely for their generosity and promising that he would make it up to them from the pay he intended to receive from the Army. His friend Baldassare accompanied him to the recruiting station, where he presented himself and acted as an interpreter for Giovanni. The sergeant at the recruiting station, a tall, burly Irishman with three bright yellow stripes on the sleeve of his blue uniform coat, looked down at the young prospect with a jaundiced eye, a brier pipe twitching under his bushy mustache.

"An' why, I ask ye." He sneered. "Why should I be takin' the likes o' this sorry immigrant into Uncle Sam's service? Can ye tell me that? Why, he's not even a bit able to speak proper English! Jaysus, Mary 'n' Joseph!"

"Please, your honor," Baldassare put in, "he's a good man, and makes a wonderful music with his trumpet."

"The devil, ye say!" The large sergeant ran a skeptical eye over the bashful Italian.

Baldassare smiled brightly and poked Giovanni in the side while whispering something into his ear. At his prodding Giovanni grinned and fumbled in his carpetbag until he drew out a battered but highly polished trumpet. The young man then reached into his pocket for the mouthpiece, wiped it carefully on his sleeve and mounted it on the instrument. Taking a deep breath, Giovanni began to play with a passion and beauty that soon brought both Baldassare and the large Irishman to tears. When he had finished, he looked up to find the sergeant dabbing surreptitiously at his eyes while Spalletti shot him a sly wink.

"Faith, if that's not a beeootiful thing, that is." The beefy Irishman clapped a large paw on Martini's shoulder. "M'lad," he said, "I've got just the place fer ye!"

His horse shied slightly to the left, and Martin pulled back on the reins with one hand while gripping his trumpet with the other. A slight breeze had come up, and Martin's mount apparently didn't care for the scent of the Indian scouts who were loitering nearby.

Custer turned to regard the Indian scouts,* who, along with Herendeen, Charley Reynolds, Gerard, and Bouyer, had gathered in a loose group near Lieutenant Varnum. Behind Varnum were the other civilian scouts and interpreters: Billy Jackson, who was part Blackfoot, Will Baker, who was half Ree, and Billy Cross, a half-breed Sioux who, like Bouyer and Bloody Knife, had old scores to settle with his former relatives in the large village nearby. Looming above this last group was Isaiah Dorman,† a very large black man, who sported a worn, ill-fitting cavalryman's shell jacket and carried a shotgun loosely under his arm. Just off to the side of this group Custer noticed his brother Boston deep in conversation with Autie Reed and the reporter, Kellogg. The bespectacled journalist was hastily making notes on a pad of gray paper and intermittently shoving his wire-rimmed spectacles back up to the bridge of his nose, only to have them slide down again a moment later. Boston noticed his brother George moving toward them and started to say something, but George waved him off as he headed straight for the gathering of scouts. Autie Reed and Kellogg stopped talking and edged in to listen to what the general was about to say.

Custer walked up to the scouts and waded right into the center of the group, motioning for them to remain at their ease. Removing his white campaign hat, he slapped the brim against his thigh and stood there look-

---

* *Although not widely known or commented upon, Custer's scout detail included at least four Sioux warriors: White Cloud, Ma-tok-sha, Caroo, and Whole Buffalo. Very probably these were members of Red Cloud's Bad Faces, which was also Crazy Horse's band. Red Cloud, who had won his war against the whites in 1868, refused to join Sitting Bull's rebellion, although his son, Jack Red Cloud, had fought at the Rosebud. During this fight Jack Red Cloud had been humiliated by a party of Crow warriors, who had taken from him his father's Winchester and warbonnet and, laughing derisively, had driven him off in disgrace.*

† *Little is known of Isaiah Dorman, who had served the Army as a courier for some time. He may have been a former "Buffalo Soldier" of the Ninth or Tenth Cavalry Regiments and was known to have lived among the Sioux for several years. He had apparently married a Santee Sioux woman and is said to have been known personally by Sitting Bull. The Sioux called him Azinpi or Teat, presumably because his skin color resembled that of a buffalo cow's nipples.*

ing about the circle for a moment, running his fingers through his damp, close-cropped hair. After a moment he tossed the hat carelessly onto a patch of sage and began to address the scouts in English while at the same time using his hands to sign out his meaning.

"We have a hard day in front of us. Our Crow brothers are right. The Sioux know that we are coming, and we will have to do as the Crow say. We will attack them before they can run away from us." He waited a moment as Bouyer and Reynolds translated, although it was fairly obvious that all understood his meaning.

"Boys," he went on, "I want you to take the ponies away from the Sioux camp. Make up your minds to go straight to their camp and take their ponies. Boys, you will have a hard day; I want you to keep up your courage. You will get a lot of experience today." The assembled warriors nodded vigorously in assent and scrambled to their feet. One of the Rees, named Stabbed, came forward and addressed his fellow scouts.

"You hear Son-of-the-Morning-Star, brothers. This will be a hard fight. Brave up! Don't be afraid, but go straight for their horses and run them off. If any Lakota tries to stop you, kill him and take his horse and his gun too!"

Stabbed snatched off a leather medicine bag that hung from a thong around his neck. Borrowing a canteen from the large black man, he opened the bag, poured some water into it, and worked the bag between his fingers to mix the water in with the bag's contents. Then, reaching into the bag, he pulled out some moistened dirt.

"This sacred clay I have brought with us from our home." He walked around to each of the Ree scouts and daubed some of the reddish brown mixture onto their chests. "Hear me, Starter-of-All-Things. Protect these warriors from the bullets and arrows of the Lakota. My Father, I remember this day the promises you have made to me; it is for my young men I speak to you. Help them to take their guns and their horses!" Stabbed turned to his friends. "Brave up, boys! Kill these Lakota dogs! Take their guns! Young men, keep up your courage, don't feel that you are children. Today will be a hard battle. You will return with your faces black!" * The Rees broke out in a bloodcurdling shriek and began to sing.

Mitch Bouyer moved across the circle to where Lieutenant Colonel Custer was retrieving his broad-brimmed hat. "General," he said softly, "I

---

* Among the Rees and Crows the taking of scalps was not as important as the act of counting coup. Stabbed's admonition to the other scouts reflects the relative importance of their missions—the most honor was to be had in taking an enemy's gun, then his horse. To "return with a black face" refers to their custom of painting their faces black when returning from a victory.

been with these Injuns thirty years now, and this is the largest damn village I ever saw! I say if we go in there, we won't come out again."

Custer gazed levelly at the scout, his eyes hard and unflinching. "I heard you the first time, Mitch." The two men stood there motionless as the scout studied his commander's face.

"Right you are, General. I believe you did."

Reynolds stood by listening quietly, saying nothing. The signs were all there, he thought, if anyone cared to read them properly. But he doubted anyone would—anyone, that was, who could do anything about it. Damn soldiers. Once they got their minds set on anything, it was hell trying to get them to see reason. Hell, he hadn't expected to see that large a village himself, but he sure as be-damned knew it was there now. Seemed to him that Custer, the whole bunch of 'em for that matter, had got it in their minds that there weren't but a few hundred Sioux out there. That, Reynolds figured, was the problem with soldiers' logic—or white man's logic, which was the same thing. If you got to expecting a thing to be a certain way, why that's just the way it had to be. Now he felt he was finally starting to understand how they had managed to kill each other in such staggering numbers during the Civil War. All of these men had studied Napoleon at West Point and had taken his ideas into that war. There is no God but Napoleon, and Jomini* is his prophet. Napoleonic tactics and modern technology had combined to produce a bloodbath beyond imagining at Cold Harbor, Fredericksburg, Antietam, and a hundred other places. But they had never seemed to figure that out. They knew the "correct" way to fight a battle, and that's just what they did. Now they thought they knew what they were up against in that damned valley up ahead. Damn soldiers, Reynolds thought. They never learn.

He looked up to see the reporter, Kellogg, who had sidled up alongside him.

"Mr. Reynolds," Kellogg said. "What are they singing about, sir?"

Reynolds didn't even spare the reporter a look but continued to watch the Rees, who were preparing for battle, painting their faces, checking their weapons, and chanting in their strange, guttural tongue.

"They are singing their death songs, Mr. Kellogg," he said flatly. "As we should be singing ours. Do you have a death song, Mr. Kellogg?"

---

* Jomini, Antoine Henri, Baron de (1779–1869) Swiss-born general who served under Napoleon Bonaparte. Along with Clausewitz he was considered one of the most influential military theorists of the nineteenth century. His seminal work Précis de l'art de la guerre (1838) argued that the conduct of warfare could be reduced to a few immutable principles such as the massing of forces to strike at one decisive point. His work was taught at West Point with what could almost be described as a religious zeal.

As Reynolds turned and moved away, Kellogg blanched noticeably. With his glasses sliding inexorably down his nose, he stared at the strange beings who squatted singing amid the dust and sagebrush on this hot Sunday morning in June.

1135 Hours
Along Davis Creek

Captain Myles Keogh urged his horse into an easy canter as he swept down the line of troops toward Company I. Comanche, his large claybank gelding, seemed almost to sense his rider's eagerness. Something was in the air, and the horse, nostrils flaring widely, responded to Keogh's every touch with a ready will despite the heat that was already building in the clear, bright sunshine. Many in the regiment thought Comanche to be one of the finest but most dangerous animals in the outfit. He was unusually large, with gentle brown eyes that belied a fierce, aggressive nature. Keogh, it seemed, was the only one who could handle him, although lately some of the troops had noticed that Comanche had taken an unusual interest in Gussy Korn, the young German who sometimes acted as Keogh's orderly. Comanche had an irritating habit of nipping his keepers in the rear end. Even the farrier was leery of him and would not go near the claybank unless Keogh or Korn stood by holding on to the horse's halter and rubbing his nose.

But Gussy had a remarkable talent with the brute, who whinnied whenever he caught Korn's scent and would rub his large head up against the German's chest and nuzzle under his arm like a large dog seeking affection. Sergeant Bustard, who called Comanche "a devil with a U.S. brand," claimed that horses could smell fear and that the only reason Korn could approach Comanche was because "Gussy's just too dumb to be scared of 'im." Fred Lehman joked that Comanche was the only horse he knew who "liked Korn better than sugar." A poor pun but one that always made Beans McNally laugh.

One thing that everyone agreed on was that Comanche's personality was perfectly suited to the dark Irishman who commanded Company I. Captain Myles Walter Keogh was not a man to be trifled with. A burly, dangerously handsome man with a luxuriant, black mustache, Keogh was considered, along with Captain Benteen, to be one of the regiment's most formidable fighters. The only difference between them, claimed Bustard, was that Benteen relished the act of killing while Keogh simply loved the fun of a melee. To him, war was more of a sport than a business.

The expatriate son of an Irish lancer, Keogh was a born soldier and adventurer. As a youngster he had run off to Africa to seek his fortune, only to dash off to Italy when the pope called for Catholics to defend the Holy See against the Piedmontese. A reckless fighter, entirely without fear, Keogh had delighted in battle. Tales of his prowess in the field reached the ears of Pope Pius IX and the pontiff had personally hung about his neck the Medaglia di Pro Petri Sede, the papacy's medal for valor. The large gold medal was the rough Irishman's most cherished possession, and he wore it constantly around his neck in a fine leather pouch suspended by a thong.

By the time the war with the Piedmontese was over, another war had broken out in America between the North and the South. The now-veteran Keogh had made his way to the New World and found himself a position with a volunteer cavalry regiment, where again he distinguished himself with his daring and aggressive spirit, and rose to the rank of colonel. When that war was over, it had not taken him long to obtain a commission as a captain in the much smaller postwar Army. The brash, two-fisted, hooligan-turned-officer had made the Seventh his home, and it suited him to a tee. Even the regimental song, "Garryowen," * was said to be his doing, for soon after Keogh had joined the outfit at Fort Riley, General Custer had been heard whistling the tune frequently. It was just like Keogh to like that song, with its lyrics alluding to drinking bouts and brawls. What amazed some was the affection with which the puritan George Custer seemed to regard the unruly, and frequently drunken, Irishman. Sergeant Bustard once remarked on this strange relationship to Sergeant Major Sharrow.

"Well, Jimmy," Bill Sharrow said, "I think it's not such a strange thing. The general, you see, was once quite the young rakehell himself, what with boozin' and singin' and playin' cards half the night wi' his brother, young Tom, and the lads. But it's the Missus what reformed him, m'boy. Swore it all off fer her sake alone."

"You don't say!" Bustard exclaimed. This was a side of the general he'd not seen.

---

* "Garryowen," which in Gaelic means "Owen's Garden," was indeed a popular song with the Fifth Royal Irish Lancers, Keogh's father's regiment. It refers to a suburb of the city of Limerick, Ireland, where the Lancers were stationed. Soon after the Seventh Cavalry was formed at Fort Riley, Kansas, the regiment adopted the popular quickstep as their marching song. The first lines give an indication of the tenor of the tune: "Let Bacchus' sons be not dismayed, but join with us each jovial blade. Come booze and sing and lend your aid and help us with the chorus. Instead of spa we'll drink down ale and pay the reck'ning on the nail. No man for debt shall go to jail, if he from Garryowen hale."

"Aye, that he did! Oh, ye'd not have known him for the same man, ye wouldna! Oh, he's a swell now, a little puritan and no mistake. A proper gentleman. But, ye know, old Cap'n Keogh's just the sort o' fella, all piss and vinegar and a bearcat for nerve, that the general would be if'n he could. Which, of course, he can't—not as long as Libby has a say. I 'spect he might see a bit o' himself in the Cap'n, and so he sort of turns a blind eye to some of his shenanigans."

"Well, if that's the case," asked Bustard, "how come the general and Cap'n Benteen ain't particular close? Old Skull-and-Crossbones is as big a boozer and card man as ever Keogh was."

Sharrow looked at Bustard, his head cocked to one side.

"I'll tell ye, Jimmy, there's nary a mystery there. Colonel Benteen is an angry man. He drinks mean and plays cards mean. The general's done gone up the pole* an' Benteen don't like it. He says the leopard don't never change his spots and believes the general's a hypocrite. Benteen can't quit and don't want to, an' anyone who does is an affront to his nature. Whereas Colonel Keogh, on t'other hand, is a happy man. He drinks and plays cards and sings 'cause he enjoys it. It's hard not to like a man who does it up brown like that. Oh, he's a ruffian and no mistake. You don't ever want to cross him drunk or sober, has a hell of a temper, so he does. But when a fight's done, it's done an' he'll let 'er go. Colonel Benteen can't and that's all she wrote."

Captain Keogh, cold sober, was not a particularly happy man at this moment. There was every indication that the outfit would be into a fight fairly soon, but while he usually looked forward to a bit of action, there was something about the way things were developing that just didn't sit right with him. He'd told Tom Custer about Yates's report but he'd not told the young fool to go blabbing to his big brother, spinning tales about Sioux war parties in the rear. Oh, there'd been Injuns back there, to be sure, but Keogh didn't think Sergeant Curtis'd know a Sioux from a Hottentot if his life depended on it.

---

* "Gone up the pole"; reformed, a teetotaler. This would be the nineteenth century equivalent of "gone on the wagon." Libby Custer had indeed put her foot down as regarded her husband's extracurricular social life, and George, ever the obedient husband, had entirely sworn off drink, gambling, and rough language. He frequently scolded younger brother Tom, who refused to be reformed, for his continued excesses and was even known to have put him under arrest a number of times for his rowdy behavior. Being put under arrest in the frontier army was considerably less serious than it appears to the modern reader and was more akin to putting an unruly child in the corner for a "time out." Contemporary letters and journals treat the practice lightly, implying that it was not a serious punishment but rather regarded as an accepted excuse to nurse a bad hangover.

Damn Curtis for a ninny! Keogh thought. He should've sent one of his lads back with the word and kept on their trail to see where the hell they were off to. There'd be no catchin' 'em now, and the Lord only knew where they were or what devilment they were up to. If Curtis had been a decent shot, they'd have a body or at least a damn blood trail to follow. While Tom and Jimmi Calhoun had raced off to tell brother George, Keogh had at least had the presence of mind to send Herendeen and Billy Jackson off to try to pick up the Indians' trail.

Herendeen had indeed found some pony tracks, but whoever they belonged to had quickly erased all trace of their presence soon after they'd left the trail. Now the outfit was operating in the dark. George Custer was probably right to assume the worst, lacking any firm intelligence, but Keogh didn't like it one bit. Damn Curtis for an ignorant dolt. If he were Keogh's man, he'd thrash him within an inch of his worthless life.

First Sergeant Frank Varden was in the process of dressing down a young private when Keogh reined up alongside the pair.

"O'Bryan," Varden was saying, "you sorry excuse of a greenie! Never have I seen a more slovenly, dull-witted misfit! Look at the state of that damned carbine! What'd ya' do with 'er? Stuff the goddamn barrel wi' mud, ya dunce? Looka them lousy ca'tridges!"

A disheveled Private O'Bryan was staring forlornly at a small pile of .45/55 rounds Varden held in an outstretched palm. Each was covered with a fine crust of verdigris* giving them a dull, greenish cast.

"They're goddamned greener'n you, ya' dope! Run a damned rod through that piece and skin them ca'tridges off and be quick about it! You try poppin' that shooter at a Injun, he'll have yer worthless scalp afore ye kin yank yer first shell out'n the breech! God, give me strength!"

"First Sergeant!" Keogh growled at the old veteran.

Varden flung the offending cartridges at the young private and whirled to salute his commander.

"Cap'n Keogh, sir!"

"First Sergeant, give me one and six for detail wid the pack train. If we've got animals that're ailin', best move 'em back wid the packs. Detail

---

* The .45/55 cartridge (caliber .45 bullet, 55 grains of powder) was the standard-issue ammunition for the Springfield trapdoor cavalry carbine (although many soldiers preferred to use the more powerful .45/70 round designed for use in the longer infantry rifle). In the field, many soldiers carried their ammunition in homemade leather cartridge belts for easy access. Under the humidity of field conditions a chemical reaction between the copper and leather often produced verdigris, a green crystalline crust, on the shells, which could cause them to jam in the rifle.

t' report t' Cap'n McDougall o' B Comp'ny. Put O'Bryan on report and any other fool whose cartridges are a disgrace. If they come out o' this fight, I'll break 'em sure, by Jaysus!"

"Sir!" Varden snapped off a salute and strode off toward the rest of the company, his mouth set firmly and fire in his eye. He'd deal with O'Bryan later, never fear.

"DeLacy!" he yelled. "Sergeant DeLacy, fall out to your left!"

Varden stalked down the ranks of Company I, his teeth clenched, eyes squinting as they examined every trooper and mount in seconds.

"Cooney, fall out and fall in with Sergeant DeLacy." Nothing escaped Varden's piercing gaze.

"Gillette, tighten that cinch and adjust that curb chain!" He stopped in front of Private Driscoll, snatched the man's revolver from his holster, thumbed open the loading gate, and drew back the hammer to half cock. Sliding the cylinder along his sleeve, he listened to the series of clicks, then worked the extractor to pop a round out into his palm. He rotated the shiny cartridge deftly between thumb and forefinger, nodded, slipped the round back into its chamber, and flipped the loading gate shut with a snap. Most of the company had been issued the new Schofields, part of a field test, but Driscoll was one of those who had decided to hang onto his Colt. Varden nodded approvingly. He didn't much care for Major Schofield's model himself. With their innovative breakaction the Schofields might be faster to reload but had a nasty habit of popping open when drawn from the holster, with the automatic ejector scattering cartridges every which way. It was a flaw that could prove awkward in a fight. He handed the Colt back to Driscoll without comment.

"Jones, fall out and fall in with Segeant DeLacy." The first sergeant stopped in front of Private Gustave Korn and eyed Korn's mare suspiciously.

"Korn, that beast don't look too healthy. You'd best go with 'em." Korn's eyes widened, and Varden thought the man would burst into tears.

"Beg to report, First Sergeant!" Korn pleaded.

Varden hesitated. "Well, Korn, what is it? Spit it out, man!"

"Please, First S-Sergeant," Korn stuttered. "Schatz don't look good, but she's a goer, she is. I swear, First Sergeant, she run like de damn wind, by *Gott*. So she will."

Varden looked Korn up and down and noticed that, whatever the condition of his uniform, his carbine was spotless and the copper cartridges peeking from his prairie belt fairly glittered in the sunlight. He reached out and placed his hand on Schatz's muzzle and smiled as the horse tossed her head and snorted. Her eyes were bright and ears erect and alert.

"Alright, Korn, as you were." He glanced quickly to Korn's left. "Johnson, fall out and fall in with Sergeant DeLacy!" Varden looked back at Korn and nodded to himself. Good man, Gussy, he thought.

As First Sergeant Varden moved off down the line, Paddy Kelly looked over at Gussy and the two grinned broadly at each other. Neither of them had any idea of what was going on, but whatever it was, these two bunkies would see it through together. Kelly didn't say it, but he was thrilled that Gustave had stood up to Varden. He couldn't say it in front of the other fellows, but Paddy Kelly's stomach was turning over inside. He wondered if this was what it felt like to be scared, and he wondered if there was really anything to be scared about. Good old Gussy, he thought, thank God you're still here.

Gussy patted Schatz gently on the nose and breathed softly into her nostrils. "There, there, *mein* Schatz. We stay with the boys, *ja?*" When he noticed Paddy was still looking at him, he grinned again and winked at his bunky as if to say, "Not to worry, old friend."

First Sergeant Varden stepped in front of Soapy Lloyd and was about to send him off to join the detail when Sergeant Bustard stepped up behind the old veteran and whispered in his ear.

"Could I have just a word with ye, Frank?"

Varden frowned at the question but took a step backward as Bustard whispered earnestly. As Bustard talked, Varden's eyebrows dropped and he glanced quickly in Lloyd's direction. After a moment he nodded shortly and moved back to Private Lloyd.

"Lloyd . . ." he began.

"Right, First Sergeant," Soapy interrupted, "off I go," and he started to move forward, only to be stopped in his tracks by Varden's large hand, which was planted in the middle of his chest.

"As you were, Private Lloyd," Varden growled. "I know yer type, ye blackguard ye. Ye'd like ta be off wi' the pack train, ye would. First chance ye got, ye'd skip out for the goldfields and Uncle Sam's property wi' ye. Why, I've a good mind t' let ye go and have the damned redskins do for ye." First Sergeant Varden paused to glower at Soapy who, by the look on his face, had obviously been contemplating just such a scheme.

"But," continued Varden, "that would ruin my chances t' deal wi' ye, meself. Back into ranks, ye heathen. Ye'd jest better be on yer best behavior this day, m'lad, for I'll have my eye on ye and no error. McNally! McShane! Owens! Fall out and fall in with Sergeant DeLacy!" Varden paused to shoot one more glare at a deflated Private Lloyd before turning back to give DeLacy his instructions.

"DeLacy, you're in charge o' this detail. Report to Cap'n McDougall o' B Company, and he'll place ye wi' Mr. Mathey's command. Ye're t' stay wi' the pack train and do as Lieutenant Mathey or Cap'n McDougall tells ye. Don't dawdle and don't let those boys get behind Old Barnum or he'll kick their tiny brains in." He looked at the detail. "And if any of ye slouch or skip off, God help ye, ye'll wish that damned mule had kicked yer brains in afore I'm done wi' ye! Izzat clear?"

"Yes, First Sergeant!" they chorused back weakly.

"Fine. Alright, DeLacy, off ye go."

Sergeant DeLacy touched the brim of his campaign hat and swung into the saddle, motioning for the rest of the detail to follow. In a moment he had turned his mount and trotted off to the rear, the six young troopers bouncing along in the dust behind him. First Sergeant Varden watched the small troop ride off then turned back to Bustard.

"Well, Jimmy, we've a long day ahead and no error. We'll have t' depend on our young corporals t' keep the lads steady. We may well jest be chasin' our tails t'day, but we'd best be prepared t' fight." Bustard nodded solemnly, his lower lip protruding from beneath his bushy mustache.

"Corporal Wild! Corporal Staples! Corporal Morriss! Front an' center, lads!" Varden bellowed. "I need a word wi' ye."

First Lieutenant James Porter made a few hasty notes in his company log, checking his watch and jotting down the time, weather, and approximate location of the outfit. He had overheard Varden's assignments and briefly noted the names of the pack train detail so that they could be accounted for later. He heard a series of rolling clicks and looked up to see Captain Keogh alongside him, a custom-made Webley revolver in his hand. Keogh was checking the pistol's action and making sure a cartridge was in each chamber of the cylinder. Porter knew that Keogh customarily loaded only five rounds in his piece, leaving a sixth chamber empty under the firing pin.

The old man must be expecting trouble, Porter thought to himself. Tucking his notebook into the pocket of his tunic, he reached for his own revolver, a new government issue Schofield, and checked his loads as well. Just to be on the safe side, he reached back into his saddlebag and scooped up a handful of extra rounds, which he slipped into the pocket that held his notebook.

"Well, Jamie," Keogh said, a large grin creasing his face. "Are ye ready for a fight?"

"Yes, sir, I expect so. Do you think we'll really see action today, Cap'n?"

"Aye, well." Keogh removed his black slouch hat and ran his fingers through his mane of black hair. "That remains t' be seen, lad. Could be we'll chase a bit o' moonshine an' dust the day long. But ye never know f' sure."

The large Irishman replaced his hat and reached into his shirt to pull out a leather bag on a thong. Without bothering to remove the heavy Medaglia, he pressed his lips to the bag and thought to himself, Saints, preserve us this day. Keogh looked around for Varden and saw him coming down the line of troops, leading his horse.

"First Sergeant, prepare to lead out, column o' fours, if ye please!"

"Sir!" Varden turned, swung into the saddle, and wheeled his horse around to face the company.

"Lead out! Prepare to mount! Mount!" The first sergeant eyed the ranks as troopers settled into their McClellans, horses pawing the ground and snorting.

"Fours right into column! March!"

Keogh and Porter eased their horses off to the side as Company I moved easily into position to the creak of leather and jingling of spurs and curb chains.

"Halt!" Varden ran his eye down the company line looking for anything out of place, then wheeled his own mount to the left and moved in front of the two officers. He snapped off a smart salute.

"Sir, the comp'ny is formed!"

"Thank'ee, First Sergeant. Post!"

Keogh returned Varden's salute, and the first sergeant wheeled away to take up his assigned post to the right of the lead set of fours. With the dust swirling around Comanche's hooves, Captain Keogh moved off to the left of the company and peered toward the regiment's front, where the other companies were just moving into column. Keogh tugged on his gauntlets and raised his left hand to indicate that the "Wild I" was ready to move.

When he could discern a light cloud of dust being raised by the company to his front, he turned in the saddle and roared, "Comp'ny I, fours at the walk. For'rd, marrrch!"

Keogh's gloved hand dropped to his side and Company I eased forward at a sedate walk. Keogh looked off to his left front at the Wolf Mountains.

Somewhere over there, Keogh thought, we'll see what this day has in store for us.

Añpohañ (Noon)
Along the Greasy Grass

When he had left Sitting Bull's lodge, Crazy Horse stretched his muscles and looked about him at the sprawling city of little camps. For as far as he could see, the lodges of the people followed the winding course of the river. Circle after circle lay along the banks of the Greasy Grass. Here at the southernmost end were the Hunkpapas, Sitting Bull's people, with their circle extended almost into the trees at the place where the river made several large loops among the cottonwoods and bluffs rose high above the lodgepoles. Farther downstream were the Blackfeet and Miniconjous, the latter sitting right along the river where it began to straighten out. There was a good ford here that made it easy to run the ponies across into the hills. Next were the Sans Arcs and the Brulés. Farther along, just past the lodges of the Two Kettles, there lay a small creek that ran diagonally across the valley to empty into the river. Just beyond this creek lay the circle of the Oglala, his own people. And finally, at the farthest end of the valley were the Northern Cheyennes with their friends the Arapahos.

The people filled every part of the valley. From the Hunkpapas to the Cheyennes, from the river on the northeast to the tablelands on the southwest where huge herds of ponies grazed in the sun, the people's lodges were pitched in the long grass. Crazy Horse nodded and thought to himself, *Lel uñnkúñpi kin he washte'.*"*

It was indeed a good thing to have all the people together like this. He could not remember a time when they were so strong as now. Usually a large encampment like this would not be to his liking. A solitary man, even his own lodge sometimes felt too small and crowded with people for him. He liked the emptiness of the plains and the quiet of the forest. He liked the solitude that allowed him to hear the beating of his own heart, the whispered thoughts of his own mind. It was odd, he thought, but he

* *"That we are here is good."*

was actually enjoying the movement and color and noise of the large gathering. How very odd! He even felt more energetic today, despite the heat that was already building. Like Sitting Bull, he had not participated in the dancing and singing last night, but unlike the old man, he had slept heavily, his sleep free of troubling dreams or visions. Now he was beginning to feel hungry and headed back for his own circle. Black Shawl would have surely cooked up something delicious by now, and his mouth fairly watered at the thought of what she might have concocted.

He slipped around a pair of dogs who were quarreling over an antelope skull, each in possession of one of the antlers, and headed down the valley through the bustling camp. Those who were about seemed all to be in a happy mood.

"*Cañnako*, Brother!" they called in greeting.

To which he nodded and occasionally replied, "*Hau!*"

Passing through the Miniconjou circle, his attention was drawn to a ruckus of high-pitched voices shrieking and laughing down by the river. Looking to his right, he saw the source of the commotion—scores of boys and girls splashing in the cool waters of the Greasy Grass. The younger ones were restricted to the shallows of the ford and were watched over by elder brothers and sisters. A smile flickered across his face but died quickly as the sight of the laughing children brought back the painful memories of his own daughter, They-Are-Afraid-of-Her. It was as if a dark cloud had passed suddenly in front of the sun. How old would she be now? He couldn't think anymore. It all seemed so long ago, the tiny red bundle on the burial scaffold on the empty plains. The snow swirling around him with tears staining his face, the wind keening in his ears as if Wakan Tanka himself sang her death song. Perhaps she would be splashing in the river today or picking berries with her mother had it not been for the white man's disease. The white man again, he thought, and his grief turned to anger. It was as if the snows that had covered his daughter so long ago were closing around his heart. He lifted a fist to heaven and screamed in protest, "*Le makóce mitáwa kiñ he e!*"* Let them come to us, he thought, and we will treat them as we did the Three Stars.

When he glanced around, he noticed that people were looking at him. Many considered him a strange man, even in his own clan, and now several people nearby were watching him with curiosity to see if he was about to do something odd. Several young women nearby were staking out some hides in the sun and had seen him shaking his fist at the sky.

* *"This land is mine!"*

Now they were giggling among themselves as they kneeled over their work, and he thought he overheard one of them whisper *"Gnashkiñyañ!"* to her friends as her fingers described a small circle on her forehead. The others giggled and snorted, some hiding their faces behind their hands or turning away, their shoulders shaking in mirth. Crazy Horse smiled at them sheepishly and started walking again.

Maybe they're right, he thought, maybe I am acting a little crazy these days. It is foolish to live in the past, he scolded himself, looking down at his moccasins as they trudged along through the grass. When he looked up again, a couple of the *akicitas** were looking at him. They too were smiling at the young warrior. Crazy Horse glowered at them. Layabouts, he thought. Had they nothing better to do than to laze about listening to women's gossip. As he moved on, he admitted that they probably didn't. They would certainly not have much difficulty with their duties today. Most of the young braves were too tired out from last night's festivities to get into much mischief. Oh, there might be a wrestling match or two among the younger ones and perhaps even a bout of hair pulling between a pair of girls, disputing the affections of a young brave no doubt, but other than that they would probably spend the day ogling the young women and stopping by their friends' lodges to gossip and dip their fingers in the stew.

He came to the small creek and leaped nimbly across, then hopped quickly to one side as a rattlesnake slithered by in the grass. He watched as the coppery line glided quickly away and was about to find a stick to kill it when a voice called out to him from a nearby lodge.

"Hau, Crazy Horse. *Cañnako,* Brother."

Crazy Horse looked up to see his friend Two Moon, a Cheyenne, his face creased in a broad grin.

"Hau," he replied. "I see your face, Two Moon."

Two Moon extended a hand to clasp Crazy Horse's shoulder in greeting. "You are welcome in my lodge, Crazy Horse. I see you are going home, but come and sit with me for a while. We will have something to eat."

Crazy Horse looked off toward his own circle of lodges, shrugged, and nodded that he would visit for a while. He was hungry enough that he could have something to eat here and still do justice to whatever Black

* Akicita, *a sort of tribal policeman. This duty, which was rotated among the warrior societies, was designed to maintain some order in the camp, breaking up fights, resolving disputes, and generally preserving tranquility within Lakota society.*

Shawl may have made. He followed Two Moon back to his lodge and ducked under the rolled-up skins to take a seat on the robes that had been spread in the grass. Two Moon joined him, and the two watched as Two Moon's wife filled wooden bowls from a steaming kettle.

"I think this is a ceremonial camp today," Two Moon said, "so we will eat dog in honor of last night's celebrations." Crazy Horse nodded, pleased. This was a great delicacy and something he hadn't expected.

"Where are you coming from?" Two Moon asked, his mouth full of meat.

"I was with the Hunkpapa Sitting Bull," replied Crazy Horse. "He is a strange man but *wakan,* so I was interested in what he had to say."

Two Moon was about to ask a question when there was a howling noise outside of the lodge. The two men looked up to see a group of young braves in a half-circle around another lodge. They were laughing among themselves and howling like wolves.

"What are they making such a fuss about?" Crazy Horse asked.

"Oh, pay no attention to those young people. They are just being foolish. It is the way of so many of the young men these days. That is the lodge of Box Elder, and they are making fun of the old man." Two Moon leaned under the lodge skins and yelled at the youngsters.

"Run along, you foolish boys. Go to the pony herds and do something worthwhile. If you must do mischief, go find some snakes to kill and make yourselves useful. Bah!"

"I thought Box Elder was a *wicasa wakan,*" Crazy Horse said, puzzled by the display. "Why should the young people be making such a racket and bothering a holy man in this way, howling like wolves?"

Two Moon shook his head. "Because the young ones have no respect for their elders anymore. Box Elder had a vision that told him that soldiers were coming to this camp today and the boys all laughed at him. They say he's a stupid old man and no better than wolf bait. It's a disgrace the way they carry on."

"What do you think about what Box Elder said, Two Moon?" Crazy Horse asked, his voice soft and his eyes focused on his friend. "Do you think there's anything in what he says?"

"No, no." The Cheyenne waved his hand in the air. "Of course not. Even the Long Knives would be foolish to come against the people when there are so many of us. It's probably just a bad dream. The older people have trouble sleeping well when there's so much noise all night, with the young ones dancing and singing and playing jokes until the sun is coming up. But it's no excuse for those youngsters' shameful manners. I tell you, it is a sad day when the old ones are subjected to such nonsense. It makes me wonder what is happening to make the children so disrespectful. You're not eating, brother. Surely, you have not had your fill."

Crazy Horse had indeed stopped eating and was now staring blankly out at the vast encampment seemingly lost in thought.

"Something is troubling you, Crazy Horse. What are you thinking about?"

The Oglala didn't reply but continued to look out on the acres of lodges, the valley filled with the smokes of a thousand or more campfires, the dogs and children running between the tipis, ponies grazing peacefully in the distance. Flies gathered in his bowl and flitted up his fingers, but Crazy Horse didn't notice them. For a moment he felt as if the world had gone suddenly silent around him and all he could hear was a great rushing in his ears like the roaring sound the Elk River* made when it passed over the large rocks. The touch of Two Moon's hand on his shoulder brought him back to his surroundings. The Cheyenne had a questioning look on his face.

"There is something very unusual here," the Oglala said finally. "I have been talking with Sitting Bull, the Hunkpapa, as I said. The old man reminded me of his vision of soldiers falling into camp and said that this was yet to be."

Two Moon frowned. "Did he say that this would happen today?"

"No." Crazy Horse shook his head. "No, he did not say this would be today. But it seems odd that he would wait until today to ask me to come to his lodge to tell me of this."

Two Moon nodded slowly. "Yes," he said, "this is unusual."

Crazy Horse shrugged. "Perhaps this will be soon, I don't know. The wolves tell us that Three Stars has gone far away and is now sitting on Goose Creek. They say that all the soldiers are doing is fishing and hunting, and they do not think they will come again very soon. We whipped them very badly, I think. They say that the Grabber† is still with the soldiers and does not dare to go far from their camp."

Two Moon nodded. "This is a good thing for him. A Lakota would surely kill him if he caught him away from the others."

---

* Elk River was the Lakota name for the Yellowstone.
† "The Grabber," also known as Standing Bear, was born Frank Grouard to a Polynesian mother and a white missionary father sometime around 1850. Captured by the Sioux as a young man, he had been adopted by Sitting Bull and raised as part of his family. This mysterious character apparently lived a double life, living for months with the Sioux and then returning to the white man's world, only to drift back to the Sioux when he had tired of civilization. At this time he was serving as a scout for Brigadier General Crook's expedition and had participated in the battle of the Rosebud.

"This is true. And I think it will be some time before Three Stars fights with us again."

"You are probably right. What else did the Hunkpapa say to you?"

Crazy Horse brushed the flies away from his bowl and dipped some more stew out with his fingers.

"Yes, I should mention that. It too was very odd. I was going to talk to the Oglala first about it, but since you ask, he said that Wakan Tanka had told him something about the *wasichus'* property." Two Moons leaned forward and listened intently as the Oglala related the old man's strange instructions.

At the opposite end of the village Gall was also thinking about Sitting Bull. Together with Crow King, he and Sitting Bull had founded the Strong Heart Society for the elite of the Hunkpapa circle's fighting men. The three of them had been friends for many years now, and it bothered Gall that he found himself drifting apart from the old man just as the Lakotas were becoming so unified. Maybe Crow King was right. Maybe he was becoming jealous. No, he decided, it wasn't simply that. For one thing, despite what Crow King said, he was not getting old. He was still a fairly young and vigorous man. Certainly he didn't go out with the war parties as much as he once had, but then there was nothing unusual about that. Unlike the young men, a mature warrior had nothing to prove. He felt no need to impress young girls anymore. He was happy and content with his family.

Gall had no reason to be jealous of Sitting Bull. He did not want to be a *wicasa wakan*. He did not want to be a famous man. No, there were other things that had begun to sour his relationship with his old friend. There had been that incident with the Grabber, for instance. Gall did not trust the man, and it was not just because he was a *wasichu*. There was something about the man that Gall thought was dishonest. You could never be sure when the Grabber was telling the truth, and you could never count on him to be loyal. The Grabber ran back to the whites too often. But Sitting Bull always stood up to defend this snake, even when Gall told him that the Grabber had been working for the soldiers and that one day he would lead the soldiers against the Hunkpapas. Gall had wanted to kill him then, but Sitting Bull had protected him, called him his son. Gall had been furious.

There had been a great argument, but Sitting Bull would not listen. He never listened. That was the problem. Now the Grabber was with the soldiers again. Gall had even seen him at the fight with Three Stars. They should have killed him a long time ago. But Sitting Bull would not listen.

He was becoming an arrogant old fool. He thought he knew everything. Well, thought Gall, he didn't know everything about the Grabber. It still infuriated him to think about it. He brooded about the Grabber incident and wondered how many other things Sitting Bull had gotten wrong. Someday, he thought, Sitting Bull will make a big mistake and the Lakotas will pay dearly for it. Overhead, the sun was just reaching above the lodgepoles.

1205 Hours
At the Divide Above Ash Creek

The regiment moved out of the bottoms along Davis Creek, coming into a stretch of open ground that rose gradually up a gentle hill. Here the grass was sparse and burned by the sun into a lifeless sandy color. Captain Frederick Benteen eased alongside of Company H, which was now in the van, his face set in a grim smile. Well, he'd not eat too much dust today, he thought. The only drawback Benteen could see to this arrangement was that that little popinjay Custer was also with the lead element. Benteen despised the man like no one he had ever known.

Hell, he didn't care much for the rest of the regiment either, if it came to that. That shanty-Irish drunkard, Keogh, who thought he was God's own gift to women. Little more than a Feeney ruffian. God help McDougall. Another of Custer's Gang. He'd heard that Keogh was even now carrying around a picture of the unfortunate man's sister. Disgusting. But then, she was a rag-headed little trollop herself and probably deserving of no better.

God, how he hated them all. George Custer and his whelp of a brother. Heaven only knew how that whining little sot had won two Medals of Honor.* Then there was that lousy little Italian DeRudio. What the hell could the War Office have been thinking to give a commission to that horrible little man—a foreigner. And Mathey, another damned foreigner—a foul-mouthed, Bible-thumping Frog. Jesus, what a crew.†

On the brighter side, Lieutenant Colonel Custer seemed to have his

---

* Thomas Custer had indeed been twice awarded the Medal of Honor for gallantry in action during the Civil War. It was something about which Tom liked to tease his brother George, who, it appears, was a bit jealous of Tom's medals.
† Captain Benteen's personal letters reveal a remarkably vitriolic nature, in that there was hardly an officer in the Army, let alone the regiment, with whom he got along, describing many in great detail as "whelps, drunkards, sots, ruffians, and cowards," etc. Of all the officers in the Seventh Cavalry there were only three, Lieutenants Hare, Wallace, and Varnum, about whom Benteen had anything positive to say. For a man who was a heavy drinker and gambler, it seems odd that Captain Benteen should have gone to such great efforts to make himself a singularly unpopular man with his fellow officers.

mind on other things at the moment. Otherwise, Benteen was sure, the son of a bitch would be riding alongside him prattling away in his brainless manner. Well, at least he didn't have to listen to that. The old cavalryman turned in his saddle and glanced back at the column that was plodding along behind him. All down the column thousands of steel-shod hooves were churning up the fine soil, obliterating every trace of the hundreds of travois and ponies that had scarred the ground. Powdery clouds of dust rose into the still summer air to settle back on the troopers' threadbare uniforms, giving the whole outfit something of a ghostly appearance. To Benteen it looked, for a moment, like an army of phantoms was passing through this godforsaken country.

Phantoms chasing phantoms. He almost laughed out loud at the absurdity of it all. If there ever were any Indians in this area, he thought, they sure as hell must have seen us and be miles away by now. Recalling a brief conversation he'd had with Dr. Lord the night before, he shook his head in disgust. Lord was a spindly little fellow, not cut out for this campaigning business, but he was probably right when he'd said he didn't think they'd see an Indian all summer. Benteen turned back to the front and watched the backs of the men riding just a few yards ahead—Custer and his pet Indian, Bloody Knife, "Cookey" the adjutant, an orderly who carried Custer's personal guidon, and that idiot Italian horn-blower—all of them looking intently at the ground they were passing over and no doubt listening to that filthy savage spin tales of how fresh the "sign" was. Damned fools.

Bloody Knife was pointing out the sign to his friend and commander, explaining as best he could what the myriad of drag marks, pony tracks, and animal droppings told him about the people who had left them behind. Lieutenant Colonel Custer was listening closely to his scout, turning now and then to Lieutenant Cooke to translate and to indicate that Cooke should make a note in his log.

"See these drags, Son-of-the-Morning-Star?" Bloody Knife was saying. "Some of them are very old—look how the edges are soft and round. See how that dung is old and dried up. These Indians are the ones we have been following all this time. They came through this place maybe a week ago. Many lodges. Now look here. See how all these drags are clean. The edges are sharp like the edge of a knife, hard, new. Also many lodges. This village is getting bigger every day. It is hard to know how many are in the village, but there are many." *

* At this point Bloody Knife and the other scouts were probably unaware of how large the village really was. Most of the hostiles' tracks had been obscured by the passage of an

The Ree reined up and slid from the saddle, landing lightly in the dust. Custer threw up a gauntleted hand, bringing the entire column to a halt as he too swung out of the saddle to stand next to Bloody Knife. The scout pointed to a pile of horse dung in the middle of the wide trail. Squatting on his haunches, he poked a finger into the mess, then picked up a ball of dung and held it under his nose. He sniffed the dark object intently and squeezed it between his thumb and two fingers.

"Hunh! Fresh," he declared. "These ponies were here this morning. The coyotes did not get to them yet, and the sun has not yet made them dry." He looked up at Custer. "It is as I said. These people are very close. Maybe a few miles ahead. No more."

George Custer nodded. He knew Bloody Knife was right. He looked to the west and took a few steps toward the top of the small divide. "You know this country, friend. Tell me what it looks like and where they will be. I want to know where to go so that I can make a success."

Bloody Knife grunted in assent and pointed out the features of the land that lay ahead of them. "Now we start to go down this hill. Where those trees are, is a creek. We call it Ash Creek, but the Head-Cutters call it Sundance Creek* because they make medicine on it sometimes when the cherries are ripe. There is good water there for the horses. This water goes toward where the sun sets and empties into the Greasy Grass. You call it Little Bighorn River. It runs to the north. There is a big valley there. That is where this village is."

"Where do you think this village will be, Bloody Knife? I mean exactly. Is it north of this creek or south?"

The scout shrugged.

"I do not know. Maybe north, maybe south. Maybe both. It is a big village. But I think it is this way." He pointed off to the north.

Custer grimaced. He needed more information. He flung an arm to

---

immense buffalo herd, which was following the same watercourses as the Sioux. After the battle on the Rosebud, Crazy Horse and his warriors came across the trail of this buffalo herd while returning to their homes and decided to follow it. The warriors were hauling their wounded along in travois, and it is likely that these were the tracks that Custer and the scouts saw and mistook for those of the village, leading them to underestimate seriously the size of the village. The Indian scouts apparently did not fully appreciate the size of the Sioux village until they reached the lone tipi, where the trail of the buffalo herd veered off to the north and away from the Little Bighorn.

* Ash Creek, also known as Sundance Creek, would later be called Reno Creek by the soldiers. "Head-Cutters" is a derogatory Crow name for the Sioux, derived from the latter's old practice of taking the heads of their enemies. Although Bloody Knife was Ree (Arikara), he had probably picked up the expression from the Crow scouts.

the rear and pointed back at the Wolf Mountains, where the Crow's Nest was located.

"Damn it, Bloody Knife," he insisted. "When we were up there, your wolves said they could see the village. I need to know exactly."

The Ree shook his head.

"No. They could see the pony herd and the smokes of this village. They could not see the village. There are steep hills and trees between there and where these people have their camp. I tell you where I think they are, but that is all I can tell you."

George Custer stood and stared out at the rolling terrain that lay ahead, all sagebrush and sunburned grass. The sun was now directly above them, and the still air had become uncomfortably warm. He shucked off his gauntlets and stuffed them into the pocket of his buckskin jacket, which he then removed and lashed to the crupper of Vic's saddle before hoisting himself back into the McClellan. His dark blue fireman's shirt was already soaked with sweat, and he mopped his brow with a corner of the long red cravat that he wore around his neck. In a moment Bloody Knife was back in his saddle and coming alongside. Custer turned in his saddle and waved the command forward to pass over the divide and down the reverse slope.

When they had ridden a few hundred yards, Custer reined Vic to a stop and turned again to Bloody Knife. "Can these people hear our trumpets from where they are?"

The Ree shook his head.

"Good. Private Martin, sound Officers' Call!"

Orderly Trumpeter Martin wheeled his horse in place and brought his trumpet up smartly to blast the signal back to the rest of the regiment. Even before the first few notes were free of the bell, small plumes of dust could be seen hurrying along the flank of the column. Captain Benteen, although he was the closest company commander, made a point of not being the first to arrive, waiting instead for the others to come up before urging his mount forward at an easy walk. Within a few moments the regiment's officers had formed a loose circle around George Custer, the company commanders toward the inside of the circle, the younger lieutenants, the scouts, and the interpreters on the outer fringes.

Toward the rear of the group, reporter Mark Kellogg struggled to inch his obstinate mule closer in so that he could better hear the conference. Every time he managed to get into a decent position, the stubborn animal would lower its head and back away from the circle, braying loudly and flailing at the air with its heels. Boston and Autie Reed, watching the reporter's discomfiture with great amusement, poked each other gleefully and exchanged grins. When the regiment's officers had all gathered around, Lieutenant Colonel Custer removed his broad-brimmed hat and looked about the circle.

"Gentlemen, my compliments," Custer began. "Thus far the move has gone quite well. With any luck, the hostiles' scouts will not yet have informed the camp of our presence and we may well retain some of the element of surprise."

Custer glanced around the circle of rapt faces, wondering if they believed this assessment. He himself doubted that it was very accurate. What was more likely was that they would catch up to the Sioux just as they were breaking down their lodges and trying to get the hell out of the way. But he didn't see any point in making the troops think that this would be any more complicated than it already was.

"We do not, however, know precisely where this camp is located. Thus our movement to contact will necessarily take the form of a reconnaissance in force. This is not what I had hoped for, but as you know, we now have no choice in the matter. As best as we can tell, the enemy is located about eight miles due west of this point, probably at the mouth of this creek which you can see below us." He watched the faces of the officers for their reaction and noted that where the younger men appeared bright and eager with the prospect of seeing some action, the real veterans were solemn and thoughtful. They knew that an Indian fight could be a dicey affair.

"While it is not my custom to explain my decisions," he continued, "as we will soon be in action under, shall we say, unusual circumstances, I felt you should know my plans and my reasons for making them. The regiment will be divided into four operational battalions. Major Reno will command the first battalion, consisting of Companies A, G, and M. When we hit the village, Major Reno, I intend that your battalion will make the supporting attack."

Major Marcus Reno, a rather plump figure with a round, baby face, said nothing but swallowed hard and nodded, trying his best to look nonchalant. He had never been in an Indian fight before and was jittery about this whole affair. What if he came out looking the fool? He glanced nervously at his three company commanders—Moylan, Weir, and McIntosh—for some reassurance. Moylan, the burly Irishman in charge of Company A, winked at him as if to say everything would be alright. Weir and McIntosh were sitting their horses casually nearby and seemed unmoved by the prospect of being in combat. Reno noted that McIntosh was actually yawning, and he was suddenly reminded that "Tosh" was half-Indian himself—Cherokee or something like that, wasn't it? The major made a mental note to have a quick chat with "Tosh" when they moved out. Maybe he'd be able to gain a little insight into the "Indian mind," which certainly couldn't hurt.

Custer turned to his next most senior officer. "Companies H, D, and K will comprise the second battalion. Captain Benteen, you will of course command this battalion and you will have two missions to accomplish. I want you first to screen our flank to the south. Pick a lieutenant and some of your best men whose mounts are the freshest and push them ahead of you while keeping the battalion within striking distance. I want you to examine the upper end of the Little Bighorn valley to ensure that there are no hostiles above the mouth of this creek. I don't want any of the hostiles to slip out of the net or turn our flank to hit Major Reno's battalion in the rear or to threaten the packs." He paused for a moment.

"This will also satisfy General Terry's desire that we screen well to the south to prevent the hostiles' getting around us. Clear?"

Benteen nodded, a wry smile playing across his lips, and touched fingers to the brim of his hat in a careless salute. This was going to be a wild goose chase. The damned hostiles would be packed up and miles away before the outfit came within a hundred miles of them. Well, he thought, it's no skin off my nose. If G.A.C. wants me to go off valley hunting, so much the better. At least I won't have to listen to him prattling on about Aldie or Winchester or some such nonsense.

"Good," Custer continued. "When you are convinced there is no threat to our flank, I want you to double back, pick up our trail, and join the main command. If what our scouts are telling us is true, we may want you badly." Custer turned to the other commanders. "Captain Keogh, you will command the third battalion, consisting of Companies I, C, and L. This battalion will be part of the main attack." Tom Custer and Jimmi Calhoun looked at each other and grinned. They would be working with Keogh, who had a reputation for always being in the thick of it.

"Captain Yates, you will take the fourth battalion, consisting of Company F and Company E. The regimental headquarters will be located with your battalion. You will also be part of the main attack—which I will direct. Clear?" Keogh and Yates nodded silently. "Captain McDougall," Custer went on, "I have not forgotten you. You will have charge of a separate command consisting of your Company B and the packtrain along with the reinforcements detailed to you earlier."

There was some tittering in the ranks as the younger officers saw McDougall's face drop with the knowledge that he would be stuck back with the mules and thus miss all the fun. Custer's face flushed with anger.

"That will be enough of that, gentlemen!" he snapped. "Captain

McDougall's company has only recently joined us from police duty in Louisiana.* While I have every confidence in Captain McDougall's abilities, too many of his enlisted men have no experience of Indian fighting, and I will not put them unnecessarily in harm's way. The veterans you commanders have sent down to augment his force will help to steady the younger men. Further, it is vital that the packs with our ammunition and rations be kept secure and available. I consider this an important mission and will not have anyone denigrating the men assigned to it."

The chortling in the ranks quickly faded into a few embarrassed coughs and some throat-clearing. Custer noted with satisfaction that some of the younger officers' ears had reddened, and he didn't think there would much more nonsense from them.

"Begging the general's pardon." Benteen's raspy voice broke the uneasy silence. "But I am curious about this arrangement of battalions. It seems an unusual way to divvy up the outfit."

Custer's ears now crimsoned slightly, but he looked straight into Benteen's eyes and decided that this might be a legitimate question despite the tone in which it had been delivered. He cleared his throat and addressed the assembled officers.

"As Colonel Benteen has observed, I have arranged the regiment in a somewhat unorthodox formation, which I hope will afford us both strength and flexibility to deal with any situation that may arise." He glanced back over to Benteen. "Now," he resumed in an even, reasonable tone, "you will have noticed that I have assigned Company G to Major Reno's battalion, and Company K to Captain Benteen's battalion, Companies E and L to remain with my battalions. In this way I hope to spread out the less experienced troops among some of our veterans so that they'll have a steadying influence. Some of you gentlemen will recognize that this is the same tactic the Duke of Wellington used at Waterloo, and I trust it will serve us as well as it served him."†

"Well, I sure hope Mr. Sitting Bull didn't study under Napoleon!"

---

* Captain McDougall's Company B had indeed been stationed in Shreveport, Louisiana, on "reconstruction duty" until 19 April 1876. The company began arriving at Fort Abraham Lincoln on 1 May, but the whole unit did not arrive until 17 May, the day the expedition started. En route the company's numbers had been depleted seriously by desertion.
† Frequently overlooked is the fact that the Seventh Cavalry had not served together as an integral unit for quite some time, having been hastily assembled for this expedition. Company G had just arrived from duty in Shreveport, Louisiana, Company K from McComb City, Mississippi. Companies E and L had marched in from Fort Totten, Dakota Territory (D.T.), and Companies H and M had marched in from Fort Rice, D.T. All of these units converged on Fort Abraham Lincoln between 1 and 17 May 1876. The companies arriving from duty in the South had suffered high rates of desertion during their transfer to Dakota Territory.

cracked Tom Custer. The remark sent the officers into fits of laughter, and even George Custer couldn't repress a smile.

Mark Kellogg, who didn't quite get the joke, grinned broadly anyway and began scribbling in his notebook. Sitting Bull—the Napoleon of the Plains! he thought. Now there's a quote for you. He could see the lead for his story already, with references to the hostiles meeting their Waterloo at the hands of America's young Murat. Wait, Murat had been Napoleon's cavalry general, hadn't he? Well, he could work out the details a little later. Have to make sure to have references to guidons fluttering in the wind, lance points and sabers glinting in the sunlight—the public wouldn't know that the sabers had all been boxed up and left back on the *Far West*. By golly, this would be one hell of a story. Clement Lounsberry would be kicking himself for having missed out on this campaign. It was beginning to look as if things were finally about to get interesting, and there was only one man who would be able to report on the events of this day for the whole country to read. Why, they'd hang on his every word from New York to San Francisco! With any luck they'd be asking him to speak at the Centennial down in Philadelphia. He'd probably even be shaking hands with the president. The reporter smiled and imagined himself chatting with the great Henry Morton Stanley, himself just back from the war in Abyssinia: "I say, Mark, old fellow. Damn fine work out there in the Dakotas. Capital piece of reporting, don't you know. Say, have you ever given a thought to roaming about Africa for a bit?" Oh, yes, this was it— his ticket out of Bismarck for good. Mark Kellogg could hardly believe his luck.

Lieutenant Varnum was also thinking about luck, his luck, Custer's Luck. The man was legendary for his fantastic good fortune. Everyone talked about how George Custer always managed to come out on top through luck. But Varnum wasn't so sure anymore. From what he could see thus far, there was damn little luck involved. The general's orders were a revelation. In the two short hours since they had first looked down into the valley of the Little Bighorn, the situation had changed radically and Custer had seemed perfectly in control of everything. He had revised the plan, accounted for possible contingencies, reorganized the regiment, and given short and succinct orders that were easily understood. Further, the reorganization had not only taken into account the relative strengths and weaknesses of the companies but had been made with perfect attention to the regiment's seniority list. It was amazing. And yet Custer made it all seem so natural. No, Varnum decided, there was damned little left to chance. He guessed it might be true what people said about a man making his own luck.

1245 Hours
Below Ash Creek

First Lieutenant Francis Marion Gibson leaned over his horse's neck, clucked quietly in her ear, and tapped her flanks gently with his spurs. The muscular little mare didn't need any more encouragement than that, and Gibson let her gallop toward the top of the ridgeline, reins held lightly in his right hand, his left arm hanging loosely by his side. Glancing over his shoulder, he could see that Sergeant Connelly was still alongside of him as they raced across the sun-parched prairie through sagebrush and clumps of spear grass, the horned toads and lizards scurrying madly to keep from under the flying hooves. A hundred yards behind them the rest of their detail, Privates Black, Haley, and Jones, urged their mounts into an easy canter, not wanting to be left behind but not particularly anxious to join in the headlong rush over ground that they knew was pockmarked with prairie-dog holes, a sure way to break a horse's leg—or a man's neck.

Gibson and Connelly easily outdistanced the rest of their detail, slowing to a walk only as they neared the crest of the ridge and stopping a few yards short of it. Being careful to keep back from the horizon, the two men slipped out of their saddles—Sergeant Connelly holding the horses as the lieutenant snatched a pair of binoculars from where they were lashed to his McClellan—and advanced at a crouch to the crest of the ridge. Throwing himself to his belly, Gibson slithered forward through the sagebrush and over sharp rocks until he could peer at the valley beyond.

"Son of a bitch!" he exclaimed, not even bothering to uncase the binoculars. Exasperated, he rolled over on his back and blew loudly. "Shit!" Here the regiment was getting ready to move into action any time now and what was he doing? He was out here skylarking around chasing goddamned tumbleweeds. It was enough to make a man scream. He slammed his fist into the ground in frustration.

"What's the problem, Lieutenant?" Connelly hissed.

"Come on up, Pat," the lieutenant called. "Not a damned thing to see here."

Connelly shook his head and led the horses up to join the young officer. As he drew up next to Gibson, the sergeant squatted in the dust to look out across the broken country below. Captain Benteen had pushed them out ahead of the battalion to see if they could pick up any Indian sign in the upper Little Bighorn valley, but all Connelly could see was an empty wasteland baking under a western sun. Connelly threw his hat on the ground and swore softly under his breath.

"Goddamned nothing." He looked at Gibson, who was lying on his back, an arm thrown across his eyes to shield them from the sun. "Hells bells, Lieutenant, there ain't nothin' out there but another goddamned ridge."

"Right you are, Sergeant." Gibson rolled over onto his elbows and dug the field glasses out of their scuffed leather case to peer intently at the terrain below. "Not a living thing in sight. Not so much as a goddamned snake."

Gibson slammed the glasses back into their case and hauled himself upright, brushing the dirt from his uniform, a futile gesture considering the sorry state it was in. Sergeant Connelly stood up, picked up his dusty campaign hat, which he slapped against the yellow stripe that ran down the seam of his blue trousers, and then jammed it back onto his head.

"When the boys get here," Gibson said, "I think I'll send Jones back with a message to Colonel Benteen and ask him what he wants us to do. There's not a damn hostile in sight, and I figure we ought to be heading back to the command pretty soon."

Connelly turned back in the direction from which they had come, looking for any sign of the battalion that was trailing along behind at a leisurely walk. He reached over to the lieutenant and borrowed the field glasses, which he then played over the barren terrain from which a heat haze had already begun to shimmer, looking for some indication that the outfit was coming up behind them. But there was nothing to be seen. Not even the barest trace of dust rising into the empty sky. The only movement on the vast expanse was that of the three cavalry privates, the rest of their scouting detachment, who were just cantering up to where Connelly and Gibson stood waiting in the bright sun. As the three rookies drew to a halt, Lieutenant Gibson walked over to Private Jones and took hold of the bridle of the youngster's horse.

"Private Jones," said the lieutenant, peering up at the young trooper, "take a short rest but don't dismount. I want you to take a message back to the commander." Jones nodded solemnly.

"Report to Captain Benteen and present my compliments. Say that another ridge denies us a view of the Little Bighorn valley. There is no sign of the hostiles, and I will await his further instructions. Clear?" Private Jones nodded and gave a salute to his young commander. Gibson returned the salute. "And, Jones, take it easy on your mount. Looks like it'll be a long day. A steady trot should suffice. Alright?"

"Yes, sir," Jones replied. Lieutenant Gibson nodded with a smile and patted the horse on its neck, which was already moist with effort.

"Alright, Jones, have a drink of water with your mates and off you go." Gibson let go of the horse's bridle and walked back to where he had left Sergeant Connelly. The two men stood and watched as Jones moved alongside his companions, took a long swig from his canteen, and with a quick nod to Black and Haley, turned his mount and trotted off briskly in search of the rest of the battalion.

"Lieutenant Gibson," Connelly said. "With your permission, sir, I'll take Black and head on over to that next line of bluffs and have a quick look-see. Shouldn't take but a couple of minutes to get on over there, sir."

Gibson shook his head quickly. "No, Sergeant," he said, "we'll take Black and Haley and head on over there together. Jones'll have no trouble finding us again, and we still haven't got a good look at the upper valley, which is what we're getting paid for."

Connelly nodded quickly, suppressing a small, proud smile. That's my lad, he thought. You'll make a first-rate soldier, my boy, a good officer.

"I wonder what the hell is taking the rest of the column so long to come up?" Gibson said, more to himself.

Sergeant Connelly pretended not to hear this comment, swinging into the saddle and motioning for Black and Haley to come alongside, but silently he was thinking, Well, you might ask, Lieutenant, but I doubt you'd like the answer to that question any more than I or the general would.

Sergeant Major Bill Sharrow galloped right up to the head of the column and turned his horse easily to come alongside Captain Benteen. Drawing himself up to his full height, he snapped off a sharp salute.

"The gin'ral presents his compliments, sorr, and says that if ye can't see anything from the next line o' bluffs, he desires that ye move t' the next line after that 'til ye've a good view o' the valley. If ye see any traces o' Injuns, ye should report back t' the gin'ral 'mediately, and if there is no sign o' Injuns ye're to quickly rejoin the main command. Sir!"

Captain Benteen did not look at the sergeant major but kept his eyes focused dead ahead at the next line of bluffs. He didn't return the man's salute but merely nodded to acknowledge Sharrow's presence. He rode ahead in silence for a moment, then, still staring ahead, responded coolly to Sharrow's message.

"That is understood, Sergeant Major. I understood that when the first messenger arrived"—his lips curled in a sardonic smile—"or did the general think the redskins might have chopped up the first man?"

Sergeant Major Sharrow didn't care for the man's tone but kept a cool head, although it required all the restraint he could muster, and replied evenly.

"No, sir, that was not his concern, but he had noticed that more'n one ridgeline intervaned and thought t' grant ye the latitude to pursue yer mission, which he felt sure was what yer honor would wish."

"My compliments to the gin-rell, Sergeant Major," Benteen replied icily without sparing the man a glance. "You may inform him that we will fulfill this mission and join him directly."

Sharrow said nothing but snapped off a salute, turned his horse, and galloped off in the direction from which he had appeared, a small cloud of dust marking his wake. Trumpeter Private William Ramell grasped his instrument and wiped the mouthpiece off on his sleeve, looking over at his commander, half-expecting him to give the order to sound the signal to advance at a trot. But Captain Benteen said nothing. The white-haired cavalry officer, his face set and staring to the front, continued to ride along easily, keeping the battalion at its leisurely pace.

Ramell said nothing and quietly let his trumpet slide back into place, easing it around to bounce lightly against his sweat-stained back. Ramell thought that the sergeant major's message should have had 'em all off at a trot, but apparently old Skull-and-Crossbones saw it different. Just keep yer mouth shut, Billy, he thought. That's the old man's lookout. Uncle Sam don't pay ya thirteen dollars a month to go around making decisions fer cap'ns with a burr under their saddles.

Lieutenant Gibson's lips curled in a slight smile as he played his field glasses over the landscape below. At the last line of bluffs the country had suddenly opened up onto a vast river valley, the trees along the watercourse a bright green, and level, lush grassland spreading for miles toward the distant tablelands. A few hundred yards from the river a small group of pronghorn antelope lay resting in the grass, a lone buck standing watch over his family group and occasionally dropping his head to crop at the sweet grass.

"All serene," the lieutenant announced, passing the glasses to Sergeant Connelly. "That must be the Little Bighorn down there," he said, "and not a noble savage in sight." He pointed to the group of pronghorn. "See those steaks on the hoof down there, Pat? You can bet that if Mr. Lo was hanging about they'd not be so casual."

Connelly peered through the glasses at the antelope and nodded.

"I could sure deal with a bit o' fresh meat tonight, Lieutenant. Nice t' know that Mr. Redskin ain't hunted the place out yet." He smacked his lips loudly. "Ah, well, more's the pity." Hunting, they both knew, was out of the question, for a while anyway. Even the general, who was usually as keen as the next man for a good hunt, had put the quietus on that sport for the duration. "Yep," Connelly noted, still staring through the field glasses at the antelope, "more's the pity."

"Private Black!" Gibson hollered over his shoulder. "Any sign of the column yet?"

Black, who had remained in the saddle, nodded quickly and pointed off toward the horizon. "Yes, sir!" he called back. "Jest caught a glimpse of 'em comin' over a rise back a ways. Figure they're still about two miles or so back of us, Lieutenant."

Gibson nodded and turned to Sergeant Connelly, who handed the field glasses back to the lieutenant.

"Alright then, Pat, let's head on back and pick'em up. If there's Injuns out there, they sure aren't at this end of the valley. The general's got 'em pretty much to himself for now, but if we hurry, we just might get to join in the roundup."

He slammed the field glasses back into their case and slung them over the back of his McClellan. Both men tossed their reins over the horses' necks and swung into their saddles, turned and urged their mounts into a canter, and headed back to report to Captain Benteen.

1400 Hours
Along Ash Creek

Second Lieutenant Benjamin "Benny" Hodgson was in an extremely good mood, and his idle chatter was just what Reno needed to help him calm his jangled nerves. Normally assigned to Company B, Hodgson should by all rights have been tagging along with his company commander, who was stuck guarding the pack train, but Reno, who was particularly fond of the young officer, had asked that he be detailed to serve as his battalion adjutant. Captain McDougall had had no objections.

"Hell, Benny," McDougall had drawled, "I guess I've got enough fellas hanging about to guard a few coffee beans and hardtack." He looked at Custer. "If the general doesn't object, I don't see any reason to keep you out of the fun."

Lieutenant Colonel Custer had just smiled and waved the youngster on to join the attack force. Hodgson was looking forward to his first big Indian fight and was fairly bubbling over with enthusiasm. At the moment he was regaling Major Reno with a story he had been told by Captain Keogh.

". . . so Captain Custer is still asleep in his pup, deep in the arms of Morpheus, and the general is looking all over the camp for him when Captain Keogh shushes him and points at Tom's tent, where the toes of his boots are just stickin' out from under the flap and a grand snoring issuing forth. Well, sir, the general is fit to be tied and is about to roust him good when he gets a better idea and this funny smile comes all over him. He puts a finger to his lips and bids Keogh to silence, moves over to the campfire, and picks up a stick with a good flame going. Then he slips all around Tom's tent lighting the grass on fire and hops back to watch the fun. Well, it doesn't take but a few seconds for the pup to catch and before you know it old Tom is wide awake and skipping about like a wild Indian in a scalp dance, trying to stomp the flames out while the general and Keogh are fairly rolling in the grass, tears streaming down their faces!"

Hodgson could barely contain himself as he pictured the scene in his mind's eye. He started to chuckle, and in a moment his shoulders were shaking with mirth.

Marcus Reno smiled lightly and shook his head. Benny seemed to think the story hilarious, but it left Reno merely puzzled. He was not a great admirer of George Armstrong Custer. Certainly the man had a great Civil War record, but in person Reno found it more difficult to actually like him. Rather than the thoughtful young Napoleon he had expected, Custer was more of a spoiled child than anything else. Mercurial, hot-tempered, arrogant, and fairly full of himself, Custer often behaved more like a mischievous boy than a general, always playing practical jokes on his intimates, dashing off away from the column to go hunting, indulging in histrionics. Reno thought the man was rash and unpredictable and gathered that General Terry was not unaware of this tendency.

From the time they had left Fort Abraham Lincoln, General Terry seemed to be keeping the boisterous "Boy General" on a short leash, as if he was gauging whether he could really trust the man's judgment. He was sure that Custer wouldn't have noticed it, but Reno thought he had de-tected something in the way Terry had looked at G.A.C. during that conference on the *Far West* which indicated that Terry was not completely at ease with the Seventh Cavalry's commander. He had first suspected that not all was right in that relationship when Terry had put Reno in charge of the first scout down the Powder River and across the Tongue to the Rosebud. Custer had been furious that he had not been given the mission himself, and Reno suspected that someone had told Terry that Custer was anxious to be out on his own. It was not hard to guess who that someone probably was. Fred Benteen had made no secret of his low opinion of his commanding officer.

"I'll tell you this, Reno," Benteen had said one evening, "old G.A.C. is just champing at the bit to be off on his own and away from old Terry, and the chief don't like it one bit! The boy wonder brought that damned re-porter along—despite what Sheridan said about not taking any newspa-permen on the campaign—and Terry probably figures the little bastard is angling to show up the whole command so's to get himself plastered on the headlines and out of the doghouse with Grant." Benteen heaved a stick out into the darkness surrounding them. "The guttersnipe's probably in his damned tent right now scribbling down a pack of lies to send to his fawning publishers in New York—there's a pack of damned idiots for you!"

"You mean he's writing another book like *My Life on the Plains?*"*
Reno asked idly.

Benteen's response was a derisive snort. "More like *My Lie on the Plains,* you mean. What a load of bosh. It amazes me the sort of absolute drivel that those ignorant peasants in the masses will suck up as God's honest truth. That's the sad state of public taste these days. They don't want the truth. Give 'em bread and circuses any day and they'll fair trip over themselves to get to it. That's what G.A.C. ought to be doing instead of prancing around out here in the goddamned wilderness. He ought to be churning out dime novels for Beadle's.† *Goldrush George; or, The Foppish Fool of the Frontier.* Bah. What a lot of rubbish."

Reno said nothing, surprised that Benteen would even deign to talk to him—they had once quarreled bitterly in the sutler's store and Benteen had finished up by calling him a "son of a bitch," something that had not endeared Reno to the cantankerous captain. He may not have particularly liked George Custer, but he was taken aback by the venom of Benteen's attack.

Reno had to admit that his flamboyant commander had some fairly evident flaws but, by the same token, he was also a pretty competent soldier. While other units just sort of poked along in garrison, Custer drove the regiment hard, insisting on perfection in appearance and drill. No detail was too small to escape the general's scrutiny, from the care and feeding of the horses to the quality and quantity of the rations issued, and from the sharpshooting contests he organized to the number of books and magazines made available to the sergeants and enlisted men. The regiment was apparently his passion, and God help the man who interfered in its operation. It was simply not Reno's style. An indifferent drillmaster and not much for socializing after hours, Reno much preferred to spend a quiet evening with a good bottle of port and a book or perhaps playing billiards. What he wouldn't give to be safe at home station enjoying a nice game of billiards right now.

Reno leaned forward in the saddle to ease his aching buttocks and

* *George Custer's* My Life on the Plains *first appeared as a series of articles in twenty installments for* Galaxy *magazine and covered the period from January 1872 to October 1874. The articles were reprinted as a book by Sheldon & Company, New York, in 1874.*
† *Erastus Beadle was a New York City publisher who established a new romantic genre with the publication of the first dime novel in 1860. Beadle's immensely popular series would eventually span over thirty years and include thousands of titles, with the stories revolving around the heroics of such characters as Deadeye Dick and Calamity Jane.*

turned to look back over his right shoulder. There on the other side of Ash Creek he could see the lead elements of Keogh's and Yates's battalions easing along through the grassy swale that spread out from the watercourse. Lieutenant Colonel Custer's personal flag, a blue and red swallowtailed guidon with white crossed sabers, flapped limply in the slight breeze created by the movement of the guidon bearer's horse. As he watched, Reno saw a lone rider gallop out ahead of the command and splash across the creek several yards ahead of his battalion. As the rider drew nearer, Reno recognized the familiar figure of Chief Trumpeter Henry Voss. In a few moments Voss had come up and saluted smartly.

"The general's compliments, sir," Voss rattled off, "and would you move your battalion to the opposite bank and join the general directly, sir."

Reno returned Voss's salute.

"Thank you, Chief Trumpeter," he said politely. "I will join the command directly."

Voss turned and galloped ahead and back across the ford as Reno turned in his saddle to look back to where he could now see Custer waving his hat in the air and beckoning for Reno to join him. The major turned back to Lieutenant Hodgson.

"Well, Mr. Hodgson," he said, "the chief beckons. Guess we'll trot on over and see what's happening. I'll go on ahead, and you move the battalion over afterward." He pointed to the point on the creek where Voss had crossed over.

"There looks to be a natural ford up ahead. Watch the horses. Don't let 'em bunch up or stop to drink, but bring 'em straight across. Alright?"

Hodgson saluted briskly, "Very good, sir!" Then he turned to pass the word to the company commanders as Major Reno spurred his horse forward, following the path Voss had taken. Just as he was climbing the opposite bank, he looked up to see the Crow and Ree scouts in the company of Lieutenants Hare and Varnum galloping toward him, with Mitch Bouyer and George Herendeen bringing up the rear. The fast-moving party was headed downstream, speeding in the direction of the village, and so intent on their mission, whatever it might be, that they didn't even glance his way as they thundered past, clods of dirt and grass scattering into the air behind flying hooves.

As Reno approached the command, he noticed that Custer was deep in conversation with Charley Reynolds, Fred Gerard, and Bloody Knife, and the small group was just breaking into a light trot. Lieutenant Cooke spurred his horse out from the group and pulled Reno aside just as Custer and the scouts moved by.

"Major Reno," Cooke said quickly, "as your battalion comes across, take the lead and move us down the creek toward that tipi."

Cooke pointed in the direction the scouts had taken, and Reno could just make out the tops of the lodgepoles extending above the treetops several hundred yards downstream. Reno nodded quickly and turned to see Lieutenant Hodgson and the rest of the battalion coming up from the ford as the main command moved slowly past them. He jabbed his spurs into the flank of his horse and galloped down to intercept the battalion.

"Benny. Fours left, trot!" Reno called and moved past Hodgson, leaving him to echo the command down the line.

"Fours left, trot!" Hodgson bellowed, and the battalion swung up alongside Keogh's and Yates's battalions and moved quickly into the lead, Reno bouncing along ahead of them.

Reno had just come up behind Custer's party. When they moved around a bend in the creek, the tipi came suddenly into view. The remains of a second lodge were collapsed nearby. The still-intact structure was the center of a flurry of activity. Some of the Crows and Rees had slashed through the side of the lodge and were leaping into and out of the opening, brandishing their knives. They had found the solitary lodge occupied by a Sans Arc brave—laid out on a scaffold in his finest clothing. He was stone dead, the corpse already beginning to swell and stink in the fetid heat. The rest of the Indian scouts were chanting and stripping off their shirts and daubing their bodies with bright pigments that they had poured from small leather bags and mixed with their own spittle. A high bluff rose behind the tipi and, off to the right, Reno caught a glimpse of Lieutenant Varnum and his orderly, Private Strode. The two had evidently been up on top of the hill and were just now making their way back down toward Custer and the scouts. Custer did not hesitate, but dashed into the center of the scouts and wheeled his horse in a tight circle bellowing at his Indian allies.

"Why are you stopping here?" Custer demanded. "You were supposed to ride straight through to the Sioux village and take away their horses!"

Strikes Two, a tall Ree snorted. "What do you think we're doing, Long Hair?" he said with a hint of sarcasm in his voice that set the other Rees laughing as they continued to strip off their garments.

Lieutenant Colonel Custer did not quite hear Strikes Two's comment but flushed at the other scouts' laughter and motioned for Gerard and Bouyer to come up to translate his words so that there would be no possibility of his meaning being misunderstood.

"I told you," he growled, "that you were to stop for nothing, but to ride straight for the pony herd. You have disobeyed me. Move aside and let the soldiers charge past you." The Crow and Ree scouts looked up at Long Hair with puzzled looks on their faces as he continued his harangue. They were surprised by his sudden impatience. Surely he must know that you don't just ride into battle; you have to strip down and prepare yourself. They always did this. Usually, Long Hair understood them so well and now he seemed to be talking crazy.

"If any man among you is not brave, I will take his weapons away from him and make a woman of him." As Gerard and Bouyer finished translating, White-Man-Runs-Him stepped forward.

"Tell Long Hair," he said, smiling up at Bouyer, "if he does this to all of his men who are not as brave as we are, it will take him a long time." The other Crows burst into hysterical laughter. Bouyer translated for Custer and, as Gerard explained the remark to the Rees, they too began howling with laughter. Immediately another Ree, Young Hawk, sprang forward brandishing his rifle.

"We are eager for battle, Son-of-the-Morning-Star!" he exclaimed, and burst into a shrill war whoop that was immediately taken up by the other Indian scouts. Custer looked at Gerard, who nodded to indicate his belief in the statement, and the lieutenant colonel's face broke out into a broad grin.

"Alright then," Custer exclaimed. "Go ahead, wolves! Take their ponies! Go!"

The Crow and Ree scouts burst into an earsplitting shriek that echoed from the bluffs and sent a chill skittering down reporter Mark Kellogg's spine. He had often written about savages screaming their dreadful war cries but had never experienced them in real life, and he suddenly felt a horrible sickness, his stomach contracting into a balled fist of muscle. Kellogg's mule had started braying with the whooping of the scouts, and as Kellogg tried to control the terrified animal, he looked down to see that his hands were trembling fiercely. As the mule balked and kicked up his heels, the scouts leaped onto their ponies and thundered downstream, their shrill cries disappearing in a whirlwind of flying hooves and dust.

George Custer watched as his savage allies raced away down the creek, then turned to Lieutenant Cooke.

"Cookey," he whispered, "where the hell is Benteen?"

The bewhiskered adjutant shook his head in ignorance as Lieutenants Hare and Varnum rode up to make their report. Varnum, as the senior man, rode right up to Custer and saluted.

"Sir," he blurted, "we've been up on the bluffs above the lodge, and there's a pretty good view of the valley from up there."

"Very good, Mr. Varnum. What could you see?"

"Indians, sir! Looks like one hell of a big camp, and they're raising quite a bit of dust down there." He paused for a moment. "I think the camp's starting to break up, sir."

"Damn!" Custer slammed a fist onto his saddle. Where the hell was Benteen? He looked around quickly and caught sight of Major Reno standing in his stirrups. "Major Reno!" he yelled, beckoning the major over to him. Reno nudged his horse and cantered over to Custer's side, snapping off a salute as he came up.

"Sir!"

"Major Reno," Custer said, his voice raw with energy, "the hostile camp has been located and it looks like they're on the jump. I want you to lead out with your battalion. Put 'em at the trot and hold that gait 'til you get down to the river. Follow the scouts on down. I'll bring the rest of the outfit right after you." Reno nodded, wheeled his mount around and spurred off to his command. Within moments Custer could hear him roaring at the top of his lungs. *"Battalion! By twos! At the trot! Forrraard!"*

The battalion leaped forward to a symphony of creaking leather and a crashing jingle of bits and spurs, canteens, tin cups, and carbines banging against the black leather of the sweat-stained McClellans. Men grunted and swore, leaning forward and urging on their mounts. The horses stamped and snorted, tossing their heads and straining against leather and steel as hundreds of steel-shod hooves churned through the dirt and a cloud of dust rose to mark the passing of Reno's battalion. As Reno's unit moved past, Custer and Cooke galloped over to rejoin Keogh's and Yates's battalions. Custer spoke rapidly to his captains, then wheeled his horse to follow Reno as Keogh and Yates formed their battalions into parallel columns of twos in the grassy meadow. Keogh looked at Yates, who nodded and then, raising a gauntleted hand, turned in his saddle to roar back at the assembled battalions: *"Battalions! Center forward! Twos left and right! At the trot! Forraaard!"*

The ground seemed to shudder as a fog of dust rose around a thousand hooves and the command thundered forward, beginning its descent into the valley of the Little Bighorn. As the companies passed by the burial lodge, one of the troopers darted from the column. Slipping from the saddle, he knelt at the base of the tipi and snatched up a sheaf of dried grass in his fist. Several of his friends whooped their encouragement as the trooper fished a match from his pocket to light the dry grass. Waiting until the match had caught and the grass was crackling loudly, he tossed the flaming bundle into the large tear the scouts had slashed in the lodge skins. Within a few moments flames were licking up the sides of the structure, sending a thick, greasy black smoke curling into the still, blue sky.

1415 Hours
Along Ash Creek

Boston Custer squirmed uneasily in his saddle and peered at the broken country ahead, hoping to catch a glimpse of some sign that would mark the progress of the main command. George had joked about sticking that rascal Tom with the mules, but here he was instead. It really stuck in his craw sometimes that George was such a stickler about regulations. With the possibility of going into action a very real prospect, the general had insisted that everyone take up the position that he had been assigned, and in Boston's case this meant getting stuck back as a quartermaster with the damned mules. It was a damned shame, so it was! Boy, but he'd really pay Tom back for this one, he thought, conveniently ignoring the fact that it had been the general's decision that had relegated him to the rearmost element.

Boston thought he spotted a faint wisp of dust rising lazily above the tops of some cottonwoods just below the horizon. No, not dust, it was too dark. Was that smoke? Was something burning up ahead? A grass fire? That was odd, he thought, and mentally calculated the approximate distance to it. At this rate he figured he'd be lucky if he caught up with 'em by dinnertime. Damn the luck! He looked back over his shoulder at the ragged column of pack mules that was inching along the trail behind him and gnashed his teeth with impatience.

As far as Bos Custer was concerned, "column" was too kind a description for the outfit he was with. It was more of a disorganized gaggle of fractious animals and sweating, swearing young troopers. The soldiers were straining at the lead ropes and bridles of the uncooperative and braying beasts, which were doing their obstinate level best to go anywhere but where the frustrated soldiers wanted them to go.

"Get yer sorry ass moving there," screamed a young corporal, "ye stupid, wall-eyed bag o' buzzard bait!"

The corporal had dug his heels into the spongy turf along the creek bank and was leaning back at an impossible angle, trying with all his might to yank the head of the intractable animal away from the watercourse and back toward the dusty trail. All up and down the line the same vignette was being enacted, with greater or lesser degrees of success, as the inexperienced and hapless soldier-packers struggled to force the perverse mules into some semblance of order and threatened to turn the warm summer air blue with their foul-mouthed denunciations of their charges.

As Boston looked on, there was an audible pop as one of the hitch ropes snapped under the strain and several large sacks of feed slid from the back of the mule they called Old Barnum, then exploded in a shower of corn that scattered into the dust around his hooves. Almost instantly there was a small stampede as several of Barnum's fellow mules rushed to partake of the unexpected treat, braying and butting heads as they tried to nose each other out of the way. The young corporal who had been trying to dissuade his animal from wading into the creek now found himself being dragged bodily across the trail as his fickle companion decided that he was more interested in the corn than the creek.

A hundred yards away Captain Thomas McDougall was, if anything, even more irritated than Bos Custer. McDougall used his teeth to tug a grimy gauntlet off his right hand and then pressed down hard on his eyes, his fingers massaging the bridge of his nose. He had developed a splitting headache and was about at the end of his rope. The packtrain was a disaster despite the best efforts of the civilian packers and Lieutenant Mathey. Mathey was tireless in his efforts to keep things moving along smoothly, dashing up and down the serried ranks of struggling figures on his sweat-foamed gelding, slapping a mule on the bottom here, offering a word of encouragement to a young trooper there. The green troops and even greener mules had combined to produce a commander's worst nightmare —a unit that did not so much respond to orders and direction as it sort of oozed and shambled along at its own erratic and unpredictable pace.

McDougall's brother officers referred to the packtrain as "Mathey's Circus," and the restive, heavily laden mules were doing their best to live up to their reputation. The one the troops called Old Barnum was appropriately named, as he seemed to serve the same function as a circus ringmaster, being always at the center of the animals' undisciplined escapades. If Old Barnum stopped suddenly, the entire string would take it as their signal to take a break, coming to a complete halt or wandering off the trail to crop at the grass or nibble on the lower limbs of the occasional cottonwood tree along the creek. McDougall recognized that the packtrain was supposed to be trailing along well behind the rest of the outfit, but this was starting to get ridiculous—there were mules scattered everywhere.

"Mr. Mathey!" he bellowed.

The beleagured Mathey turned his mount and galloped over to his senior officer, rivulets of sweat cutting through the dust caked on his face and running alongside his heavy black mustache, which was now white with dust. The wiry young Frenchman pulled up sharply and removed his campaign hat with a sweeping gesture and a slight bow.

"Yes, Captain!" he barked. "At your service!"

"Edward," McDougall began, using Mathey's Christian name, "what in God's name is the problem here? Can't we get these damned beasts to go any faster?"

Mathey drew a sleeve across his sweaty brow and shook his head sadly. *"Mon capitaine,"* he breathed out, "it is what it is! We do the best we can with these damned animals, but do not expect miracles."

"It'll be a goddamned miracle," McDougall said, "if we ever catch up with the blasted outfit again."

Mathey shrugged with what McDougall imagined to be typical Gallic sangfroid.

"Thomas, my old friend," Mathey said, gently sweeping an arm back toward the mule-littered landscape, "what we have here are a very few real pack mules and the dregs of the wagon train. There are maybe two dozen of them that have ever carried a load before. The rest"—he shrugged again—"are the leads and swings from the wagons. They pull good, but they are not good carriers.

"Now," Mathey went on calmly, "we've got a few *aparejos*, which is a damn good saddle and just what we need, but not enough to go around. The *aparejos* I put on the ammunition mules, and I make damn sure that Wagoner and his boys are packin' them so we know those loads don't come off. The rest of that mob we've got to load with the sawbucks. They come loose too easy and they slide like hell. Most of these boys don't ever see a mule before that's not pulling a plow and they got no idea how to tie down a load. Hell, you've seen the mules' backs, *mon capitaine*. Most of 'em are rubbed raw and festering like hell—sure, they're skittish and ugly. Why, Thomas, I say we are damn lucky to have got 'em this far without half of 'em buckin' off their loads and heading for the hills."

McDougall nodded slowly, his headache pounding behind his eyes.

"Yeah, Edward." He sighed. "Sorry I skinned you. I know you're doin' the best you can, considering. But damn it, we're scattered from hell to breakfast now. Why, the goddamned company must be two miles back already. The Old Man'll be after me with a sharp stick." McDougall shot an evil glance at Old Barnum, who was now braying loudly, causing the captain's headache to throb even harder.

"That goddamned devil-spawn of a jackass," McDougall said. "He's the goddamn ringleader. Why, I've a mind to shoot the son of a bitch myself and leave his worthless carcass here for the buzzards."

Mathey grinned and reached out to put his hand on McDougall's arm.

"Easy there, Capitaine. You don't want to shoot Old Barnum. He may be a pain in the ass, but the son of a bitch is the damned natural leader of this circus. You see how the rest of 'em kind of look out to see what he's up to? Hell, you shoot him, the rest of the bastards think he's taking a nap and they all lay down and wait for him. No, we leave Barnum alive." Mathey paused for a moment as an idea shimmered into the back of his brain. "Say, I think maybe we're not using our heads here." He turned and shouted over his shoulder.

"Mr. Wagoner! Wagoner! Somebody send Wagoner over to me!"

A cry echoed down the line for "Wagoner to the front!" and moments later a bearded and dust-covered civilian cantered up alongside the two officers and touched his fingers to the brim of a battered straw hat that threatened momentarily to unravel around his bearlike head.

"Mr. Mathey. Afternoon, Cap'n, hell of a burlesque, ain't it?" he drawled, jabbing a thumb back in the direction of the roiling mass of mules and troopers behind him.

"Mr. Wagoner," Mathey inquired, "can you take Old Barnum there in your charge? I ask myself, what if you make him your bell? You think the others fall in line pretty soon?"

Wagoner frowned for a moment and rubbed a filthy hand through his beard, digesting the lieutenant's suggestion. He looked to where Old Barnum had dropped on his hind quarters and was now sitting patiently in the middle of the trail, his large brown face displaying as much detachment and disinterest as a mule can assume. Around him several other mules gave indications that they were about to follow suit. The burly packer slid his fingers up under his ratty hat to scratch his scalp vigorously, and then spat a brown stream of tobacco juice into the dust.

"Well, hell's bells, Lootenant," he said finally. "It's worth a damned try. Independent old cuss, ain't he?" muttered Wagoner in an admiring tone. "Well, maybe if I nursemaid 'im a bit, he'll head up and lead 'em out just from pure contrariness."

Not waiting for a response, the veteran mule skinner headed straight over to where Old Barnum was studiously ignoring the ravings of a young private who was yanking mightily at the mule's bridle. Mathey looked on as the private gratefully surrendered Barnum's lead to Wagoner, who immediately stuck his face into the mule's and appeared to be conferring with the stubborn creature. The mule skinner reached into a frayed pocket and shoved something into Barnum's mouth, whispering quietly into the mule's ear all the while. To Mathey and McDougall's mutual astonishment Old Barnum stood up, let out an ear-shattering bray and placidly followed Wagoner to the head of the column, the mule skinner flashing a grin and a wink at the two officers as he passed by. In a few moments Wagoner had hung an old copper cowbell around Barnum's neck, and the huge animal was walking serenely ahead as if it was what he had intended to do all along. As if by mutual consent, a few other mules ceased their antics and fell in behind Barnum, to be followed by a dozen more, leaving their frustrated attendants gawking open-mouthed at the odd parade.

"Well, I'll be damned!" exclaimed McDougall.

Mathey shook his head in wonder and turned to move down the line of mules which was just beginning to move again, urging the stragglers into line and laughing quietly to himself. McDougall sat his horse and watched with relief as his charges began to move steadily down the trail, hardly noticing as Boston Custer pranced up alongside on his spirited pony.

"Say, Thomas," Boston exclaimed, "what's the rumpus? Got 'em movin' again, I see."

McDougall nodded as Boston tugged back on his reins and patted his pony's withers to settle him down. Somwhat self-consciously Boston pulled out a small silver hunter and popped open the lid, making a mental note of the time. It was about seventeen minutes past two o'clock. It seemed like it should be later than that. He shook the watch and held it up to his ear wondering if the damned thing had stopped again.

"Tom," the youngster said, "if there's no objection, I'd like to sprint up ahead and see what the boys're doing."

McDougall nodded tiredly. "Go on ahead, Bos. I guess we're going again, so there's no reason to keep ya hanging back. As long as you're going, give my compliments to the general and tell him we're on the move. Let him know about where we are so he can gauge his speed."

Boston Custer, a broad grin on his face, nodded, slapped his hat down firmly on his head, and wheeled off to find his brothers. With any luck, he should be able to catch up with 'em before they opened the ball. His buckskin pony responded with a will, and the pair flew down the trail toward the valley of the Little Bighorn, leaving the packtrain and its long-suffering escorts to continue their Sisyphean labors.

As McDougall watched Custer disappearing down the trail, Pretty Face, a Ree scout, rode up alongside him and pointed in the direction the youngster had taken, gesturing emphatically and exclaiming in his own tongue. McDougall did not speak Ree and gestured to indicate that he didn't understand what Pretty Face was trying to say.

"Smokes!" Pretty Face stammered in broken English. "Someone makes smokes!"

"What the hell?" McDougall started as he saw what the Ree was pointing at. "Grass?" he asked, pointing at the smudge on the horizon. The Ree looked puzzled, so McDougall slid out of his saddle and snatched a fistful of grass from the ground. "Grass smokes?" he asked again. The Ree shook his head emphatically and looked around for something, finally grasping the fringes on McDougall's buckskin campaign shirt.

"Smokes!" he said, sharply tugging on the buckskin.

Someone was burning hides up ahead? McDougall wondered if the column had already hit the village and set it afire. But no—if they had, there would surely be more smoke than what was now visible. McDougall shook his head, puzzled. Something was not quite right there, but it was best to be on the safe side. He looked around for Mathey.

"Lieutenant Mathey!"

Mathey rode over to join him, a questioning look on his face. "Sir?"

"Edward, I want you to find First Sergeant Hill. Have him put together a platoon from the escort and take the lead and tell 'im to be on the qui vive." Mathey nodded, frowning. "Then close up the column as tight as you can get it and advance the ammunition mules to the head of the train."

Mathey saluted, wheeled his horse in a tight circle and dashed back down the column in search of the first sergeant. From the look of things, Mathey thought it was going to get pretty hot around here very quickly, and he hoped like hell that Old Barnum didn't decide to change his mind about cooperating.

Minutes later Boston Custer was cantering alongside the creek, glancing occasionally at the ground to confirm that the main column had passed this way, when he caught sight of a large body of horsemen just opposite him and about to cross over the watercourse to come onto the main trail. Boston immediately recognized Captain Benteen in the lead. He figured that Benteen must have finished his screen to the south and not come across any Sioux because the man's face was purely deadpan. The lead troopers appeared to Boston to have the glazed look about them that men have when they are numbed by boredom. They didn't look as if they'd stirred up much dust getting here. Custer flashed them a broad grin and waved as he passed by.

"Hallooo, Benteen!" he called. "Say, Gib, didja pitch into anything?"

Lieutenant Gibson laughed and called back. "No! But at least we ain't been wading around in mule shit, Bos."

Bos Custer laughed heartily and spurred his pony into a gallop, leaving the battalion as it splashed up out of the creek and turned to the west, following the broad trail.

Captain Benteen glowered after the retreating figure and nudged his mount off to one side to watch as his battalion wheeled into column. Concentrating on Boston Custer's back, he did not notice the slight wisp of dark smoke rising into the air. Glancing in the direction from which Boston Custer had come, he caught sight of the first of the packtrain and its escort about half a mile behind him on the trail and decided to wait for them to come up. Moving back to the head of the battalion, he spotted a low marshy area where the creek broadened out in a slight depression. He motioned for Gibson to join him.

"Gib," he said, "McDougall and the packs are coming in now. Move the outfit down to that morass over there and let everyone get watered up. Make sure the troopers get their canteens filled upstream of the horses so we don't have to deal with a slew of bellyaches in an hour or two. I want it done fairly quickly and before the packtrain gets in. Clear?"

Lieutenant Gibson nodded, snapped off a salute, and cantered down the column's flank to pass the word.

Watching the boy ride off, Benteen paused to figure how long it would take the packtrain to arrive and decided that it would be a good fifteen minutes or so, which should be just enough time to get his outfit watered and moving again before the mules started to mix in among them. Reaching behind his saddle, he pulled out the field glasses he had recovered from Lieutenant Gibson and focused them on the approaching mules. In the lead he recognized the figures of McDougall's first sergeant and Lieutenant Mathey, that damned Frog. Mathey exhibited the suave mannerisms of his homeland but, when he grew excited, his language was such as to cause a sailor to blush. The man was a disgrace and a buffoon. His fellow officers had taken to calling him Bible Thumper, doubtless a sardonic alias, but Frederick Benteen found nothing humorous in the man.

"Damned foreigners," he muttered under his breath. Micks, Krauts, Frogs, and Eyeties—the gutter sweepings of Europe. The whole goddamned Army was becoming full of the bastards.

1432 Hours
At the Mouth of Ash Creek

White-Man-Runs-Him worked his rawhide quirt savagely against the flanks of his pinto, urging the nimble creature on and shrieking loudly as the rest of the scouts fanned out to either side of him. A few yards behind, Lieutenants Varnum and Hare scrambled to keep up on their large grain-fed mounts, but the scouts' barefoot ponies maintained a comfortable lead. As the riders neared the mouth of the creek, the ground began to open up into a broad and level meadowlike expanse covered with a thick growth of rank, green grass and bordered on either side by creeks flowing together just before they fed into the Little Bighorn River. Here the wide trail left by the hostile village was much more obvious, as it veered sharply off to the left, crossed over the river, and disappeared again to the right around a timbered bend in the river.

Just as the lead scouts were approaching the northernmost fork of the creeks, Lieutenant Varnum managed a final burst of speed from his mount and raced in front of the Crows and Rees to try to stem their headlong rush. Waving his hands wildly, Varnum indicated by signs that some of the scouts should wait at the juncture of the creeks while others should accompany him to the top of a nearby hill. As the group slowed to a walk, Lieutenant Luther Hare galloped up to Varnum and reached out to tug on the man's sleeve.

"Damn, Charlie!" he sputtered. "Why're we stoppin' here? I thought the general said to head straight for the herd?"

"What herd, Luther?" Varnum shot back. "We don't really know where exactly the damn herd is yet. I ain't goin' in there blind. And the Old Man may've said to hit 'em hard, but if we skip off and leave him without knowin' exactly what the layout is, you can bet he'll have our hides for certain sure."

Hare knew intuitively that Varnum was right. The general would not want to be left wondering what was ahead if they had an opportunity to find out. Nodding vigorously, Hare wheeled his horse around and gathered up the Rees while Varnum led a party of Crows in an easy lope up the nearby butte. This small party had no sooner gotten to the top of the butte than Reno's battalion trotted into the meadow below and Varnum observed the pudgy major raising his hand to bring the unit to a halt. Fast on Reno's heels was the main command, George Custer clearly visible, with his blue shirt and long red scarf billowing in the still air as he galloped to the head of the combined units. Mitch Bouyer, Bloody Knife, and the ubiquitous Cooke followed close behind the general, while George Herendeen and Charley Reynolds made up the rest of Custer's party. The small group rode straight in among the gathering of Indian scouts Varnum had left in Hare's charge, and from what he could tell, Varnum guessed that Luther Hare, now pointing to the top of the butte, was explaining the chief of scouts' actions.

Varnum could now see that Custer was looking up the butte and waving his broad-brimmed hat in the air and nodding his approval, and the young officer breathed easier knowing that he had apparently guessed right. Turning to peer down the valley, a few seconds told Varnum all that he needed to know. Far down the valley, beyond the trees, a large dust cloud was forming on the tablelands where he could now make out the shimmering mass of the pony herd, and closer in he could now see the tops of scores of lodges. Motioning to the Crows, he turned and raced back down the butte just as Herendeen was coming up. Herendeen waved as he passed by, and Varnum and the Crows jounced out onto the flat to gallop over to where Custer was now closeted with Reno and several of the regiment's other officers. Varnum didn't hesitate but dashed straight into the small circle and snapped a salute as he blurted his findings.

"They're out there, General! Hundreds of 'em," he gasped. "Got a good view of the pony herd and a bunch of the lodges. They're stirring up a heap o' dust, General!"

Before Custer could acknowledge Varnum's report, everyone was distracted by the distant voice of George Herendeen yelling down from the butte that Varnum had just left. Leaning back in his saddle as his horse came skidding back down the side of the butte, Herendeen was waving his hat in the direction of the camp and shouting at the top of his lungs.

"There are your Indians, General!" he called out. "Running like devils!"

The effect on the small group was electric. Every face was now turned toward George Custer, their eyes betraying a mixture of excitement, anxiety and, in some cases, outright fear. Custer shut his eyes briefly, a hand to his forehead as he grappled with the situation.

Damn it, he thought, they're scattering. If we wait any longer, it'll be like trying to hold water in your open fingers. Where the hell is Benteen? Too late. We just can't wait. Have to move quickly. He looked up and turned to Varnum.

"How close to the village, Mr. Varnum? Give me your best estimate!"

Varnum pointed across the Little Bighorn, where a stand of timber protruded into the valley bottom from a wide bend in the river. "Just around that stand of timber I'd say, sir." Varnum guessed: "Maybe two miles at the farthest."

"Mr. Cooke," Custer barked. "Time, please."

Lieutenant Cooke drew out his watch and glanced at it quickly. "Two forty-three, General." Cooke paused. "Precisely." Custer nodded and turned to his second-in-command.

"Major Reno," he said, pointing across to the broad valley, "you will take your battalion and move forward at as rapid a gait as you deem prudent. Water your stock at the ford, but make sure the horses don't drink too much because they have to travel a good deal today." Reno nodded as Custer continued. "Cross the river and charge afterward and I will support you with the rest of the outfit." Reno saluted and wheeled away to rejoin his battalion. As the major started down along the creek, Custer called out after him. "And take the Ree and Sioux scouts with you!" Custer turned to Cooke and Keogh who sat nearby.

"Go on after him and make sure he knows what to do and then come back." The two nodded and raced after Reno's battalion, which was just moving into the ford and had stopped briefly. Charley Reynolds and Fred Gerard looked at each other, shrugged, and galloped after them.

Lieutenant Varnum, momentarily forgotten, popped off a salute and turned to follow the battalion when he caught sight of his old friend Lieutenant "Nick" Wallace. Varnum waved and called out merrily.

"Come on, Nick, with the fighting men," he teased. "Don't hang back with these coffee coolers."

Wallace looked pleadingly at Custer, who laughed, waving him away with his hat.

"Oh, go on, Mr. Wallace. We'll get by without you."

Wallace flashed a grateful smile and spurred his horse after Varnum, soon catching up with him and Hare, who had swung out alongside the column. Side by side, the three lieutenants plunged their horses into the icy waters of the Little Bighorn and splashed out onto the plain beyond, chattering happily like boys off on the first outing of the summer. Custer then turned to Mitch Bouyer, who had shuffled in to fill the space vacated by Cooke and Keogh.

"Mitch, send a couple of the Crows over that butte up there to tell me where the Sioux are." Bouyer nodded and, motioning Half-Yellow-Face and White Swan over to him, quickly repeated Custer's instruction. In the distance Custer could hear Reno calling out to his battalion: *"Battalion! Fours left! At the trot! Forrraaard!"*

Half-Yellow-Face and White Swan, who were listening intently to Bouyer's instructions, looked up startled when a trumpeter sounded Advance and Reno's battalion began to move forward. Forgetting all about Bouyer, the two scouts whooped and sped off after Reno's battalion.

"Bouyer!" Custer barked. "That's the wrong way. Where the hell are they going?"

Bouyer, shaking his head in consternation, watched as Half-Yellow-Face and White Swan disappeared down the valley along with Reno and most of the other scouts.

"Hell if I know, General," Bouyer said, shrugging. "They musta got confused." He then turned to the remaining Crows and spoke to them in their own language.

"White-Man-Runs-Him, Curley, Goes Ahead, Hairy Moccasin, you will come with me and we will ride over that ridge and look at the lodges." The Crows nodded quietly and fell in alongside Bouyer as he turned and galloped up the hill that Varnum and Herendeen had climbed a few minutes before.

As Reno's battalion trotted out onto the level valley floor, Lieutenants Varnum, Hare, and Wallace cantered alongside and quickly outdistanced the rest of the outfit, with the exception of several Ree scouts who yipped and howled as they sped along the grassy turf. Far out ahead of them they could see scores of tiny mounted figures scampering back and forth across their front and raising clouds of dust in their wake. The entire unit began a gradual oblique to the right, keeping the river on their right flank. The column began to accordion as some of the horses surged forward while others began to tire and flag. Major Reno could not yet make out the village but could see only the tops of a few lodges just beyond a large stand of timber that jutted out into the valley from along the bend of the river. Maintaining his gait, he turned in the saddle and bellowed, *"Fours right into line!"*

Without slowing its pace, the column began to wheel around behind Reno as the troopers started to spread out over the floor of the broad valley, faces tense with anticipation, hands fidgeting nervously at the flaps of holsters or gripping the stocks of carbines, the battalion opening like a blossom to spew tiny blue spores that floated in a ragged line across the sagebrush and grass.

•

Lieutenant William Winer Cooke stood in his stirrups and watched as Reno's column began to deploy and move forward against the tiny figures that floated through the dust farther up the valley. Satisfied, he turned to Keogh, nodded curtly, and the pair wheeled about to splash back across the ford toward the main command, where Custer was looking at his scout Bloody Knife. Nearing the command group, Cooke noticed Tom Custer talking to the odd little reporter fellow with the spectacles. Kellogg was balanced carefully on top of his mule and leaning forward over the animal's neck, which he was now using as a sort of desk as he scribbled furiously in his notebook. Well, Mr. Kellogg, thought Cooke, I should think you'll have a deal to write about before this day is through.

Bloody Knife looked up at the sun, which had begun advancing to the west, his hands lifted in what to Custer seemed a gesture of worship. The Ree, finished with his quiet chanting, lowered his arms and addressed a final comment to the bright disc.

"I shall not see you go down behind the mountains tonight," Bloody Knife said solemnly in his own language, and turned to Custer, who was staring at him curiously.

"What," asked Custer, "was that all about, Bloody Knife?" The Ree looked into the clear blue eyes that stared out from a sunburned and lightly bearded face.

"You are making a big mistake, Son-of-the-Morning-Star," the Ree said, sweeping his arm around him. "All of these people will get killed." Custer's face turned a bright crimson, and the Ree thought the man would explode with anger.

"Damn your eyes!" the cavalryman barked. "You don't know what you're talking about. We'll whip these damned Sioux yet, and if you're afraid to come with me, then get out of my sight. Go back with the women and let us soldiers do the real work. Go on, go home."

The Ree just stared evenly at the livid colonel. He knew that Long Hair did not like to be contradicted once he had made a decision, even if it was a bad one, which this certainly was. Bloody Knife ignored the temptation to say that this man was being stupid. Clearly there was no point in arguing with a man who had already made up his mind, but there was also no point in ending a long friendship in anger.

"I am going down to join my people now," the Ree said quietly, tossing his head to indicate the direction that the Ree scouts and Reno's battalion had taken. "I have an old debt to repay. Good hunting to you, old friend." Bloody Knife paused, reached out, and grasped Custer firmly by the hand.

"You and I," Bloody Knife said solemnly, "are both going home tonight by a road we do not know."

Without another word, the Ree broke his grip, yanked his Winchester from its scabbard, spun his pony around, and galloped shrieking and yipping across the river and out onto the plain beyond, the sun flashing on the barrel of the rifle as he rode away.

PART THREE

"A Good Day to Die!"

COLLISION

Q: State as near as you can, the number of Indians that engaged Major Reno's command at that place, and whether during the engagement there was any increase or decrease in the number of Indians, and what movements if any were made by the Indians with reference to Major Reno's command at that place.

A: It is almost impossible to estimate the strength of mounted Indians. There was a very large force there soon after the command was dismounted, and there was a large force circling around us all the time, and passing around to the left and rear. . . . There was very heavy firing going on on both sides; I was lying in the edge of the woods with Girard [*sic*] and Reynolds and was anxious to get a drink out of Girard's flask, and was paying more attention to that than to the Indians.

Statement of Lieutenant Charles Varnum, 7th U.S. Cavalry
(Extract from Official Records, Court of Inquiry
Convened 13 January 1879 at Chicago, Illinois)

Here the Dakotas attacked them and the shooting made a continuous roar on both sides, soldiers and horses were killed very fast.

Statement of Young Hawk, Ree Scout

I had sung the war song, I had smelt the powder smoke. My heart was bad—I was like one that has no mind. I rushed in and took their flag; my pony fell dead as I took it. I cut the thong that bound me. I jumped up and brained the long sword flag-man with my war club, and ran back to our line with the flag. The long sword's blood and brains splashed in my face. It felt hot, and blood ran in my mouth. I could taste it. I was mad. . . . I was crazy; I feared nothing.

Statement of Rain-in-the-Face, Hunkpapa Lakota

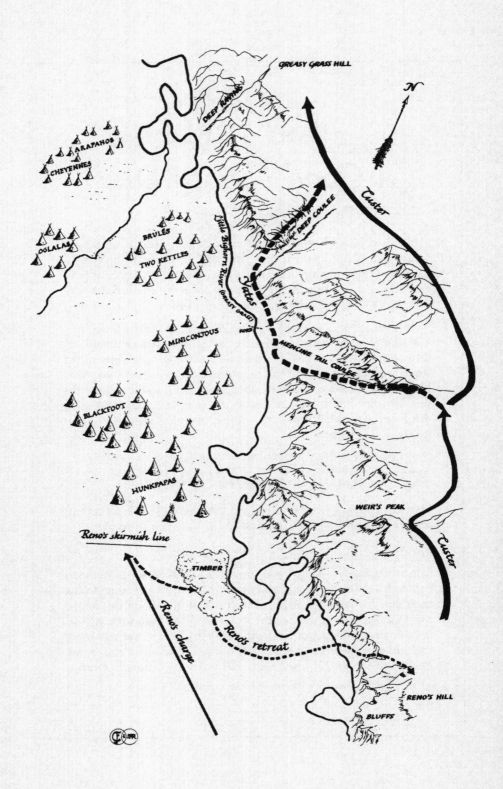

Witakiñyañyañka (*Early Afternoon*)
Along the Greasy Grass

Her-Holy-Door looked down at her son, who was sleeping peacefully in the shade of their lodge. It was a hot day and Tatanka Iyotanka had had a very long night and needed his sleep badly. He was not as young as he used to be, and the demands that the people made on him were becoming too much. His sleep was too often troubled by dreams, and his appetite usually suffered if he'd had a particularly bad night. A mother noticed these things, although he was too stubborn to admit it to himself. The old woman picked up a horsetail whisk and shooed away some flies that had been buzzing around Sitting Bull's slumbering form. Her son's arms were still healing from the Sun Dance ceremony two weeks earlier. Sitting Bull had pledged a gift of flesh to Wakan Tanka. As the others had danced and chanted, Jumping Bull had slowly cut one hundred small bits of flesh from Sitting Bull's arms, and the myriad cuts had been slow to heal. The flies were getting bad here, and it was a constant battle to keep them from tormenting her son's wounds.

Her-Holy-Door thought they would surely have to move fairly soon, as such a large camp quickly became so littered with refuse and offal that the flies, multiplying by the thousands, would soon become all but unbearable. A wisp of dust drifted in under the lodgeskins and the withered old woman looked out to see what was causing it. Out on the plains in the distance she could see riders, men and boys, dashing through a growing cloud of dust as they whipped their ponies around in a large circle. She leaned out and called quietly to Moving-Robe-Woman, the daughter of her son's friend Crawler.

"What is all that commotion over there?" Her-Holy-Door asked crossly. "They're making a lot of fuss and dust and my son is trying to sleep."

The young woman stood up on tiptoes. Shielding her eyes from the sun, she peered out into the dust and shook her head slowly.

"I don't know, Grandmother," she called back. "It looks like some of those crazy Sans Arcs are just riding around yelling." She turned and cocked her head. "Maybe they see some buffalo coming down the valley," she opined with a slight smile.

"Bah!" the old woman retorted. "If there were any buffalo, those young fools would soon chase them off with all of their noise and dust. Can't they see that it's too hot for that nonsense? Some people are trying to rest."

She looked back down on her sleeping son and whisked away another fly that had settled on the end of his nose. Young fools! They had no respect for anything anymore. Her-Holy-Door glanced back out at the scurrying figures and decided that she would be glad when it was time to move again. It was just too noisy with all these crazy young braves gallivanting around and showing off in front of the young girls.

Far downstream to the north, in the Cheyenne circle at the lower end of the camp, Crazy Horse was still visiting with his old friend Two Moon. The time had slipped by easily, gurgling quietly over their conversation like the waters of the Greasy Grass passing over stones, and Crazy Horse found that he was now much more relaxed than he had been when he had first come from visiting with the old Hunkpapa. Two Moon's wife, She-Is-Clever, was indeed a good cook, and Crazy Horse found himself eating considerably more than he had intended. It was a good way to spend an afternoon, although he thought he should probably be going pretty soon. Well, maybe one more helping of stew wouldn't be so bad.

Two Moon's wife had gone out to fetch another bowl of stew a few moments before but had not returned, and Two Moon was glancing under the lodgeskins to see what was keeping her so long. He looked at his guest, shrugged, and eased himself up to go see what was causing the delay. She was probably just gossiping with her sister again, a pretty young girl but one who just couldn't seem to stop talking. It was no wonder that her parents had named her Magpie Woman. Ducking under the side of his lodge, Two Moon saw that Magpie Woman was indeed with his wife but, oddly enough, neither of them was talking. Rather, both of them were staring up the valley at something.

"What are you two women doing out here?" he pretended to scold. "Have you forgotten your manners? There is a hungry guest inside."

"Hush!" said She-Is-Clever without turning around. "*Tiyañkayo.* Be patient. *Haho nas Hist.* Look and listen, you man."

Two Moon wandered over to see what the women were staring at and noticed that all around them people had stopped to stare up the valley toward the Hunkpapa circle, where dust was rising into the air and tiny figures were scurrying toward the pony herds.

"Someone said that some Sans Arcs say that there are buffalo coming down the valley," crowed Magpie Woman. "It's about time, because I was getting tired of the same old dog every day."

Two Moon rolled his eyes upward, thinking that it was just like Magpie Woman to complain about having too much of a delicacy. She was never satisfied with anything. The man who finally married her, he thought, would certainly have his hands full and good luck to him. Two Moon heard something behind him and turned to see Crazy Horse ducking out from under the lodgeskins.

"What's going on, brother?" the Oglala asked.

Two Moon pointed up the valley at the rising dust cloud. "These women say that the Sans Arcs say that there are buffalo coming this way."

Crazy Horse looked at the dust cloud and the tiny figures dashing back and forth. He frowned and thought that this was a very strange thing indeed. He shook his head, puzzled.

"This does not make any sense, brother," he said finally. "That is where our camp was before and where we left the dead from the fight with Three Stars. Why would the buffalo come where they can smell so many people? There should not be any buffalo there. They should be going away from this camp not coming toward it."

Two Moon frowned and looked at his old friend. There was truth in what he said. The buffalo would not come so near so many people gathered together. In all his years he had never known even the strongest medicine that would bring Uncle Pte to venture near the people. He felt Crazy Horse's hand on his shoulder.

"There is something that is not right," Crazy Horse said. "I am going to get my gun, and we will ride down there and see what is going on."

Two Moon cast a sharp glance at the women, who had not heard what Crazy Horse had said but were now chattering away merrily about what they would do with some fresh buffalo steaks and a tender tongue or two. The Cheyenne nodded to his friend and slipped back into his lodge to load his gun.

Sitting Bull stirred fitfully in his sleep, his dreams flashing and changing before him. An eagle soared past him and whispered as it passed, "Listen to me, Tatanka Iyotanka."

The old man followed the eagle, climbing over gray rocks that towered above him, their peaks lost in the clouds above. He pushed his way upward through clouds that felt more like the powdery snow that comes in the Moon of Popping Trees, and his fingers grew numb and bled on the rocks as he crawled and scrambled ever higher. His limbs grew heavier and he felt he would never be able to find the eagle again to hear what he wanted to say to him when he suddenly broke through the clouds and crawled up onto a smooth boulder that was warmed by the bright sun beating down on it from above. Directly in front of him the eagle sat in his nest and fed scraps of raw meat to its squalling young. The eagle looked at the old man and spoke.

"Go back to your people," the eagle commanded. "They are waiting for you to tell them what they should do. Hurry."

Sitting Bull reached out to touch the bird, but it began to screech and changed suddenly into a bright red fox that leaped over the old man's head, shouting, "Quickly! Come quickly!" and disappeared into the snowy clouds below. Sitting Bull stepped into the clouds and drifted down and down until he found himself standing on a broad plain covered by sagebrush and grass. The fox was scampering away through the brush, and the old man felt the ground shaking under his feet as the fox shrieked "Quickly!" and disappeared.

The ground continued to shake, and Sitting Bull heard a thundering noise growing louder, ever louder, and he looked up to see a huge buffalo bull charging toward him and bellowing "Quickly! Quickly!" The thundering grew and grew in his ears, and the whole world seemed to be shaking around him, the dust rising in his nostrils and choking him.

"The Chargers are coming!" a woman screamed. Sitting Bull awoke with a start, his heart racing in his chest, his head swimming crazily, the ground still shaking under him. His lodge was filling with dust, and outside the people were running everywhere and women were screaming.

"*Siye'! Siye'! Akicita wasichu! Inyañka!* Watch out! Watch out! White soldiers are coming! Run! Run!"

He heard the crack and pop-pop-popping of gunfire. Shots were being fired from somewhere! He rolled out of the robes and scrabbled through his belongings to find his guns, thinking of his other dream of soldiers falling into camp.

1501 Hours
On the Bluffs Above the Little Bighorn

Lieutenant Colonel George Armstrong Custer used his spurs to nudge Vic lightly, and the powerful animal surged up the sandy slope heading toward the bluff where Mitch Bouyer was waiting with the Crow scouts. With Vic's hooves scrabbling at the loose soil, horse and rider lunged up over the edge and pulled up alongside the solemn group, which was gazing dumbstruck into the valley below.

"Good God!" Custer gasped. Hundreds of feet below them a vast level plain swept out and away from the tree-bordered river at the base of the bluffs. He had been led to expect a camp of some four hundred lodges or so. A large village, of course, but not unmanageable. But this was considerably larger than that. Why, there must be nearly a thousand lodges down there if there was one. How many warriors must a camp of that size hold? Two thousand? Four thousand? It was a far cry from the eight hundred warriors they had expected to find. Well, this was obviously going to be a bit trickier than any of them had supposed. He leaned forward in the saddle, straining to take in the scope of the village that spread for miles into the distance, a chaos of activity, with tiny figures running in every direction, stirring up clouds of dust.

That was odd. He had expected the Sioux to run, but the lodges were still standing, and none of the tiny figures seemed to be occupied in breaking them down for flight. And all of the little figures appeared to be women and children. There was hardly a warrior in sight. A few mounted braves seemed to be driving the pony herds toward the upper end of the camp nearest Reno, but that was about all. Could most of the warriors still be asleep? At this time of day? Were they off hunting? If that was the case, they might be able to round up the women and children fairly easily. If the warriors returned, then they would not dare to resist, and he could avoid a fight altogether. Something didn't make sense, but he couldn't quite put his finger on it.

Reno! he thought suddenly, and turned to look down beyond the upper end of the village, where he could now see Reno's tiny battalion spread across the valley floor—a spindly blue wisp. Reno obviously hadn't seen the village yet. That stand of timber at the bend in the river was still hiding it from Reno's command, and they were now galloping headlong toward the invisible village. Custer snatched his hat from his head and waved it wildly in the air urging the outfit on. Good show, boys, he thought. That's the spirit!

As he watched, the fragile line of blue lunged forward suddenly. The distant notes of the trumpet floating softly up the bluffs told him that Reno had sounded the charge. They must have seen him waving his hat and were closing in to get on with it. Even now he could make out the dim shouting and hallooing of the troopers as they sped down the valley.

Good! he thought. That should keep the Sioux busy for a while and give me time to get the rest of the outfit into position. Custer backed Vic off away from the edge of the bluff and turned to see the rest of the command puffing up the long slope. Frowning, he watched as the command came on, and found his mind drifting back to Bloody Knife's parting words.

What an odd thing for Bloody Knife to say, he thought, "a road we do not know." Such an unsettling expression, and colored with the gloomy resignation that had stared out from his friend's eyes. Wasn't that what they were all doing, every day of their lives? Who really knew what the future held? Who could tell where the road they traveled would lead? He felt a sudden chill, and an air of foreboding settled into his bones. It was an unpleasant and unfamiliar sensation for him. Usually the prospect of battle was an intoxicant—raising his blood pressure, sharpening his senses, adrenaline flowing through his system like a torrent—filling him with a sense of elation and yes, freedom. He looked forward to the rush of wind in his face, the acrid smell of gunpowder, the noise, the exhilaration. But today he felt strangely depressed and joyless.

"Damn that old Ree!" he thought fiercely. The man's damned dreariness was contagious, and there just wasn't time to be worrying about such nonsense.

He noted that some of the climbing horses were already winded from the effort and beginning to drop farther and farther behind. As the outfit poured over the top onto level ground, some of them were able to glimpse Reno's troopers charging ahead in the valley below. The men began whooping and cheering at the sight. Infected by the enthusiasm of their riders, some of the horses began to break into a gallop and surge ahead of the others.

"Hold your horses in, boys!" Custer barked hoarsely. "There's plenty of 'em down there for all of us."

He nudged Vic forward, moving him farther away from the edge of the bluffs and forcing the column to veer slightly to the east, where they could not see the scene unfolding below them.

"Can't let them get too good a look at the village, let 'em see how many there are, yet," he thought, afraid that some of the younger men might spook a little too early. Best not to let 'em think too much about an action beforehand. Best just to push 'em in full tilt with their blood up and let their momentum carry 'em through. Well, Reno was committed and there was now no going back. Custer knew he couldn't let Reno fight too long unsupported. If the warriors were indeed still in the village, they would soon figure out that Reno's wasn't that large of a battalion, and if he didn't somehow take the pressure off of him, the Sioux might well collapse his outfit like a house of cards. Something like that could make Washita look like a Sunday outing.

He had to hit them quickly and from so many different directions that he could throw them off balance, make 'em panic.

Have to drive them downstream, he thought. That way, if they run, it'll be smack into Gibbon's people.

All he had to do was act quickly and decisively. But first they had to get down there and across the river. Couldn't go down here, the damn bluffs were too steep. He looked farther along the ridgeline. There must be somewhere further downstream where they could get down to the river, get into the hostiles' flank or rear. An old watercourse maybe, a ravine or coulee—something.

"Armstrong."

Tom Custer had ridden right up to him while he had been lost in thought.

"Looks like Reno's going in fast. Maybe he'll do for an Indian fighter after all," he added cheerfully. "Say, what's the trouble?" George Custer shot a glare at his brother that caused the younger man to lapse into silence and sit back in his saddle. Tom glanced over his brother's shoulder and got his first look at the village.

"Whew!" Tom exclaimed, whistling. "That's a bit larger than we'd expected, ain't it? How many of 'em ya figure're down there?"

"Where the hell's Benteen?" Custer demanded. Tom shrugged and shook his head.

"Well, never mind that, no time now. Tom, I want you to send a man back. Make sure he's a good rider. Get him through to McDougall and get the packs up quickly. Don't let him dawdle. We need 'em and we need 'em now. Have 'em cut across to the high ground. If he sees Benteen, he's to hurry him up. Tell him we've hit a big village."

Tom, taken aback by the abruptness of George's tone, nodded dumbly and wheeled about to gallop back toward his company.

"Sergeant Kanipe!" Tom bellowed. "Front and center! At the gallop!" Daniel Kanipe, a slight man with a boyish look to him, spurred his mount out of the ranks and reported to his commanding officer. Captain Thomas Custer had an anxious look on his face.

"Kanipe, go find Captain McDougall and the packtrain. Have 'em bring the packs across to high ground. They're not to stop but come straight through. If any of the packs come loose, don't stop to fix 'em, just cut 'em loose and come on fast. Big damned village. If you see Captain Benteen on your way, tell him to come quick."

Kanipe nodded quickly, yanked his mount's head around and, jabbing his spurs savagely into the horse's flanks, clattered away down the trail, a swirling cloud of dust marking his departure. Tom Custer watched the courier skidding down the ridgeline and then turned back to find his brother George.

George Custer's mind was racing as he quickly took in the lay of the land. They had to get farther downstream. He wheeled Vic around and dashed to the head of the column, Tom Custer, Cooke, Bouyer, and the Crows close on his heels. The command scrambled up a long ridge from which the troopers could now look down at the valley floor to see hundreds of Sioux boiling out of the village to meet Reno's charge. Custer observed the scene grim-faced. It looked like the warriors were home and they'd have to fight this one out after all. As they watched, the thin blue line rounded the stand of timber that jutted from the river bend and ground to a sudden stop. Reno's people were dismounting and spreading out across the plain in a skirmish line, every fourth trooper slipping to the rear with three other horses in tow, a steady pop-pop-pop of rifle fire drifting up from below.

Alright, Custer thought. That's better, Reno, old fellow. If you can just stay cool and keep pouring it into 'em, you can probably hold 'em off for quite a bit now, and that should give me just about enough time to get around on their flank and hit 'em hard. Good man. Carefully studying the ground ahead as he rode, Custer saw a promising dip in the ridgeline. Veering off to the east, the command started down into the mouth of a ravine, the village and Reno quickly slipping from view. After a few hundred yards Custer reined up suddenly and turned to Myles Keogh.

"Myles," he said quickly, "take the outfit down into this coulee a couple hundred yards and hold 'em up. Make a final check of your weapons and ammunition. Make sure they can get to their cartridges in a hurry." Keogh nodded and assumed direction of the command while Custer, Tom, Cooke, and the scouts angled off to the left and scrambled up a rise to take another look at the terrain.

Sergeant Daniel Kanipe urged his horse along at as quick a pace as the broken country would allow, the tiring animal passing several troopers along the back trail whose own horses had already given out. These stragglers had all dismounted, some to care for their animals, to whom they had naturally become greatly attached, or to lead them on gently by their reins. Kanipe gave each of the men a brief nod as he passed. He could tell by each one's glum looks that the troopers were discouraged and frustrated. After having come so far, to miss out on the fight was almost too much for them to bear. Kanipe knew that any rebukes he might have doled out would pale in comparison to the unmerciful ribbing these fellows would have to endure from their mates when the day was over and everyone was sitting around the campfire telling tales about the fight.

As he came back out onto the flat, he was startled by a "yip-yip-yip" and twisted violently in his saddle to see a screaming mob of Indians in hot pursuit. Kanipe felt his stomach roll over in sudden fear, until he caught a glimpse of the bright red strips of cloth fluttering wildly above the left elbows of the warriors and recognized his pursuers as some of their own Ree allies. There were also a few of the "friendly" Sioux who had joined the Army, he imagined to pay back their tribesmen for some petty grievances. The Indian scouts were not in the least interested in Kanipe but rather intent on driving a small herd of captured Sioux ponies back toward the pack train.

Heaving a great sigh of relief, Kanipe nudged his mount off to the side of the trail and let the shrieking and jubilant raiders thunder past him, driving their booty ahead of them at a full gallop. When the scouts had disappeared over the next rise, Sergeant Kanipe waited for a moment for the dust to drift away and then started back down the trail. In the cloud of dust that had drifted across the trail, he had completely missed the passage of another horseman headed the other way.

Boston Custer had seen the onrush of Indian scouts and dodged nimbly around to their south so that as the scouts were passing Kanipe, who was going west, Boston was on the opposite side of the trail heading east toward his brother's command as fast as his pony could carry him. In the distance he could hear the pop-crack of rifle and pistol fire and was anxious to get up with the boys before he missed out on all of the fun.

A few more minutes of hard riding brought Sergeant Kanipe face-to-face with a body of mounted men that he immediately identified as Captain Benteen's battalion. Kanipe had no difficulty locating the crusty old captain, who was plodding along at the head of the column and held up his hand to bring the command to a halt as the courier dashed up to him.

"Chasing the Rees, Sergeant?" Benteen asked, his voice heavy with sarcasm. "Not enough of the Sioux left to go around, I take it?" He glanced over his shoulder at Lieutenant Gibson, who grinned easily at Benteen's droll humor. Kanipe, upon whom the joke was obviously lost, did not smile but looked curiously at the white-haired cavalryman with the sour expression.

"Oh, never mind, Sergeant," Benteen went on. "You're obviously not here on an excursion, so state your business. Quickly now."

"Y-Yes, sir," Kanipe stammered, a bit nonplussed. "The general presents his compliments—"

"Yes, Sergeant," chided Benteen, his eyes squinting, lips twisted in irony. "I'm just sure he does. Doubtless he is solicitous for my health as well."

"I beg your pardon, sir?" Kanipe was not sure, but he had a feeling that maybe the captain was trying to make some sort of joke and so he smiled somewhat uneasily.

"Nothing." Benteen sighed, shaking his head. He concluded that this sergeant was a damned dense fellow, a dullard and thus perfectly suited for one of Tom Custer's crew. "Get on with your report, Sergeant."

"Kanipe, sir, Daniel Kanipe, Company C," he said, starting over again. "The general presents his compliments and desires that you join the main command immediately, sir. We've hit a big village, sir."

"How big is this village, Sergeant Kanipe? Did you see it?"

"Yes, sir, sort of," Kanipe shot back. "We just got a glimpse of it from the ridgeline, but it was the biggest damned village I ever saw. Old Reno . . . begging your pardon, sir, Major Reno's battalion was charging in hell-bent-for-leather when I last saw 'em, sir. Should be one hell of a fight, sir!"

"Alright then, Sergeant," Benteen said. "Anything else?"

"No, sir. I'm to head back and find Captain McDougall and have him hurry the packs up across to the high ground." Kanipe finished his report and waited for Captain Benteen to respond.

"Well, then," Benteen said harshly, "I expect you'd best be on your way then, boy."

"Yes, sir!" Kanipe fired off a sharp salute and spurred his mount down the line of the battalion as he headed back to find Captain McDougall and the packtrain.

"Good luck, boys!" Kanipe called excitedly as he galloped past the dusty troopers. "They've opened the ball up ahead!" He tore off his campaign hat and waved it furiously at his comrades, who cheered and catcalled loudly as the dust-covered sergeant sped down the line.

"Better save us some coffee there, Sarge!" one called out.

"Don't go sweet-talkin' them mules, Danny Boy!" hollered another.

Kanipe smiled broadly at the good-natured ribbing and dug his spurs deeper into the flanks of his mount as he pounded down the trail toward McDougall and the packtrain.

Hearing the boisterous outbreak from the battalion, Frederick Benteen scowled blackly and waved his hand to start the outfit moving again.

"Big village indeed," Benteen mumbled to himself. "If George Custer told me the sun was shining, I'd make damned sure I had a slicker handy."

"Did you say something, sir?" Lieutenant Gibson had ridden up alongside.

"No, no, Gib," Benteen replied calmly. "Just thinking out loud, I suspect."

"Uh, sir," Gibson ventured quietly, "should I bring the outfit to the trot?"

"I can't imagine why you'd do that, Mr. Gibson. If we've a fight ahead of us, as the general seems to think, I rather think we'd do best not to arrive on the field with our mounts fagged out. I doubt the general would be very pleased with such an ill-conceived decision. Don't worry, Gib, I won't mention that you suggested such a thing."

The rebuked Gibson allowed his horse to drop back behind the battalion commander and rode along in silence and uneasy confusion. If the battle had already been joined, shouldn't they be beating a path to the sound of the guns? At least that's what they'd taught him at the Point.

Well, he thought, that may well be so, but I've learned a thing or two since I got out here on the frontier.

One of the things he had learned was that it didn't pay to second-guess Frederick Benteen. The young lieutenant turned in his saddle to look back along the column of troops as the battalion continued to move forward at a walk.

Wiatañoñmya *(In the Afternoon)*
Along the Greasy Grass

Gall scrambled out of his lodge in a burning rage. Above him the lodgepoles had been shattered by the first volley of shots, and the hides were rent by holes where the heavy lead bullets had torn through them. This would have, in any event, angered the man, but it was the second volley that had turned his heart black and put the killing rage upon him. The *wasichus*, realizing that they were shooting too high, had dropped the muzzles of their carbines for the second volley, and it was this crashing thunder of shots that had ripped directly though Gall's lodge, tearing his soul from his body.

In truth Gall lived, was untouched by the bullets, but behind the jagged strips of buffalo hide that dangled limply beneath the bullet holes, Gall's entire family, his two wives, his three children, all lay crumpled in death. The blood oozing slowly from their still-warm bodies stained buffalo robes and mixed with the dirt beneath. Like a wolf that is wounded and in pain, the Hunkpapa warrior howled eerily in a grief that turned suddenly into blind rage, throwing a red mist of hatred across his tear-filled eyes.

He started to reach for his rifle but hurled it viciously aside in favor of a more fitting weapon—a flexible willow wand to which a smooth round stone was tightly bound with strips of rawhide. For Gall there would be no sniping at his enemies from a long distance. Today nothing would satisfy him but the solid feel of his enemies' skulls being crushed beneath this club, which he would wield with his own arm. He would look his foes dead in the eye as he crushed the life from them.

"*Hiyupo!*" he screamed to the heavens, raising the club high over his head. "*Hokahe!* It is a good day to die!" He caught a pony that was rushing by riderless and swung up onto its back. Gathering the reins in his fist, Gall kicked the pony's flanks and rushed headlong into the swirling dust at the upper end of the camp.

•

Tatanka Iyotanka stood motionless outside of his lodge, seemingly unaware of the bullets that zipped and snapped around him. Everywhere Sitting Bull looked, there was confusion and terror as the people ran as if possessed by demons. Some of the men were pushing the women and children away from the lodges and pointing to the north, telling their families to run for the tablelands where the pony herds were grazing.

Women shrieked and the children tumbled, wailing in the dust as they scrambled, terrified, underfoot. The younger women and some of the men scooped up the smaller ones in their arms and rushed them away, but many of the aged ones were far too old and infirm to run and sat rooted by their lodges as the choking dust and the noise rose around them, their mouths working soundlessly. After a moment Sitting Bull discerned a high-pitched, wailing chant and realized that the old ones were singing death songs for the younger warriors.

Her-Holy-Door, as she insisted loudly and with vigor, was not about to run. Where would she go? Why should she leave her lodge for those crazy *wasichus* to shoot holes in it? Sitting Bull, who was trying his best to reason with his aged mother, was shaking his head in exasperation when his adopted son, One Bull, rode up leading several ponies and passed the lead rope of a beautiful black gelding to Sitting Bull.

"Here, Father," he yelled, "let's get the helpless ones to safety!"

Sitting Bull nodded quickly and turned to boost Her-Holy-Door, protesting loudly, up onto the back of the pony. He then did the same for one of his sisters and leaped onto the pony's back behind them.

"Stop complaining, Mother," Sitting Bull insisted. "You must look after the little ones so that we can fight these people. We don't have time to do both things."

His mother quickly ceased her scolding but soon took up chanting a death song for her son, the eerie warbling soon lost in the thunder of hooves as they galloped down through the camp toward the Cheyenne circle. One Bull and his brother White Bull helped to carry some of the women and children out of the fray, dropping them to the ground as they came up on the tablelands, where the pony herds were now being driven the other way, back into the camp, by men and boys hurrying to get into the fight.

Leaving their precious cargo in relative safety, the three men wheeled their ponies and raced back to the Hunkpapa circle, where Sitting Bull ducked into his lodge to grab his weapons. The roar of musketry and shouting was now deafening. The old man emerged and reached up to One Bull to present him with his shield, bow, and old war club.

"Here, my son," he said solemnly. "My old weapons will bring you good hunting."

One Bull was stunned. Never in his wildest dreams had he imagined that the old man would offer him his own weapons. This was indeed powerful medicine and a great honor. He didn't know what to say.

"Go on, take them, my boy," Sitting Bull insisted. "Don't be afraid. Go right in there."

The young man nodded breathlessly and snatched the weapons and shield, slinging the shield and quiver of willow shafts across his back and wrapping the leather thong of the war club around his wrist. Not knowing how to thank the *wicasa wakan*, he quickly handed down his Winchester and unbuckled a belt with a holstered revolver.

"Thank you, Father," he said earnestly. "Here, take these guns and come with us."

Sitting Bull smiled grimly as he accepted the weapons, then swung nimbly onto the back of his pony. Turning the young gelding around in a tight circle, he bellowed to the surrounding lodges, "Brave up, boys! It will be a hard time. Brave up!" Then, shrieking and whooping, the three warriors galloped off into the curtain of dust and gunsmoke that concealed the enemy soldiers.

At the far end of the camp Crazy Horse had returned to his lodge seemingly oblivious of the pandemonium that surrounded him. He and Two Moon had only had to ride halfway up the length of the valley to realize that the village was under attack. Rather than rush headlong into the fray, the two had parted company and headed back the way they had come, both of the same mind. They would gather their warriors and prepare themselves for battle. For Crazy Horse this was not a diversion but a necessary thing. One did not ride heedlessly into a fight. One must be properly painted and dressed. A warrior without his medicine was a fool and of no help to anyone.

In the amber light within his lodge, with dust motes swirling in the air like dirty snow, Taschunka Witko stripped off his shirt and, reaching into a small parfleche box, produced the mummified remains of a small red-backed hawk, which he fastened carefully in his light hair. From the same box he pulled a small, smooth pebble, which he suspended behind his left ear with a strip of sinew. Then, dipping moistened fingers into a bowl of pigment, he began to daub small white hailstones on his arms and chest, then dipped into the pigment again and drew two fingers from the top of his forehead across his right eyebrow and down his right cheek, tracing a jagged white lighting bolt on his face. When he was satisfied with his work, he wiped his fingers on a tuft of sweet grass and sat with his eyes closed, listening to the singing, outside, of one of the younger braves.

He could tell from the words of the song that the young man was a member of the Kit Fox Society.*

"Hear me, Inyan Tunkasila." The voice rang clear and strong, chanting the words:

> "I am a Fox,
> I am supposed to die
> If there is anything difficult
> If there is anything dangerous
> That is mine to do!"

Crazy Horse opened his eyes and rose to stride out from his lodge. The words the boy was singing echoed in his head, but they did not work on his heart, which had grown cold and hard. Let the young braves have their passion, he thought, slinging an eagle-bone whistle around his neck and working the action of his Winchester. He had more serious work to do today. He gathered up the reins of his spotted pony and led him to the opening in his lodge, then ducked back inside to retrieve a small leather pouch and the bowl of white pigment, which he used to dot the animal's flanks with hailstones.

Reaching into the pouch, he drew out a handful of dust gathered from a gopher hole and sprinkled it over the pony's withers and rump. The "fooling gopher dust" would serve to turn the soldiers' bullets away from the animal. Swinging lightly onto the pinto's back, he raised his rifle overhead and shrieked a war cry as a large group of Oglala braves gathered around him on their war horses.

"*Toke!* Listen to me! Be strong, my friends," he exhorted. "Make these soldiers shoot three times fast so their guns will stick and you can knock them on the head with your clubs!" The braves nodded vigorously, recalling how this had worked during the fight with Three Stars.

"Remember the helpless ones," he went on, turning his pony in a tight circle. "*Haiye!* A great day is here. It is a good day to die! *Hokahe!*"

"*Hokahe!*" The Oglalas shrieked back as Crazy Horse placed his eagle-bone whistle between his lips and, blowing it loudly in a high-pitched squeal, galloped toward the rising cloud of dust and gun smoke at the upper end of the village. The others whipped up their ponies and thundered after Crazy Horse, yipping and screeching, feathers fluttering wildly from lances, arrows nocked on bowstrings, and rifle levers clacking

---

* The Kit Fox Society was an Oglala warrior society whose members supposedly emulated the kit fox in speed and cunning. They held Inyan (literally, the spirit of the rock) in reverence and referred to him as Tunkasila, or Grandfather. During wartime the duty of the Kit Foxes was to defend the elderly and the weak or infirm.

as rounds were jacked into their breeches. *"Hokahe!"* It was a good day to die.

At the upper end of the camp Sitting Bull, One Bull, and White Bull had managed to scramble into a coulee that ran down toward the river and gave them some protection from the bullets slapping the dust around them. Sitting Bull noticed that Gall was among the warriors already gathered in the ravine. Less than an arrow's flight away they could barely make out a ragged line of dismounted soldiers who, viewed through the swirling dust and gun smoke, had the appearance of tiny, shapeless demons who were spitting small bursts of flame and belching smoke. Peering out over the top of the coulee, White Bull caught sight of a swallow-tailed pennant waving just above the fire-belching demons.

"Whoever is brave," White Bull cried out, "will capture that flag!"

White Bull waved a long, hooked coup stick at the tiny banner. At almost that same instant a volley of shots crashed from the soldiers' line, kicking up plumes of dust in front of the warriors and tumbling Chased-by-Owls, a Two Kettle brave, from his saddle, to flop limply in the dust at the bottom of the coulee. Young Bear Soldier slipped from his pony to help the man, but when he rolled him over on his back, he saw that a bullet had entered Chased-by-Owls's left temple, traveled completely through his head and carried away the man's eyeballs as it passed out the other side, so that Bear Soldier now stared directly into two gaping and empty red sockets. The young man recoiled in horror and, reeling away, vomited loudly into a clump of sagebrush. None of the other braves elected to rise to White Bull's challenge and the white men's flag was ignored.

"Hoppo!" roared Gall, whose heart was hardened. "More will die today. Brave up, boys! Let's charge those *wasichus!"*

Slapping his pony with his quirt, he scrambled up out of the coulee, screeching and whirling his war club over his head. *"Oktyee! Oktyee! Oktyee!"* Fast on his heels a swarm of warriors boiled up out of the dust, screaming, whooping, and shooting as they thundered into the curtain of dust and smoke. Lying low on the necks of their ponies, the warriors streaked over the hard-packed ground, arrows and bullets spinning away from them as they fired blindly into the brown fog of battle.

Nearing the soldiers' line, a continuous crashing of rifles shoved the mass of warriors away to careen crazily along the front of the flashing muzzles. They had galloped completely around to the other end of the blue ranks, before they wheeled around to slip behind the enemy's rear, racing madly for the soldiers' horses, which were being held by a group of terrified young troopers. Eagle-bone whistles shrieked above the din.

"Hau!" screamed One Bull. "Look! Get the horses, boys! There are more bullets in their little sacks. *Hau! Hau! He!"* A dozen braves crashed through the sagebrush, racing for the horseholders in a whirlwind of dust and flying hooves.

"Has'! No!" shrieked Gall surging into the lead. "The hell with the horses. Kill those men!"

1530 Hours
In the Valley of the Little Bighorn

Lieutenant Charles Varnum clutched the reins of his horse and led the animal behind him as he walked slowly along behind the skirmish line. Reno's troopers had spread out among the tufts of grass and sagebrush and were now kneeling in the dirt, rivulets of sweat running down their temples and pooling under their armpits as they worked the actions of their Springfields with mechanical efficiency.

Under his breath the young officer was soundly cursing a penurious Congress and War Department, which had consistently refused to budget for ammunition for marksmanship training. As a result, Varnum knew, only the veterans on the line had ever fired their weapons more than a few times a year. The lieutenant grudgingly recognized that his hope that the men would actually bring down one of the screaming warriors who flitted through the dust ahead was grounded more in a dependence on dumb luck than on actual skill.

They would just have to depend on the troopers' keeping up a steady volume of fire in the hope that a few of the flying lead projectiles would take out those warriors hapless enough to stumble into their path. At least the hours of dry-firing drill had managed to impart the mechanical functions necessary for the troopers to make the weapons fire at all. Hammer to half cock, flip open the latch, crank the trapdoor forward to eject the shell, thumb another round into the breech, crank down the trapdoor, hammer to full cock, cheek to buttstock, peer down the sights, squeeze the trigger, bang, feel the thump of the recoil, hammer to half cock, flip open the latch . . . again and again the movements were repeated as an acrid cloud of thick, bluish gray smoke rolled and eddied around the muzzle blasts.

Varnum had pulled out his revolver and felt its reassuring heft in his grasp as it hung by his side, the sweat of his palm making the wooden grips slick and warm to the touch. A glint of movement caught his attention and his gaze wandered up above the skirmish line to the bluffs just beyond and across the river, where he could just make out a column of mounted men passing over the ridgeline. The Gray Horse Troop, Company E, he thought, that would be "Fresh" Smith's men. They must be trying to move around to the flank of the village. He looked back to the skirmish line. Another few minutes, he thought, and at least the damned hostiles would have someone else to worry them for a bit. It seemed to him that things were starting to get somewhat too warm for his liking around here.

"Steady, boys," he called out with a calm he did not feel. "Mark your targets. Keep your muzzles low. Don't fire too high now." The lieutenant smiled as he considered the irony of his instructions. As if it were even possible to do much aiming at all. The dearth of marksmanship training was bad enough, but there was hardly even a decent target to draw a bead on. There was no solid wall of massed enemy battalions moving inexorably forward, bayonets fixed, disciplined, determined, and readily identifiable. Instead, the enemy was really not much more than a huge cloud of dust and smoke through which flitted hundreds of individual shadows, melting in and out of the gloom to loose streams of arrows or fire a series of blasts from repeating rifles.

He glanced over at the men in their dusty blue shirts, now almost black with sweat, and noticed that most had snatched several rounds from their pouches and thimble belts and laid them in small piles within easy reach on the ground. A couple of the older veterans had thought to remove their campaign hats, flipping them upside down in the dust and dropping their rounds into the relatively clean felt crowns. It was an old trick to reduce the chance that extra grit would be fed into the breech along with the soft copper cartridges. As he moved down the line, he saw Captain Moylan standing, legs braced apart, directly behind the troops, swearing softly to himself as he squeezed off round after round from his heavy Colt revolver into the swirling brown mass to their front. When Varnum had gotten to within a few feet of Moylan, the older man caught a glimpse of movement out of the corner of his eye and called out to the lieutenant over the roar of gunfire.

"This is one hell of a mess, ain't it, Charlie?" Moylan roared out with a grin.

Varnum waved his revolver carelessly. "Reckon so, Cap'n."

He was about to add a light comment but stopped short as Moylan's face paled visibly and the man spun toward him, the barrel of his heavy pistol swinging in an arc across Varnum's nose to discharge with a thunderous roar near the lieutenant's ear.

"In the rear!" Moylan was shouting. "Watch to the rear!"

Varnum could not actually hear what Moylan was saying, with his ears ringing loudly and the sour taste of gunpowder in his mouth, so he spun about to see what the captain had fired at and watched in horror as a dozen warriors, Winchester and Henry rifles blazing, streaked behind the skirmish line.

"They're headed for the horses!" Moylan yelled.

Acting solely out of reflex, Lieutenant Varnum swung into the saddle and spurred his mount savagely in a desperate race to reach the horses first. The horses, whose saddlebags carried the extra ammunition, were shying and rearing frantically as the terrified troopers, each with one hand tangled in the reins of four horses, were trying to hold the animals while being jerked helplessly around. Several of the youngsters were trying to work their revolvers with their free hands. Varnum leaned forward in his saddle, extending his right arm to its full length, the heavy Colt cocked and leveled. As his mount got into its full stride Varnum felt himself ease into the rhythm of the gallop and allowed the pistol to float naturally down across the flank of one of the Sioux's lead ponies. The Colt jumped in his hand and he saw the pony he'd been aiming at tumble forward into the sagebrush, pitching its rider headlong into the dirt. Varnum could tell from the angle at which the warrior hit the ground that his neck was broken. The pony struggled up and limped, dazed, toward the village, a dark ribbon of blood streaming down its left foreleg.

The stumbling pony had not disrupted the charge of the other warriors, and the lieutenant now bent low over his mount's neck to surge past the shrieking party, which was still moving toward the horse-holders. He reached his goal moments before his opponents and managed to get the cavalry mounts turned and headed for the timber along the river, their keepers tugging them behind as they ran breathlessly across the hardpan. The only thing that saved Varnum from being overtaken and clubbed from his horse was the timely arrival of three of his scouts, White Swan, Bob-tailed Bull, and Half-Yellow-Face, who galloped screaming out of the timber, their carbines leveled at the onrushing Sioux.

As if on a signal, the three scouts discharged their weapons in a thunderous volley just as the Sioux did likewise, shrouding the entire scene in a cloud of dense, rolling gun smoke and dust. Reaching the timber, Varnum slid from the saddle, whirled, and, dropping to one knee, held his Colt out at full length to meet the charge of Sioux warriors. It was then that he noticed the swirling dust cloud that vibrated with the screaming of wounded horses and men. Moments later the figures of Bob-tailed Bull, Half-Yellow-Face, and White Swan plunged out of the dust, their ponies dancing wildly as the scouts screeched over their shoulders and shook their rifles triumphantly at the unseen Sioux.

"Come on, boys!" Varnum shouted hoarsely as he squeezed off a blind shot into the smoky haze behind the scouts. Bob-tailed Bull grinned and brandished his carbine in the air as the three horsemen bounded into the line of timber to make for a small clearing halfway to the river.

One Bull looked around dazed as the dust and smoke swirled crazily around him. His friend Black Moon lay sprawled in the dust, his vacant eyes staring sightlessly into the sky. There was nothing to be done for him, but Good-Bear-Boy was still alive and crawling painfully away from his pony, which was thrashing wildly in its death throes. One Bull dropped quickly to his friend's side and hoisted the grimacing youth onto the back of his own pony. The young man had been shot clean through both of his thighs and the thick, warm blood made his legs slick and hard to grab onto.

"Come on, Good-Bear-Boy," One Bull urged, "help me get you onto this pony."

The younger man grunted and used his elbows to try to lever himself over the back of the animal. With the wounded man slumped securely over the pony's withers, One Bull leaped up behind him and urged the skittish pinto back toward the Hunkpapa circle.

Gall, whose pony had been shot from under him, glanced around quickly and seized the reins of a riderless horse that was cantering past him. From the look of the blood-spattered, high backed saddle, he thought this animal must have belonged to a Cheyenne. Those Shyelas were notoriously good lancemen, and they said that the high saddle helped them to use a lance more efficiently. Gall grabbed the pommel and hauled himself up, then yanked the horse's head around as he looked to gather a group of warriors for another charge.

As Gall was using the dust to cover his escape, Lieutenant Varnum was busy trying to get the horses moved farther back into the timber, where they could be kept from the clutches of the Sioux. Normally it was the sergeants who were the horse-holders, but since there was a dearth of steady marksmen in the outfit, the sergeants had remained on the line. The young troopers who had been designated as horse-holders in their place were the rawest of recruits and were noticeably shaken by their close call. Varnum saw that their eyes rolled violently in their pale faces, some with mouths hanging open slackly and others with their jaws clenched tightly in a fear that bordered on panic.

Not a good sign, he thought anxiously to himself. If any of them broke and started to run, they could have a damn rout on their hands. The lieutenant knew just enough about fighting Indians to know that to run in a fight like this one was an invitation to disaster. He'd just have to put up a bold front to try to keep the youngsters from skipping on him.

I could sure use a little of Custer's Luck about now, he thought.

Varnum dropped the Colt back into its holster and strode easily among the troops, checking cinch straps and curb chains, slapping one horse gently on the flank, blowing easily in the nose of another, as he chatted absently with the young men who seemed as pale and insubstantial as ghosts, flinching at every zip of a bullet through the trees overhead.

"Don't forget to check your loads, boys," he said calmly. "May need to bang out another round or two before the day's done, you know. Mr. Lo can be a persistent sort of a cuss when he's a mind to."

He grinned wryly as he threaded his way among the men, really no more than boys, many of whom were now longing desperately for the verdant cool of Galway or the snug warmth of a kitchen in Bremerhaven, the smell of cabbage boiling on the stove and salt air wafting through an open window, and wondering why they had ever left home. The lieutenant himself, if truth be known, was thinking that the bone cold of a Massachussetts winter with the scent of maple syrup on the boil seemed a damned attractive alternative about now. He shook his head to clear it of such idle thoughts. There was simply too much to do, he reminded himself sharply, to start daydreaming right now.

Suddenly the woods echoed to a thunderous crash as the skirmish line fired off a volley, and Varnum heard the shouting of the officers as he turned just in time to see the skirmish line begin to fold in on itself. The battalion was dropping steadily back toward the cover of the timber. Moylan's people held the far right, nearest the river, and pivoted as the rest of the outfit wheeled around to form a sort of an L-shape along the edge of the grove.

Out on the prairie the dust was boiling beyond the far end of the ranks as yet another party of Sioux charged recklessly toward the troops. As he watched, Bob-tailed Bull, who had been serving as his first sergeant for the Ree scouts, plunged past him out into the open at a full gallop, reloading and firing his carbine with incredible speed. Varnum realized that the man was covering the withdrawal of the left of the line, now hard-pressed by the onrushing Sioux.

The lieutenant hastily lashed his horse to a tree and sprinted out to the edge of the wood line, drawing his Colt as he ducked through the trees and underbrush. He reached the open just as a volley of gunshots erupted from the Sioux and in time to see Bob-tailed Bull's pony rear violently in a cloud of gun smoke. The Ree scout thudded heavily to the ground like a loose sack of grain, his head bouncing on the hard-packed soil. Dark blood pooled quickly around the man's body. From the chunks of flesh that lay scattered and hanging in nearby sagebrush, Varnum guessed that Bob-tailed Bull must have caught the full force of the volley square in the chest. Damn it!

The chief of scouts raised his revolver but before he could thumb back the hammer, he was distracted by a screeching "Ki-yi-yi!" that rose to mingle with the shrill keening of the eagle-bone whistles. He looked to his left to see the scout White Swan charging headlong toward a bonneted Cheyenne warrior. The gap between the two duelists closed at incredible speed as the hooves of their ponies churned through the sagebrush, each aiming his rifle directly at the other. A split second later both weapons discharged with a roar that sent both Indians plunging into the dust.

The Cheyenne jerked spasmodically for a moment and lay still, the fluttering feathers of his bonnet covering his blood-smeared face. White Swan too was on his back in the dirt, but soon rolled himself painfully over and began using his elbows to drag himself slowly back toward the timber. There was a large red stain spreading over one thigh and leaving a dark streak in the sand as the scout slithered haltingly toward him, and Varnum could see that the man's left hand had been all but shot away, the arm ending in a bloody mess from which the fingers dangled precariously by the odd scrap of skin and sinew. Immediately the wounded man's friend, Half-Yellow-Face, darted into the open and dropped to one knee in the dust next to White Swan, firing his pistol blindly into the cloud of smoke and dust that roiled around the dead Cheyenne.

"Half-Yellow-Face!" Varnum shouted. "Run back! I'll cover you!" and he stepped into the clearing, his Colt bucking violently in his hand as the Crow gathered his injured friend and half-dragged, half-carried him back into the relative shelter of the wood line. By this time the rest of the command had slipped back from the skirmish line and spread out along the edge of the timber, where they continued to bang away with their Springfields, augmenting Varnum's efforts to cover the scouts' agonizingly slow retreat.

This is not working out well, Gall thought as he tried to control his pony, which was crow-hopping wildly after having had a hole drilled clean through one of its ears by a bullet from Varnum's pistol. He managed to turn the animal back toward the village and raced to get out of range of the soldiers' guns. The Cheyenne—Gall thought his name was Whirlwind —had had half of his face torn away by the Crow's shot, and the man's blood was splashed across Gall's cheek and forehead in large red spots. He wiped the Cheyenne's blood from one eye as he hurried away, considering his next move. Slipping through the covering dust cloud, he looked down at the ground that the soldiers' line had occupied and noticed with disgust that not a single *wasichu's* body had been left behind stretched out on the prairie. He snarled in anger and glanced toward the village.

Sitting Bull, Gall thought savagely, you old fool! This is what your pride has brought us. Our children killed, our young men dying in the dust, and damned *wasichus* we can't seem to kill!

1536 Hours
On the Bluffs
Above the Little Bighorn River

Mitch Bouyer looked back down the steep slope to see Lieutenant Colonel Custer bounding up the slope, lying low over his mount's neck. The man was obviously in a hurry to join Bouyer and the four Crow scouts, who had slipped off to the left to get yet another view of the hostile encampment. Bouyer wondered idly what the general's reaction would be once he got a sight of the village from this vantage point. He did not think it would be a pleasant moment. It certainly hadn't been for him. The ride up from the ford where Reno's people had crossed the river had finally given him and the Crows this fairly unobstructed view of the village. What a shock it had been to realize that whatever they had seen before had been mere glimpses of a few of the camp circles, just a fraction of what was a far larger encampment, larger in fact than anyone could have imagined in their worst nightmare. What was it the soldiers had guessed? Four hundred lodges? Even Bouyer could tell at a glance that there were well over a thousand lodges in that valley. And he figured he hadn't seen half of what was really down there.

The entire valley floor was one large camp sprawling for miles and miles. Bouyer could hear the heavy gunfire drifting up from below and now knew that Reno must be fighting for his life. The poor bastard probably still had no idea how many Sioux were massed and on their way. Bouyer knew what Custer would do. Would have to do. The old man had committed Reno to this fight and would have to try his best to pull him out of it. There was no way out that Bouyer could see. The others might not realize it yet. They probably wouldn't figure it out until it was too late, but this, as far as the scout was concerned, was as plain as fresh hoofprints in new-fallen snow.

It was such a shame, Bouyer mused. He had so loved this country and the life it had allowed him to lead, one of luxurious freedom and independence. He loved these people and now it was over. He missed the grand days he had spent with John and Louis Richard and "Big Bat" Pouirer when they had first hunted this area with Jim Bridger and run messages for the soldiers when the first forts were built. Oh, they'd had their scraps with the Sioux before but nothing they couldn't patch up afterward. For the most part, the Sioux had let 'em be when they weren't on a killing spree or in a generally nasty mood, which lately had become a more frequent occurrence, but mostly they had all given each other a fairly wide berth. That was all finished now. Mostly he would miss Magpie Outside and the children.

They would be sad when he didn't come back. She was a good woman. Probably better than he could have hoped for, a good wife, a fine mother. Tom LeForge would have to tell her what happened and he knew it would be hard on old Tom, but he would do what he had to, what he had promised. He would make sure she was cared for—and the children. A bad business this. He looked up to see the Crows watching him and could see that they knew what was going to happen, but before he could say anything, Custer rode up to them and had his first real look at the enemy he was facing.

"Good God in heaven!" Custer sat his horse, open-mouthed, staring in disbelief at the size of the village that stretched out below them. "I never could have imagined . . ."

"None of us could, General," Bouyer said quietly, although to himself he thought, Except for the Crows and Rees who tried to tell ya!

Custer looked over at the scout but saw that there was no reproach in the man's tone nor, more important, in his eyes. Custer looked away again down into the madness of the valley floor.

"Reno's fighting like hell down there." Bouyer's voice again, softly and matter-of-fact.

Custer nodded briefly, swallowing hard and taking in a huge breath. He looked at the Crow scouts, who sat their ponies quietly and waited for his instructions. It seemed that there was no emotion playing over their faces, but he thought he detected a quiet air of resignation in their eyes. Such handsome men, he thought, strong, noble faces that spoke of bravery, determination, and a fierce pride. Yes, these were men he could respect, but where he would have to go, he did not think he could ask them to follow, knowing full well that if he asked they would do so without hesitation. Custer flushed suddenly, still angry over his last encounter with

Bloody Knife. What the hell could have gotten into him and the other Rees? They were acting like a bunch of skittish schoolgirls.

"Mitch," he said finally, "I want to talk to them." Bouyer nodded and called the Crows over so that they could hear the general's words even as he translated for him.

"*Ä hahé ak'tsì'te!* * Boys," Custer said loudly, his chin in the air, shoulders thrust back, "you have done what I wanted you to do and your job is finished."

The Crows looked at him curiously and then at each other as Custer went on.

"You have done a good job here. If we win this battle today, you will all be famous men in the Crow nation. If I am killed, well, you will still get this land back and live on it forever."

As Bouyer translated, the Crows sat their horses nodding silently. This was strange talk from Son-of-the-Morning-Star, they concluded. He was talking like he was a Crazy Dog,† as if he no longer wished to live.

"I don't know if I will pass through this battle," Custer said. "If I do, I will recommend all of you and you will be much honored. My other scouts are worthless. The Rees are acting like women, but you have found the enemy for me. Even if the Sioux massacre me, they will not win, for they have disobeyed the Great Father in Washington and they will be punished and you will have this land back. You have found the Sioux for me, but now it is time for the soldiers to fight them. This is not your fight, and I want you to go back to the packtrain."

He nodded to Bouyer to indicate that he was finished, and after the scout had translated his last words, he leaned over in his saddle to say quietly: "That goes for you too, Mitch. Might as well go on and get yourself out of here."

Hairy Moccasin, Goes Ahead, and White-Man-Runs-Him moved their ponies forward and each shook hands solemnly with the general before turning back down the slope and riding slowly back toward where the packtrain was thought to be. Only Bouyer and the young Crow named Curley remained behind. Custer looked at them curiously.

---

* "Well done, Scouts!"

† Crazy Dog was a Crow warrior society that embraced a fighting style not unlike that of the Viking Berserker. It was a very exclusive group and was often called upon to perform the function of camp police. A portion of this group might elect to become the even more eccentric Crazy-Dog-Wishing-to-Die. This was one who had sworn to fight to the death whatever the odds and behaved in a reckless and contrary fashion, much like the Lakota Heyoka, and vowed to ride in among the enemy to strike the first coup, deliberately courting death.

"Go on, Mitch." Custer smiled. "Get out of here, get some rest. I expect we'll be through here in a couple of hours."

Bouyer shook his head slowly. "Come this far, General," he said, "figure a bit longer won't hurt all that much. Kinda interested in what yer gonna do next."

George Custer looked into the scout's eyes but could not read anything there. The man was as composed and nonchalant as if there was nothing particularly unusual about the circumstances. Glancing at the young Crow, Custer asked if he was going after his friends or not. The boy Curley sat there on his pony, his face set, and shook his head at Custer's gestured question.

"Curley's his own man, I guess, General." Bouyer answered for the boy. "He ain't seen much fighting yet and probably figures he can't start off without getting a bit of experience first."

"Hell, Mitch, he's just a damned youngster," Custer insisted quietly. "You ought to run him off."

Bouyer looked at Curley and then back at the general.

"Can't do it, General," he said slowly. "Besides, he ain't much younger'n about half of them boys back down in that coulee yonder." Bouyer nodded in the direction where Captain Keogh was waiting with the main command.

Custer again shook his head. "Alright," he said. "If you fellows want to hang around a bit longer, you might as well make yourselves useful. Stay up here for a while and keep your eyes open. Make sure our friends down there don't get up to any mischief." Bouyer nodded.

Custer shook his head at their obstinancy. He'd thought they'd want to take a short rest and catch up on their sleep while the rest of the outfit finished up with the Sioux, but he figured they were entitled to make their own choices. He just hoped they wouldn't regret them a bit later.

Well, there were other things to think about right now. He had to figure a way to take some of the pressure off of Reno and buy enough time to get the rest of the outfit up with the spare ammunition. If he could just get most of the outfit back together, they should be able to swing around behind these ridges and hit the Sioux hard enough in the flank or the rear to take all the fight out of 'em. Then it would just be a matter of keeping them corralled until Gibbon's people could get into the lower end of the valley. After that it would be a relatively simple thing to start 'em all back toward the reservation.

Well, whatever they did, they'd have to be damn quick about it. He turned Vic around and let him pick his way back down the rock-strewn slope, and allowed his mind to turn over the various possibilities. He had to decide quickly. But whatever he did, he'd have to put on as bold a front as possible. The Sioux were probably pretty well stirred up by now and, with as many of them as there were, half-measures would be as bad as none at all. They might take it for a sign of weakness and try to resist or just scatter for the hills before he had time to reorganize the outfit. If any of the troops wavered for even a moment, it could be disastrous.

Well, he'd certainly been in tricky situations before, and in virtually every case it had been the bold move that had unbalanced the enemy just long enough to allow him to strike the decisive blow. It had worked at Aldie and Winchester and had broken J. E. B. Stuart's people at Yellow Tavern. One of the troopers had even managed to kill Stuart himself at that one. And it had saved the command from almost certain disaster at Washita. Audacity! What was it that Danton had said? *"L'Audace, et encore l'Audace, et toujours l'Audace!"* *

Keogh, Tom Custer, and Cooke had gathered at the head of the column and were talking together in low tones, wondering what was happening, when George Custer scrambled up alongside and called Cooke over to his side.

"Cookey," he said, speaking levelly but with a sense of urgency, "send the orderly back to Benteen. He's to ride as fast as he can. He's to tell Benteen we've hit a big village, come quickly and bring the packs with him. Make sure he brings up the packs! We've got one hell of a fight brewing and we're going to need lots of ammunition. That should get his attention. Old Benteen may be a porcupine of a fellow, but I've never known him to dawdle when there's a chance he can get his hands bloody." He grinned at Keogh and Tom as Cooke bent over his small notebook and scribbled hastily with his pencil.

Cooke ripped the sheet of paper from the small book and folded it carefully, then called to Orderly Trumpeter Private John Martin.

"Martin! Come over here!" he shouted.

As Martin came up, Cooke handed him the note and explained his instructions carefully.

"Martin, you're to take this dispatch directly to Captain Benteen. Take our back trail and ride as fast as you can. Come back if you can, but if there's any danger, you go ahead and remain with your company once you get there. Is that clear?"

Martin nodded quickly as he took the note in a grimy hand.

"All right then, son," Cooke said. "Off you go and be quick about it.

* *"Audacity, and again audacity, and always audacity!"*

We don't want these Sioux to skedaddle and scatter. Go on." Martin saluted and wheeled his horse around to scramble back up the coulee they had just descended a few minutes before.

Custer, who had been joined by Autie Reed and the reporter Kellogg, watched as Martin headed toward the mouth of the coulee, then swung Vic around and called out to the column.

"Courage, boys! We have got 'em!" he shouted. "As soon as we get through, we'll return to our station!"

Martin slipped easily over the rise to level ground and jabbed his spurs into the flanks of his horse just as he heard the voices of the men still with the general erupt into a raucous cheering that echoed up from the coulee behind him. Lieutenant Cooke's note was stuffed securely in his pocket.

1540 Hours
Above Cedar Coulee

Private Gustave Korn was closer to tears than he had been since he first left his home in Germany. Schatz had somehow managed to pick up a sharp rock shard that imbedded itself deeply in the quick of her right forehoof, causing her to go lame within moments. For a few seconds Gussy thought that she had just stumbled and allowed herself to be nudged out of the way by the rest of the column, but it soon became apparent that something was seriously wrong with her hoof. Gussy slipped out of the saddle and watched in frustration as Sergeant Bustard and the rest of the fellows in Company I trotted up over the rise and out of sight. The Lehman boys were thoroughly caught up in the excitement of the moment, and Henry called out laughing as he passed by.

"Guess you'd best let Schatz ride you for a bit, Gussy."

Paddy was at least more helpful and dropped back alongside to wait for his bunky.

"What's the problem, Gussy? Is she alright? I can wait a bit fer ye."

Gustave appreciated Paddy's concern, but after examining Schatz's hoof, he saw clearly that she was lame and would never be able to catch up with the rest of the outfit. He shook his head glumly and motioned for Paddy to go on ahead without him.

"*Nein*, Paddy," he croaked. "*Mein* Schatz, she's done hurt bad. I see what I can do and mebbe we catch up with you in a bit, *ja?* You best to go mit der fellers—we be okay."

Paddy Kelly was unsure of what to do as he glanced back over his shoulder at the company's dust cloud. He didn't want to leave Gussy behind, but then he sure as hell didn't want to be stuck out here in the middle of nowhere. For a moment his loyalty to Gussy made him hesitate, but this was quickly overtaken by his fear of being left alone in this wilderness even if accompanied by his bunky. Even less did he relish the idea of being chewed on by Sergeant Bustard for hanging back in a fight. He quickly rationalized to himself that the rest of the outfit was coming up with the packtrain pretty soon and Gussy would probably be fine. Besides, there were several other fellows strung out here on the back trail whose horses had also either come up lame or simply fagged out. There were enough fellows to keep Gussy company for a few minutes, and maybe they would indeed all catch up with him in a few minutes. Leaning over, he rubbed Schatz gently between her ears, nodded to Gussy, and turned back to gallop after the rest of the company.

Gussy, who was consumed with removing the stone from Schatz's hoof, never considered that he had been left somewhat exposed until he looked up from his work and glanced around him. The sun was beating down mercilessly from overhead, and the countryside—barren, brown, and dusty—stretched for miles in all directions. He listened to the sound of fighting that drifted up from the valley, a strange pop-thump-crackling noise as if someone's barn had caught fire and the corn stored there for the animals had caught in the blaze and was popping and whuffing off in all directions. Despite the heat, Gussy suddenly felt a terrible chill run down his spine. Schatz whinnied plaintively and backed away, tugging at the reins.

"There, there, Schatz," Korn said soothingly. "Easy, girl, we get you out of here, you bet. Dem redskins is still a ways off, okay."

"Hey, Korn! Is that you?"

Gussy looked around quickly and breathed a sigh of relief as another trooper plodded wearily out of the dust cloud, his horse trailing along behind listlessly. As the man came closer, Gussy recognized "Pistol Pete" Thompson, a private who was assigned to Tom Custer's Company C. Thompson's hat was shoved toward the back of his head, and sweat seemed to ooze from the man's every pore.

"Damn, Gussy, it's hotter'n hell itself out here."

"Ja, I suppose," Korn replied slowly. "But, it probably be a mite hotter for dem fellers down there, you bet."

Thompson looked over toward the bluff that hid the valley from view and from behind which came the staccato rattle of gunfire and distant whooping. It must be one hell of a fight to be able to raise so much dust that it seemed to hang in the air just beyond the edge of the bluff like it did. Thompson shook his head.

"Damn," Thompson said. "I guess old Reno's sure got his hands full down there. Poor little fella's probably browned his damn trousers pretty good by now."

Thompson snickered to himself, and Gussy was unsure of what to say. He was fairly shocked by Thompson's irreverent attitude toward a superior officer. Back in Germany no private soldier would even consider making such a remark, even if there wasn't anyone around to hear him. This irreverence was something that Korn was not yet used to, and it made him a little uncomfortable although, at the same time, it did have a strange sort of appeal to it—the fact that even the lowliest private would consider himself a proper judge of the character of his betters, as if he didn't recognize them as better at all but only different, and either more or less competent than he—it was intoxicating.

"Well, Gussy," Thompson went on, "I think we'd better see if we can get the hell back out o' the way a bit. If old Reno or Moylan scares any of them Sioux up thisaway, I sure as hell don't want to be standin' out here in the goddamn open with my thumb up my ass. What say we find us a good place to lay low for a bit?"

Korn nodded quickly. Thompson might be an insubordinate soldier, but he was probably not stupid, and there was a good deal of sense in what he said about being caught out in the open if the Sioux did happen to come along while they were separated from the rest of the outfit.

Gussy wrapped Schatz's reins around his left hand and shifted his carbine up from where it hung at his right side, suspended by the sling that crossed over his broad chest. He unsnapped the weapon from its swivel and flipped open the breech, blew the dust out of it, and reached around his back to slide a cartridge out of his thimble belt, then thumbed the round into the weapon and snapped it shut with a loud click.

He had reached far around behind for the cartridge, thinking that if they did happen to get into a serious scrape, the rounds that were closer to the front of the belt would be a hell of a lot easier to get to in a hurry. He noticed that Thompson had slung his carbine over his saddle and instead slipped the heavy Colt out of its holster. Pistol Pete had never been very comfortable with the Springfield anyway, and besides, the damned Colt held six rounds to the carbine's one. It was a thought the young private found particularly appealing, especially now.

As the two men started down the back trail, they noticed a small cloud of dust heading up to meet them. From the size of the cloud it was probably a single rider moving at a fairly good clip. The fact that Thompson was alongside was comforting to Gussy, but he wasn't about to take any chances and he dropped to one knee, bringing the carbine up to his cheek and hauling back the hammer to full cock. If it was a damned redskin, he'd have to be awful damned good and quick to get away from Gustave Korn. Thompson fingered his pistol nervously and sidled over behind his mount, just in case he needed to use the animal as a sort of breastwork, peering uneasily down the trail. Just then the lone rider popped over a small rise, and Thompson immediately recognized him as Captain Custer's brother Boston, who had been back with the packtrain.

Boston Custer never slackened his pace but came straight toward the two men who were halted in the middle of the trail. One of them appeared to be hiding behind his horse.

"Hello, boys!" Boston shouted. "Where's the general?"

The stocky little fellow with the carbine quickly lowered the weapon and stood up straight, pointing past a small rise behind the two. Custer didn't stop but tossed a quick wave to them and hurried off toward the rest of the outfit.

Poor fellows must've had their horses give out on 'em, he thought, clucking silently to himself. Too bad they would miss out on all the excitement. Well, that's just a couple more redskins for me, he chuckled. Damned if he was going to let Armstrong, Tom, and Autie Reed have all the fun—the greedy little beggars. He knew darn well that if he'd hung back with the packtrain the whole fight'd be over and done and he'd be the butt of their ribbing for months, if not years, to come. Well, he certainly wasn't having any of that, no, sir!

Boston heard the banging of shots coming up from the valley and spurred his little pony forward. Well, boys, he thought, Boston Custer ain't gonna miss out on this little donnybrook. He surged up the slight rise and almost collided head-on with another rider who was hurrying back toward where Boston had left the two stragglers.

The trooper reined up sharply and tried to apologize in broken English, continually touching the brim of his hat and referring to him as "Your honor." Boston just smiled and waved it off.

"That's alright, trooper," he said lightly. "Where's the general?"

The young trooper smiled nervously. "He's down thataway, sir!" Martin stammered as Boston broke into a wide smile and galloped off toward the command. Martin swallowed heavily and turned to continue down the back trail. Damn! He had almost knocked the general's brother off of his horse. He wasn't sure, but he didn't think that would look very good. Luckily, Boston Custer hadn't seemed even to notice. The young man on the pony was obviously much more interested in catching up with the rest of the outfit. John Martin breathed a heavy sigh of relief and congratulated himself on being a very lucky man. He had no idea how lucky he really was.

1550 Hours
In the Timber Along the Little Bighorn

As far as Charley Reynolds was concerned, things could hardly look much worse than they did now. Here they were, holed up in this damned brush pile with more goddamned Indians screeching and scooting about than he'd ever seen in one place in his life. A cloud of acrid gunsmoke, trapped by the canopy of cottonwood leaves, drifted among the ash saplings and the combatants like a dense morning fog. He and Fred Gerard had managed to slip back off of the firing line for a few minutes and were busily checking the loads of their rifles. Gerard had a nice Henry repeater, and Reynolds had somehow managed to get hold of a Spencer from one of the bandsmen back at the Yellowstone. He liked the fact that it fired the heavier .50-caliber round. Also that you could load seven shots up the tubular magazine and fire as quickly as you could work the action.

Gerard yelled out that he figured there were probably a lot of young troopers here who were wishing like hell that the Army hadn't rejected the rapid-fire Spencers, Winchesters, and Henrys because they "tended to waste ammunition." Charley spit into the thick grass and observed acidly that the Sioux at least had apparently not been restrained by some pea-brained, bean-counting, procurement officer in Washington and were not in the least concerned about wasting ammunition. Thousands of rounds were even now popping and zipping through the trees all around them. He looked over at Gerard, who ducked as a small cottonwood limb, cut by a Sioux bullet, dropped down across the man's shoulder.

"Son of a bitch!" Gerard swore. "It's getting mighty hot hereabouts, Charley."

Reynolds nodded grimly as he jammed a couple more rounds into the loading tube of his Spencer and noticed with alarm that he didn't have much more than a dozen rounds left in his saddlebags. He thought he'd best start looking around for one of those Springfields pretty soon. The way things were going, there should be a couple of spares lying about any time now. At least there might be a bit more ammunition to go around for them. But this hope was quickly dampened with the loud cries that began drifting back from the firing line at the edge of the timber.

"Ammunition! Bring up some more ammunition!"

Moylan and some of the other officers were yelling over their shoulders—a sure sign that supplies were running low up on the line. Reynolds caught a glimpse of movement out of the corner of his eye and noticed Lieutenant Varnum shepherding several of the horse-holders and their charges up toward Moylan's position as a couple of men slipped back to meet them, snatching handfuls of cartridges from the saddlebags. Damn. They were dipping into the reserves already. No, not a good sign at all.

Second Lieutenant Benny Hodgson was close to going into shock. The jovial young officer, usually so full of fun and always ready with a good story, had gone into this action full of excitement and anticipation, emotions that had quickly been overwhelmed by confusion, uncertainty, and fear. It was not supposed to be this way. They were supposed to be chasing the Sioux, not the other way around. Now they were hunkered down in a tangle of trees and underbrush, firing blindly into a wall of dust through which shadowy figures leapt and cavorted. The Sioux were screaming at the top of their lungs and blowing those maddening little whistles, which overlay the booming of rifle and pistol fire with an earsplitting screech. Looking down at his Colt revolver, he swung open the loading gate and worked the extractor rod furiously to eject the spent shells. He reached into the black leather cap box at his waist, fished out the last five rounds that he had, and tried without much success to jam them into the smoking chambers of the heavy pistol. To his panicked mind the cartridges seemed to have swelled to three times their normal size and simply would not slide into the tiny chambers, but the truth was that his hand was shaking so violently that the soft noses of the bullets clattered ineffectually against the revolver's cylinder. It was only with the greatest effort that the young officer was able finally to jam his last few rounds into the weapon.

Benny Hodgson's mouth tasted funny to him, both bone-dry and wet at the same time, and suffused with a strange taste that reminded him of rusty iron. The men around him, who were all especially fond of the inexperienced and easygoing Hodgson, would likely have noticed the small trickle of red running out of the corner of his mouth had they not been so busy with their own concerns. Few would have realized what had caused the young officer to bleed so. In fact, Benny Hodgson himself would have been surprised to know that he had bitten nearly completely through his own lip in his fear.

•

"Damn it all to hell!" Moylan swore loudly. "We're damn near out of ammunition, Charlie. Where the hell is Benteen and the goddamn pack-train, for Christ's sake?"

Lieutenant Varnum, who didn't have the answer to the captain's question in any event, didn't bother to answer but squeezed off another shot from the carbine he had snatched from one of the horse-holders. He was rewarded by the sight of a young Sioux buck being knocked over backward by the impact of the heavy slug. He worked the Springfield's action violently while rummaging through his pockets for another round and swore softly to himself, oblivious to Captain Moylan's tirade just three feet away.

Bloody Knife was under no illusions that he would survive this fight. He had merely resolved to take as many Lakota with him as possible—and one in particular. No one really knew the depths of his hatred for these people, and many would probaby have been surprised to learn that the Ree was himself half-Sioux. His father had in fact been Hunkpapa, a friend of Sitting Bull's, and Bloody Knife had spent his boyhood with these very people whose circle was now a few hundred yards away. For Custer's friend and trusted scout this was a homecoming he had long desired. He had hated his childhood, for the Hunkpapas, a vain and arrogant clan, could be spiteful and vicious. No one knew this better than Bloody Knife, who as a child had been beaten, kicked, spit upon, and ridiculed by the other boys, especially the one called Gall.

For reasons that Bloody Knife had never understood, Gall had nurtured a burning hatred of the young boy whose mother was a foreigner—a Ree. Throughout the child's life it was Gall who had always been the leader of the others when they attacked the young half-breed, beating him with switches or bows, slapping him and leaving his nose bloody and his eyes blackened and puffy. When Bloody Knife had tried years later to visit his aging father, it was Gall who had tried to kill him, in violation even of the camp's own rules of hospitality. And it was Gall, frustrated by the *akicita* in his attempt to kill Bloody Knife, who had vented his rage on the Ree's two younger brothers. The vengeful Hunkpapa, leading a small war party, had lay in wait for the boys who had wandered from their village to hunt rabbits. Almost within sight of their mother's lodge Gall had supervised their torture, delighting in prolonging the agony of the youngsters. When he had finished, he ripped their corpses into small pieces and left them for the wolves to devour.

Now Bloody Knife smiled. He had finally had his revenge and, even as the Sioux bullets cut through the trees around him, he could not help but smile as he thought of his coup. When Reno's command first charged down the valley, Bloody Knife was anxious to even the score with Gall. While the other scouts were busy cutting into the Sioux pony herd, Bloody Knife had made straight for the home of his enemy. Leading a small party of Ree scouts to within a few yards of the village, he pointed out to them Gall's lodge in the Hunkpapa circle. It was not hard to find, for the man was an arrogant braggart as well as a bully, and the paintings on the lodge proclaimed to all: "This is the lodge of Gall. A great warrior! A great hunter! A ruthless slayer of enemies! Look at all of my great deeds!"

A ruthless slayer of women and defenseless boys would be nearer the truth, Bloody Knife thought. The four Rees slipped quietly through the brush at the edge of the timber and found a spot where it was impossible to miss their target. Bloody Knife, Forked Horn, Young Hawk, and Goose had fired all together into the side of Gall's lodge and exalted to hear the screaming and moaning that had issued from behind the shredded hides as the smoke curled from the end of their carbines. Bloody Knife didn't know if he had hit that dog of a Lakota, but he indulged himself by imagining the Hunkpapa with a ragged, festering wound that would cause him to linger in unbearable pain as he died. He would probably have taken grim satisfaction in the knowledge that while Gall had not been wounded, the volley had destroyed everything and everyone the Hunkpapa loved, and had torn the man's heart as surely as if Bloody Knife had put a bullet through it.

Riding alongside the vengeful Bloody Knife, Major Marcus Albert Reno was in a quandary. What was he supposed to do now? Custer had said he would support him with the whole outfit, but where the hell was he? Reno kept slipping off to the upstream end of the position and scanning the plains for some sign of the rest of the regiment. The valley behind him was empty except for the shrieking Sioux, who rolled back and forth on all sides, spitting bullets and willow-wand shafts that whispered past him through the trees.

Oh, God, he thought, what the hell am I supposed to do now?

There were not nearly enough men to hold this godforsaken woodpile, and now he could hear the men screaming for more cartridges. He sniffed the air and detected some new smells—the unmistakable odor of wood-smoke and the sweet scent of burning sage. Good God, the Sioux must've set fire to the brush. They were trying to burn them out. This was all so wrong. Reno hunkered in his saddle as an arrow shushed by and stuck quivering in a nearby cottonwood.

They'd have to get out of here. Get to a place where they could pull in tighter. Get away from these damned shrieking demons. Reno started looking back toward the river and up at the bluffs beyond.

Maybe if we could get to some high ground, he thought. Maybe we could get linked up with Benteen's people and get dug in where we could see these bastards to shoot at 'em.

Bloody Knife, who thought that the soldiers were doing fairly well where they were, glanced over at the round-faced Little Soldier Chief and knew immediately that things were about to change for the worse.

"*Mount!*" Reno screamed the order as loud as he could.

But the word came out as sort of a hoarse croaking sound, and only the few soldiers in the immediate vicinity even heard the major's rasping command. Most of the battalion, scattered throughout the timber and all but deafened by the continuous thumping of the heavy carbines, heard little more than their own labored breathing and the rush of blood through their ears. Bloody Knife saw the soldiers nearby scramble back from the firing line and grab the reins of their horses from startled younger troopers.

Fools, Bloody Knife thought angrily. This is madness. With the Lakotas this close, if we show any sign of weakness, the Head-Cutters will swarm over us like maggots on a buffalo carcass. He knew he had to stop the Little Soldier Chief from running. The Ree scout reached out and seized Reno's arm in an iron grasp, shaking him violently.

"If you run—" Bloody Knife began, but never finished the sentence. A .44-caliber rifle slug punched through behind the scout's left ear, traversed his brain, and exploded the right side of his face in a red mist of flesh, bone fragments, blood, and brain tissue. It sprayed outward in a vaguely circular pattern to splatter the face and chest of Major Marcus Reno, carrying away the man's straw hat and filling his open mouth with blood and gray matter. The scout's body remained upright in his saddle for a moment and then toppled heavily to the ground. His right hand was still locked in a death grip on Reno's arm, and nearly dragged the hapless officer from his horse, which was shying and whinnying wildly.

Marcus Reno was stunned and horrified as he sat gasping in his saddle. Hacking and spitting violently, he tried to dislodge a half-inch chunk of Bloody Knife's brain that had stuck in the back of his throat, at the same time prying the Ree's dead fingers from his arm. He coughed the fragment free and vomited over his horse's withers. Shuddering fiercely, the major slapped and clawed at the blood and tissue that covered his face and uniform, wiping the blood from his eyes and trying to regain control of himself. He slipped from the saddle and looked at the men and horses milling frantically around him.

"*Dismount!*" he shrieked, and reached into his pocket for a grimy white handkerchief, which he wrapped hastily around his head to keep the blood-matted hair from his eyes.

Think! he told himself urgently. What should we do? Oh, God, what was that damned Ree trying to tell him? "If you run . . . ," he'd started to say. If you run, what? If you run, you may still live? If you run, there's still time to get out of this mess? Is that what the Ree meant to say?

He cast around desperately, looking for an answer, but all he could see was the confused and terrified faces of the men gathered around him, some still on their horses, others standing mutely by their mounts, but all of them looking to him for direction.

Damn you, he thought, I don't know what you want from me. Damn you, Custer. Where the hell is my support? He couldn't wait any longer. They had to get out now.

"*Mount!*" he screamed, and hoisted himself into the saddle. The men around him quickly followed suit, the small knot of soldiers pushing and shoving against each other as they waited anxiously for the next order.

Lieutenant Varnum rushed into the small clearing where Fred Gerard and Charley Reynolds were rummaging through their saddlebags.

"Charley! Fred!" Varnum yelled. "How're things going?" Without looking up from his saddlebag, Reynolds spat into the brush.

"Things look mighty bad, Lieutenant," he said, and pulled a small metal flask from his saddlebag, noting with dismay that a small round hole had been drilled clean through it, allowing the contents to drain completely. Gerard also was fishing for a flask. He produced it with a flourish, twisting the lid off of it with a single quick turn.

"Let's have us a drink, boys," Gerard proposed. "It may be our last." He tipped the small canister back before offering it to Charley Reynolds. Reynolds too took a swig of the whiskey, and drizzled a bit over his festering thumb before passing the flask over to the lieutenant, who looked around quickly before taking a drink himself.

"They're going to charge!" someone bellowed from farther down the line, and the cry was repeated up and down the edge of the timber. "They're going to charge!"

"What?" gasped Varnum, choking on the fiery liquor. "Who's going to charge? Are we charging the village again?"

Reynolds and Gerard just looked at each other and scrambled up onto their horses as the lieutenant struggled to get one foot in his stirrup and then boosted himself up and into the saddle. He yanked his horse's head around and galloped off toward where he had last seen Major Reno. Slipping through the dense-packed ash saplings as he raced back through the timber, Varnum noticed that the heavy roar of Army carbines was slackening to a feeble bang now and again. Everywhere men were shuttling back through the woods, hatless and wild-eyed, scrambling for their horses. What the hell was going on? Bursting into a small clearing, he saw mounted men forming into a ragged column and dragging their horses' heads around toward the river. Where was Reno? he asked himself. What was everybody trying to do? Finally he caught sight of the round little major, a white rag tied around his head, waving his pistol wildly in the air and shouting.

"Form up! Form up! Column of twos at the gallop!" Reno yelled. "Make for those bluffs! It's our only chance!"

Varnum was stunned. No! his mind screamed at him. Stop! If we run, the Sioux'll chop us to bits. He couldn't get the words out and struggled to keep his seat as frightened men and horses pushed past him, scrambling to get away.

Wikuciyela *(Late Afternoon)*
On the Cutbank of
the Greasy Grass River

It was Sitting Bull who first noticed that the banging of the *wasichus'* rifles was growing quieter and quieter. It worried him that there was so much confusion in the camp and he could not see through the thick cloud of dust and gun smoke that veiled the trees where the white men had gone. He knew that something was wrong, and he imagined that the white soldiers were getting back on their horses to charge the village again. This was bad. Already several of his friends lay dead or wounded from the whites' bullets, and everyone else was running around like frightened antelope. Some of the braves were running blindly into the dust cloud; some were trying desperately to get their families away. He saw some of the women hurrying to take down their lodges to flee. If the whites should come again now, there would be a terrible slaughter. He raced his pony up and down through the lodges waving his rifle and shouting.

"Watch out for a trick!" he bellowed. "The soldiers are charging! Watch out for a trick!"

But no one seemed to pay any heed to the old man as they scrambled back and forth, screaming and calling out for their families. Fight them! he thought wildly, gritting his teeth and shaking the Winchester over his head. Don't run from these people. The dust rolled and eddied around him like a small whirlwind, and then, as if by magic, a hoarse cheering rippled through the confusion.

"*Haho! Haho!*" people shrieked. "Crazy Horse is coming! Crazy Horse is coming!"

Sitting Bull whirled his pony around to look back toward the camp and saw a tremendous cloud of dust moving like a storm, boiling and rising through the maze of lodges. Women began trilling their tongues, men yipped and roared as eagle-bone whistles shrieked wildly over the thunder of a thousand hooves. Gall, his face a mask of rage, and shaking his war club, cantered around the old medicine man.

"Trick, old man?" he snorted. "We'll show these *wasichus* a trick, you old fool."

Spitting at the dust beneath Sitting Bull's pony, Gall wheeled his pinto around and streaked back toward the timber, the stone club whirling around his head just as Crazy Horse and his warriors burst from the village and surged into the wood line keening their war cries. The ponies crashed into the underbrush with the fury of a hailstorm as furtive, blue-clad figures scattered through the leaves and thickets before them. Now the killing could start in earnest.

Eagle Elk was too excited to shoot his rifle at first, swinging it like a club as he darted through the confused soldiers who hunched over their saddles and tried to run from him. Time and again, the heavy butt of the gun slammed into white men's skulls, emptying the shiny black saddles of their riders. *"Hunh!"* he grunted each time he felt the satisfying crunch of bone under his flailing assaults. This was almost too easy, the soldiers milling about like confused buffalo waiting to be hit. All around him other warriors were screeching and shooting in a fury of blood lust as the whites toppled to the ground where still more warriors waited with their knives and hatchets to hack and slash.

Eagle Elk cantered through the underbrush, grinning and whooping his delight. Ducking under a low branch, he spotted a familiar face. It was the strange black-white man they called Anzinpi. The big man with the shiny black skin was lying on the ground, his back propped against a fallen tree, blood soaking through his soldier jacket, his eyes dim and his mouth hanging open.

Isaiah Dorman gazed down at the large hole in his gut and knew that he was dying. Already he could feel the world swimming in and out of focus as the sounds of battle faded behind the faltering thump of his own heartbeat, which pounded through his ears. He cursed his decision to come back into this country. Dorman knew the old days were fading fast and had figured it would be nice to see the land one more time before his old friends among the Sioux were moved onto some reservation and the damned miners tore the hell out of everything, looking for gold. Well, it sure had been a damn-fool notion, he concluded. Too late now.

He looked up to see a young Brulé standing over him. Dorman's own shotgun was in the boy's hands. The boy hauled back on the hammers and fired the weapon straight into Dorman's legs, shredding his boots and trousers and splashing blood everywhere.

Isaiah moaned and gurgled, his head rolling backward with pain and then dropping onto his chest, blood trickling from the corner of his mouth. Damn waste, he thought. Couldn't the boy see that his legs were already broken?

Eagle Elk rode up to watch as Dorman began murmuring in Lakota.

"Don't count coup on me, brothers," the large black man gasped feebly. "You've already killed me anyway."

Eagle Elk was surprised to hear the man speak his language, but there were others who were not moved by the wounded man's pleas. Two youngsters ripped at his clothing, stripping him in seconds, whooping and dancing with glee as an old Hunkpapa woman pushed them roughly aside. Eagle Elk thought things must be going very well if even the women and boys were streaming out to join in the fight. He watched with amusement as the old woman scolded the boys sharply, shaking a long pointy piece of iron at them. It was a picket pin that she had snatched from one of the soldiers' saddles, and she wielded it like a large butcher knife.

"Go kill some of those other soldiers, worthless boys!" she shrieked. "Don't dance around here doing nothing." The youngsters scampered off into the woods as the hag turned back to the dying scout.

"I know you, Anzinpi!" she screamed into Dorman's face. "You worthless dog. Why did you come back here with these soldiers?" The old woman dropped to her knees and snatched up a large rock as she shoved the picket pin in between the black man's legs. "If you like this country so much, I'll make sure you stay here!"

Eagle Elk turned his pony and started back toward the river. There was nothing more for him to do here. This was work for the women and boys. As he headed back toward the fighting, he heard the rock ringing against the picket pin and the black-white man's screams echoing through the woods.

George Herendeen's horse was running at full tilt along the riverbank when it hit the deadfall and tumbled headlong over the brush, pitching the scout into a thicket several yards away. Herendeen landed flat on his back, his breath whooshing out of him with the impact. He lay there for a few seconds, stunned, until he realized that besides having had the wind knocked out of him he was otherwise intact. He knew that this condition would not last for long if he didn't get the hell under cover and fast.

Rolling onto his stomach, Herendeen slipped his pistol from its holster and looked around anxiously for a good spot to lie low for a bit. Luckily there were only a few Sioux within several yards of him and their attention was directed entirely toward Charley Reynolds and Fred Gerard, who were galloping madly past him. Gerard managed to plunge his horse into the river and scramble up the other side, but Reynolds, whose horse had not been quite as fast, didn't make it that far. Herendeen gritted his teeth as he saw Charley jerk upright in the saddle before tumbling backward, his Spencer flying off to splash into the Little Bighorn. Reynolds' left foot had caught in the stirrup and Herendeen watched in anguish as his friend's body bounced limply along behind the spooked horse before snagging on a crook of driftwood.

Damn it, Charley, he thought. Guess these bastards done for you after all.

As the pursuing Sioux leaped down after Reynolds with their butcher knives flashing, Herendeen decided that this was not a good place to be and used his elbows to back himself quickly into the thicket. Once out of sight, he scrambled up onto his knees and scuttled through the dense undergrowth looking for a more remote hideout. A nearby patch of chokecherries seemed to offer a plausible "go-down," and he dropped down onto his belly to slither in under the tangled mass of greenery.

Herendeen was more than a little surprised to find that he was not the only inhabitant of the chokecherry thicket when he looked up into the barrel of a large army Colt pointed straight at his nose. On the other end of the pistol was a bedraggled cavalryman with stripes on the sleeves of his blue coat.

"Whoa, there, Sarge," Herendeen gasped out, "I got enough worries with my enemies without my damned friends pointin' smoke wagons at me."

The sergeant let out a large breath of air and lowered the pistol slowly as Herendeen glanced around to count nearly a dozen soldiers huddled in terror. As he scrabbled in among them, the sergeant grabbed Herendeen's arm to drag him into the small circle.

"Get your ass in here then, Mr. Scout," he whispered, "an' keep yer damned head down or we're all dead men. What in the hell's going on out there?"

Herendeen didn't need to be told that this was pretty fair advice, and he shifted around to face out toward the crashing and whooping that drifted in from the other side of the thicket. The scout's pistol was cocked in his hand and his eyes were narrowed down to thin slits as he peered intently through the tangle of bushes.

"Well, Sarge," he said finally, "I kin tell ya it sure ain't no church picnic out there. And I'd be obliged if you'd keep that young pup over there from snuffling for his ma or he'll have the whole goddamned Sioux nation slicin' us up fer supper."

Sergeant Charles White swung around to thump the whimpering private with the barrel of his revolver.

"Shaddup, Neely," he snarled, "or I'll throw yer worthless hide out o' here and let them redskins haul yer freight."

One of Neely's friends grabbed the terrified youngster in his arms and cradled his head, rocking him slowly as the boy's shoulders heaved violently. White nodded at the older man and turned back to Herendeen.

"Christ, what a fix," he whispered. "What're we going to do, Mr. Scout?"

Herendeen grinned crookedly at the big sergeant who, he noticed, had had a bullet crease his forehead so that he looked a bit like he'd painted himself like a Sioux.

"Herendeen's the name, but we needn't be formal. Call me George."

The sergeant nodded. "White," he said, "Company M. The fellas call me Buck."

"Well, Buck," Herendeen whispered, "I'll tell you, I've been in worse scrapes 'n this with Injuns, though it looks mighty bleak about now. They're a lazy bunch of scamps when it comes to it, and I say that if we keep our heads and lay low for a bit we might come out o' this with our hair yet. So let's keep the boys quiet, keep your shooters handy, and do just what I say. We ain't goin' nowhere for a bit. Them devils still have a piece o' killin' to do."

1600 Hours
At the Ford of the Little Bighorn River

Lieutenant Varnum jammed his spurs deep into the flank of his horse and felt the animal lunge forward. The huge gelding was a muscular thoroughbred that he'd purchased straight from a breeder of racehorses in Kentucky, and probably the fastest horse in the regiment. Not having had much of an interest in the outfit's passion for horse racing, Varnum had never been particularly impressed by the animal's speed. He was much more interested in the horse's fine lines, large barrel chest, and smooth gait. He had figured that Black Jack would be a lot more comfortable ride than many others he had looked at. It was only at this moment that he fully appreciated the gelding's tremendous speed and long legs. The lieutenant leaned forward in the saddle and slackened the reins to let the horse race forward at a breakneck pace past the ragged column of fleeing men.

"Stop!" he bellowed as he thundered down the line. "For God's sake, men, don't run. We've got to stand and fight 'em."

But his ravings went unheard as the frightened and sweating troopers lashed their horses forward in desperation. Where the hell had Reno got to? Varnum spotted his commander far ahead of the battalion and just splashing up onto the other bank of the river. He touched Black Jack with his spurs, and the horse leapt down into the water with a tremendous splash. He pushed quickly across the shallow river and scrambled up the opposite bank to confront the major, who looked like a costume-ball pirate with that ridiculous kerchief on his head.

"Damn it, Major," he yelled, "you've got to stop them! The Sioux are cutting 'em to ribbons." But he knew it was already too late. As he turned to fire back across the river, Varnum could see that the Sioux were everywhere, hacking, stabbing, and shooting into the huddled mass of troopers who tried desperately to shake off their tormentors. One warrior, his face painted red and yellow and screeching at the top of his lungs, seized the reins of Captain Tom French's horse. Varnum looked on in wonder as

French coolly leveled his pistol at the Sioux and blew a huge hole through the center of the man's chest before turning to plunge his horse into the river. In a moment he had scrambled up alongside Varnum, smiling grimly.

"Damn, but he was a sassy bastard, Charlie," French said as he raised his pistol and squeezed off another shot at the mass of warriors swarming the opposite bank. Varnum decided that this had ceased to be a retreat and was fast turning into a complete rout as soldiers and Sioux brawled savagely with one another in the churning water, clubbing, slashing, biting, and tearing at each other's hair with desperate fury. Varnum and French worked their revolvers furiously as they saw Lieutenant McIntosh trying to urge his skittish horse off of the steep cutbank a few yards across from them.

Tosh McIntosh had just made it to the cutbank when a Cheyenne, his upper body painted red, his face a hideous yellow, leaped up at the officer and dragged him out of the saddle. The Cheyenne's hatchet blurred as it flashed up and down, sending droplets of McIntosh's blood arcing into the nearby river. Varnum and French fired at the same time, blowing the Cheyenne's head into a pink spray. The body tumbled backward over the riverbank and sank back into the water to swirl away downstream.

Benny Hodgson did not see Tosh McIntosh die. He was far too preoccupied dodging willow and dogwood shafts and lashing his horse forward. The horse, with one feathered shaft already protruding from its right shoulder, was moving as fast as it could in its terror. As Hodgson urged it over a final small rise, the horse dropped onto its haunches as it began to slide down the muddy, hoof-churned embankment into the water below. It was Hodgson's misfortune that at the moment he hit the water Eagle Elk threw his Winchester up and fired a single round at the fleeing soldier. A poor shot on his best day, Eagle Elk was amazed that not only had he hit the soldier in the thigh, but at such an angle that the bullet also passed clear through the horse's heart and lungs. The animal dropped like a stone into the river as Lieutenant Hodgson thrashed wildly in the water trying to kick out of the stirrups. Trumpeter "Bounce" Fisher plunged down the bank a moment later and kicked his left foot free of the stirrup.

"Lieutenant," Fisher yelled, "grab my stirrup! I'll pull ya over."

Hodgson, sputtering and coughing up water, snatched Fisher's stirrup and held on desperately as the trumpeter kicked his mount through the river and up the other bank. When Hodgson's wounded leg thumped against a large rock, he yelped with pain and let go of the stirrup, to roll back toward the river clawing desperately at the muddy bank. The lieutenant managed to stop himself just as his boots slid into the water, and rolled onto his back, grabbing his revolver. Hodgson managed to squeeze off two rounds before a volley of rifle fire sent four bullets ripping through his chest and arm. He sank back into the mud, small pink bubbles foaming out of his mouth.

Sergeant Botzer could hardly believe what was happening. Was it only this morning that he and Henry Voss had been talking about flapjacks? Now he was riding for his life with damned screaming savages everywhere he turned. The old veteran whirled around in the saddle and fired his pistol into the side of a Sans Arc brave who had ridden up alongside and was slapping at the German with the flat of his bow. The Indian had a look of disbelief on his face as he buckled at the waist, to slip under the pounding hooves of his own pony. But as Botzer turned away, his head slammed into an overhanging tree limb. The sergeant cartwheeled backward out of the saddle and tumbled senseless to the slick riverbank. His horse plunged wildly into the water while Botzer's body slid slowly down the bank as a pair of Cheyennes fired half a dozen dogwood shafts into the unconscious old soldier. On the opposite bank of the river Benny Hodgson gasped out his last breath.

Varnum looked around in desperation. It appeared to him that everyone who was going to get across the river had already done so, including a small mob of Sioux who were racing along the bank at a dog trot, stopping only long enough to send an arrow or a bullet toward the backs of the fleeing soldiers. Time to get the hell out of here, he thought, and turned his horse toward the long hogback ridge that angled back and away toward the bluffs high above them. A hundred yards farther upstream a ragged line of troops splashed out of the water and struggled slowly up the steep slope on the other side. As Varnum started up the closer hogback he heard a number of men calling out his name.

"Come back, Mr. Varnum!" someone shouted. "Over this way!" Varnum hesitated for a moment and looked up at the hogback where he could see one of the regiment's surgeons, Dr. DeWolf, looking absently toward a point higher up on the ridge. A rifle cracked from up above, and DeWolf toppled back down the hill, his body sliding and skidding over the rocks and scrub.

"There's Injuns up there!" someone was yelling, pointing uphill. Following the line of the man's arm, the lieutenant now caught a glimpse of a figure with black hair and feathers scooting along the ridge line directly above him. Varnum ducked down over Black Jack's withers and spurred away toward the men on the next hogback, even as they began firing at the Sioux who had slipped around to shoot down on the soldiers near the river. Varnum urged his mount forward toward the rest of the survivors and away from the carnage as the screams of the wounded reached up from the timber below. Those poor souls, he thought, they'll think death is a blessing before the bastards're through with 'em.

Gall was flailing his war club wildly, bringing the heavy stone head thumping down again and again on the white man's skull as he pounded it into jelly. Gall's face was contorted by a wicked smile, and he growled and grunted like a wolf with each stroke as he straddled the corpse, splattering blood and brains through the undergrowth. When Sitting Bull rode up to him, the frenzied warrior did not hear the old man call his name or even look up at the pony as it wheeled around him, so intent was he on obliterating the white face that had stared up at him in terror a few minutes before.

"Gall!" the old man shouted, and tapped his shoulder with the barrel of his Winchester. Startled, Gall looked up, uncomprehending, at the old man on the black pony. Sitting Bull knew madness when he saw it, and it was surely madness that he saw now in Gall's blank and staring eyes. Gall's arms were red and dripping to the elbows, his face streaked and spattered with sweat and blood, and his stone club was a mass of clotted blood and hair. Sitting Bull was troubled by the man's appearance. Especially the soul-piercing brilliance of the eyes.

"Old friend," he said gently. "That man will never be more dead than he already is. Come, get up. This day is not over yet."

Gall growled and spit into the crimson mess that lay under him, his chest heaving and spittle dripping down from his mouth. He seemed not even to recognize the medicine man who had been his close friend and companion these many years.

"*Hokahe*, old man!" he said, his teeth clenched. "Here is a trick for the white man. I can make his head disappear." Gall laughed wickedly, dipped his fingers into the man's brains, and stuck them into his mouth chewing with delight.

"What do you think, old man? Are you afraid that if I eat the white-eyes' brains I will become more stupid, like they are?" He threw back his head, laughing hysterically and howling like a mad wolf as he shook his war club at the nearby bluffs. "Come down from those hills, white-eyes!" he screamed. "Gall is still hungry! *Aowoooohhh! Aawooohhh!*"

It was clear to Sitting Bull that there was no use in talking to Gall as he was now, with the killing frenzy on him. He had known men whose grief had made them so. The death of loved ones could change a man terribly. But so could the killing of enemies. Sitting Bull looked around him where the small patch of timber was overrun with women and children who had come rushing out of the village trilling their tongues and waving sticks, clubs, and knives. Now they had set about their grim work with a vengeance. Already this place had the stink of death about it, blood mixed with urine and excrement, the stench of fear.

Even the grass and leaves ran red with the sticky blood that turned black in the sun as knives and hatchets slashed and cut at the dead and living *wasichus* that littered the woods. Even the river had been churned into a reddish brown color as it carried the corpses of soldier and Lakota alike whirling downstream past the rest of the camp. The corpses of men and horses would quickly begin to bloat and rot in this heat, and Sitting Bull knew that very soon this water would not be good to drink for a long while. They must think about moving the camp.

He turned and saw the young men running through the woods and back toward the village shrieking their victory songs, stopping only to shoot randomly at the hill where the soldiers were still clawing their way up to the top. All of the people he saw carried some trophy they had picked up from the whites—pistols, cartridge belts, rifles, hats, scalps. Some led away the large American horses with their blood-spattered saddles. One carried the little flag with the tails like a swallow. Two young girls skipped along swinging a bloody object between them. Squinting down at it, Sitting Bull saw that it was the severed head of an Indian that they held by the hair. Although half of the face was gone, he thought the man looked somehow familiar. Had it not been so ruined by the bullet, he might have recognized the face that, as a young boy, had slipped into his lodge to hide from Gall and the others when they tried to beat him. Bloody Knife's father had been a good friend to Sitting Bull.

The old man heard a strange bleating sound and turned to see a Sans Arc who wore a bloody blue jacket with yellow stripes on the sleeve. The Sans Arc's cheeks were all puffed out as he tried to blow into a shiny metal horn with a fancy braided rope on it. This was not right, Bull thought. Wakan Tanka had warned him that the white men's things were to be left alone. They would break the medicine. Tatanka Iyotanka fired his rifle into the air and cried out in his loudest voice.

"Hear me, Lakotas!" he sang. "Let the rest of those men go and do not touch these spoils. Wakan Tanka has said that if you set your hearts on the things of the white man you will bring a curse on this nation. Hear me, Lakotas! Throw these things away!"

But no one seemed to hear. The boys laughed and ran, waving their treasures in the air. The women and girls trilled and chattered and gathered the knives and the shiny little pots that the soldiers drank out of. The warriors chanted their songs of victory and fired their new pistols at the distant bluffs. Sitting Bull looked down at Gall, who gazed up at him grinning and drooling over the white man's corpse.

"Touch not their things," Gall sneered. "Might as well tell the snows not to come, old man. Go ahead, tell the sun not to set. Tell the wolves to be gentle with the weak buffalo calf. Look around you, Sitting Bull! White men falling into camp, you said. Well, they are here now. They are the gift of Wakan Tanka. I thank the Wakan Tanka for these stupid soldiers who have no ears. Now, go away and let me enjoy my gift." Gall tossed his club to the grass, drew out a long knife, and was in the process of cutting the corpse's heart from his chest when Sitting Bull turned his pony about and started back toward the village.

1605 Hours
At the Medicine Tail Coulee

Boston Custer's pony clattered down the dusty ravine as his rider urged him past the long column of troops, who were moving forward at a steady walk. The youngster's face was creased by a wide grin as he realized he'd arrived in time to join in the fun. Wouldn't Armstrong be surprised to see him, he thought. Boston Custer was not about to be left behind with the mules while the rest of the Custer boys were out here in front shooting the place up. No, sirree. He waved his hat in the air and hallooed out for George and Tom as the pony skittered over the loose rocks and soil. He reined the quick little animal to a stop just as he came up alongside Tom and the general.

"Afternoon, fellas," he said brightly as he dropped his hat back onto his head and tapped it into place with the palm of his hand. He noted with some satisfaction that neither George nor Tom seemed especially pleased to see him and guessed that his arrival had spoiled some little plot they had hatched to make him the butt of family jokes for months to come.

"What the devil are you doing up here?" George Custer snapped. "You're supposed to be back with the packtrain. And just what the hell do you mean galloping down here raising a cloud of dust behind you? I'm trying to keep the dust down so that the Sioux don't have a welcoming party out for us, damn it!"

Boston was taken aback by the general's sharp tone. It appeared that George was genuinely angry with him. Even Tom was glaring at him, and Boston lapsed quickly into a stuttering apology that George cut off with an upraised palm.

"Never mind saying you're sorry, Bos," Custer scolded. "As long as you're here, you'll fall in with the rest of the outfit and do as you're told until this business is over. Stick with Autie Reed and Mr. Kellogg and stay out of the way." Boston nodded acquiescence as his older brother laid down the law. "Now, as long as you're here, I assume you kept your eyes open on the way, so tell me what you've seen and where Benteen and the packs are."

"Yes, sir," Boston stammered. "I came right past Reno's people and they were fighting like hell down there. Making one hell of a racket, they are. Also, came right by old Benteen just below that tipi that's burning back there a ways. He's right behind me and should be up with us any time now."

George Custer nodded, his lower lip jutting forward as he worked out the distances in his head. The lone tipi was about six miles back. He looked at Boston's pony and noticed that the animal was neither lathered up nor breathing hard, so the boy couldn't have pushed too hard to get here. If Benteen was right behind him, he should already have gotten his first message at least and be moving forward at the trot. The second messenger should be reaching him any time now to speed him up even more. Not too bad. With any luck, Benteen's outfit should catch up with him in the next fifteen minutes or so.

Good! he thought. We can do one last check of the saddles and gear, move forward at a moderate pace, and Benteen should be coming up just about the time we're in position to hit the village. Excellent! They were shaving it a bit fine but, all in all, things seemed to be working out pretty well.

Mitch Bouyer slumped glumly in the saddle, shaking his head and muttering to himself. This sure was turning into one hell of a day. He closed his eyes for a moment. He hadn't realized that he was so tired. The young Crow Curley seemed to be enjoying himself immensely. The boy had never been in a big fight before and was keen as mustard to come to grips with the Head-Cutters. He had become so excited that he fidgeted constantly in his saddle as he watched the fighting below them.

"Two Tongues," the boy said, tugging insistently at Bouyer's sleeve. "Look at the pony soldiers. The Little White Chief is running away!"

"What the hell!" The startled Bouyer looked up suddenly and saw that the boy was telling the truth. Down on the valley floor it appeared that the Sioux had seized the upper hand and Reno's people were falling back rapidly. In a few moments it was clear that Reno's position had crumbled and a panic of blue-shirted men were running for their lives with Sioux and Cheyenne swarming all over them.

"Shit!" Bouyer exclaimed. He looked quickly down the coulee where the last of Custer's people were just disappearing around a bend. "Curley," he said, "we've got to catch 'em. Got to tell Long Hair that the Little White Chief is beaten. We'll have to cut across country and ride like hell. Let's go!"

Curley whooped and wheeled his pony around to follow Bouyer as he spurred off across the ridgeline, beating his horse's rump with the barrel of his rifle. The two men lay across the necks of their mounts as they raced along the rim of a coulee, clods of dirt and small rocks arcing into the air behind the flying hooves. Bouyer knew that this was a damned bad break. Without Reno down at the upper end of the village, the Sioux would be able to bring all of their people out against Custer as the outfit came into view. It could be a disaster. He hoped like hell that Benteen and the packs came up pretty quick. It looked like they were going to have their hands full.

Trumpeter Private John Martin galloped back over the flats, taking the same trail the outfit had come up on. His horse was darn near played out by now, but Lieutenant Cooke and the general were depending on him.

"Just imagine," he said to himself, "you can barely speak the language and already a general is depending on you to deliver a critical message before a great battle! *Maraviglioso! É troppo magnifico!*"*

Maybe Baldassare Spalletti had not been so far wrong when he suggested that Martin should join the Army. What a tale he would be able to tell his children and his grandchildren now. How John Martin, born Giovanni Martini, delivered the message that won the last great battle against the savages. *É molto bene!*† As Martin raced along the trail, he could hear the crackle of gunfire off to the rear and urged his horse onward with another jab of his spurs.

"Rider coming in!"

Lieutenant Gibson shouted a warning as the galloping figure of the courier closed in on the front of the column. Gibson immediately recognized the young Italian trumpeter from Company H who had been designated as an orderly for the general. Martin or something, he thought, although it seemed like an odd name for a fellow with an accent like that. Gibson figured that Martin must have some sort of dispatch to deliver. The lieutenant couldn't be sure, but he guessed that Benteen probably wasn't moving fast enough to suit the general and was about to be reminded of the fact in no uncertain terms. General Custer was not one to mince words when he wanted something done and done quickly. Benteen raised his right hand to bring the column to a halt as Martin reined up and saluted smartly. The old captain cleared his throat and slapped the dust off of his uniform while deliberately ignoring the courier.

---

* *"Marvelous! It's just too magnificent!"*
† *"This is very good!"*

"The general sends his compliments, sir," Martin managed to blurt, remembering the standard form of address for such occasions. He reached into his pocket and fished out the folded scrap of paper, which he presented quickly to Benteen. The white-haired cavalryman glared at Martin for a moment before snatching the proffered note and unfolding it with a show of studied indifference.

> Benteen,
> Come on. Big village. Be quick. Bring packs.
> W. W. Cooke
> ps. bring pacs

"Tell me the situation, Private Martin!" Benteen spat the words quickly.

"*Cosa?* Uh, what, sir?" Martin struggled to understand the question.

Benteen rolled his eyes upward and slammed his fist on the saddle bow, his face turning bright red in his fury.

"Damn you," he screamed. "What the hell is going on up there, you blockheaded idiot? What are the damned Indians doing? Speak up and speak English, damn your eyes!"

Martin saluted again, nervously racking his brain for the right phrase in English.

"The Injuns," he blurted, "they are skedaddling! Sir!" He smiled proudly.

"Bah!" Benteen scowled, crumpling the note in his gloved hand and jamming it into his vest pocket. "The Injuns, they are skedaddling," he squeaked, mimicking an Italian accent. "I'll just bet they are. Probably scattered from hell to breakfast already, unless I miss my guess. Old G.A.C.'s got 'em spooked and running like rabbits, I'll bet. Right now he's probably whining for me to come up and help him corral the whole lot before Terry comes down and skins him for making a royal hash of this whole business."

Benteen noticed that Lieutenant Gibson was listening closely to his outburst and quickly shut up. No point in giving the game away to the pups now, he thought. They'd soon see for themselves what a damned incompetent braggart Custer was. Well, this might prove to be rather an enjoyable afternoon after all. By the time old Terry gets up, he thought, we'll be standing around with nothing but a bunch of old lodgepoles and a couple of broken-down ponies to show for our troubles, and G.A.C. blubbering that it wasn't his fault. Oh, yes, this would be a treat, watching the little bastard squirm. By the time Terry and Sheridan finished skinning the Boy General, he'd be the laughingstock of the Army. Oh, see how the mighty have fallen.

Benteen waved Martin away, and the young Italian, not sure what to do but remembering Cooke's instructions to stay with the outfit, decided to work his way back down the column to fall in at his usual position with Company H. The boys in the outfit were glad to see him and hallooed and whooped at his return.

"Yo, Johnny!" Henry Bishley called out. "Where ya bin, boy?"

"What's going on up yonder?" his friend Trumpeter Private Billy Ramell asked eagerly.

"The Injuns," Martin, grinning, repeated loudly, "they are skedaddling!" A large whoop went up from the troops nearby. It looked like they were going to see some action pretty soon after all.

Lieutenant Gibson heard the ruckus and looked back at the cheering troops with a smile. It still amazed him that even the most tired and bedraggled private seemed to forget all of his troubles and aching bones at the least hint of a donnybrook. Hunger, thirst, long hours without sleep, dust, horseflies, saddle sores, everything was forgotten when the word passed up and down the line, "Action front!" The pulse quickened and blood pumped furiously through your veins. Stomach muscles tightened and every sense seemed to come alive and sharpen. Gibson could feel the current of excitement ripple through the ranks.

"Lieutenant Gibson!" Benteen roared. "Alright, Mr. Gibson, let's close 'em up tight. Let's go see what the rumpus is up ahead. And keep those men quiet back there. I won't have this outfit turn into bedlam." Gibson saluted, and cantered down the line calling out to the sergeants as he passed.

Benteen raised his hand and called back over his shoulder: *"Battalion, column of fours. At the trot, Forraard!"*

Benteen's hand dropped, Trumpeter Private Ramell raised his instrument to sound the Advance, and as the brassy notes rang out in the still air, Benteen's column lurched forward to the jangling of bits, tin cups, and picket pins.

A few miles away George Custer's mind was racing as he considered how to deploy the outfit when they came into contact with the village. Ideally, he thought, if they could get to the lower end of the village, they could race right through the center of the camp. Hit from two directions at once, the Sioux were prone to panic and collapse. Then they could start coralling the women and children while at the same time destroying lodges and property. Once deprived of their shelter and food stores, the Indians generally became a fairly docile lot and could be persuaded to move back to the agencies so that they could, once again, enjoy Uncle Sam's bounty—at least until they got themselves reestablished. Well, that was the agents' problem and not his. The only problem was that Reno might not be able to keep the hostiles busy long enough for the outfit to get clear around to the other end. And just where the hell was Benteen?

As the column proceeded down the coulee, Custer noticed that the rough trail swung off to the left and began to drop away quickly toward the valley. Of course, he reasoned, any seasonal watercourse would naturally move toward the river, and, judging from the size of this coulee, it would very probably empty into a fairly wide and open area as it fed into the Little Bighorn. This would probably also be a perfect place to ford. He raised his hand and signaled for the outfit to swing around to the left. As the column rounded the bend in the coulee, there it was. Custer grinned broadly. It was just as he'd thought; the coulee widened as it descended from the bluffs and ended in a broad, level area where the river ran shallow and, just across the river, there was the center of the village. Better yet, there was nary an Indian in sight.

Mitch Bouyer, popping over the rim of the coulee, caught sight of the column just as it came within view of the village. Damn it! he thought. Hold off, boys! I'm coming in! Smacking the rump of his horse with his rifle, he urged the animal, skidding and sliding, over the edge and plunged down toward the troopers, yelling at the top of his lungs, with Curley hot on his heels.

"General!" he bellowed. "Wait! Don't go down there! Reno's been skipped out!"

1610 Hours
At the Medicine Tail Coulee

"What in the devil?" George Custer asked as he reined back on Vic and slid to a stop in the middle of the coulee, his staff thumping into each other as they too reined in their horses, bringing the entire outfit to a dead halt. "Mitch, what the dickens is the matter with you?"

Bouyer yanked back on the reins of his horse as he clattered down the last few yards to the head of the column.

"Damn it, General," he gasped, "Reno's broke, and all hell is about to break loose down there!"

Bouyer, flushed and panting, was pointing down toward the distant ford with his rifle. Custer stared at the man open-mouthed as he tried to grasp the significance of what was happening. He moved Vic a few feet away from the rest of the staff and drew Bouyer away with him.

"Damn it, Mitch," Custer whispered urgently, "what the hell is going on down there? What did you see, man?"

Bouyer caught his breath and started blurting his news.

"General," he said, "Reno's broke and runnin' for his life. There must be thousands of 'em down there. Even more'n I thought. They swarmed into the timber, and the next thing you know Reno's people were going like hell tryin' to git back across the damn river. Looks like the Sioux're cuttin' 'em up bad. Real bad! Benteen still ain't nowhere in sight, an' it's just us out here. General, them Sioux ain't in a runnin' mood today, an' we got us a problem."

Custer drew a deep breath. This was bad news indeed. Now what? He had to think. He looked back up the coulee at the column, which waited, bits jingling and men shifting anxiously in their saddles as the horses snuffed and pawed the ground. The plan would have to change again. Custer closed his eyes and pressed his fingers tightly to his forehead, his brain pounding as he tried to work through a plan of action. Getting across the river now was out of the question. Instead, he'd have to figure a way to use the river to their advantage as a sort of obstacle. Keep the Sioux bottled up and off-balance on the other side while the outfit found a good place to dig in and get organized. If they could just put enough pressure on 'em from the flank, that might give Reno enough breathing space to pull his people out and rejoin the outfit. He looked off to the right and up toward the rolling hills beyond the rim of the coulee.

High ground. Had to get the outfit to high ground: get some good fields of fire, pin down the Sioux, and play for time. Had to give Benteen time to come up with his battalion and the packs. But what if Benteen was being cut up too? What about Gibbon? Gibbon was supposed to be here tomorrow. If he could get the packs up, there was enough ammunition to hold out for another day easily. Maybe, he thought, we could get someone through to Gibbon and hurry him up. He looked back down at the ford. Damn! If it looked like an easy crossing for the Seventh, it would be just as easy a crossing for the Sioux. Had to control the ford; deny the enemy use of it. Even if only for a few minutes. He wheeled Vic around and yelled back toward the staff.

"Mr. Cooke," he shouted. "Send Mr. Crittenden up, and quickly!"

Moments later Lieutenant John Crittenden galloped up alongside and was waiting eagerly for instructions. Crittenden, an infantry officer, was not officially a member of the regiment. One of Jimmi Calhoun's oldest friends, the two of them had thought it would be a lark to chum along on this expedition. The pair had wheedled and cajoled until John Gibbon had just thrown up his hands and allowed Crittenden to attach himself to Custer's command as a sort of "liaison officer" between the infantry and the cavalry. Well, Custer thought, the youngster might as well start earning his pay as a liaison. The general yanked a small notebook from his saddlebags and scribbled into it hastily, then ripped the sheet off and handed it to the lieutenant.

"John," he said, "I want you to get this dispatch through to Colonel Gibbon. Give him my compliments and tell him we're in a tight corner here. We'll need his help as fast as he can get here. If the infantry is too slow, he must at least push the Second Cavalry through to us. Jim Brisbin'll know what to do."

Crittenden nodded in silence as Custer went on.

"Now, you head north and swing well away from the camp. Gibbon can't be much more than ten or twelve miles out, so ride like hell."

Crittenden snatched the paper, stuffed it into his shirt pocket, and snapped off a quick salute. Custer nodded and watched as the young infantry officer wheeled his sorrel-roan and spurred away up the long slope. Custer now turned back to the outfit and started his plan in motion, calling Captain George Yates and Lieutenant Algernon "Fresh" Smith over to him.

"George, Fresh," he barked, "Reno's thrown back, and I need you to buy us some time. You are now our left wing. Take your battalion down and control that ford." He pointed down the coulee toward the camp. "Don't cross the river, but make as bold a show as possible. The object is to keep the hostiles from crossing over. I'm taking the right wing up to that high ground and we'll support you with fire. If things get too hot, you're to retire and rejoin the main command. Keep closed up as tight as you can and keep the hostiles at arm's length. Whatever you do, don't let 'em get in among you and don't run. Stay cool. Fire low and keep it steady. Benteen's coming up with his battalion and the packs, and you're to keep the hostiles from coming up to cut him off. Clear?" Both men nodded quickly. "Alright then, off you go and Godspeed!"

Moments later the coulee was churned into a mass of dust as Companies E and F lunged down toward the ford at the gallop while the rest of the command wheeled around and started to scramble up the side of the ravine, heading out onto the rolling, sunbaked hills above the river. As the lead elements climbed up onto a small knoll, Custer gathered the other officers around him and quickly outlined his new plan.

Mark Kellogg was becoming confused. He'd been talking to Crittenden and Calhoun when the former had been called off to join the general. When Crittenden was spotted dashing away to the north, Kellogg turned to Jimmi Calhoun and asked him what was happening, but Calhoun had merely shrugged.

"Your guess is as good as mine," Calhoun said. "Maybe he's off to see where the other end of that village is or something. I expect the general's trying to find the best place to hit 'em."

Kellogg didn't know enough about what was happening to make a rational guess, but unless he was very much mistaken, something was amiss. As they'd started down the coulee, he'd fully expected that the outfit would break into a charge and make a dash through the sea of tipis down below. Instead, the outfit had come to a halt for a few minutes and then split into two groups. Some of the boys headed toward the village, but the rest of the command headed up onto this damn hillside. What about the attack? What the hell was Custer up to now? Kellogg wasn't a soldier, but even to him it just didn't seem to make a whole lot of sense. Hell, he thought, not much of anything makes much sense about now.

•

Bobtail Horse had not yet participated in any of the fighting. When all the commotion had broken out, he was in the middle of making a charm from an elk tooth and didn't bother to look up from his work. The Cheyenne was a careful man, and he felt that this charm was a powerful part of his medicine. There was no question of his doing anything as foolish as going into battle until he was quite sure of his medicine. Now that he was done, he picked up his rifle and went out into the bright sunlight to get his pony, which was hobbled a few feet away. It was only as he went to toss the rawhide reins over his pony's neck that he looked up to see a blur of dust and mounted men moving down the coulee across the river from the Miniconjou's circle.

He blinked once or twice as his eyes adjusted to the glare and then leaped onto his pony with a yelp. Those men were *wasichus!* Bobtail Horse had no idea what to do as he looked around desperately for help. The Cheyenne circle was all but deserted, with most of the braves up near the Hunkpapas, where all the shooting was going on.

"Brothers!" he shrieked. "Soldiers are coming! Brave up! Brave up!"

Just then two of his friends rode up grinning and singing a victory song. Roan Bear was actually leaving the singing to Calf, a Crazy Dog warrior who, still elated from the fight near the Hunkpapas, was making up lyrics that stretched even Roan Bear's credulity. Tagging along behind the two was White-Cow-Bull, an Oglala friend of Roan Bear's, who was making faces behind Calf's back and causing his friend to giggle uncontrollably.

"Roan Bear!" Bobtail Horse cried out. "Come quickly, there are soldiers coming across the river. What'll we do?"

Roan Bear threw back his head and laughed. "Where have you been, Horse, sleeping all day? We just chased those *wasichus* back across the river. They were running like frightened rabbits."

"No!" Bobtail Horse yelled. "Not those *wasichus!* There are others coming down near the Miniconjous right now. Look." Horse pointed his rifle toward the ford as the other three looked on increduously.

"*Haho!* Look," said the Oglala. "Your friend is right. Here they come."

In a flash, Calf whooped and wheeled his pony off to gallop headlong toward the ford. The others looked at each other for a moment and then turned to race after him. Bobtail Horse thought that this was crazy. How could just four men hope to hold off so many soldiers? But there was no time to think about it. He grasped his rifle tighter and headed for the river.

1615 Hours
At the Medicine Tail Coulee

Sergeant Johnny Ogden had always been especially proud of his horse Sky Dancer. The large eight-year-old mare stood a full fifteen-and-a-half hands tall and had a chest like a water barrel. Thanks to her smooth gait and powerful stride, there wasn't another animal in the Gray Horse Troop that could touch her for speed, and it was this fact that had kept "Bulldozer" Ogden nicely in the chips. Ogden had raced her at every opportunity and "Sky" had responded with a will. With every victory Ogden, not one to kill the golden goose, always used some of the proceeds, which were considerable, to procure a little extra in the way of a treat for his four-legged companion and racing partner. The frequent lumps of sugar, halved apples, and extra corn had had the desired effect on Sky, who quickly recognized that indulging her natural instinct to run invariably resulted in some tangible reward.

So it was only natural when the Gray Horse Troop began its charge toward the river that Sky Dancer assumed that this was just another race, with some tasty morsel waiting for her should she outdistance her companions. It seemed odd that her rider was tugging so hard at her mouth with the heavy curb, but, as the trip had thus far been lacking any special supplements for her diet, she dearly wanted the sweet or juicy taste that would reward a strong gallop—enough to overlook the cruel pressure of the bit biting into her mouth and tongue. Sky Dancer, who could not understand her rider's screaming, assumed that she was being urged to go faster and quickly pulled ahead of the other horses to splash across the river and out onto the plain beyond. She didn't stop running until she noticed that the weight of her rider was no longer there. With no more pressure from the bit she slowed to a walk and was soon grazing content-edly on a patch of buffalo grass and waiting patiently for her sugar lump.

"Jesus Christ!" First Sergeant Hohmeyer swore as he watched Johnny Ogden's body disappear under a throng of screaming women and youngsters, all waving clubs and butcher knives. Hohmeyer, along with Corporal Hagan, had barely managed to turn their own mounts at the last minute, just as their hooves churned up the bluish clay on the riverbank. The pair yanked their horses' heads around and scrambled back up the slope to the rest of the outfit, which was just deploying into skirmish formation. Captain Yates was bawling out orders to the two companies and waving the men into position parallel to the river.

"*As skirmishers,*" Yates bellowed. "*On the center. . . . Fours take intervals. . . . Halt! Skirmishers, commence firing!*"

All along the skirmish line the heavy bang of the carbines rang out again and again as troopers rammed cartridges up the Springfields' breeches and fired blindly into the lodges across the river, a dense cloud of gun smoke rolling out and across the fast moving water. Horses danced and shied as the fire-belching weapons roared out over their heads. Captain Yates had taken up his position behind the center of the line and was watching anxiously as the men worked their carbines furiously. Glancing back up the hillside, he could see Companies C and L forming into firing lines. Company I must be just beyond them in reserve. The men above were dismounting and moving their horses to the rear as Myles Keogh rode back and forth along the line, sitting erect in the saddle, seemingly as calm as if this were a simple drill. Yates could not make out the general but knew that the man would be somewhere toward the center of the formation, probably chatting with Tom and Calhoun.

Mad Wolf was shaking his head in wonder as the four braves dashed toward the river. What was wrong with those young men? He could understand the Oglala's behavior—he was, after all, one of those strange Crazy Dogs—but the others were just being foolish. There were simply too many soldiers coming down that coulee for four men to charge against them. The old Cheyenne watched as a *wasichu* with yellow stripes on his arm charged across the river and right into the muzzles of Roan Bear and Calf's rifles.

Well, that, he thought, was a stupid thing to do, even for a white man. The women and boys were swarming over the foolish white man before he stopped rolling in the dirt. The old man was a little more satisfied when he saw the four braves leap from their ponies and into the bulberry bushes near the ford, where they started shooting up at the soldiers as fast as they could work their rifles. He grunted his approval and turned his pony away toward the Hunkpapa circle. He thought that those people should be finished with the whites down there by now and decided that he would just ride down there and gather them up to come help these crazy boys.

"Set yer sights at five hundred yards, boys!" Keogh bellowed. "Mark yer targets and shoot low. And don't hit none o' them Gray Horse Troop."

The men of Company I had dropped to one knee and advanced their carbines, fiddling nervously with the sliding range scales on the rear sights. Sergeant Bustard had remained standing behind the line and was now stalking up and down, looking over the men's shoulders as they fumbled in their thimble belts for the requisite five rounds called for in the manual. He stooped over Paddy Kelly and reached down for the youngster's carbine.

"Lower line there, son," he said, easily adjusting the carbine's sight. "Five hundred yards, not seven. You'll be shootin' up the man in the moon with that set. There ya go! Now, stay calm and listen to the Old Man— he'll talk ya through it easy now." Paddy nodded quickly but noticed that his throat was too dry even to croak out a brief thank you. Bustard patted the young Irishman on the shoulder and moved farther down the line.

"Alright, fellas," Bustard called out, "steady now, wait for the word. Damn it, Lloyd, where the hell ya been keepin' them cartridges? Stuck up your butt? Christ almighty! Clean the damn things off, ya walleyed guttersnipe!" Several of the boys snickered as Lloyd hastily polished a couple of rounds by wiping them on his trousers.

Lieutenant Calhoun stood to the rear of the companies and cast a professional eye over the formation while First Sergeants Porter, Varden, and Butler bustled around making sure the horses were linked securely together and the saddlebags, containing spare ammunition, had their straps unbuckled. All kept watch on the operations of Yates's and Smith's people down near the ford. It was First Sergeant Butler, a large distinguished-looking man with a clipped New Yorker's accent, who first noticed the dust cloud boiling up from behind the tree line across the river. It was moving rapidly up from the south or left of Yates's battalion. James Butler watched for a moment and then turned to shout back at Captain Keogh.

"Colonel Keogh," he bellowed. "Look to our left front, if you please, sir! Here they come now!"

Keogh nodded and watched quietly as the rolling dust storm swept up through the village and burst like a thunderstorm in a melee of thousands of screaming, yipping warriors.

"Jaysus, Mary 'n' Joseph!" he swore quietly, crossing himself and lifting the *Pro Patria* medal to his lips to plant a quick kiss on it. Look at 'em all, he thought. Yates'll never hold 'em back. He strode up to the firing line, extending his hands straight out to either side. First Sergeant Butler glanced up at the captain and decided idly that the man with his rakish mustachio and dark good looks seemed remarkably like a Fenian Mephistopheles doing an impression of Christ.

"*Skirmishers!*" Keogh bellowed. "*At five hundred yards, maark your targets! Steady now. Com-mence firing!*"

The line erupted with a massive roar as the first volley was cut loose at the swarming hostiles. Keogh didn't think it would stop them, but it should at least slow their progress long enough for Yates to pull his battalion out of the way. Thank God the boys down there hadn't dismounted. Almost immediately Yates did precisely what Keogh had thought he would do, wheeling his battalion off to the right and moving them rapidly downstream at the oblique. Yates was trying to move up to rejoin the rest of the outfit. Good man, Keogh thought, now all we've gotta do is keep 'em off ye a bit longer. George Custer appeared over his shoulder like a ghost.

"Myles!" Custer yelled to be heard over the roar of the carbines. "We've got to keep 'em off of Yates and Smith while we move the rest of the outfit forward!" Keogh looked over as Custer pointed to a prominent knoll several hundred yards farther along.

"That piece of ground," Custer shouted, "should command most of this valley. If we can rally up there when Benteen comes up with the packs, we can launch an assault down toward the other end of the village. At worst, we'll be able to hold the beggars off 'til eternity!"

"Well, General darlin'," Keogh shouted with a grin. "Let's hope it don't come to that."

Custer laughed and slapped Keogh on the back.

"Alright, Myles!" Custer yelled. "We need to move now. Leave Calhoun's company as rear guard and leapfrog C and I back to the next ridge. When you're in position, give cover to Jimmi so he can pull his boys back. Clear?"

Keogh nodded quickly and moved off to tell Calhoun how they would manage the withdrawal, while Custer moved rapidly toward the small knot of officers and civilians gathered near Company I. Mark Kellogg and young Autie Reed stood speechless to one side, their mouths working noiselessly as they tried to comprehend the noise, smoke, and confusion that billowed around them. George Custer didn't even bother to look their way, heading straight for Boston, who was gesticulating wildly at Tom. George pulled Boston around to look at him.

"Boston!" he shouted. "Where the hell is Benteen? I thought you said he was right behind you."

Boston Custer shrugged haplessly. "He was, Armstrong. I don't know what the hell's keeping him." But George Custer was already moving away and swinging up into the saddle.

Damn Benteen, Custer thought savagely. What the hell could be keeping him? If Boston had passed him coming up, there was no reason why he shouldn't be here already. The prickly bastard must be dawdling, trying to make him sweat before charging in to the rescue. Custer decided he'd have a piece of Benteen's hide for this.

"Cookey!" Custer yelled. "Sound To Mount. We're moving the outfit to higher ground."

Lieutenant Cooke nodded and grabbed a nearby trumpeter, who quickly sounded out the brassy notes that had all but Calhoun's company moving back to their horses.

Curley, still sitting his pony alongside Mitch Bouyer, watched the proceedings with genuine interest. He had never seen how white men fought a full-scale battle and was fascinated by how they all seemed to move as one —not running off to charge the Head-Cutters and count coup on them like the Crow. This was a funny way to make war. He looked back down toward the ford and grunted to get Bouyer's attention. As the smoke thinned slightly, he could see hundreds of the Head-Cutters splashing across the river on their ponies and swarming up through the coulees and ravines that cut deep into the hillsides all around them.

"Look, Mitch," he said, "they are coming up around us in the coulees."

Bouyer nodded and spat into the dust. Damn if this wasn't a hell of a mess. And getting messier by the minute.

1620 Hours
On Reno's Hill

Lieutenant Varnum dropped wearily to the ground and groped in his pockets for some more revolver cartridges. God, but he was tired. After riding all last night and all morning, then fighting a battle this afternoon, the climb up the bluffs had been just about the final straw. He didn't think he could go another step.

For reasons that his tired mind could not yet fathom, the Indians seemed to be leaving them alone for the present. He glanced to his left and saw Major Reno a few yards away, sitting dejectedly in the dirt, his head cradled in his hands and his revolver lying on the ground next to him.

Damn you, Reno, Varnum thought savagely. You're the commander. Act like it!

Varnum struggled to his feet just as Luther Hare rode up, a smoking pistol in his hand but his hat long since gone, probably left somewhere in the timber below.

"Where you off to, Luther?" Varnum asked.

"I'm going back to see where the hell McDougall is with the packs." Hare glared at the oblivious Reno. "Damn it, Charlie," he whispered hoarsely, "what the hell just happened here? Tosh and Benny're dead and Charley Reynolds too! God knows how many more of the fellas have bought it." Hare was livid, tears of rage and grief coursing down his face, which was smudgy and black from gunpowder.

"The damned Sioux got the bulge on us is what happened, Luth," Varnum shot back. "We're lucky any of us got out of there alive. I wonder where the hell Custer's got to?"

In the distance they heard the scattering pop of rifle fire and looked toward the sunbaked hills to the north. Hare began reloading his pistol. From the sounds of things Custer too had found the Sioux and was now having a go at them a bit farther downstream. Hare and Varnum looked at each other and then at Major Reno, each thinking that they had probably not seen the last of the Sioux for that day. Before either of them could say anything, the sound of hoofbeats drew their attention from the sight of the despondent Reno. They looked off to the south to see Frederick Benteen's battalion trotting easily up the trail.

Major Marcus Reno's eyes grew wide as he saw Benteen's outfit coming up into the position. He sprang to his feet and seized a trumpeter, ordering him to sound the Halt, which the man began to do over and over again as the portly major heaved himself into the saddle and galloped across the hilltop, shouting to be heard.

"Benteen," Reno cried out. "Stop! For God's sake, man. I've lost half my command."

Benteen flung up his hand, bringing his column to a sudden halt as Reno ran up alongside and grabbed the bridle of Benteen's horse. Varnum and Hare could see the moon-faced Reno gesticulating wildly as he pointed down toward the valley and waved a hand back toward the survivors of his battalion. Captain Benteen sat astride his horse stone-faced as the major recounted his disastrous charge and retreat.

Moments later Benteen slid to the ground and strode purposefully up and down the bluffs. The sour-faced captain waved his battalion into positions forming an oval-shaped perimeter around the makeshift hospital that had been set up in a small, saucerlike depression. He directed the horse-holders toward the center of the position, providing a sort of horse-flesh shield for the wounded, who had been laid evenly around the sides of the slight depression. While Benteen was organizing the defense, Reno gathered a small group of men and slipped over the side of the bluffs, heading back down toward the valley below.

"Luther," Varnum said. "Best go get McDougall. I think we're gonna need that ammo pretty damn quick. Hey, where the hell's Reno think he's going?"

Lieutenant Hare nodded, wiping his nose on the sleeve of his shirt. "He's probably going down to try to get Benny's body buried. Although I don't know how the hell he thinks he's gonna do it. There ain't a shovel in the outfit." Hare glanced angrily down the hill after his commander, then turned his horse and moved quickly down the back trail. "He's a damned fool, Charlie!" he called over his shoulder. "I'm going after McDougall."

Varnum looked around him and quickly concluded that Hare was right. Reno was indeed behaving like a damn fool; first letting the Sioux bounce 'em out of the timber and getting half of the battalion cut up trying to get away. Now the idiot was off skylarking around after Benny Hodgson, who was dead, when he ought to be up here trying to get the living organized in case the Sioux came back. More like *when* the Sioux came back, for he had no illusions that the Indians had given up on them.

Varnum glanced over at Captain Moylan, who was stalking around the open-air hospital, tears running down his cheeks, as he tried to get his wounded—nearly half of his company—under some cover. The acting surgeon, Dr. Porter, was crawling from man to man doing what little he could to help. Bones had to be set, arrowheads or bullets dug from groaning soldiers, bandannas pressed into service as slings or bandages. Christ, what a mess.

By the time Marcus Reno reached the body of his friend, he was nearly beside himself with grief and depression. He rummaged through Benny Hodgson's pockets gathering the few scraps of paper and gently worked Benny's West Point class ring off of his cold finger. Hodgson's watch was already gone, no doubt a trophy for some young buck. Sweat and tears mixed freely in Reno's eyes, stinging them cruelly as he reached down to cut a small lock of hair from Hodgson's head. He knew that Benny's mother would want something to remember her son by.

Looking back up the hill, he quickly realized that there was no way that he would be able to drag the body out of here, and without a spade or pick, it would be impossible to bury him until the packtrain came up with some tools. He glanced around at the small detail that had slid down from the bluffs with him and noticed they were all staring uneasily downriver toward the sound of recurring gunfire. They couldn't stay here much longer. He called out to a sergeant who had waded into the Little Bighorn to drag Tosh McIntosh's body out onto the far bank. The young lieutenant's body had been badly cut up before a vindictive brave had kicked it rolling down into the river.

"Sergeant Pahl!" Reno yelled. "Let's go. We'll bring a detail down later. We have to get back up to the command."

Pahl waved in acknowledgment and waded laboriously back across the Little Bighorn, glancing anxiously over his shoulder while holding his cocked revolver up out of the water. As the man scrabbled up the near bank, Reno led the detail back up the steep slope, slipping and scrambling over loose rocks and grabbing onto sagebrush bushes to pull themselves hand over hand to the top.

Lieutenant Varnum, who'd been joined by his friend Nick Wallace, moved over to help Reno's detail up over the edge. The troops had no sooner bellied, panting, over the rim when a rustling of bushes on the slope below caused them all to flatten themselves on the ground with their weapons pointing downhill.

"Easy with them shooters, boys," the rough voice of George Herendeen called out from a nearby patch of sage. "Soldiers comin' in with me, so keep them fingers off the trigger."

As the officers watched, Herendeen scuttled up from below, followed quickly by a dozen dirty and terribly frightened young troopers. Bringing up the rear was Sergeant "Buck" White, a revolver in each hand and a bloody strip of a rag tied across his smoke-blackened forehead. Well, Varnum thought, that's a few more able-bodied men than we had a minute ago. He wondered if there were any more of the men still holed up down below, although he rather doubted it.

"Buck," Varnum said, "you seen anyone else down there before you came up?"

Sergeant White spit a stream of tobacco juice over the side of the bluff before he turned to answer Varnum.

"Yes, sir," White said. "There's a passel of the boys still down there. Sergeants Botzer, Considine, and O'Hara; Corporals Lell, Hageman, Martin, Scollin, and Streing; Privates Gordon, Klotzbucher, Lorentz, and Sniffin. They're all down there, an' more, I expect." White paused, his eyes drifting meaningfully in the direction of Major Reno. "Exceptin' that every one of 'em's stone dead."

Reno groaned softly as he dropped to sit heavily in the dirt, his head cradled in his hands.

"Oh, my God," the major mumbled quietly. "Oh, my God."

As the men stood idly watching Reno, the distant sound of gunfire was punctuated by a loud crackling, as if a fight was heating up. Varnum started at the sound.

"Jesus Christ, Wallace," he exclaimed. "Did you hear that?" The roar of another round of firing echoed from beyond the nearby hills. "And that? Custer must be having a pretty warm time of it down there."

Lieutenant Wallace nodded dumbly, and Varnum found himself wondering what had become of the rest of the command. Had they too been thrown off? Were they corralled up on a damned hilltop like this one? Had they linked up with Terry and Gibbon and started pushing the Sioux back this way? Varnum yawned and shook his head to try to clear the cobwebs. God, but he was tired. He stumbled over toward the southern edge of the perimeter and sat down heavily in the brown grass. Stretching himself out at full length, he rolled onto his belly behind a stunted sage bush and blinked rapidly, trying to focus on a distant ridgeline. He looked down at his hand and tried to think how and where he had picked up the carbine he was grasping but just couldn't seem to remember. Sliding the carbine forward, he poked the muzzle out from under the sage bush, flipped open the breech to make sure it was loaded, and then fiddled with the range scale to adjust the sights. Have to make every shot count, he thought groggily.

Private Anton "Tony" Siebelder dropped down into the dirt nearby and laid a handful of cartridges out in the dirt next to him. Looking over at the young officer, Siebelder smiled and snorted with amusement. Here they were, half cut to ribbons and surrounded by more goddamned savages than he'd ever seen in his life, and the chief of scouts was darn near done in. The lieutenant had fallen fast asleep on the butt of his carbine.

Fred Benteen was smiling grimly to himself. What a thoroughly botched job this was, he thought. That spineless moron Reno has gotten half of his damned battalion shot to hell and come running up here like a whipped urchin. Now he was down there mooning over his dead friend Hodgson. Too bad about Hodgson, he seemed like a nice enough sort. Probably lucky to go when he did, as these bastards would have ruined him or done for him in the long run anyway. Sioux probably did him a favor putting him out of his misery. Benteen looked at Moylan, the great oaf, standing there blubbering like a damned infant. He snorted in disgust. Bunch of worthless scoundrels! And old G.A.C. nowhere in sight. Probably off whooping it up like the damned immature pup that he was.

Well, he thought with smug satisfaction, here we are again, old man. These puling infants have made a fine mess of it, and it's left to the iron man, Fred Benteen, to clean up after 'em. He pulled out his watch and looked off to the north.

" 'The Injuns are skedaddling' indeed," Benteen said half to himself. "Probably skedaddlin' right this way too. Well, we'll soon have a warm welcome set up for you, Mr. Lo, just see if we don't."

1633 Hours
On the West Rim of Deep Coulee

Captain George Yates could hardly believe what was happening. He'd expected that there would be a fairly large village, but this, this was incredible. The damned Sioux were everywhere. He glanced ahead to where Fresh Smith rode at the head of his company. Smith had already been hit twice and was bleeding like a stuck pig. Now he was being held in his saddle by his orderly. Only the quick thinking of Privates James Brogan and Owen Boyle had kept the young lieutenant from tumbling off into the river below. Brogan and Boyle had seen Smith reel in the saddle, his buckskin jacket slick with blood where a musket ball had torn into his chest. Boyle reached across and grabbed him, holding the lieutenant upright while Brogan snatched loose his lariat and lashed the young officer securely to the rings on his McClellan. Now both companies were scrambling back up along the coulee's rim with Yates's company bringing up the rear.

Yates twisted in his saddle and fired two rounds point blank into an Arapaho warrior who had emerged suddenly from the coulee to his right. Yates's second shot slammed directly into the Indian's chest and sent him cartwheeling back down the ravine, his bow bouncing crazily into the air before hanging up in a sage bush. Damn, Yates thought, this is too goddamned tight. Behind him he could hear the deep bass voice of First Sergeant Kenny, who had hastily organized a makeshift rear guard of the company's best marksmen.

"Fire!" Kenny bellowed. "Cather, skip that big bastard out! The one with the bonnet."

The coulee boomed and echoed with the roar of carbines and pistols, the sound rolling and rebounding from its steep sides. Over all was the screaming of warriors, troopers, and horses and the shrill screeching of eagle-bone whistles rising eerily above the boiling clouds of dust and gun smoke. Feathered willow and dogwood shafts buzzed out of the brown fog to arc up and over the fleeing troops, a telltale thunk announcing when they had struck flesh or bone. But, in the roar and confusion, arrows and bullets were indiscriminate killers, as likely to hit friend as foe, and more than one Miniconjou or Brulé fell writhing in the dust with an Arapaho or Oglala shaft protruding from a ragged wound.

Sergeant John Vickory paused to shove another round into his carbine and looked up just in time to see the bow that slammed into his nose and knocked him sprawling from his saddle, blood gushing from his nostrils. Before the stunned sergeant could heave himself upright, a Crazy Dog, using his bow as a club, smashed the back of Vickory's head in with a single blow. When Corporal Charles Coleman saw his friend John Vickory killed, he leapt from his saddle in a blind rage, shoved the muzzle of his carbine into the surprised Lakota's open mouth, and pulled the trigger. The back of the Crazy Dog's head dissolved in a pink halo, tiny fragments of eagle feathers drifting crazily in the gun smoke like the puffball spores of a dandelion carried away on a breeze. Before he could reload, "Duffy" Coleman too was down in the dust, half a dozen Cheyenne and Arapaho arrows quivering in his side and back.

Yates looked desperately up the hill and spotted the main command a hundred yards above him. Keogh's people had arrived first and were already off of their horses and spreading out into a ragged skirmish line. Thank God, he thought, as the first volley roared out from above and the air to his right and left was rent by the zipping sound of .45/70 bullets hurtling toward the Indian ranks.

"Go! Go! Go!" Yates found himself screaming at the top of his lungs. "Faster, damn it!"

The companies surged forward just as hundreds more painted and feathered demons came screaming and boiling up out of the ravines on his right and left. Horses reared and whinnied in pain and terror as the hillside exploded around them, arrows hissing and bullets tearing through leather and flesh.

Mitch Bouyer, who was watching Yates's withdrawal from above, turned to his Crow friend Curley and pulled him roughly away from the firing line. Bouyer started yelling into the boy's ear in English before he saw the incomprehension in Curley's face. Bouyer switched quickly to Crow.

"Curley," he yelled, "you are young yet and don't know a lot about fighting. I want you to stay as far from the shooting as you can." Curley shook his head angrily.

"I will fight, Mitch," the boy yelled back. "We will kill many Head-Cutters."

"No! Damn it," Bouyer insisted, dragging the youngster farther back from the skirmish line.

"Listen to me, boy. I want you to stay ready in case we have to send a message to No Hipbone!"* Bouyer then pointed at Custer, who was turning his horse easily in a small circle while popping away at the swarming Sioux with his small English pistols.

"That man," he said, "will stop at nothing. Once he starts forward, he never goes back. I think he will take us all down there into the village and we will all be killed. This is not how the Crows fight. This is not how you should fight."

Curley looked into Bouyer's eyes. The eyes were kind and honest. There was no deceit in his friend's steady gaze. He decided that Mitch was being truthful with him and nodded quickly.

"Good," Bouyer said. "Now, stay close to me and we will keep close to Son-of-the-Morning-Star. He will want us to take a message soon." Curley nodded again, and the two turned their horses to move closer to the general. Custer appeared to be muttering to himself as he fired his pistols into the masses of Sioux and Cheyenne who kept surging up the hillside like a ragged surf, and did not notice the two scouts who were watching him intently.

"Pass 'em through!" Keogh shouted as what was left of companies E and F scrambled over the last few yards of sand and sagebrush.

"Fire!" Another volley belched fire and smoke down into the massed warriors darting through the brush and dust clouds around Yates's battalion.

Private Paddy Kelly, who found himself at the center of Keogh's line, was shaking uncontrollably as he loaded and reloaded his smoking weapon. He had never been so terrified in his life. The Irishman mumbled constantly to himself, reciting the rosary over and over again as the Springfield thumped mercilessly against his sore shoulder. Kneeling in the dirt next to him, Sergeant Jimmy Bustard cursed loudly and cackled like a madman with every bang of his carbine.

"Eat that, ya bug-eyed bastard!" His carbine clacked and clicked as another cartridge was rammed home. The hammer clicked back and the carbine roared again.

"Go on to hell, you son of a bitch!" Another spent cartridge chinked into the dirt as Bustard roared with laughter. Behind him a horse screamed

---

* No Hipbone was the Crows' name for General Alfred Terry, a very slender man. The Crows said that Terry was "a man without hips," and the name stuck.

and collapsed in a thrashing heap, breaking both legs of the young trooper he had fallen on.

To Bustard's right, Soapy Lloyd was, for the first time in weeks, completely silent as he worked his carbine with desperate speed. In his mind though Soapy was cursing his own stupidity, and that of everyone around him. They'd gotten him into this fix. Another couple of days, he thought, and I'd have been a hundred miles away from here and scraping gold out by the shovelful.

Damn you all! he thought, and cursed everyone he knew. As he squeezed off shot after shot, the faces of the Sioux and Cheyenne blurred and took on the faces of his old tormentors: Solomon & Hart, who'd let him go from what now seemed like a fairly cushy job as a paperhanger; Old Man Niblo, who had insisted on having Everett cut off his credit at Niblo's saloon, and Everett for actually doing it; and that stupid newspaperman who had written that gold-in-the-Black-Hills rot. Ignorant bastard. He hoped they'd all rot in hell for the mess they'd put him in this time. Soapy smiled evilly and pulled the trigger again.

Captain Tom Custer pounded his brother George on the shoulder. The din of battle was deafening and he had to shout to be heard.

"It's no good, Armstrong!" he yelled. "They're too close. We need some more elbow room or they'll be all over us in no time."

George Custer nodded and spurred Vic over toward where Myles Keogh was directing his battle line. The Irish giant was standing spread-legged directly behind the skirmishers and roaring out orders in a baritone brogue as he banged away with his own revolver. Custer leapt down into the dust next to him and yelled into his ear to be heard above the din.

"Myles! We've got to get higher up." Custer pointed up along the ridgeline toward a small knoll several hundred yards farther north. Keogh nodded grimly as Custer rattled off his instructions.

"Calhoun as rear guard. I want two battalion volleys before we move. That should push the hostiles off long enough to get us started and signal Benteen to hurry his ass up here with the packs!" Keogh nodded vigorously and trotted down the line to where Jimmi Calhoun was directing his own company's battle.

Mark Kellogg was cowering behind his mule as Keogh jogged by. He had dropped his pencil somewhere and his notes were now fluttering aimlessly between sage bushes or trodden under hooves and bootheels. All were entirely forgotten now. Before starting on this expedition he had stuffed an old cap-and-ball pepperbox pistol in his saddlebags thinking that, at worst, he might need it to do in a rattlesnake or two. Now Kellogg clutched the little five-barreled piece to his chest and stared wildly at the nightmare of dust and sudden death that whirled dizzily around him. An arrow buzzed out of nowhere and chunked into his mule's saddle, the feathers waving wildly as the animal bucked and kicked in his terror. Oh, Christ, Kellogg thought darkly, looks like Lounsberry may wind up writing this story after all.

Myles Keogh was ready. With his own Company I keeping up a steady rattle of musketry, he'd had First Sergeant Butler hastily form Companies C and L into two ranks, each bent in a sort of V-shape, with the point facing directly toward the Little Bighorn River. Now with the ranks formed, Company C dropped to one knee as Company L stood directly behind them. First Sergeant Butler smiled to see the formation and thought Her Majesty herself would be pleased with their soldierly appearance. He nodded to Keogh, who drew a deep breath.

"Battalion load!" Keogh bellowed. "Volley fire! Fire by rank! Battalion . . . rear rank, aaiim . . . fire!" A sheet of flame shot from the formation with a thunderous crack; smoke and dust in billowing clouds rolled down over the masses of Sioux and Cheyenne below.

"Front rank, aaiim . . . fire!" Another volley roared across the valley and echoed through the dust-choked coulees, accompanied by the satisfying shrieking of the wounded and dying warriors who had tried frantically to duck out of sight at the last second. Before the smoke had cleared, Company L had reloaded and resumed a steady fire while Company C and Company I had remounted and were flying rapidly up the ridgeline toward the small knoll above.

Lieutenant John J. Crittenden had managed to get as far as the north slope of the ridgeline before he ran into his first setback. No sooner had he crested the ridge when a savage figure seemed to rise out of the very ground in front of him. Entirely nude except for a breechclout, the warrior had painted his entire chest and face a garish yellow and his legs and hands bright red. Had Crittenden known anything of the Oglala culture, he might have had a better idea of the type of opponent he was facing, for the man's appearance spoke volumes about him.

He would have known, for instance, that the man with the upraised war club was a member of the Kit Fox warrior society, and the fact that he wore his hair loose indicated that he was prepared to do desperate deeds in battle. From the eagle quills standing upright on the man's scalp, he would have been able to tell that this Kit Fox had already killed two men in battle. Further, the black paint on the man's mouth and chin could have told him that this warrior had brought back his enemies' scalps. The red stripes radiating from the man's chest and neck showed that he had been in five battles, and the red dots on his upper-left forearm that he had been wounded by spears or arrows. Perhaps it was better that Crittenden could not tell these things, for the sight was hideous enough without the added knowledge that the young lieutenant was facing a hardened veteran.

Luckily for the lieutenant, the warrior's sudden appearance so spooked Crittenden's horse that it reared up, flailing its hooves wildly, one of which struck the Oglala a glancing blow on the left temple and knocked him senseless into the dirt. Crittenden gasped as he fought to control the animal and counted himself the luckiest man alive, having lost nothing more than two buttons that had snagged on the saddle's crupper and been torn away. Dragging his revolver from its holster, he spurred his mount forward down the slope and around the Oglala's body. He had not gone another fifty yards before his luck changed once again, as half a dozen mounted warriors leaped screaming up out of a hidden ravine.

Crittenden yanked his horse's head around, fired two shots at the warriors, and veered off to the right. Before he could get another fifty yards on, another war party loomed up ahead of him. Crittenden wheeled his horse about again and raced headlong back toward the command, a dozen warriors now yipping and whooping on his heels. The lieutenant leaned over the neck of his mount and hung on for dear life as he skirted around the eastern slope of the ridge before dashing up and over the top. He arrived just as the command fired the second mass volley and began its withdrawal. The lieutenant looked anxiously around and caught sight of Jimmi Calhoun's company still on the firing line. Urging his horse forward, he leapt from the saddle next to his friend and breathed a heavy sigh of relief. The warriors who had been chasing him veered off as the other two companies moved between them.

"John!" Calhoun exclaimed. "What the hell are you doing here? I thought the general sent you after Gibbon?"

"Bit of a problem, Jimmi." Crittenden was panting. "Damn Sioux are thick as locusts up there. Thought I'd best join up with a few friends. Safety in numbers, you know."

Calhoun squeezed off a shot at a middle-aged Sans Arc who had just raised a Winchester to fire. The warrior seemed truly surprised as his hands dropped helplessly to his sides and he looked down at a gaping wound in his own chest, blood spurting in a graceful arc into the dust in front of him. The Sans Arc sank slowly to his knees and flopped over facedown in the dirt. Calhoun thumbed open the loading gate on his Colt and jacked out the spent cartridges as he turned to his old friend.

"Out of the frying pan, into the fire, if you ask me, J.J.," Calhoun shouted. "There's damn little safety here."

Wickuciyela *(Late Afternoon)*
*On Greasy Grass Hill**

The banging of the guns had grown to a deafening roar. Everywhere Crow King turned there were hundreds of warriors—Kit Foxes, Strong Hearts, Otters, Beavers, Heyokas, Bare Lances, Bull Soldiers. Every society of every clan seemed to be represented. Some were beautifully painted and in full regalia: warbonnets, breastplates, armlets, and buffalo-hide shields. Others were nearly nude, wearing little more than a breechclout and moccasins.

But all of them carried weapons of some sort—bows, lances, tomahawks, butcher knives, war clubs, pistols, rifles, even old trade muskets. And all of them seemed to be screaming, chanting, or blowing eagle-bone whistles. All was confusion, dust, smoke, and noise. The *wasichus* too were shooting and screaming. Crow King could only catch fleeting glimpses of them through the dust, but every time the smoke began to drift away from the hill, he could still see them in little crowds shooting in all directions, or swinging their rifles like clubs while their horses reared and plunged behind them.

Crow King saw that this was not a good place to use horses. Everywhere, the hills were torn by coulees and ragged, deep ravines where the dirt was loose and treacherous. He noticed that most of the people were now leaving their ponies behind and racing on foot up the crooked ravines, using what cover they afforded to stay away from of the soldiers' guns. Good. This was a good way to fight. Looking to his left, he saw a large group of Cheyennes behind a small hill. All of them had the new fast-shooting guns, and they were firing as fast as they could work the levers, popping up, shooting, and them ducking behind the hill again. Just next to them some Arapahos were shooting bows almost straight up so that the arrows were flung high into the air before they arced down again right on

---

* Now known as Custer, or Last Stand, Hill. Greasy Grass is also the name given to the ridge just beyond this hill.

top of the soldiers. Some young boys were lying behind them and handing up new arrows as fast as the warriors could loose them.

When he turned to look to his right, Crow King saw Gall rush by, followed by a large war party made up of Hunkpapas, Miniconjous, and Sans Arcs. Gall had a mad look in his eyes. His arms were bathed in blood to the elbows, and large splotches of blood spattered his face and chest. Gall had been busy today. Crow King was a little surprised to see that Gall was carrying only a stone club in his hand. The club was raised high over his head and pointed straight up Medicine Tail Coulee as the man screamed at his followers.

"Hokahe! This way, Lakotas!" Gall was shouting. "Come this way. We will be right in their faces before they can see us. Brave up, boys! It is a good day to die!"

The Lakotas shrieked in unison and disappeared at a run up into the dust and smoke that filled the coulee. Crow King grinned and shook his rifle after the Hunkpapas. They were good fighters today. He looked at the Cheyennes and decided that the Hunkpapas should not count all the coups today. Running over to the men who were shooting he yelled: "Come on, you Shyelas! Come on, Arapahos! Don't let the Lakotas take all the honors. Only the earth and the sky live forever. Come on! *Hokahe!"*

The warriors all looked at him curiously for a second and then leapt, whooping, to dash over the little hill. Moments later they were all racing up a small ravine headed for the place where Crow King had seen a group of soldiers a few minutes before. He knew that if they followed this small ditch it would take them nearly to the top of the hill without being seen. And, if they ran quickly, they might even beat Gall to the top of the hill. Oh, yes, this would be a good trick on the *wasichus.* They would surprise them from two sides.

Crazy Horse was just riding back through the village when he turned and saw Crow King leading his war party up the ravine. He watched for a moment as the warriors scrambled, howling, up the hillside. Let them go, he thought. I've done enough today already. Crazy Horse kicked his pony's flanks and continued on his way back toward the Oglala circle. The soldiers in the timber had been easy to beat. A few charges and they scattered like frightened antelope. It was not much of a challenge to chase these *wasichus.* They were across the river now, and he didn't think they would dare to bother the Lakotas again today. Let them run away.

He rode slowly through the lodges where the women and children were just now returning to their homes. Even the helpless ones knew that there was nothing more to fear from the soldiers, and they were rushing back to watch the warriors fight. Several times he had to stop his pony suddenly to keep from trampling some youngster who was running head-long toward the fight, waving a toy bow or a stick. As he approached his own lodge, he urged his pony to jump across the small stream, and then he heard someone calling his name. Crazy Horse turned to see the Hunk-papa they called White Bull cantering up on his buckskin.

"*Kta*, Crazy Horse, wait!" White Bull called out. "Where are you going? This fight isn't over yet. We need you."

"*Iñs hecel?* Who cares?" Crazy Horse replied laconically. "These sol-diers are running away now. I say, let them go. I've had enough fighting today. You don't need me anymore."

White Bull rode up alongside Crazy Horse and looked at him with curiosity. The Oglala didn't bother even to look his way and appeared truly disinterested in the battle that was still raging less than an arrow flight away. He saw that Crazy Horse had much blood spattered on him. It had smeared some of the painted hailstones that decorated the man's body. He'd obviously been in the thick of the fighting already. Now that they were winning, it seemed unbelievable that the man had just lost interest. What an odd fellow this Oglala was.

"Crazy Horse," White Bull went on, "the battle is now moving toward your end of the village, and we need your help to finish these *wasichus* off." White Bull turned and looked anxiously at hundreds of Oglalas and Brulés who had begun to follow this strange warrior. The man insisted that he was not a chief, but his leadership was undeniable.

"Look behind you, Crazy Horse," he urged. "All of these warriors are following you and waiting for you to lead them back into the fight. Surely you don't want to take all of these people away just when we need them most?"

Crazy Horse looked behind him and was surprised to see that what the Hunkpapa said was indeed true. Hundreds of warriors had gathered to follow him back toward the north end of the village. What was the matter with all of them? he wondered. They can fight without me. Why don't they just go on? I'm not their chief!

"*Has' Wahtes'niit'a!* I'm sick and tired of it!" Crazy Horse spat. "If you're so eager for battle, White Bull, why don't you just lead them? Go ahead, I won't stop you."

"I would," White Bull retorted, "and I will, but they say they will only follow you. Come on, Crazy Horse," he pleaded. "Just come with me. I'll lead the way, you just have to come along so that we have as many warriors as possible. Wherever you go, they will go. Come on!"

Crazy Horse reined back his pony and looked back to discover that the other warriors had all stopped as well. This was ridiculous. He breathed in deeply and let out a long breath in exasperation.

"Alright," he said finally, but without much enthusiasm, "let's go. But we'll do it my way. We'll ride up to the north end of the camp where the Shyelas are. We'll get some of them together and cross the river down there. We'll go around the base of that hill." He pointed across the river toward the long brown slope whose top was now wreathed in a thick cloud of dust and gun smoke. "The *wasichus* will try to get to the top of that hill, where they can shoot down into the camp until more soldiers come to help them."

White Bull frowned at this. He had not considered that there might be more soldiers coming even now. Crazy Horse seemed to read his thoughts.

"Yes," Crazy Horse said quietly, "there are more soldiers coming. You know that they will not stop coming, they will never stop now. So, if you want to finish this battle, we must do it quickly."

Without another word, Crazy Horse turned and kicked his pony, urging him into an easy lope. He would go to the Shyelas and see if Two Moon was back from his fight. If they could get two large war parties to strike the soldiers from two sides, they might be able to end this thing soon.

Despite his best effort to get up the ravine as quickly as possible, Crow King found that his war party reached the top about the same time as Gall's. As they neared the top of the ravine, it gradually became more shallow and they had to crouch lower and lower as they scuttled through the loose soil between the withered tufts of grass that dotted the cut's sides. Most of the warriors were bleeding from skinned knees and elbows, and some had to stop frequently to dump loose pebbles from their moccasins. All of them were sweating heavily and caked with dust. When Crow King found himself with his elbows nearly touching the ground, he noticed that the sound of the soldiers' guns had grown so loud that they must be only as far away as one could easily throw a rock. He stopped and waved to his followers to stay down in the ditch and wait for his signal.

A ragged volley roared over their heads, and Crow King rose, screaming his war cry and blindly firing his Winchester as fast as he could work the action. At his signal dozens of Arapahos and Cheyennes scrambled from the ditch whooping, shooting, and flailing the air with clubs and hatchets. Charging into the smoke, Crow King saw that they had gotten closer than he expected. The soldiers were right in front of him. He could plainly see the shock and terror in their eyes as the war party leapt into their midst with a horrible fury. A soldier with bright red hair pointed his rifle directly at him, but when the hammer fell, there was no explosion. The gun had misfired and Crow King yipped in triumph as he swung his own rifle to smash the soldier's head like a ripe pumpkin.

The beleaguered soldiers had no idea that the end was so near. Gall's war party struck from the opposite direction at about the same time, and within seconds the whole skirmish line had dissolved into a maelstrom of screaming, frantic men grappling in the smoke and dust. They clubbed and slashed at each other, going down into the dust wrestling, clawing, scratching, and biting. Bullets were quickly abandoned in favor of knives, gun butts, hatchets, and teeth as the two sides merged into a single writhing mass of sweating, bleeding bodies.

In the middle of this brawl the two friends, Lieutenants Calhoun and Crittenden, fell within feet and seconds of each other. Jimmi Calhoun lay facedown across the rump of a dead horse, his lifeblood seeping slowly into the dirt, the world spinning crazily around him. As the world grew darker, he heard a distant, guttural chanting as a young Lakota warrior began to sing in a high and breathless voice:

> "ite`isa byeh
> aö`pazan
> owa`le
> c'a
> he' camon ye"*

The chanting grew fainter and ever more distant, to be replaced gradually by a dull rushing sound, as of a mountain stream plunging down a chute of rapids. Calhoun exhaled and sank into the cooling darkness that closed over him like water.

---

* "Black face paint / (and a) feather / I seek / so / I have done this." *A Lakota war song. The killing of an enemy entitled a warrior to paint his face black and wear an eagle feather in his hair.*

1650 Hours
Along the Ridgeline

"Jaysus!" Keogh yelled. "They're inta Calhoun! *Company I, mount! Rally on me!*"

The wild-eyed Irishman swung into the saddle and wheeled his horse around, shouting for the company to form into a line. Yates and his company fired madly as they tried to withdraw slowly up the ridgeline, stopping momentarily to fire and reload as they walked steadily backward. They were trying desperately to buy time for the rest of the outfit to assemble near the regimental headquarters. Tom Custer's Company C had been joined by Smith's Company E, now that Fresh Smith was laid out in a makeshift aid station under the care of Dr. Lord.

The aid station had been set up hastily on a small knoll at the end of the ridgeline where George Custer had now located the regimental headquarters. Even now the general and "Queen's Own" Cooke were supervising the slaughter of some of the headquarters' own horses, arranging their bodies to form a sort of barricade behind which the wounded, those who were in reach, could be dragged for safety. Tom Custer, assisted by Yates and First Sergeant Kenny, had managed to keep the companies closed up tight as they made their torturous way up the ridgeline behind Keogh's screen of troops. Now it looked as if their screen was about to evaporate before their eyes.

Myles Keogh realized the danger now posed to the outfit's withdrawal. If Calhoun was overrun, there would be little time to reorganize in a decent defensive position. He had to move quickly. He wheeled Comanche about and burst through to the front of the line of mounted troopers.

"*Chaaarrge!*" Keogh screamed.

Trumpeter Private McGucken sounded the Charge, and the whole line lunged forward at the gallop, revolvers leveled and spitting fire into the hordes of Sioux and Cheyenne warriors now intermingled with Calhoun's men. The men of the "Wild I" let loose with an earsplitting Rebel yell as they smashed headlong into the Indians, who raced out to meet them halfway up the ridgeline. As the two masses met and mixed, the soil was kicked into a whirlwind of dust and gun smoke, obscuring the desperate conflict from all onlookers. Even those in the middle of the fight could catch only fleeting glimpses of their fellow combatants.

Soapy Lloyd, his revolver empty, heaved the weapon into the face of a Kit Fox and snatched up his carbine. He quickly slammed a cartridge into the breech, never noticing the dull green coating of verdigris that had formed on the copper casing. Throwing the weapon to his shoulder, he fired just as the Kit Fox recovered his balance and sent a slug tearing through the warrior's windpipe. What Soapy didn't know was that, as the weapon fired, the heat from the exploding gunpowder had melted the cartridge's green coating, causing it to bond instantly with the steel of the breech and locking the empty cartridge securely in the weapon.

When he flipped open the trapdoor, the extractor, instead of flipping the spent cartridge out into the scrub, succeeded only in ripping the base clear off of the shell. It took Lloyd only a split second to realize his dilemma. He yanked out his hunting knife and jabbed frantically at the ruptured shell casing. A split second later a Bull Soldier shoved a lance clear through Soapy's chest, the lance point pushing a large chunk of his sternum in front of it. Soapy looked down at the thick-feathered shaft protruding from his chest and rolled from his saddle, collapsing in a heap. The Bull Soldier grabbed up the jammed carbine and shook it triumphantly over his head. He unbuckled Lloyd's cartridge belt and tried to push another round into the breech, puzzled that it would not fit no matter how hard he pushed. Sergeant James Bustard used this opportunity to employ his lariat with its heavy iron picket pin like a flail and caved in the distracted Bull Soldier's skull like an overripe melon. But Bustard's triumph too was short-lived, and seconds later he lay facedown in the dust with a half-dozen chokecherry and dogwood shafts in his body.

Paddy Kelly stared open-mouthed as Fred and Henry Lehman were tumbled from their saddles by a screaming horde of Cheyennes. Kelly had already emptied his pistol, but kept cocking it and pulling the trigger convulsively. With the noise and confusion he never noticed the dull click as the hammer fell again and again on the empty shell casings.

"Holy Mary, Mother of God," Kelly cried out, working the heavy Colt in terror, "pray for us sinners, now and at the hour of our—"

A heavy stone war club swung by a large Hunkpapa turned Paddy's world into a blinding white flash that dissolved into darkness and oblivion. Gall uttered a satisfied "Hounh!" as the war club did its work on the Irishman's skull. He spun with the momentum of the blow and saw the

Oglala Eagle Elk and his Miniconjou friend High Horse grappling with a single trooper, who rolled and thrashed in the dirt. The white man was powerful and flung High Horse around, beating the dust with him like a discarded buffalo robe, as Eagle Elk danced to one side, slashing at the pair with the flat of his bow. To Gall it appeared that Eagle Elk was hitting his friend as often as he was hitting the *wasichu*. The excited Oglala dodged in front of Gall just as he heard a muffled thump.

Eagle Elk pulled his friend High Horse away from the soldier, and Gall saw that the bluecoat's throat was slashed and gushing blood. The soldier slid back on his heels and collapsed in the dust, his smoking revolver clasped tight in a death grip. When Gall looked at the two Lakotas, he saw that the soldier had managed to discharge his revolver point-blank into High Horse's chest. A wailing and frantic Eagle Elk was now dragging his friend's limp body down the hill. Gall growled his fury and kicked viciously at the dying soldier's head.

Myles Keogh was in a killing frenzy. His horse Comanche was down and rolling in the dust. The game was up and Keogh knew it. The company hadn't been able to get enough momentum before they collided with the Sioux, and now they were at a distinct disadvantage. A man on horseback can do tremendous damage to a man on foot, provided he can throw the weight of himself and the horse at his opponent at a gallop. But that hadn't happened. The Sioux had quickly seen the danger and rushed out to meet Keogh's onslaught before it could reach full speed. The charge had immediately ground to a halt in a churning mass of horseflesh and human bodies.

Keogh's troopers could no longer concentrate on firing their weapons, for each was surrounded by three or four warriors wielding hatchets, clubs, and even rocks. Hundreds of brown hands grabbed at bridles and reins, tugged at boots and lariats, or waved blankets in front of the rearing horses. The terrified mounts neighed and plunged, pitching their riders into the masses of warriors amid a cacophony of screaming, gunshots, and screeching whistles.

Seeing that all was lost, Keogh vowed silently to take as many redskins with him as possible as he emptied his revolvers into the swirling dust cloud, bellowing and snarling at his tormentors. When his revolvers were empty, he hurled them at a yellow-and-black-faced Cheyenne, startling the man long enough to enable the Irishman to snatch away the warrior's lance. He'd have preferred to use his saber, but the unit had left them all back at the Yellowstone, carefully packed in crates. This would just have to do. Keogh used the lance like a bayoneted rifle going into the "en garde" position, parrying, thrusting, and stabbing. A circle of dead and wounded warriors mounded up around him as he wielded the captured lance and laughed demonically, daring the others to come on.

"Come on, ye black-hearted bastards!" Keogh taunted them. "Come git yer reward!"

Some of the warriors drew back from the Crazy Dog white man with the curling black mustache and the killing fever in his eyes. As the fight swirled around them, a Brave Heart thrust through the small knot of onlookers, pushing out his chest and brandishing his own lance at the *wasichu*. The Brave Heart rushed at Keogh with a yell, only to have his legs knocked out from under him as the Irishman swung his lance like a stave, smashing the Brave Heart's knees. Keogh drove his lance point through the man's back and jerked it free in time to parry another warrior who had darted in from the side. Keogh reversed the weapon to slam the butt into the warrior's testicles, then kicked the man's face into jelly with his boot heel. Roaring with laughter, the battle-maddened Keogh whirled to meet the next man, but the warriors had had enough.

It was a tired-looking, middle-aged Sans Arc who put an end to the standoff. The panting warrior picked up Paddy Kelly's carbine and casually fired a government-issue slug through Keogh's heart. The Sans Arc stood over Keogh's body and was about to take his scalp when he noticed the leather thong and pouch around the dead man's neck. The warrior decided that this *wasichu* was wearing powerful medicine. Perhaps, he reasoned, this was why he fought like a Crazy-Dog-Who-Wants-to-Die. Whatever the reason, the Sans Arc concluded that it was best not to fool with such medicine, put his knife back in its sheath, and trotted easily past the body. He would content himself with looking for another white man on whom to try out his new gun.

Two hundred yards farther up the hill Mitch Bouyer could see that things were now mighty bad indeed. His own horse was down and he himself had taken a .58-caliber musket ball through the left thigh. The bone was unbroken, but a large chunk of flesh had been torn away and made walking a painful exercise. A little to Bouyer's rear Tom Custer was bellowing an order for those under his command to load and fire a simultaneous volley. Twice the massed carbines roared in unison, their thunderclaps rolling over the barren countryside. Bouyer shook his head and limped over to where Curley was standing near his pony, calmly firing his rifle over the animal's back. He laid a hand firmly on the boy's shoulder, being careful to call his name as he did so.

"Curley," he called. "Listen to me, boy. This battle is over." Curley looked saddened and shot a quizzical look at his friend.

"What about these shots, Mitch?" He asked. "Is this not some signal to the others?"

Bouyer looked quietly into the Crow's eyes before he answered.

"Yes," Bouyer rasped, wincing with the pain in his thigh, "it is a signal, but I think it is too late. Son-of-the-Morning-Star thinks that if we can get to the top of this hill we can hold them off until the rest of the regiment comes up to help. I do not think this will happen. Benteen will not come, and I think that in a little while they will rub us out. Do you understand?" The Crow nodded glumly.

"Alright then," Bouyer went on, shoving a cased set of field glasses into the boy's hands. "I took these from an officer who has no more need of them. I want you to go to that ridge over there." He pointed off to the northeast. "Stay well away from the Sioux and watch with these glasses to see what happens here. Then you ride away as fast as you can go. Go to No Hipbone and tell him we are all killed."

Curley took the field glasses and draped the strap over his shoulder. He ripped his pony's picket pin free of the ground and looked about as if hunting for something. Curley noticed a dead Sioux pony lying nearby, went over to it, and pulled a bright red blanket free of the carcass. Part of the blanket was worked with distinctive Sioux designs, and he wrapped it around his waist, making sure that the designs showed clearly. He then quickly undid his hair, running his fingers through it to let his tresses hang loose rather than in the Crow style he usually wore. His disguise complete, Curley shook hands with his wounded friend, leapt onto his pony, and galloped away in the direction Mitch had indicated. A few moments later he disappeared down a ravine and was lost from sight. Bouyer watched him go, muttering a Crow prayer under his breath.

"Hé Hé Hé í'tsikyãta!" Bouyer said. "Go safely, brother, and if you meet an enemy, may you kill him without injury to yourself."

Another burst of heavy firing drew Bouyer's attention back to the fight, and he dragged himself painfully back toward the ragged skirmish line that Tom Custer was trying to get organized, just below the little knoll where George Custer had set up his headquarters. The men gathered around the general were now all kneeling, or leaning over the flanks of dead horses with carbines propped up on the carcasses. Those who had any strength left were still firing gamely at the closing circle of warriors or handing loaded weapons forward to others.

Mitch reached the skirmish line and took up a postion between a pair of haggard-looking sergeants. The scout bent to adjust the filthy tourniquet he had wrapped around his leg and was thinking that this was turning out to be a hell of a day when a lead slug drilled a hole through his brain and put an end to the painful throbbing in Mitch Bouyer's leg. The sergeants never noticed Bouyer slump to the ground but dug deeper into their pockets for cartridges and banged away blindly at the curtain of dust that hung all around them.

Hundreds of yards away Curley maneuvered his pony deftly as it picked its way through a scrub-covered ravine. The Head-Cutters had not yet closed the circle around the soldiers and it was a fairly simple matter for him to slip through the lines and away from the fight. Curley looked anxiously around him and, seeing that no one was following, dug his heels into the pony's flanks and urged him into a lope. He resisted the temptation to gallop, as that would have kicked up a dust cloud and possibly drawn some unwanted attention.

When he had reached the ridge that Mitch had pointed out to him, Curley reined back on his pony and turned to look back toward the fighting. Satisfied there were no Sioux nearby, he balanced his carbine across the saddle, dug into the leather case suspended around his neck, and pulled out the field glasses. These were wonderful things, he thought, these medicine eyes that let you see for long distances. The white men's medicine was truly strong, and he felt the Crow had made a good bargain by joining them to fight the Head-Cutters. In the end, he knew that the Head-Cutters could not hope to win.

He peered through the glasses and was temporarily disoriented as they swept over the vast expanse of scrub-covered hills. He realized that if he moved the glasses too quickly he got dizzy, and it was better if he used his own eyes first before trying to look through the field glasses. Curley could see the battlefield in the distance. It was easy to pick out because of the huge cloud of dust that hovered around the hilltop and rose into the sky like smoke. But even with the help of the field glasses, it was difficult to see what was happening. The bang of weapons and the screaming of men and horses drifted out to him and echoed from the surrounding ravines, but all he could see was dim figures shrouded in smoke and dust scurrying through the murk like frenzied ants whose home has been kicked by a careless foot.

Curley remembered a time in his childhood when he and a friend had collected a stick full of black ants and thrust the stick violently into a mound of dirt inhabited by red ants. The two boys had sat and watched fascinated as the red ants swarmed out of their hill to kill the invaders. It looked much like this, he thought curiously, except the ants had not raised the dust so. The boy thought sadly of his friend Mitch, who must now be traveling down the ghost road. He raised a hand and quietly recited an old prayer.

"Eternal are the heavens and the earth," Curley said. "Old people are poorly off; do not be afraid. You are gone. Do not turn back. We wish to fare well."

The boy turned his pony and rode away as tears coursed down his smooth cheeks.

Intahepi (Before Evening)
On Greasy Grass Hill

Crazy Horse had had just about enough fighting for one day and was now regretting his weakness in letting White Bull coax him into this last fight. As far as he was concerned, the *wasichus* were so badly beaten now that they would be no threat at all to the camp. He would just as soon let these people run away to tell the other whites how powerful the Lakota had become. He couldn't help feeling that if they insisted on killing them all there could only be more trouble.

He remembered one of his first fights against the whites, when Red Cloud had been the Oglalas' leader. After the Fight of the Hundred Dead,* Red Cloud had refused to let the warriors try to attack the white man's fort. Red Cloud had said that it was bad policy to try to rub out all of the white soldiers.

"If you try to kill them all," the old warrior had warned, "you will find that more of them come. They are like bees when you strike their nest with a stone. They are so many that they will sting you to death."

Red Cloud had convinced the tribes to hold back, and just as he said, the white men had stopped coming. They had even taken their soldiers from the forts after Red Cloud touched the pen at Laramie. Red Cloud had won his war, and now Crazy Horse wondered if they would win this war too. If Red Cloud was to be believed, there was always a danger that they would go too far and make the soldiers come like bees. This sort of thing made his head hurt when he was so tired, and he decided he would worry about this later. Right now he would just try to end this fight quickly.

As they crossed the river, a large party of Cheyennes rode up and joined in, hundreds of hooves splashing through the shallow water below the beaver dam, the warriors chanting and grinning at each other. The

---

* The Fight of the Hundred Dead was the Lakotas' name for the Fetterman massacre of 1866. The "white man's fort" was Fort Phil Kearney on the Bozeman Trail, which, along with Fort Reno and Fort C. F. Smith, was abandoned to the Sioux by the Laramie Treaty of 1868, ending Red Cloud's War.

Shyelas had painted themselves for battle, and Crazy Horse could tell that both the warriors and their ponies were still fresh. Good, he thought, they can do most of the work now. He caught sight of Two Moon and guided his buckskin over to his friend's side.

"*Cañnako*, Crazy Horse!" The Cheyenne was pleased to see him again. "Are the Lakotas ready to finish this fight?"

"*Hokahe*, Two Moon," Crazy Horse replied. "They say it is a good day to die."

"But a better day to kill, eh?" Two Moon shot back with a wide grin.

Crazy Horse maneuvered his buckskin so that he and Two Moon were taken a little aside from the rest of the warriors as they started up the long slope of Greasy Grass Hill. When they had gone a little way, the Oglala reined in his pony and pointed up the hill.

"I have a plan," he said, "that will finish this fight very quickly. Are your braves ready for a hard fight?"

The Cheyenne stopped, looked at his old friend, and nodded in interest. Crazy Horse was a good fighter. Many said that it was Crazy Horse's plan that had won the fight with Three Stars, and Two Moon quickly decided that whatever Crazy Horse had to say was worth hearing. He noticed that his friend had a faraway look in his eye, almost as if he no longer cared very much for this fighting. Perhaps he is just tired, Two Moon thought, but quickly shrugged off the idea.

"We will split our forces into two separate war parties," Crazy Horse explained. "You take your people up this ravine here and work around to the right. I will take the Lakotas and we will go back around the base of this hill. We must go first because we have a longer way to travel. We will come around from behind the soldiers on the hilltop and ride them down. You Shyelas will strike them from the front, and that way we will have them between us. Do you agree?"

Two Moon nodded his assent. It was a good plan. Crazy Horse went on: "Good. First let us send our braves who are the very best shots. They should all have the fast-shooting guns. They will ride around to the north and way to the east of these soldiers. When they get to the far ridgeline, they can shoot into the soldiers from far away. That will keep the soldiers from looking as we ride up."

Two Moon grinned. This was an even better part of the plan, a wonderful trick to play on these soldiers. He turned to his followers and quickly rounded up a small party of his best shots, all carrying the new Winchester, or the heavier Henry, rifles. Crazy Horse too picked out some braves with these weapons, and they sent the whole group racing off around the northern end of the hill to get into position. The remaining warriors, now numbering in the hundreds, waited anxiously, their ponies prancing nervously in the coulees, as they assembled into two large war parties.

The air felt charged with electricity as it does when a thunderstorm is moving closer over the plains. The excitement rippled through the warriors, who bantered with each other and boasted of the coups they had counted already. The younger men especially were eager to be off to battle once again. It was a good day for counting coup and gathering many battle honors. They would talk about this fight for many years to come. After a few moments Crazy Horse nodded and signaled for his war party to follow him as he urged his buckskin into an easy lope and disappeared around the base of the hill.

The Cheyennes watched eagerly as the Lakotas moved out of sight, Two Moon sitting his pony and holding a restraining hand upraised as he waited for Crazy Horse to get his people into position. The time seemed to drag on interminably as Two Moon visualized the route the Lakotas would have to take and counted off the minutes it would require for them to get there. After a few moments he could hear the rapid banging of the Winchesters and Henrys coming from beyond the hilltop and knew that the marksmen were doing their job. He waited a few minutes longer and then turned to the warriors behind him. It was time.

"Brave up, boys! Brave up!" Two Moon shouted. "Let not a man escape. It is a good day to die! *Hokahe!*" A tremendous shout went up from the war party as the braves screamed and yipped their readiness to fight. "*Hiyupo!*"

A hundred eagle-bone whistles began to shrill and screech, and the entire mass lunged up the slope in a cloud of dust. Ponies plunged and scrambled in the scrub and loose soil, slipping and pawing for footholds as they leapt forward, their riders quirting them viciously. The warriors screamed as they swung their war clubs and hatchets and shoved their rifles forward over the blankets and saddle bows, levering the rounds into their chambers. The whole mass thundered through the coulee and up the hillside to burst over the crest in a deadly whirlwind.

George Custer had just reloaded his pistols, a pair of nonregulation Bull Pups, as the first wave of warriors surged out of the dust cloud that eddied up out of the coulee below. There was an audible gasp from the few men remaining in the position as they braced themselves for the onslaught. Custer looked around him and took a mental inventory of his command. Tom was here, bleeding heavily from arrow wounds in his arm and thigh. Tom had left Lieutenant Harrington in charge as he slipped back from his skirmish line to have Dr. Lord put a dressing on his wounds. But Lord was pitched forward in the dirt with two arrows protruding from his back and his arm nearly torn away by a .50-caliber slug. The Sioux came again before he could get back to his company. Now Tom knelt near Boston and Autie Reed, each with a Springfield carbine leveled at the onrushing Sioux. Lieutenant Cooke was already down on his knees, reeling and clutching at a wound in his chest. There were maybe a hundred other soldiers, most already wounded, left to meet this new assault.

Custer could hardly believe that things had gone so wrong. Reno was broken and running. Benteen had still not arrived, and the rest of the regiment was scattered across this damn hilltop in small groups and isolated pockets of two and three men. No matter what they did, it seemed that they just never got enough time to pull themselves together. No sooner had one wave of Sioux washed over them than another appeared out of the murk, stampeding the horses, knocking men from their saddles, and punching holes in their skirmish lines. There was simply no time to recover, to reorganize, tighten the lines, fill in the gaps. He looked off to the north and thought of John Gibbon just a few miles away. If only Gibbon's scouts would appear off to the north, it might startle the Sioux long enough to give him time to get the rest of the outfit reorganized.

It just didn't seem possible that it should all end like this. After all those years in the war, with shrapnel and minié balls flying everywhere, with J. E. B. Stuart's people on the spree in their rear, with reb artillery tearing through the ranks with grape—to have come through all that with hardly a scratch and end on some godforsaken bump of ground in the middle of nowhere, it just couldn't be happening. What would Libby say? And what about Mother? Oh, God, what about Mother? He looked around and saw the faces of his brothers and Autie Reed, grimly set and waiting for the next onslaught. Oh, Mother, he thought, forgive me. George Custer clenched his teeth and stood in the midst of his ravaged command, cocking his pistols and bracing for the next charge.

No! he thought fiercely. We'll pull through this one yet! They'd just have to get through this next assault. He glanced at Tom and felt his knees buckle under him. For a moment he thought he'd been kicked in the side by one of the few remaining horses. George Custer looked down to see a large, bloody stain spreading across his shirt. Good God, could he have been hit? It didn't seem possible. There was no pain, just a strange numbness and loss of breath. He dropped one of the pistols and tried to steady himself on the rump of a dead horse. He felt strangely cool, even in the fierce heat of the sun. Couldn't think about it now. He raised up the other pistol and tried to get his eyes to focus on the dim shapes that weaved through the darkness gathering around him. So strangely dark. Then the world exploded in a flash of light and all was darkness and silence and peace.

Mark Kellogg's mule was dead. The animal had taken a .58-caliber slug through the brain and dropped like a rock at Kellogg's feet, dragging the startled reporter down with him. Kellogg had wrapped the reins around his forearm and it took him what seemed like hours to struggle free of the restraining leather straps that were tangled up under the dead animal. He scrabbled around in the dust on hands and knees searching for his pepper-box pistol and finally found it lodged under the mule's rump. He had to tug mightily on the small grips to dislodge the piece and then quickly checked it to ensure that the percussion caps were still in place.

Kellogg had lost his hat, and the swirling dust stung his eyes fiercely. The sweat pouring off his brow had dribbled onto his spectacles, where dust had now collected to turn them to a dusty-white translucence so that he saw everything as through a milky curtain. It was difficult for him to tell friend from foe, and he waved the little pistol frantically in all directions, hoping to scare off anyone who approached him. When a dark, feathered shape loomed up over the mule's carcass, he pulled desperately at the trigger, only to hear a dull snap as the percussion cap failed to explode.

The Oglala called Many Lice whooped with elation when the skinny man's gun didn't fire. He could see that the man was too terrified to try again, for the pistol was shaking violently and the crotch of the man's trousers were dark from where the white man had fouled himself. This would be an easy coup. Many Lice leaped over the mule and slapped the man's head with the barrel of his revolver to send him sprawling into the dirt, then lifted his head and screamed in triumph.

"Many Lice to count first coup!"

The Oglala then cocked his revolver and fired it straight into the white man's face. But Many Lice would never tell of this coup. The shot that he fired had indeed plunged through the white man's brain, but when Many Lice had loaded the old cap and ball revolver, he had been in a great hurry. In his haste to get into the fight he had forgotten to push grease into the ends of the bullet chambers, and as the weapon went off, a fragment of burning powder was deflected from the frame of the Army Remington and into the next bullet chamber, where it set off the powder that was trapped around the lead. This chamber set off the next chamber and so on, so that the entire cylinder exploded at once.

The explosion blew Many Lice's pistol into eight large fragments, the barrel going one way, the loading lever another, bits of the frame and trigger guard rocketing off in opposite directions, the latter carrying away three of the warrior's fingers with it. But the fragment that did the most damage was a half-inch-long piece of the Remington's hammer spur, which flew straight back to pierce Many Lice's eye and lodge securely in his brain. Many Lice toppled backward over the dead mule and lay faceup in the scrub, his heels still resting on the mule's flank.

A throng of other warriors surged past the bodies of Kellogg and Many Lice, leaping over dead horses and men and wrestling in the dirt with the living. The roar of gunfire mingled with the whooping of war cries and the screams of the wounded and dying as a thick pall of dust and gun smoke rose to blot out the fierce Montana sun. In the false dusk of battle, mistakes were made: pistols misfired, arrows missed their intended marks. Men blew holes in their own bodies in their terror and excitement. Some soldiers killed themselves rather than fall into their enemy's hands. But these were few. Most were much too busy trying to survive or to kill. These fought like demons with clubbed rifles, pistol butts, knives, fists, even with their bare hands and their teeth, gouging out eyes and biting off the noses or ears of their foes.

White Bull met a man like this. He was a big soldier with stripes on his arm and the gun he fired at the Hunkpapa scorched White Bull's face with burning powder, but the bullet missed its mark. White Bull leaped from his pony and bore the man to the ground, knocking the soldier's pistol spinning into the sage. The two rolled over and over in the dust, clubbing and clawing each other. The big sergeant grabbed White Bull's pistol while White Bull quirted the man repeatedly in the face.

The soldier let go the pistol but grabbed White Bull by the hair and pulled his face into his own where he tried to bite the Hunkpapa's nose off. It was only at the last second that White Bull was able to jerk his head back and land a stunning blow with his pistol butt on the soldier's head. The sergeant dropped back into the dirt as White Bull cocked his revolver and blew a hole in the man's head at point-blank range. The Hunkpapa pulled himself to his feet, reeling with exhaustion, then stooped to snatch up the soldier's cartridge belt before staggering drunkenly away.

A few yards away Lame-White-Man was scrambling up a gully to get back into the fray. The old Cheyenne war chief had slipped back down to the river to rally his people once again and was eager to be in on the end of this fight. It was getting harder to see up on this hill, with the smoke rolling down into the ravines, the acrid smell of gunpowder burning his lungs and making his old eyes well up with tears. He caught a glimpse of another warrior sliding over the edge of the gully, a rifle flashing in his hands. Lame-White-Man grinned broadly. The Lakotas were doing good work today, and there were still some whites left to be killed. He was about to call out encouragement to the other warrior when the man saw Lame-White-Man and, much to the old man's surprise, fired his rifle, blowing a neat hole between the old Cheyenne's eyes. Lame-White-Man pitched forward into the dust, his limbs twitching violently as the blood ran out into the dirt and matted the hair around the large, bloody crater in the back of his head.

"Somebody scalp that Ree!" someone shouted, and the Hunkpapa who had fired the fatal shot leapt down with his hunting knife to rip away Lame-White-Man's scalp. The Hunkpapa held the bloody trophy above his head, shrieked in triumph, and raced back to the fight.

Moments later another Cheyenne, Wooden Leg, came across the mutilated body of Lame-White-Man. Wooden Leg howled with fury. The Lakotas had done this! The damned fools! In their madness they were killing their own friends. Wooden Leg stooped to hoist his friend's body onto his shoulder and stumbled back down the hill, tears of rage and grief streaming down his face. In his anger the howling of men and the banging of their guns seemed to drift into the distance.

PART FOUR
"The Darkness of Their Eyes"

ABEYANCE

Late in the afternoon we saw a few horsemen in the bottom apparently to observe us, and then fire was set to the grass in the valley. About 7 P.M. we saw emerge from behind this screen of smoke an immense moving mass crossing the plateau, going toward the Big Horn Mountains. This moving mass was distant about five or six miles, but looked much nearer, and almost directly between us and the setting sun, now darkened by the smoke and dust ladened atmosphere; the travois with families and belongings and the pony herds was massed, the long column with wide front was skirted by the warriors on guard; thus silhouetted against the red-lined western sky-line, their departure was to us a gladsome sight.

Statement of Lieutenant E. S. Godfrey, 7th U.S. Cavalry
(Extract from Official Records, Court of Inquiry
Convened 13 January 1879 at Chicago, Illinois)

But if the vision was true and mighty, as I know, it is true and mighty yet; for such things are of the spirit, and it is in the darkness of their eyes that men get lost.

Black Elk, Oglala Lakota

1700 Hours
On Reno's Hill

Captain Thomas B. Weir, commanding Company D, stood impatiently at the northern edge of the defensive perimeter. For what seemed like an hour, he had been listening anxiously to the steady banging of rifle fire that drifted down from the hills to their north. There was some kind of a fight going on up ahead, and it made Weir nervous to be standing up here out of the way, not knowing just what the hell was going on. He thought they were supposed to be attacking the damn village, not sitting around on top of some damned dust pile cooling their heels. Listening to the firing from downstream, Weir fidgeted with his revolver and ground his teeth in frustration. Custer must be giving 'em hell up there, he thought, and we're back here sitting on our asses.

First Lieutenant Edward Godfrey and Second Lieutenant Winfield Scott Edgerly, Weir's second-in-command, had come up behind the captain and now stood nearby, their horses' reins wrapped lightly around their hands. It was Edgerly who finally gave voice to what Weir was thinking.

"Sounds like a hell of a fight down there, boys," Edgerly opined. "I expect we ought to be heading down that way pretty soon now, don't you think?"

"Well, we sure as hell ought to be doing some damn thing." Godfrey spat. "Damn it, Tom, what the hell are we sitting around up here for? If we don't move pretty soon, Custer'll be after Reno with a sharp stick!"

Captain Weir turned around and glanced over toward the center of the hilltop position where Major Reno was apparently having a heated discussion with Captain Benteen. Weir snorted in disgust.

"Those damn coffee coolers'll have us sitting here 'til goddamned doomsday," Weir said with feeling. "You're one hundred percent right, Ed. I'm going to see if I can talk Reno into letting us start moving up before the whole damn fight's over."

Weir turned on his heel and strode purposefully over to where Reno and Benteen were still arguing. Edgerly and Godfrey looked on eagerly as Weir advanced toward the senior officers present, his face tight with impatience and irritation.

"Weir's pretty steamed up now," Godfrey said with a grim smile. "Dollars'll get you doughnuts he lights a hell of a fire under those two prima donnas." Edgerly nodded in agreement.

As the two young officers watched, Captain Weir inserted himself between the quarrelling older men and spoke earnestly to Reno while pointing back in the direction of Godfrey and Edgerly. Edgerly assumed that Weir was urging Reno, as the nominal commander of the outfit, to gather the regiment together and move out to support Custer's fight, which was obviously waxing hot farther up the valley. He couldn't make out what was being said, but from the expressions on their faces, Edgerly gathered that tempers were beginning to flare. After a few moments Weir turned to Benteen, who had crossed his arms over his chest and was studiously ignoring the overwrought captain. When Weir started back toward the two lieutenants, they could see that his face was beet red and he was snarling angrily. Weir stomped over to Godfrey and Edgerly in a blind fury.

"Those goddamned, ignorant, do-nothing bastards!" Weir swore, glancing back over his shoulder. "I've never seen such a couple of sorry excuses for soldiers in my life. That idiot Reno's too scared of his own shadow to use any initiative and that white-haired, pigheaded son of a bitch Benteen accused me of wanting to leave the damned wounded to the mercy of the Sioux. Pompous old bastard!"

Weir was furious, and for a moment Godfrey feared that the man would lose complete control of himself and end up pulling his pistol on both Reno and Benteen. Godfrey didn't particularly like Benteen but it wouldn't do to have the officers "drawing down" on each other out here in front of God and everyone.

The thought had occurred to Weir. It was only with the exercise of the greatest restraint that he was able to suppress his rage at the two senior officers. Reno, he reasoned with himself, was just scared and not worth a bullet. Benteen, on the other hand, was being purposely obtuse. The cold-blooded bastard was enjoying Reno's discomfiture and wallowing in his better-man-than-thou attitude. Plus, Weir told himself, Benteen was a notorious duelist who would have jumped at the chance to pull pistols with anyone who crossed him. The bloodthirsty old coot just might get lucky if provoked. It was the sort of thing he enjoyed. Weir decided he wouldn't give the bastard the satisfaction.

"Fuck 'em!" Weir snarled. He turned to Edgerly and Godfrey. "Get your people together, gentlemen. We're going out."

Edgerly nodded vigorously and rushed off to gather his men. This was more like it, he thought. At least someone's got the balls to do something around here. Godfrey stood by Weir's side and waited until Edgerly had gotten out of earshot.

"Look here, Tom," Godfrey said quietly, "are you sure you want to do this? I agree that we ought to be doing something, but it just don't do to start out pirating on your own hook with the damned hostiles all over the place. That's how old Elliot got himself used up back at the Washita in 'sixty-eight. You decide to skip off here and Reno may roll over, but old Skull-and-Crossbones'll have a damn fit."

"Let 'im," Weir said shortly. "If he don't like it, the son of a bitch can call me out, but I'll be damned if I'll sit here like a damned bump while the general's up ahead waiting for us to prance in."

Weir stopped for a moment while Godfrey kept a firm grasp on his friend's sleeve. After a moment Weir seemed to calm down and said evenly: "Tell you what, Ed. You talk to 'em. If you decide that they're shirking, well, I'll save you a place up on the line. If you think they've got it right, well, no hard feelings and we'll see you when you come up with the rest. Okay?"

Godfrey pressed his lips shut tight and nodded, then turned and set off to talk to Benteen himself. Before Godfrey could get to him, Benteen had tumbled to the fact that something was going on at one end of the perimeter. Company D's troopers had seized their mounts and swung into the saddle as Edgerly began to form up the company behind Captain Weir. Benteen's face reddened as he realized that Weir was intent on going out on his own initiative, and he rushed forward to try to put a stop to it.

A few yards away Captain Tom French, in command of Company M, was carefully adjusting the leaf sight on his rifle. It was an old infantry-model Springfield, which he had had cut down to a bit longer than carbine length. French felt that these older .50-caliber models, in addition to their longer range, had a more gratifying result when the slug impacted. Thus far, he had taken considerable pleasure in punching large holes through the few Sioux snipers who cavorted on the far ridges thinking that they were comfortably out of range of the white men's guns. He only wished that he had a telescopic sight so that he could see the surprise on their faces when his heavy slugs took dinner-plate-sized chunks out of the cheeky bastards. Most of them had by now figured out that something was quite wrong and had prudently gone to ground, leaving the captain with little sport.

French had about given up on getting a clean shot at a wiry Arapaho who had taken up residence behind a small knoll some one thousand yards out when he saw the commotion in D Company. He quickly concluded that some of the outfit was getting ready to move out after the hostiles. He wasn't about to miss out on having another crack at the Sioux and rushed for his horse.

Captain French shoved his Springfield into the scabbard he had attached to his McClellan and pulled himself up into the saddle, eager to get back into the fight. He didn't have to say anything to his troops, who quickly followed their commander's example. Most were sick of hanging around this hilltop. Most had lost friends in the valley fight and they were again ready to come to grips with the Sioux. There were fresh scores to settle now. Before French could move the unit over to join Weir's Company D, Lieutenant Godfrey got hold of his bridle and whispered urgently up at him. French looked back to where Benteen was, nodded, and dismounted to follow Godfrey off to talk to the man.

Captain Frederick Benteen was livid. Damn that Weir, he thought angrily. The insubordinate son of a bitch was ignoring Reno's instructions to stay put. He strode over the dusty hilltop with murder in his eye, fully intending to horsewhip the man when he caught up with him. Benteen screamed for Weir to halt, but Weir ignored Benteen's ravings and waved his hand for the hastily assembled column to move forward. The ragged column lurched after the captain, stirring the dust into a blinding cloud as the horses began to trot along the ridgeline, moving in the direction of the distant sound of the guns.

As Godfrey, French, and Benteen were moving on converging paths across the perimeter, another body of mounted men thundered into the confusion of the hilltop position. Captain McDougall and the packtrain lumbered into the midst of the men milling around Major Reno, the newcomers glancing around in wonder at the scene that greeted their eyes.

What the hell happened here? McDougall asked himself as he took in the seething gaggle of men and horses that was spread over the bluffs. Everything was in disorder; soldiers were using dinner plates, tin cups, and knives to dig into the rocky soil. Some had thrown their saddles to the ground as makeshift breastworks, while others moved around the saucerlike depression that served as a hospital, carrying water to the wounded who were strewn over the ground. Major Reno said nothing to the bewildered McDougall but pushed past him to snatch a pair of shovels from one of the pack mules. McDougall watched as Reno strode off with the shovels. Lieutenants Mathey and Hare rode up next to McDougall just as Reno moved away.

"Cap'n," Mathey said quietly, "just what the hell happened up here?"

McDougall shook his head wonderingly. "Can't say, Mr. Mathey. But it looks like the Sioux got the bulge on old Reno." He looked ahead and spotted Benteen on the other end of the position, talking to Captain French and Lieutenant Godfrey, and wondered what the hell he was still doing here. That's odd, he thought. When Sergeant Kanipe had come up with his message to get the packs up, McDougall thought, hadn't he clearly said that Custer had also ordered Benteen up to join the main outfit. Puzzled, McDougall dug out his watch. That was damn near three hours ago! It made one wonder what the hell they had been doing this whole time.

Charles Varnum was dreaming lazily of a beach he had walked along when his father had been posted briefly in Florida. It was hot and he could almost hear the somnolent rushing of the waves as they washed up on the shore and slipped away again. The dream was so real that he could feel the heat of the sand rising to envelop him. He had just stopped to pick up a crab and his mouth was watering at the thought of the delicious feast he would have when he had gathered enough of the creatures that scuttled along ahead of the surf. The dream evaporated in a flash when someone kicked the soles of his boots repeatedly and he heard his name dragging him from his reverie.

"Varnum!" the voice rasped. "Varnum. Take these shovels and a detail down to bury Lieutenant Hodgson decently."

Lieutenant Varnum rolled onto his back and sat up stiffly, his head pounding brutally and his eyes blinded by the sudden exposure to light. A dark figure loomed over him, silhouetted against the sky, and it took him a few seconds to recognize the voice of Major Reno. Varnum staggered drunkenly to his feet, his head light and reeling with the effort. Damn Reno, he thought. Why don't he bury him himself? Hell, Hodgson's not going anywhere fast. He looked over to see Tony Siebelder and two other men standing nearby.

Private Siebelder had jumped up at Reno's approach and now stepped forward to take the shovels himself.

"Come on, Lieutenant," Siebelder said quietly, "Weaver 'n me'll bury Mr. Hodgson. Sullivan's comin' too. You and him just gotta keep the damn redskins off our backs for a couple of minutes while we get 'er done, sir."

Varnum nodded dully as he used his carbine as a prop to heave himself stiffly to his feet. The three privates checked the loads in their weapons and started off down the bluffs as Varnum followed dazedly along, still groggy from his short nap. Three other men, seeing the detail leave, decided to tag along just in case the Sioux did come back. As he stumbled down the face of the bluffs, Varnum saw part of the outfit beginning to move downstream. He caught sight of Weir and Edgerly in the lead and wondered what the devil they were up to.

Captain Benteen was still fuming over Weir's departure when he turned to see the packtrain come up. Godfrey and French were left startled by Benteen's abrupt departure and watched as he headed toward the packtrain. Benteen stalked toward Captain McDougall but noticed a fierce glint in the man's eye and saw that McDougall's hand was resting on the butt of his pistol. Benteen brushed past McDougall's horse and grabbed the bridle of Lieutenant Mathey's mount.

"You frog-eating, slow-poking son of a bitch!" Benteen shrieked. "Where the hell have you been with these goddamned animals? I ought to thrash the life out of you, you stupid French bastard!"

Mathey's face turned a bright crimson, and for a moment it looked as if the man would leap down on Benteen. McDougall acted quickly and used his horse to shove Benteen bodily aside.

"I beg your pardon, Captain Benteen," McDougall called loudly. "My mount must've spooked."

As Benteen stood there sputtering with anger, McDougall leaned over the saddle into Benteen's face and whispered so that only the blustering captain could hear him.

"You make one false move, Benteen, and I'll personally blow your fucking brains out. Reno's obviously out of it and you're in charge now, so mind the damned business at hand."

Benteen looked up into McDougall's eyes and saw in them the steel glint of absolute truth. The man meant every word that he said. McDougall would shoot him down in cold blood if provoked. If there was one thing Fred Benteen understood in others, it was a refusal to be bullied, coupled with a willingness to kill. McDougall had both in spades. Benteen backed off and turned to continue the organization of a defensive perimeter. His mind was racing now.

McDougall and the others obviously expected him to do something, and Weir had already ridden off followed by damn near half the command. If Custer came up now, he'd chew Reno's head off, but it would be Benteen, as the more experienced of the two, who would bear the brunt of it. The damned popinjay might even accuse him of cowardice or bring him up on charges. Damn him. He'd just call the man out. No. He wouldn't be able to do that either. Custer would refuse, and General Terry would be up tomorrow and he wouldn't stand for it. Weir and the others would take Custer's side, of course. Damn them all. He'd have to do something now or there would be hell to pay tomorrow. He trotted over to Reno and spoke loudly so that the others would be sure to hear.

"Alright, Major," Benteen called out, "McDougall and the packs are up. I suggest we slice out the ammunition mules and move the bulk of the outfit forward. The rest of the packtrain can laager up here, and Moylan can take charge of the defense. We'll use the tack boxes and grain to set up a temporary breastwork and use the mules and horses to screen the wounded from any further attacks. Does that sound reasonable to you, Major?"

Reno, who appeared to be still somewhat befuddled by the situation, was glad for any suggestion and quickly agreed to the proposal. As the troopers began to pull their horses into column, Lieutenant Nick Wallace remembered that Varnum and the burial detail were still down below. Wallace hurried over to the edge of the bluffs and called out to his friend.

"Charlie! Charlie Varnum. Get back up. Bring it in now. Hurry!"

Lieutenant Varnum thought he heard someone calling his name. He looked back up the bluffs, but his eyes couldn't seem to focus on anything. He decided that his tired mind was beginning to play tricks on him, shrugged, and looked around to find some decent firing positions for his escort. Behind him Siebelder and Weaver had taken a blanket from a dead horse and laid it out on the ground. The two men grabbed Lieutenant Hodgson's body and lifted him gently onto the blanket. Siebelder tugged off the dead man's boots, a task that was easier than trying to unbuckle the mud-caked spurs, which would have snagged on the blanket.

The easygoing Hodgson had been a popular figure with the enlisted men, and so it was not surprising that, even with the hostiles possibly lurking across the river, the veteran privates were especially gentle in handling the youngster's corpse. Siebelder straightened the dead man's uniform as best he could, and then he and Weaver carefully folded the blanket around him. The detail had only just gotten started digging a shallow grave when they heard renewed shouting from above. Varnum looked back up the hill and caught a glimpse of someone waving his arms furiously.

"What do you suppose that's all about, Lieutenant?" Tony Siebelder asked frowning.

"Hell, Tony," Varnum replied with a sigh, "I don't know. I just wish someone would figure out just what the hell it is we're supposed to be doing."

"Amen to that, Lieutenant." Siebelder said, looking around at the rest of the detail, who were waiting for somebody to decide something. "Could be," Siebelder suggested, "that they seen some more Injuns headed this way, sir. In which case we'd probably ought to get the hell out quicklike."

Varnum looked around at the bodies that were still scattered through the brush and timber on the other side of the river. Siebelder had a point. If the Sioux were coming back, this would be a hell of a place to get caught with just six men. Varnum nodded and motioned for the detail to follow him, and the whole party started the slow climb back up the crumbling hillside. As he passed the blanket-wrapped corpse, he stopped for a moment and removed his hat.

"Sorry, Benny, old man," he said quietly, "we'll be back to take care of you proper a bit later."

The lieutenant didn't think it possible for him to be any more tired than he already was, and the climb back up seemed beyond his capabilities. Never mind, he told himself grimly, don't look up, just keep climbing. He turned in the direction of the shouting, put one foot in front of the other, closed his eyes, and, with Siebelder and the others following along, willed himself up the hill.

By the time Varnum had clawed his way back to the position, the outfit was in a frenzy of activity. Nick Wallace was waiting at the top to help him up the last couple of feet.

"Come on, Charlie," Wallace urged, "you'll miss out on all the excitement."

Varnum sat down heavily at the edge of the bluffs and wiped a sleeve across his sweat-bathed brow. "The last thing I need now, Nick, is more excitement. What's up?"

"Benteen's finally decided to move out in support," Wallace said quickly. "Weir's already gone ahead with D Company. If Custer is pushing 'em this way, we should be able to hit 'em head-on."

Varnum stuck up a hand and Wallace reached out to haul his friend upright. Varnum noticed that Nick was leading a pair of horses, one of which was Varnum's. Well, he thought tiredly, there's just no rest for the wicked, or the righteous either, for that matter. It took him three tries to get his foot into the stirrup, and then he nearly slipped off the other side of the saddle as he plopped down into it. Nick handed him up the reins, mounted his own horse, and the two young lieutenants trotted out to catch up with the dusty column of troops that was headed back downstream. There was a muffled crackle and pop of gunfire in the distance, and Varnum was reminded of Napoleon's old maxim, the one they'd had drilled into their heads time and again back at West Point: "Ride to the sound of the guns." He suppressed a large yawn and wondered idly how many more times that day they would ride to the sound of the guns.

Añpotahena *(Before Day Is Done)* *On Greasy Grass Hill*

Crazy Horse was through with fighting for today. He turned his buckskin pony in a tight circle and started back down Deep Coulee, letting the animal pick his way over the treacherous slope at his own pace. Once again, his medicine had been strong and he had come through this fight without so much as a scratch, although his pony had been nicked twice by the white men's bullets. He wondered if perhaps he had done something to break the gopher dust's medicine that had allowed the *wasichus* to see his pony and resolved to be a little more careful in the future. He had done well in this battle, but what was happening now was something for which he had neither the inclination nor the stomach.

The dust still swirled around the hilltop as if kicked up by a whirlwind, but now it was only the Lakota and their allies who raised it. The soldiers were all down. Not all of them were yet dead, as was apparent from the continual shooting and the occasional screams that echoed out of the dust. Now the braves and the women would disfigure the dead and dying soldiers so that their spirits could not enjoy the other world. The dead would enter the other world with the bodies they had just after death, and an enemy could not be allowed to enjoy the other life. Eyeballs would be dug out so they could not see the other world or aim their guns. Hands would be cut away or muscles and tendons slashed so they could no longer pull a trigger or draw a bow. Their teeth would be knocked from their heads so they could not eat. Leg tendons would be cut so they could not walk, and thighs would be slashed open so they could not sit on their horses. Crazy Horse knew that the killing and dying would continue for a while yet, but it was not something that greatly interested him.

The people swarmed all over the hill, shouting and singing, chanting victory songs. Some chanted death songs for their friends and relatives. The women and children had begun to climb up the ravines and coulees to join in the aftermath of the battle. He could hear the women as they shrieked their joy, their tongues jiggling to and fro over their lips to produce a curious tremolo warbling. Everywhere he rode, the people were stripping the soldiers of everything they carried.

Guns and ammunition were of course the most prized loot, but the horses too, those that had not been killed, were also a great treasure. The big American horses with their fine saddles were perfect for hauling heavier loads on the travois. Those who could take such a horse would be able to carry away so much more than the others when they moved the camp. Crazy Horse did not care for these horses himself. They had been made too fat on grain and corn, and he did not think that they would last very long once the winter arrived. He wanted nothing that the white men had.

Not everyone shared Crazy Horse's contempt for the white men's things, and most were half-crazed as they scuttled like beetles among the dead and wounded, snatching as much as they could carry or drag away. They tugged at the clothes of the troopers, pulling away boots and trousers. The heavy wool would help to keep out the cold this winter. The boots were curious things. Most thought that the shoe part was a poor substitute for moccasins, but the upper part could be cut away to make heavy soles for moccasins for the winter or excellent pouches for carrying things. Many braves were wearing the blue wool jackets of the soldiers; the ones with the yellow stripes on the arms being highly prized, since most of these men had been good fighters and probably had strong medicine sewn into their jackets.

The boy Black Elk had got himself a fine new pistol and much ammunition. He had also found a wonderful shiny round totem on a slender chain. The totem had pictures of deer scratched into it and made a curious ticking sound when he held it up to his ear. Black Elk had strung the chain around his neck and smiled gleefully as he walked slowly back to camp with the shiny thing held up to his ear.

White Bull sat panting and wincing on a dead cavalry horse at the top of the hill. A spent bullet had glanced off the bone of his ankle, and the throbbing pain made it difficult to walk. He would have ridden home, but his horse had been shot four times and lay dead nearby. As he sat there rubbing his ankle, a Hunkpapa named Bad Soup came up carrying a soldier's carbine and with two new cartridge belts draped across his chest.

"*Haho*, White Bull," the man said, "look over here. *Haiye!* A great day is here!"

White Bull did not look up but examined his swollen ankle carefully. "What do you want, Bad Soup?" he said crossly. "What's all the noise about?"

Bad Soup pointed at the naked body of a white man nearby. "Don't you know who this is, White Bull? Look again. It's Pehin Hanska himself."

White Bull looked up, astonished. "What? What are you talking about? Who are you talking about? How do you know it is Long Hair?"

"Bah," Bad Soup said lightly. "I have spent much time among the *wasichus* at Standing Rock and at their forts. I've seen Long Hair Custer many times and I know him when I see him. Just look at him. He thought he was the greatest man alive, and now here he is. *Hinuhinu!* What do you know."

White Bull frowned and used his rifle as a crutch to push himself up, then staggered over to look at the body. The man had yellow hair and mustache, and his face and arms were burned red from the sun. He looked so peaceful that one would almost think that he was sleeping, except for the two holes that ran red, one in his head and another in his side just below his heart. Several Lakotas had gathered around and would have begun to slash the man's body, but two Cheyenne women sat near his head and waved them away angrily. White Bull thought he recognized the older one as the sister of Black Kettle, a Cheyenne chief who had been killed by the whites many years before. He thought she was called Mah-wissa but couldn't be sure.

"What are you women doing?" White Bull asked quietly.

The older woman waved a pistol at a youngster who had slipped up with a knife and sliced off a piece of the man's finger.

"He is a relative, Lakota," she said sharply. "His name is Creeping Panther. If you want to cut up white men, I'm sure you can find one or two others up here if you look hard enough."

White Bull thought that this Cheyenne woman was being a little strange. If this man she called Creeping Panther was indeed Long Hair, he was the very one whose soldiers had killed her brother. White Bull shook his head. He did not care for this woman's sharp tongue but decided that it would be undignified to question her any further. As he watched, the other woman produced a long sewing awl and pushed it deep into the dead man's ear. He found this puzzling.

"What are you doing now?" he asked politely. The Cheyenne woman looked up at White Bull as if he were simply quite dense, for her to have to explain her actions.

"Our chiefs once told him when he made peace with the Cheyennes that if he ever came against us again the Everywhere Spirit would see and he would be killed. He must not have listened too good, so now we will clean out his ears that he may hear better in the other world."

White Bull shook his head and turned to Bad Soup.

"Let's go, Bad Soup," he said. "I've had enough fighting today and don't wish to start in with these Shyela women now."

Bad Soup grinned, and grabbed the bridle of a cavalry horse that was standing nearby. He helped White Bull get up on the horse's back and turned to lead him back down the hillside. Bad Soup was in a particularly good mood, making jokes and laughing uproariously as the two jounced lazily down toward the camp. He looked back toward the two women, snickered, and jabbed White Bull in the ribs.

"I bet that as soon as we're out of sight," Bad Soup said, "that Shyela woman'll slice off his balls and take them home to use as a medicine bag."

Despite his sore leg, White Bull couldn't help but smile at the absurd picture that Bad Soup had managed to conjure up for his amusement. Bad Soup was an incorrigible jokester and clown, always telling outlandish tales and making wisecracks. He was especially fond of crude humor and enjoyed making the young girls blush with his innuendos. As they started down the ravine, a young brave skidded past them leading a large sorrel cavalry horse.

"Noisy Walker," Bad Soup called out. "Have you got a good horse there?"

The youngster smiled broadly and nodded. "Oh, yes," he said eagerly, "I know this is a good one for sure. It was Long Hair's horse!"

At the bottom of the hill and on the other side of the river, Sitting Bull watched as the people began to come down from the battle. He was disturbed to see that everywhere he looked they were taking away things from the soldiers; horses, blankets, guns, clothes, everything. This was not right. Fools! They would break the medicine. Sitting Bull nudged his black pony and rode back and forth along the river bank, yelling to the people as they came down from Battle Ridge.

"Stop!" he cried out. "Leave these things. Take nothing that the whites have. You will break the medicine and bring evil down on us all." But no one seemed to pay any attention to him. They were too excited by the battle and the great victory they had won to listen to prophecies now. Sitting Bull spotted Crazy Horse as he guided his pony slowly across the river.

"Crazy Horse," he called, "remember what the Wakan Tanka has said."

Crazy Horse glanced at the old man, a tired look on his face. He looked around at the people who were carrying off the soldiers' guns and leading away their horses. He looked back at the Hunkpapa and rode slowly past him without stopping.

"I remember what you said," Crazy Horse said quietly. "I have taken nothing. There is nothing that the whites have that I want." He tossed his head back toward the river. "I am no chief, no prophet. If you want them to stop, then tell them yourself, but I think you are wasting your breath. I am tired of fighting. I'm going home now."

Sitting Bull knew what Crazy Horse said was true. No one would listen to him now, not after the hard fighting they had done. He looked up the hill and saw that many were coming down with their friends and relatives slung limp over the backs of ponies, blood running down from their mouths and bodies. Too many were dead or would soon die from the fight. In addition to the elation of victory there was too much anger, too much grief, for his words to be heard. He knew he should be elated by their triumph over the whites, but all he felt now was depressed. This was not right. They had come so close. Everything that Wakan Tanka had told him had come to pass, and now, with their blindness and greed, the people would throw it all away. He looked up the hill and saw White Bull coming down in the company of Bad Soup and Has Horns. When they had splashed back across the river, he could see by the look on White Bull's face and the way he slumped in the saddle that he was hurt. Sitting Bull rode up alongside his kinsman and spoke quietly to him.

"You should be more careful, nephew," Sitting Bull admonished. "One day you will take too many chances." White Bull managed a tight-lipped smile.

"It is alright, Uncle," he replied, "the bullet did not break the skin. In a few days I will be fine. It is the whites who took too many chances today." He pointed back up the hill. "The man who thought he was so lucky is out of luck now. Pehin Hanska brought these soldiers and now he is dead on the top of this hill."

Long Hair! The one they called Custer brought these soldiers. Sitting Bull sat back on his pony, surprised. He had thought they were fighting Three Stars again, but it was not so. This was yet another group of soldiers. Three Stars and his army were still out there. What did this mean? Were there perhaps more groups of soldiers out there that they still didn't know about? Would they have to fight these people all summer? He thought about the significance of this. Maybe after this fight they would see how powerful the Lakotas had become and leave them alone.

No, he didn't think so. They had rubbed out Long Hair and most of his army, and he was a very powerful man among the *wasichus*. Bad Soup was always saying how the whites thought Pehin Hanska was so great. The Cheyenne feared him. Even Red Cloud had said that Long Hair was a great warrior. When the whites found out that the Lakotas had killed him, they would become angry. More soldiers would come. This was not good. He looked around at the people, who were still carrying away everything that the white soldiers had brought with them, and felt the anger rise again. As Sitting Bull's face clouded over, Has Horns rode up next to him and handed him some trinket he had taken from one of the soldier chiefs. It was a little round box with tiny scratches on it. The scratches were under something that was clear like ice but was not cold. Under the ice was a small arrow that wiggled and danced in a circle.

"Look at this," Has Horns said brightly. "I took it from a soldier chief. No matter where I carry it, this little arrow always points downstream. It must be powerful medicine. I give you this as a gift, Sitting Bull."

Sitting Bull looked at the object curiously for a moment, then his eyes grew wide and he hurled the object into the river.

"It is bad medicine," he barked angrily. "The little arrow is blue like the soldiers' coats. It's how they find each other and that is why it is pointing that way. There are more soldiers coming from the north. You must throw these things away, I tell you. The white man's medicine will seek itself out and it will lead them to us. This is what the Wakan Tanka warned us about. We must take nothing from them. It is cursed."

Has Horns and Bad Soup looked curiously at the spot where the object had disappeared into the river and wondered about what Sitting Bull had said. Neither wanted to give up the things they had just fought for. Bad Soup especially was reluctant to give up the new gun he had picked up. Before either of them could speak, there was a great shouting from the other side of the river and a confusion of warriors rushing upstream on their ponies.

"Soldiers!" someone shouted. "More soldiers coming. Brave up, brothers! Hokahe!"

Again there was a cacophony of whoops and screams and a shrilling of whistles as hundreds of warriors began to scramble through the dust, all heading to the south. It must be the ones who had run away from the fight in the valley. They were coming back for more. Bad Soup and Has Horns looked at each other. Neither said anything, but each was thinking the same thing: Sitting Bull had been wrong about the little arrow pointing toward the soldiers. He was probably wrong about their taking the guns and things too.

Has Horns was irritated that Sitting Bull had thrown away his gift. The little arrow didn't point toward the soldiers as he had said, but away from them. This would have been a good thing to have, but Sitting Bull had thrown it away. Now Has Horns was wishing he had just kept the little medicine arrow for himself. It might be hard for him to find another one.

Bad Soup thought the old man was being ridiculous. Well, Sitting Bull could stay here to mumble out his prophecies all day if he wanted to. Bad Soup was going to join the new fight. His medicine was strong today. Maybe he could get another gun and a large American horse. Bad Soup lifted his new gun over his head and shrieked out a war cry as he wheeled his pony around and plunged back across the river with Has Horns galloping after him.

1725 Hours
At Weir's Peak

"Son of a bitch! Lookit all of 'em!"

Lieutenant Edgerly could hardly believe his eyes. Although he was the one to say it, the other officers and men were thinking precisely the same thing. They had ridden up from Reno's position, following the sound of distant gunfire, until they crested a sharp ridge a little over a mile downstream from where they had started out. The men strained to see clearly the battle that appeared to be raging on a hilltop about three miles farther downstream. Off to the left they could see the large camp in the valley below, but the hill where the firing seemed to be coming from was shrouded from view by a huge cloud of dust and smoke. Thousands of tiny figures afoot and on horseback flitted through the fog of battle. Above and beyond the tiny figures, Captain Weir noticed a pair of guidons floating above the dust and pointed them out to the others.

"There they are, boys!" Weir burst out. "There's Custer's command on the hill. Must be one hell of a fight."

The others nodded solemnly and braced themselves for the advance into the battle that they felt sure was coming momentarily. For a moment no one spoke, as they were lost in their own thoughts, pondering the coming fight. The silence was broken by a young sergeant named Flanagan who edged his mount up alongside of Captain Weir's and leaned over.

"Cap'n," Flanagan said curtly, handing Weir a set of field glasses, "you'd best have a look through these here glasses, sir. I don't think that's Custer at all. I think those're Injuns down there."

Weir took the proffered glasses and focused them on the distant hilltop. Even though their magnification was not great, it was sufficient to confirm for Weir what Flanagan had suggested. The figures racing around the hilltop waving the guidons were indeed Indians and not soldiers. But if this was so, where the hell was Custer and the rest of the outfit? Several of the braves racing their ponies across the hillside appeared to be shooting down into the dirt, which meant that some of the men must be down. But there were five companies out there somewhere. He wondered where they could have gotten to. A spattering of shots echoed across the valley, and Weir recognized the distinctive throaty roar of Army Springfields.

Soldiers, he told himself. Custer must have been thrown off toward the north. That must be the rear guard hurling a few parting shots after the Sioux. It looked like they were effectively cut into two separate outfits now. Custer would probably make for Gibbon's column on the north. Weir wondered how they would manage to coordinate their actions once Custer had linked up with Gibbon. They'd have the Sioux sandwiched in between the two wings, and it would just be a matter of maneuvering to keep the hostiles in between 'em. Just a matter of maneuvering. He snorted to himself. Easier said than done. A damn tricky business it would be to try to get couriers through that mess down below.

As Weir was pondering what the next course of action might be, Lieutenant Luther Hare galloped up from the rear. Hare reined to a stop and snapped off a hasty salute.

"Captain Weir," Hare blurted. "Major Reno presents his compliments, sir, and asks that you try to communicate with General Custer and see what his desires are."

Weir was considering just how the hell he was supposed to go about this when he saw Hare's eyes widen as the lieutenant gazed past him toward the distant battlefield.

"Jesus!" Hare gasped.

Weir twisted around in his saddle to discover what had gotten Hare's attention and saw that the rolling terrain between Custer's outfit and his own was rapidly filling with hundreds of mounted warriors. As they watched, these warriors were joined by hundreds more, until the entire landscape seemed to swarm with them—shrieking, whooping, firing their rifles into the air—and all riding directly toward them. Weir thought that this did not look like a healthy situation.

"Mr. Hare," he said, "my compliments to Major Reno and tell him it may be a while. I don't believe we can get through right now, but we'll form line here and try to fight it out where we are." Hare nodded silently and turned his horse to gallop off toward the main command. Weir turned to Lieutenant Edgerly.

"Win, quick now," Weir said, "dismount your company and give me a skirmish line." Edgerly nodded, and trotted to Company D, shouting for the noncommissioned officers. Moments later they had the men on the ground and spread out along the ridgeline with their carbines pushed forward at the ready. The junior men of the company had taken charge of the horses and were moving them back behind the ridgeline and thus out of view of the onrushing Indians. Edgerly too had dismounted and, with his own carbine gripped tightly, was stalking up and down behind the skirmish line, checking the men's positions and speaking quietly to steady their nerves as bullets began to patter into the dust like huge raindrops. He noticed that one of his men had lost his carbine and was crouched in the dust casually reloading his revolver and laughing quietly to himself. Edgerly stopped and handed the man his own Springfield.

"Private Saunders," Edgerly said crossly, "just what the hell is so goddamned funny?"

Saunders reached up for the profferred carbine with a nod of thanks and a broad grin.

"Hell, Lieutenant," Saunders drawled, "these damned redskins are the god-awfullest worst shots I ever seen. I swear, Mr. Lo couldn't hit a bull in the butt with a banjo."

Edgerly just shook his head and wandered off to check the rest of the line. He thought that Saunders was one hell of a cool customer and decided that if a young private could stay that calm, the least he could do was to try to set a good example for the rest of the men, some of whom were not nearly so sanguine about the lead that was now cutting through the air around them. He glanced toward the rear and saw that more of the outfit was just coming up, and recognized Godfrey and French with Companies K and M. Following along behind them was Benteen and his own Company H.

Before Benteen could get up, Godfrey and French had had a short conference with Weir and were quickly deploying their companies off to the left and slightly more forward of the ridgeline. Edgerly left his first sergeant in charge of the skirmishers and wandered toward Captain Weir to see what was developing. As Benteen reined up alongside them, his attention was riveted on the scene unfolding on the hillsides below them.

"Goddamn!" Benteen exclaimed as he watched the dust-shrouded Sioux moving toward them like a storm front rolling inexorably across the open plains. He looked along the ridgeline where the other companies had formed up in skirmish lines and back at the onrushing Sioux.

"This is a hell of a place to fight Indians," he said to Lieutenant Gibson, who had come up with him. "I'm going back to see Reno and propose that we fall back to the last position and make a stand there." Benteen wheeled his horse around and trotted away, the rest of Company H following along in his wake and most of the men wondering what in the hell was going on.

Captain Thomas Weir saw Benteen heading back and was just wondering the same thing when the first wave of Sioux washed up against his position. The skirmish line exploded as the heavy carbines spat a wall of fire into the leading ranks of howling warriors. Horses whinnied and men screamed as the first volley ripped through animal and human flesh and deflected the first assault. As the attack wave wilted under the muzzles of the Springfields, the Sioux began to throw themselves from their horses to continue the attack on foot. They slithered through the dust and rocks, up ravines and behind sage bushes to get closer to the bluecoats, firing their rifles and flinging arrows blindly up over the ridgeline.

The blue-clad skirmishers blasted away into the dust clouds below, empty cartridge cases clattering onto the rocky soil as round after round was forced through the hot breeches. Men shouted and horses whinnied as the crashing sound of musketry rose in the still, hot air of the late afternoon. The men's throats were parched and dry, and there was no time now to stop for a pull at their canteens. Not that it would have helped, for by now most of the canteens were bone-dry and the only water around was on the other side of a horde of screaming Indians. So the men fought on in agony in the terrible heat and dust, their throats burning and the coppery taste of fear swelling their tongues.

"They're getting around us!" someone yelled, and a fresh burst of firing echoed down through the ravines on the western edge of the ridgeline. As Captain Weir moved toward the new firing, Lieutenant Hare materialized out of the dust and grabbed Weir by the elbow.

"Sir," he yelled over the roar of the battle, "Major Reno says you're to fall back on the last position and we'll make a stand there. He says we're too exposed up here."

Weir nodded quickly. For once, he thought, Reno was right. It was going to get awful damn hot up here pretty quick. He resolved they'd at least do this right. Mount a fighting withdrawal. Keep the pressure on. If they turned tail now, the Sioux'd cut'em to ribbons before they got half-way back. He glanced around him and saw that Company K was in the best position to hold off the Sioux. Trotting across the ridge, he yelled to Godfrey.

"Edward, we're pulling back to the last position. I need you to cover the move. When we get a hundred yards back, we'll turn and support you as you pull out, okay?"

Godfrey nodded quickly, and Weir rushed off to get the other companies pulled off the line. Slowly the outfit disengaged as Godfrey's company continued to fire into the curtain of dust that rolled and seethed in front of their position. When the other companies had gotten out, Godfrey began his move to the rear. They fell back slowly, yard by yard, stopping only to load and fire repeated volleys into the nearly invisible enemy. Not everyone made it back. While bunkies helped their wounded mates to hobble to the rear, one man, farrier Vincent Charley, fell unnoticed in the gun smoke and noise and lay bleeding and terrified as he waited, praying for his comrades to find him before the Sioux did. His prayers were not answered.

Hta *(Evening)*
On the Slopes Around the Soldiers

This, Sitting Bull thought, was not a good way to fight. They had killed all the soldiers on Greasy Grass Hill and turned back to finish off the rest of them. But the Little White Chief and his men sat on the top of the hill now and were making little holes in the ground like foxes or prairie dogs. It was harder and harder for the braves to get a good shot at the soldiers. The Lakotas had managed to kill many of the enemy's horses and mules, but now that the *wasichus* had dug into the ground, it seemed that every time a brave stood to shoot he risked being killed or wounded by one of the soldiers. Some of these soldiers were very good with their rifles and could kill a man from a very long distance.

The fight they had had with these people in the late afternoon had not gone very well. The warriors could not often get very close to the soldiers, and every time they did, the white-haired soldier chief would lead a charge that sent the warriors tumbling back down the hillsides and into the ravines. Sitting Bull had watched one of these charges and thought that this soldier chief with the white hair was a very brave man. He looked too old to be a soldier, but there he was, standing upright and walking around behind the other soldiers and seeming to pay no attention to the bullets that passed by him. Sitting Bull thought that the man must have some very strong medicine.

Now the sun was going down behind the hills and still the *wasichus* held out. Fewer and fewer of the warriors stayed to shoot at the whites. Many had already gone back to the camp, some to eat, and some to sleep. Others had gone to gather more of the whites' belongings on Greasy Grass Hill. Many of the younger braves were still excited from the great battle and wanted to feast and dance all night. In the distance Sitting Bull could hear the drums already beating out the rhythms for the dancers. Finally the old man climbed onto his pony and turned back to the camp. It was foolish to stay here much longer. He would have to speak to the other chiefs.

Coming back into the village, Sitting Bull found that everything was in an uproar. People scurried back and forth between the lodges as they prepared for a great night of celebration of their victory. Large fires had been kindled and the aroma of cooking meat filled the air. The drums beat steadily, and everywhere the people sang and boasted of their deeds in the great fight. Nor did he miss the other sounds that floated above the camp —the keening and wailing of those who mourned. Everywhere people were singing death songs, the women weeping as they cut off their hair and gashed their arms and legs in sorrow. Too many had died today. Yes, they had killed or driven off the soldiers, but at what cost?

Sitting Bull was worried. He did not think that all that many warriors had been killed outright, although he knew that more would certainly die in the coming days from the horrible wounds they had sustained. Still, even if the whites had lost three times their numbers, what would be the result? The whites were like the blades of grass that the ponies could eat to the ground, or could be burned off by fire, and the next spring would leap from the ground fresh and plentiful as before. The Lakotas did not grow so fast as the grass. When the next spring came, more white soldiers would come, but the Lakotas who were dead on this ground today would still be dead.

The desultory banging of guns in the distance let him know that at least some of the warriors were keeping a watch on the whites who were still on the bluffs above the river. The old prophet did not waste any time but quickly sent heralds out to the various circles to bring in the fighting chiefs for a talk. He felt that much yet needed to be done and many decisions would have to be made before the sun climbed into the sky again.

An hour later hundreds had assembled in the large yellow-painted council lodge that sat near the center of the village. Even with the sides rolled up for ventilation, the lodge was thick with the smell of sweating, bloodied bodies. The men who had gathered to hear what Tatanka Iyotanka had to say represented every tribe and clan that had fought that day. Some were chiefs, some prophets, some were war leaders. Many bore new wounds from the fight. All were puzzled by the old man's call for a council. The lodge buzzed with their muttered questions.

Satisfied that the village was well represented, Sitting Bull stood before them and waited for the noise to die down. When the rumbling of voices had quieted, Sitting Bull recounted the events of the day and re-minded them all of the vision he had had during the Sun Dance.

"All that I have foretold to you has come to pass," he said solemnly. "The soldiers have fallen upside down into camp, and Wakan Tanka has given for you to kill them on these hills and in this valley just as I said would happen. I sacrificed my flesh in the Sun Dance for this. I made the medicine that gave us this great victory over the whites."

He paused for a moment and looked around at the tired faces of the men who had fought these *wasichus* today. He now had harsh words for them and wanted to make sure that he had their complete attention.

"But," he went on with a fierce tone in his voice, "you have not done all that Wakan Tanka told you to do. You have disregarded his warning not to touch the things of these soldiers. I told you what he said—that if you touched these things they would make slaves of you. You would always covet the white man's things, and it would bring a curse down on this nation. I am ashamed." Sitting Bull was shouting now and staring down at the chiefs who sat around him. "What?" he insisted. "Am I the only true Lakota left in this whole camp?" A murmuring came from the assembled warriors until one of them leaped up and shook his fist at the old man.

"Bah!" Gall shouted. "What is this nonsense you would feed us, old man? Get down off your high horse. The great Sitting Bull. Hah! What a laugh. You gave us this victory, did you? You gave us nothing, prophet." Gall turned to the others and stalked up and down in front of them holding his blood-blackened hands like claws in front of him. "We took this victory with our own hands. We ripped it bleeding from the throats of these *wasichus.*" He turned back to confront Sitting Bull.

"Look at this blood on my hands! Where is the blood on you, old man? I see nothing because you did nothing. You sat here and made medicine while we warriors fought this battle. You have nothing to say to me. When the sun comes up in the morning, we will ride out again and we will finish this job and rub out the rest of them!"

A grumbling roar of approval rippled through the assembled warriors as Gall went back to his place and dropped heavily to the ground, his arms crossed over his chest. The warriors began to talk among themselves, recalling the individual fights they had engaged in during the hard day, boasting of their own exploits or those of their clansmen. The discussion grew louder and more animated as coups were claimed and disputed, the braves showing each other their wounds and displaying trophies taken from the whites.

Sitting Bull was stunned. Gall had always been a close friend and a supporter. He had thought that the recent trouble between them was a passing thing. Now he regretted that he had delayed going to see Gall earlier to resolve their differences. What could have caused Gall to lash out with such bile? What Gall said about him was not true, of course.

Sitting Bull had been in the fight. Many had seen him down near where the soldiers first came. Yes, he thought, I left for a while to make sure the helpless ones were safely away from the fighting, but then I returned to the fight. Normally, Sitting Bull would have overlooked such an outburst, realizing that Gall's heart was bad today with his family now dead. But the fact that the hot words had come in front of the others was unforgivable. Rumors would start, even though Gall's words were false, and the nation would begin to squabble over petty slights.

Sitting Bull looked around and saw that some of the discussions were already getting quite heated and unpleasant as recriminations were hurled back and forth. Several Lakotas were shouting at the Arapahos, claiming that their man Left Hand had killed a Sioux. Brave Bear of the Cheyennes was denouncing the Lakotas for having killed the Cheyennes' war chief Lame-White-Man.

Sitting Bull was horrified. The fight was not even over yet and already they were quarrelling among themselves. This must be what the Wakan Tanka had been trying to warn him of when he had his vision. They had taken the white men's things and they were being made crazy by them. The Lakota had made an opportunity for Gnaskinyan* to work his mischief. It was breaking their medicine, and Gall, by his words, had given the Evil One the invitation to begin sowing discord among the people. As Sitting Bull watched, the warriors began to argue about who would count more coups tomorrow when they went to rub out the rest of the soldiers. It was too much; he had to put a stop to this. Sitting Bull reached down for the pistol One Bull had given him and fired it up into the air while calling for silence.

"Enough!" he shouted. "Where is your reason? Where are your wits? I am ashamed that warriors who have won a great victory over the whites should quarrel over this day like dogs fighting for scraps. You have taken the things of the whites, and they make you crazy so that you forget the helpless ones. You forget why we fought these people. You forget your wives and your children. You forget your aged parents in your foolish pride and your greed for more of the whites' property. Stop this!"

The loud chattering died to a low grumbling sound as many of those present began to consider Sitting Bull's words. Some of the more experienced men recognized the truth of what he said and did what they could

---

* Gnaskinyan, or Crazy Buffalo, was a god. Of all the evil gods, to the Lakota he was to be most feared. He would appear in the midst of the people in the guise of the good buffalo god and cause the people to do evil things. Frequently he was assisted by Iktomi, the trickster, who filled a role very similar to Loki in Norse mythology. The term was also applied to people believed to be crazy.

to restrain the hotter heads among them. Finally the young Cheyenne Wooden Leg stood in Sitting Bull's defense.

"This man is right," Wooden Leg said loudly. "We have had to fight the whites today and may well have to fight them again tomorrow and the next day. If we begin to quarrel among ourselves, we will be like ashes blown by the wind. Our strength will be shattered, and we will be driven from this land for our foolishness. I say we listen to what Sitting Bull has to say and think hard on it before we decide what we will do. He is right to tell us to remember why we fought this battle today."

Before Wooden Leg could resume his seat, another man stood in council. Sitting Bull recognized him as Short Bull, a medicine man for the Oglala and a friend of Crazy Horse's.

"This Shyela," Short Bull said, "is right to speak as he does. Some of us may not like Sitting Bull, but this is not important. What he says should be heard. I do not care if you take the white man's things, for they are just things. But we must be careful that we are not blinded by them and blinded by petty hurts among us. If we do not remember why it is that we have fought, then our eyes will grow dark and we will surely lose our way. That is all I have to say."

The Oglala turned and sat down. Throughout the lodge the grumbling dimmed to a low murmur and finally died as the warriors, nodding, and looking sheepishly at each other, fell silent and took their places once again in council. With order restored, Sitting Bull employed all of his skills as a diplomat and statesman to smooth ruffled feathers and explain the necessity for repressing any personal feuds and jealousies in the face of the threat posed by the invasion of the whites. The chiefs listened and talked among themselves until late in the night as they weighed the problems facing them. Should they move the camp? Should they rub out the whites who were still on the hills? Maybe they should break into smaller bands so that the hunting would be easier and the soldiers would have a hard time finding them again? After much discussion a decision was finally reached, and Sitting Bull stood to summarize the plan they had agreed upon.

"When the sun rises," Sitting Bull said, "we will again attack these *wasichus* who are in their gopher holes on the hill. We will not try to rub them out, but we must keep them afraid and make them stay where they are until the people can move. This will be a hard fight, but the young men who do this must be smart. They cannot get so close that they are killed, but they must keep the whites in their holes and keep them away from the river."

The warriors nodded their agreement. The young men were of no help when it came to moving the camp anyway, and this would keep them out of the way while at the same time keeping the soldiers from the village.

Sitting Bull went on: "Very soon these soldiers will not have any water left, and they will try to get to the river to fill their little water bottles. I do not care if they do this, but they must not get close enough to see the village. If they go to the river, you should try to kill some of them so they do not come close to us. If these soldiers live, they will tell the other whites how powerful the Lakota nation is, and this is good. Maybe they will stay away. But most important, you must try to kill as many of their horses as you can. If they have their horses, they can still chase us, or some of them will be able to follow the camp when it moves. This must not happen."

The warriors nodded their assent. This was a good plan. As they stood to go back to their lodges, Sitting Bull held up his hand to announce a final decision.

"Tell the young men who will shoot at the soldiers tomorrow," he said, "that if they have to choose between killing a soldier or killing a Ree or Crow they should kill the Ree or Crow. Without these people the white soldiers are like men who are blind. They must not be able to find us again."

The council was over, and the chiefs left to go back to talk to their young men and prepare for the day that was to come. As they slipped into the darkness, Sitting Bull glanced at Gall, who, since his outburst, had sat quietly through the rest of the evening, saying nothing and staring at the ground in front of him. As Gall tried to stand, a violent wrenching seized his stomach and he dropped forward onto his hands and knees and vomited into the dirt. Gall stayed crouched in that position for a few moments as vomit and spittle dribbled from his mouth, and Sitting Bull was struck by a thought.

Iktomi the trickster often appeared as a beetle, crawling on the hands and feet of a man. Perhaps Wakan Tanka was telling him that Gall, who had been his friend for so long, was no longer that man. Perhaps Gall had become the trickster. Perhaps his old friend had now become his enemy. The old man was horrified by the thought and watched in disgust as Gall pulled himself to his feet, spit to clear the vomit from his mouth, turned, and walked into the darkness beyond. Sitting Bull watched the man go and listened in the dark to the wailing of the death songs that would continue through the night and haunt him in his dreams.

1000 Hours, 26 June 1876
On Reno's Hill

Lieutenant Varnum was feeling damned irritated at the moment. The firing of the Sioux had died down considerably after sunset. He supposed that they were afraid of being killed in the dark and not being able to find their way to the happy hunting ground or some such nonsense, but still everyone in the outfit was so apprehensive that hardly a man could sleep. Adding to the tension was the constant thrumming of drums and howlings of the Sioux echoing up from the village, which could be discerned by the flickering light of huge bonfires that the Indians had kept stoked throughout the night.

Most of the men kept busy, using every sharp instrument they could find—knives, spoons, forks, tin cups, even halves of canteens they had broken apart—to try to burrow into the hard, rocky soil. Sometime during the night there had been a light rain, but it had amounted to no more than a sprinkle—not enough to relieve the gnawing thirst of the combatants, but enough to dampen their clothes and further increase their misery as the temperature dropped through the night.

Varnum himself, despite his fatigue, had been unable to nod off until sometime after midnight but awoke at three in the morning, surprised to find himself in the arms of Private Siebelder. Apparently, as the first flush of predawn glowed on the hills, the Sioux had resumed their desultory sniping at the troops, and Tony Siebelder had decided that the lieutenant had fallen asleep in a fairly precarious position. Rather than wake the sleeping officer, Siebelder had gathered Varnum up into his arms like a sleeping infant, moved him gently to the rear, and was in the process of laying him in a small depression when Varnum's eyes fluttered open.

"Mornin', Lieutenant!" Siebelder had said cheerily. "Beg pardon, sir, but if ye'd got yer butt shot off, it'd been a hell of a thing."

Varnum yawned widely. "Maybe so, Tony," he had said, "but at least I'd've gotten some decent rest." A bullet zipped through a nearby sagebrush, and Siebelder dropped to the ground, shoved his carbine forward, and squeezed a round off toward an unseen Indian.

"Rest for you, sir, maybe." He spat. "But it'd be old Tony Siebelder'd have t' dig ya a grave, and I ain't feelin' particular energetic today. No offense, sir." Siebelder flipped open his carbine to eject the spent cartridge, and Varnum had to duck to avoid the hot shell casing that somersaulted toward him. Siebelder slammed another cartridge into his weapon and waited for the sniper to show his head. Varnum found that he was more than a little embarrassed as he realized that he had hunched behind a sagebrush no thicker around than his finger and was seriously wondering whether it might be thick enough to deflect a bullet.

So it had continued throughout the morning, with individual warriors popping up from behind a hillock to snap off a couple of rounds and then dropping out of sight again before anyone could draw a bead on the bastards. Sometimes the firing would rattle on for a full thirty minutes, cease suddenly, and then be followed by a thundering of hooves as a group of mounted warriors swooped in to try to shoot down into the defenders or slap one of them with a coup stick. These "raids" were invariably short-lived and never broke through the defenses, but it was unnerving just the same. You could never relax, never let down your guard, not knowing if the next rush would be the one to carry thousands of painted demons howling through the sagebrush.

The sun had not yet reached its zenith when Varnum's luck changed. A small nest of three or four Sioux had managed to crawl to within a hundred yards of their position and were giving the outfit the devil of a time, popping up to pump five or six shots into the horses and mules and then dropping again while the troops ducked and scrambled out of the way. Captain Benteen, who had spent the morning strolling around the perimeter as casually as if he had been walking down Fifth Avenue, was enraged. He had rushed to Varnum's position and hastily organized an assault party.

"By God," Benteen swore, "I'll be damned if I'll let these little pissants shoot any more of my damned mules. Skirmishers into line, let's give 'em hell, boys! . . . *Charge!*"

Whooping, shrieking, firing their carbines from the hip, and waving revolvers, fifty-odd soldiers leapt down the hill toward the hidden snipers, who broke from cover and scampered away. Almost immediately scores of other warriors opened a hot fire on the charging soldiers. Lieutenant Varnum stumbled forward and quickly realized that he had been shot through one leg, the bullet passing clean through the flesh and then, its energy spent, bouncing off the boot on his other leg. As he snatched the revolver he had dropped, Varnum felt himself being hauled upright by Tony Siebelder.

"Come on, Lieutenant," Siebelder hollered. "We're droppin' back an' I don't wanna have t' come out ag'in after ya."

The troops scrambled back up the hill and dropped behind what cover they could find as bullets whined and zipped through the air, clipping off sagebrush twigs and spattering the dust all around them. Lieutenant Varnum managed to roll into a shallow hole in the company of a pair of privates who were fairly well occupied in trying to keep the Indians' heads down by judicious use of their carbines. Rolling onto his back, the lieutenant tried to examine his legs to see how badly he was wounded. His left leg was sore, but his right leg throbbed with pain, and he fully expected to see bone protruding from the wound. But every time he tried to draw one leg or the other up to take a closer look, a bullet would cut into the ground right next to him so that he found he was jerking spasmodically to try to keep from being hit, like some tenderfoot made to dance by a gunfighter's six-shooter in a dime novel. The lieutenant heard a suppressed chuckling and looked up in time to see one of his fellow soldiers, Private George Mask, burst into laughter at his superior officer's supine jig. Varnum flushed angrily and thought, What the hell does he think's so damned funny?

"You damned chucklehead," Varnum barked, but even as he did, he noticed that Private Mask had abruptly fallen silent. For a second Varnum was puzzled. It seemed the private had fallen sound asleep in mid-guffaw, for his eyes were closed and his mouth hung open slackly. It was only when he noticed the thin trickle of blood oozing out from under the man's cap that Varnum realized that the laughing private had been shot clean through the top of his head and was stone dead.

After a few minutes the heavy firing died down again to a smattering of shots as the Sioux settled back to the serious business of killing the horses and pack mules. The soldiers hunkered into their shallow depressions and waited. Captain Benteen, known to be a bearcat for nerve, strode openly about the perimeter, seemingly unconcerned by the bullets that whined overhead or slapped into the dust around him. Benteen seemed to be everywhere: talking to the wounded, examining those horses and mules that still survived, strolling behind the shallow rifle pits encouraging the men to conserve ammunition and make every shot count. As he passed along the line of his own company, he noticed Sergeant Pahl rising onto his knees and sighting his carbine at a small knoll two hundred yards away. Benteen rushed over to the man and pushed him bodily to the ground just as a bullet pinged off a nearby rock.

"Damn it, Sergeant Pahl," Benteen roared. "I told you to keep down, and by God I expect you to do it."

Pahl rolled onto his back and grinned up at the old soldier, "Well, hell, Cap'n. Whyn't ye keep down yer own self. Ye're drawin' fire."

Benteen just shook his head. "Oh, never mind about me, old man," he mumbled distractedly. "Mother sewed some good medicine into my coat before we left. I'll be fine." Turning on his heel, Benteen strolled off toward the makeshift aid station, where Dr. Porter was doing his best to make the wounded more comfortable. As the captain wandered off, Sergeant Pahl shook his head and went back to his personal duel with an Arapaho sniper.

Partially concealed by a ring of hardtack boxes, battered pack saddles, and dead mules, the aid station was only slightly safer than the rest of the hilltop. During the night the wounded had consumed what little was left of the water and felt extremely fortunate when someone discovered a few cans of tomatoes on one of the dead pack mules. These had been punctured and the juice shared out among the more seriously wounded. The situation had become so grim that during the day a group of men volunteered to make a try for some water. With the outfit's best marksmen providing cover, seven troopers slid and tumbled down through a narrow ravine festooned with as many canteens as they could carry. The Sioux had tried to cut them off and managed to kill one man and wound two others, but the marksmen under Captain French's direction made the Sioux pay dearly for this minor success. The water party was just straggling back in with their booty when Benteen arrived. As the soldiers rolled in over the dead mules, dragging the canteens behind them, Porter thought again about how the animals were already bloating in the hot sun. Between the gaseous, decaying corpses and the smell of urine, excrement, and suppurating wounds, the stench was becoming damn near unbearable. The doctor made a mental note to speak with Major Reno about trying to move this position farther away from the rotting, flyblown carcasses.

"Nicely done, lads," Benteen congratulated them. "Dr. Porter, take what you need for the wounded. Whatever can be spared we'll share out among the rest of the boys." The captain didn't wait for a reply, but quickly moved off to check on Lieutenant Wallace's men.

Porter nodded absently but was more interested at the moment in the severe wound that Saddler Private Madden had received while bringing in the water. Mike Madden was in pretty bad shape. A .44-caliber bullet had ripped through his leg just below the knee, the soft lead mushrooming as it entered. The bullet had shattered the bone and done spectacular damage to the muscle and tissue around it. Porter grimaced as he prodded gently at the wound and pronounced his diagnosis.

"Madden, old son," Porter explained quietly, "she's too bad to save. I'm going to have to cut this leg off if you want to live to tell your grandchildren about this fight."

Madden moaned quietly but nodded.

"I'm afraid," Porter went on, "we don't have any anesthetics here to dull the pain, son. This'll hurt like hell. I'm sorry, but it can't be helped." Madden sucked in a deep breath as the surgeon crawled away to fetch his case of instruments and Madden's friends gathered around to help hold him down when the surgery started. Before Porter could return, First Sergeant John Ryan slipped into the small depression, a pair of saddlebags in one hand.

"Madden, ye damned blackguard," Ryan said, "just lookit what I've found stashed in yer saddlebags." Ryan reached into one of the bags and produced a sizable metal flask, which he unscrewed with a flourish as he passed it under his nose. "As I suspected, ye dirty no-good. Ye've been haulin' the creature wid ye. By God, I've a mind to bring ye up on charges." The men nearby sat hushed and motionless as Ryan shook the flask in Madden's face.

"Well," Ryan went on, "as ye done a fair decent job o' fetchin' up water, I've a mind to let ye off easy this time. Here, take this damned stuff and get rid o' it afore yon Cap'n Benteen's wise to ye. I'll say n'more."

Ryan shoved the flask into Madden's hand and, slithering over a dead mule, disappeared toward the firing line. Madden looked around at his friends and raised the flask in salute. He knew full well that the saddlebags were not his.

"Oh, an he's a darlin' man so's the first sergeant, boys," Madden said. "*Sláinte!*" Without another word he tipped back the metal can, draining the contents in seconds.

Dr. Porter arrived with his instruments just as Madden was downing the last few drops of the fiery liquid.

"Madden, ye damned scamp!"

"Ah, Dr. Porter, sir," Madden slurred. "It's ready I am. Cut away, sir."

Shaking his head, Porter set to work and sawed rapidly through the gory mess until the shattered limb came away in a corporal's hands. The young corporal blanched noticeably and then hurled the severed limb as far away as he could.

The spurred boot caught briefly on a sagebrush, causing the limb to flip once before it cartwheeled down a ravine, narrowly missing the head of a young Cheyenne who had been trying to belly up close enough for another shot at the bluecoats. The young brave was oddly unnerved by the flying limb and decided to abandon his plan. It was getting to be too much when these crazy *wasichus* began throwing their body parts at him.

Bandaging up Madden's damaged stump as best as he could, the sweating Dr. Porter looked down at his patient, who had grown pale and feverish.

"Mike," Porter asked quietly, "how are you feeling, son?"

Madden didn't answer for a moment but lay there panting and blowing out his cheeks, his knuckles white where they were wrapped tightly around his empty flask. Finally he held the metal object up toward the surgeon and lifted his head slightly.

"Mm-ehh, Doctor," he whispered huskily, "gimme another drink o' whiskey an ye kin cut off me other leg."

The day wore on. The sun rose higher, arched over the besieged hilltop, and began its slow descent into the western skies. Under its fierce rays the ground baked hard and brittle while men and animals broiled in the intense glare. The hills shimmered in the heat, and the soldiers sweat until they were sure that all moisture was sucked from their bodies and there was nothing but their blood left to ooze from their pores. Every mouth was bone-dry as the men sucked on pebbles or chewed on grass to try to stimulate some saliva. Their tongues were swollen, and when they tried to chew hardtack, they wound up blowing the crumbs from their mouths like so much fine ground flour. All around them the rifles of the Sioux popped and cracked in the still air until the soldiers felt sure they would go mad with the tension and monotony. It was not until the sun began its orange descent behind the distant hills that the shooting began to trickle off to an irregular pop every few minutes.

Emboldened by the lull in firing, Lieutenant Nick Wallace hauled himself upright and wandered over to visit his old friend. He found Varnum lying behind a sagebrush, his right leg pulled up so that he could rub his sore ankle.

"Hey, Charlie," he said, "ain't that the wrong leg?" Wallace had noticed the bloodstained bandage on his friend's left leg. Varnum looked up at Wallace, a pained expression on his face.

"Hell, Nick," he said, "the damn bullet went clean through that one and it don't bother me much at all. It only bounced off this leg, but I swear it hurts like hell." Wallace just grinned and gazed off toward the valley floor.

"What the hell?" Wallace exclaimed. "Hey, Charlie, lookit this, willya."

He leaned over to pull Varnum to his feet, and the two watched in silence as a huge dust cloud rose slowly into the air below them. With Varnum leaning heavily on Wallace, the two officers strained to see through the dusty haze. After a moment they could just make out a huge column of people and animals on the move. The camp was leaving, moving away from them. To Varnum it looked like a huge army on the march, as thousands of ponies moved toward the setting sun, the long poles of the travois dragging in the dirt and stirring it into a billowing, brown fog into which the column soon disappeared from view. As the sun set, the brown cloud settled back onto the valley floor. The firing had stopped and the valley of the Little Bighorn was empty.

1100 Hours, 27 June 1876
In the Valley of the Little Bighorn

Muggins Taylor breathed deeply and nudged his horse forward. He sank easily into the saddle and leaned forward slightly, keeping a tight hold on the reins while easing back the hammers on his shotgun. If anything went wrong, he wanted to be damn sure he was able to get out quickly. His eyes narrowed to slits, and his head turned constantly to the left and right as he scanned the open plain for anything even slightly suspicious.

Scouting for the Army was an iffy thing at best, and Muggins was of the opinion that there were only two kinds of scouts, old scouts and bold scouts. Muggins planned to be one of the old ones and so took his time as he eased his mount slowly across the valley floor. Scattered in every direction was evidence that a large camp had been here shortly before. Wherever he looked, Taylor saw broken lodgepoles, ruined and blood-stained bits of clothing, rusted camp kettles, even shattered weapons. Littered throughout were innumerable piles of fairly fresh horse dung amid a crazy-quilt pattern of crisscrossing travois drags. It must have been one hell of a large camp.

Willy, Muggins's horse, was skittish. His nostrils were flared and he tossed his head back, constantly fighting against the bit as if he wanted nothing better than to move back the way he had come. It was only with a firm hand and the cautious use of his spurs that Taylor was able to keep the animal heading toward the few lodges that stood in the center of the valley floor. Muggins could understand the horse's reluctance, for he himself could already smell the rank stench of corruption. Buzzards wheeling lazily overhead had alerted him miles before, but it was only now that he was able to get a closer look at the objects of their attention. Some of the scavengers were directly overhead, but most were slightly off to his left and on the other side of the river.

Muggins decided he'd leave that for later. Best to concentrate on this side of the river first. As he drew up in front of the first tipi, the smell of death was strong in his nostrils, and he figured that it and the few others scattered around the valley were burial lodges. He didn't much care for the idea but knew he would have to look inside sooner or later, so he slipped lightly from the saddle and, drawing his hunting knife, slashed a long rent in the side of the lodge.

The stench was nearly overpowering, and he drew back gagging for a moment before slashing a wider opening and gingerly easing the hides aside with the barrel of the shotgun. As he had thought, several scaffolds had been erected inside and bore the bodies of a number of dead warriors. He looked around at the other lodges and calculated that some forty "good Indians" had been left behind when the rest of them decamped. Judging from the pony droppings and the still-warm coals in the fire pits, they hadn't been gone more than a day.

Well, Muggins told himself, they sure as hell didn't move on 'cause it smells so sweet around here. Somebody must've give 'em one hell of a farewell party.

Judging from the wide trail that led out of the valley, they were moving north and west—toward the White Mountains and away from Crook, Custer, and Gibbon too. So, he thought, the birds managed to fly the net after all. General Terry would not be happy about this. Satisfied that none of the hostiles had hung back with a welcoming party, he un-cocked his shotgun and heaved himself back into the saddle. Moving slowly among the litter-strewn campsites, he began to recognize bits of Army equipment, remains of shirts, torn uniform parts, bits of McClellan saddles, even a Springfield carbine with its butt stock broken clean in two and smeared with a black sticky substance that had attracted a host of flies.

The insects were a genuine nuisance, the black clouds of buzzing flies swarming around in droves. Muggins thought there must be millions of them and cursed vehemently as he wiped them from his face and spit one out of his mouth. God, the stink was tremendous! The flies and the smell were so bad that he had almost forgotten about the buzzards until he got down to the river, intending to let Willy have a drink. Then he looked up and got his first real glimpse of Greasy Grass Hill.

"Oh, my God!" Even Muggins Taylor was stunned by the sight that greeted his incredulous eyes. He waded Willy across the Little Bighorn and began to count.

By the time Muggins had finished counting and crossed back across the river, the lead elements of Gibbon's column were just moving into the northern end of the valley. Taylor caught sight of the advance scouts and fired off one barrel of his shotgun, then rode to the center of the deserted campsite and waved his hat in the air. Lieutenant James Bradley and a detachment of six troopers of the Second Cavalry galloped out ahead of the column to catch up with their scout. Taylor waited for them a few yards away from the first lodge, where Bradley reined up in front of him.

"Jesus, Muggins," Bradley said, wrinkling his nose in distaste. "Either you need a bath worse than I thought or you found a few good Indians up here."

The scout nodded quietly. "Yes, sir, Mr. Bradley," Muggins said, twitching his head toward the lodge, "they's a few of 'em in there an' they're about as good as they come."

Immediately the young troopers with the lieutenant whooped and started forward, intending to rip the structure apart, until their sergeant swung his horse around in front of them and fired his revolver into the ground.

"As ye were," the sergeant growled. "Get yer sore asses back inta line, ye slovenly soldiers. I'll tell ye when ye've got leave t'go on a tear! G'wan! Git!" The troopers reined back on their mounts and filed solemnly back behind the lieutenant, who was self-consciously pulling at his nose.

"Damn, Muggins," Bradley said, "can't we get a bit further upwind of these cusses? Christ, what a stench. It's worse'n when they're alive." Taylor nodded and led the lieutenant off a few yards, motioning for the sergeant to keep the rest of the men back.

"Here we go, Mr. Bradley," Taylor said quietly as he reached into one of his saddlebags and pulled out a small metal flask from which he took a long pull before offering it to the lieutenant. "But ye'd best get used to the smell."

Bradley waved the flask away and looked at the man curiously.

"Say, Muggins," Bradley said, "where the hell's Custer's outfit? I thought they were supposed to be here this morning?"

"Oh, General Custer's outfit is here all right, Lieutenant," Muggins said slowly as he turned his horse toward the river. "Come on along, Mr. Bradley, and stay close. I'm gonna keep this here flask handy, as you might be changin' your mind about havin' a pull pretty soon."

One hour later Gibbon's column arrived in the valley with Grasshopper Jim Brisbin's cavalry detachment leading the way. They had half-expected to run into Custer and his regiment and were frankly puzzled that they had not yet encountered the Sioux. When they stumbled into the remains of the village, they were astonished. It must have been huge, like a small city. Everywhere were the traces of lodge sites and campfires. In fact, several lodges were still standing. When the men ventured cautiously forward to peer into them, they discovered the first of the dead. These were the Sioux. Major Brisbin counted thirty-eight corpses in the various lodges and all newly dead. It was obvious that there had been some sort of a fight, but with whom? Again and again the question was asked, "Where's Custer?"

Major Brisbin was just posing this question to General Terry and Colonel Gibbon when he caught sight of Lieutenant Bradley in the company of Muggins Taylor splashing back across the Little Bighorn River. Brisbin thought that Bradley looked awfully white and wondered if the heat was getting to him. Maybe he would suggest that Bradley head back to the river and take a rest under the trees for a bit.

"Ahh, Mr. Bradley, Mr. Taylor," General Terry said brightly. "Capital! I say, have you gentlemen run across General Custer's people yet?"

The two sat strangely quiet for a moment when Colonel Gibbon repeated the question and added one of his own.

"Well, Muggins," Gibbon said, "did you come across Custer? And what the hell are all of those rocks doing on the other side of the river?" Taylor shifted a quid to his other cheek and spat a thin stream of tobacco juice into the dust. Finally, Muggins spat out the rest of his chaw and cleared his throat.

"They're not rocks, sir," he said quietly. "That's the Seventh Cavalry."

The soldiers who sweated under the hot Montana sun did not have their hearts in their task. It was ungodly hard work. With few shovels in the command and the ground baked to the hardness of rock, it took a Herculean effort to get down the eighteen inches that was considered the minimum depth required to keep the dead out of the reach of scavengers. Some men dug while their comrades tried to gather the dead.

Some of the dead had laid out in the full sun for two days now and had quickly bloated beyond any hope of recognition. The men looked for whatever clues they could find. They looked for anything that was familiar: a shirt that someone's mother had sewn lovingly for an absent son, an irregular patch on a worn pair of boots, an unusual birthmark, a tattoo, a scar received in a foolish brawl among friends in the Enlisted Men's Club at Fort Laramie or in a close call with a Cheyenne at Washita. They looked for journals, for letters from wives and sweethearts who would not know for weeks what had happened to their husbands and loved ones, who could never be told how they really died.

But most of the dead were unknown. They looked nothing like they had in life. The Montana sun and a host of scavengers had done their work well. In those few instances when a man was recognized, a small slip of paper was rolled up into empty cartridge cases, which were then pounded into a stake at the head of a heap of dirt and rocks. Most of the slips read simply:

U.S. Soldier. 7th Cavalry. Fell here. June 25, 1876

Great care had to be taken when moving the bodies the few inches to their shallow graves, for the slightest jar could cause a distended stomach or bowel to burst, and spew noxious gases. Most of the men had tied their bandannas over their noses against the stench, but that didn't seem to help much.

With their uniforms whitened by the dust, they looked for all the world like phantoms as they moved drunkenly about the littered hillside and bent to the task of collecting and burying what remained of their friends and comrades. Considering the number of men working on this hot afternoon, the air was strangely silent. There were no jokes, no banter, no sergeants bawling out young recruits, nothing of what one might expect of an Army work party. If one listened hard, he could hear the muffled sobbing of men whose hearts were broken. Some talked quietly, some prayed, some swore vengeance through their tears, but mostly they concentrated on the job at hand. Or tried not to, as the case might be, for it was terrible work.

What the victorious tribesmen had done to the dead horrified the living. Heads, legs, arms, private parts, had been torn from the trunks and scattered about the hillside. Faces were crushed to jelly, eyeballs dug from sockets and laid on rocks. Entrails had been torn from body cavities and strewn over sagebushes. Many of the bodies had the appearance of porcupines, they were stuck with so many arrows. Several different warriors had fired at least one shaft into each body to mark his tribe's participation in the killing.

General Alfred Terry and Colonel John Gibbon were stunned. They had seen much of death in the Civil War. Mutilation by shellfire was, in fact, common, but never had they seen bodies that had been so disfigured deliberately by human hands. The thought that a man could do this to another human turned their stomachs.

The men had already counted 197 dead on the field and only just discovered Reno's dead in the treeline when they heard a ragged cheering from the top of the bluffs and looked up to see Lieutenant Charles Varnum sliding down the face of the hill in the company of Captain Weir. Far above them the survivors of Reno's and Benteen's battalions waved their hats and screamed themselves hoarse at the sight of their arriving comrades.

General Terry's relief at the sight of these survivors was nearly palpable. He had feared that the entire regiment was wiped out and was nearly ecstatic to hear that most of seven companies had managed to hold out against the hordes of Sioux and Cheyennes who had wiped out the men with Custer. Varnum and Weir, however, were stunned to hear what had happened to their comrades. They had felt sure that the outfit had merely been driven off to the north and fully expected to meet their commander when they came down from the hill. The news was almost too much for Weir to take. He went pale, tears staring from his eyes, as Muggins Taylor pointed up at the ragged hillside.

Weir sobbed, staring at the corpses, many of which had been stripped naked. "Oh," he said, "how white they look!" and he lapsed into silence. Varnum's eyes dropped to the ground. Gibbon and Terry were embarrassed by the sight of the veteran soldier standing there, his fists clenched by his sides and his shoulders heaving silently as noiseless tears rolled down his pale, powder-grimed cheeks.

Later that day, as the sun was just dipping toward the horizon, an exhausted Varnum sat by the river on a fallen tree. Colonel Gibbon, Grasshopper Jim, and young Lieutenant Bradley sat nearby talking quietly among themselves. A lone soldier passed by, and Varnum looked up to see a familiar trooper leading a wounded and limping horse.

"Trooper," Varnum asked quietly, "isn't that Colonel Keogh's horse?"

Private Gustave Korn stood to attention, tears staining his square, Teutonic features.

"Ja, sir," he said quietly, rubbing the horse gently on the muzzle, "it's Comanche. He's bad hurt, Lieutenant, but you won't let dem shoot her, ja?" Korn's eyes pleaded with the young officer.

"Dem savages have killed *mein* Schatz. She was a sweet thing, Lieutenant. I take Comanche and make him better, you bet. Please, Herr Lieutenant, don't you let dem shoot him."

Varnum found he could not speak. Comanche was the only thing that lived on this field from all of the five other companies that had ridden with them just two days before. The lieutenant glanced at Colonel Gibbon and stifled a sob that welled in his chest and threatened to choke him. John Gibbon and the others stood and walked slowly over to the horse, which they saw was scarred from several bullet and arrow wounds. Gibbon rubbed the animal between the ears and looked down at the stout German private.

"What's your name, son?" Gibbon asked.

"Private Gustave Korn, Company I, Seventh Cavalry, sir!"

"Private Korn," Gibbon said, "I believe General Terry would consider it a personal favor if you would be kind enough to escort this fine animal to the rear and see that his wounds are properly dressed. I am sure that some water and a few oats would not be amiss, if you wouldn't mind."

Gussy Korn saluted smartly and blinked his eyes, trying in vain to keep the tears from rolling down his cheeks. Colonel Gibbon, Lieutenant Bradley, and Major Brisbin drew themselves up and returned Korn's salute. The group stood in silence as the lone survivor of Custer's battalion was led slowly from the field.

Lieutenant Charles Varnum watched transfixed as Korn and his charge picked their way through the littered field. The sun was just beginning to set, and the large orange ball silhouetted the pair as they moved slowly toward their comrades. Custer's luck. What had happened? How had everything gone so wrong? Varnum's tired brain reeled. It was all too much to comprehend. It wasn't just the general, but Benny and Tosh, Keogh and Fresh, Tom, Autie Reed, Boston, Mitch Bouyer, Queen's Own, and Charley Reynolds. All gone.

What will we do now? he asked himself. Where will we go? But the questions remained unanswered. He felt drained. Empty. Lost. What was the difference between triumph and disaster? Was life so fragile? Everything dependent on a simple roll of the dice? A turn of the card? Was it all just luck? What about Custer's luck? It was all so confusing, so arbitrary. You never knew where the road was going to lead. He knew only that he had to go on.

AFTERWARD
"Walking the Black Road"

RECESSIONAL

The black road goes from where the thunder beings live to where the sun continually shines, a fearful road, a road of troubles and of war.

Black Elk, Oglala Lakota

That was a long time ago. I am old now and my mind has changed. I would rather see my people living in houses and singing and dancing. You have talked to me about fighting, and I have told you of the time long ago. All that is past.

Two Moon, Northern Cheyenne

Fading Voices

On the sultry evening of 5 July a number of the wives of Seventh Cavalry officers had gathered in the Custers' parlor at Fort Abraham Lincoln in the Dakota Territory. There had been no news of the expedition for days, and some of the women had become fretful. Somebody observed that the steamboat *Josephine* would be leaving for the Yellowstone the next day, and an impromptu excursion was planned. Mrs. McIntosh suggested that they assemble picnic lunches and some traveling clothes so that they could surprise their husbands as they came in from the field. Despite the lighthearted nature of the plan, the atmosphere remained inexplicably glum. Libby Custer thought that some music might help to ease the tension, and they gathered around the piano, where Maggie Calhoun picked out the notes to "The Girl I Left Behind Me" as the others sang.

But the next song was a hymn, and halfway through "Nearer My God to Thee" Nettie Smith began to sob quietly to herself and rushed from the room. Annie Yates and Libby tried to comfort her but were themselves depressed and decided to end the evening. The ladies bid their farewells, and Libby retired to her room, where she found herself unable to sleep. Maggie decided to spend the night in a spare bedroom. Several hours later there was a knock at the back door. Libby rushed downstairs in her dressing gown and pushed past her cook Eliza to be confronted by Captain McGaskey, Dr. Middleton, and Lieutenant Gurley. Above the dress uniforms their faces were grim.

A few minutes later Maggie Calhoun stumbled into the parlor where Libby, despite the oppressive heat, had wrapped herself in a shawl. Maggie took one look at their faces and knew immediately that the news all had dreaded had finally arrived.

"Come, Maggie," Libby said quietly. "We must be brave. There will be others to notify and I will need your help."

While rumors circulated the country, the definitive news of the disaster on the Little Bighorn did not reach the East Coast for several days. The timing could not have been worse, for the headlines broke during the week of the Fourth of July 1876. A great Centennial Exposition was being staged in

Philadelphia, and throughout the country celebrations were well under-way. The festive crowds were stunned by the news. The nation sank into mourning, and church bells rang out the *Te Deum* in cities, towns, and villages nationwide.

President Grant was furious. While Custer had been a thorn in his side when he was alive, Custer dead was a damned serious embarrassment. With his administration rocked by scandals that reached into his cabinet as well as his immediate family, and the nation still reeling from the Panic of 1873, a military disaster was the last thing he needed. The nation was outraged and demanded immediate and ruthless action. The Army had been grossly underfunded and a terrible price had been paid. At the Little Bighorn the tiny U.S. Army had lost sixteen officers, or 1 percent of the entire officer corps, killed in action. Artist Thomas Nast launched a series of scathing political cartoons that further fueled the nation's anger.

Spurred by public outrage, Congress quickly found the additional funds for the Army and passed the Sioux appropriation bill, forcing the Sioux to give up the remainder of their precious Black Hills. Native Americans who were already on the reservations did not fare any better, as the government seized all weapons and ponies.

For the Lakota nation the consequences were even worse. So great was the fury of the white population that the Army was forced into a campaign that would give the hostile tribes no rest. As the Sioux and their allies retreated from the valley of the Little Bighorn, the Army followed them relentlessly. Throughout the fall and into the winter of 1876–77, the Army pursued the hostile bands. For the Lakota and their allies there could be no escape. At Slim Buttes, Dull Knife, Warbonnet Creek, Wolf Mountain, and Lame Deer, the Army battled with the remnants of the Lakota nation. More warriors were killed, supplies of buffalo meat seized, lodges, ponies, and buffalo robes destroyed, and the survivors left destitute, with nothing to protect them from the rapidly approaching winter.

The tribes began to break into factions, some wanting to continue the war, others demanding that they sue for whatever peace they could still get. Personal feuds erupted between their leaders. Old friends became bitter enemies. Small bands broke away from the circles and moved to the agencies, soon to be followed by hundreds more. By May of 1877 even Crazy Horse had surrendered and gone onto the hated "white man's is-land," and Sitting Bull, with what few followers he had left, had fled across the border into Canada. The Lakota nation had disintegrated.

On 19 July 1881, Sitting Bull and his followers, now numbering but 44 men and 143 women and children, arrived at Fort Buford in the Dakota Territory. In a short ceremony the following day he handed his rifle to his young son Crow Foot. The boy then handed the rifle to the post commander, Major David Brotherton.

With his heart breaking, Sitting Bull looked at Brotherton and said: "I surrender this rifle to you through my young son, whom I now desire to teach in this manner that he has become a friend of the Americans. I wish him to learn the habits of the whites and to be educated as their sons are educated. I wish it to be remembered that I was the last man of my tribe to surrender my rifle. This boy has given it to you and now he wants to know how he is going to make a living."

The Survivors

Lieutenant Charles Varnum continued on active service with the Seventh Cavalry and fought at the battle of Wounded Knee alongside his old friend Nick Wallace; he was awarded the Congressional Medal of Honor for that action. He later served with the Ninth and Fourth Cavalry Regiments, deployed to Cuba during the Spanish-American War, and retired as a lieutenant colonel, only to be recalled for duty during World War I. He retired as a colonel and died at the Presidio of San Francisco in 1936.

Gall (Pizi) followed Sitting Bull into exile but, as Rain-in-the-Face later told an interviewer, following the confrontation after the battle "there was always bad blood between them." In 1880 he broke entirely away from Sitting Bull's band and returned to the United States, surrendering at the Poplar River Agency on 3 January 1881. Settling at Standing Rock Agency, he became close friends with Agent J. F. McLaughlin, an advocate of government education for Sioux children. In 1889 he became a judge of the Court of Indian Offenses and strongly opposed Sitting Bull's influence. He died quietly at home in 1894.

Major Marcus Reno never recovered from the defeat at the Little Bighorn. Frequently blamed for not having pressed home the initial charge or later ridden to the support of Custer's battalion, he became a pariah in the Army. In 1879 he asked for and received a court of inquiry, which largely absolved him from any blame. A heavy drinker, Reno sank deeper into alcoholism, and his behavior became more erratic. He was finally court-martialed for conduct "prejudicial to good order and discipline" and dismissed from the Army He died in Washington, D.C. on 1 April 1889 at age fifty-four.

Captain Frederick Benteen would also live under the cloud of the Little Bighorn. While all who saw him in action on Reno's Hill admitted that he, more than any other man, was responsible for the survival of the units trapped on that hilltop, several officers would accuse him of having "lollygagged" and thus left Custer and his battalion to its fate. His acerbic nature and acid tongue earned him a host of enemies and detractors. He continued to serve with the Seventh Cavalry throughout the Nez Percé campaign and received a brevet promotion to brigadier general in 1890. He died on 22 June 1898 at the age of sixty-three.

Captain Thomas Bell Weir was as much a casualty of the Little Bighorn as any man who died on the field. After the fight he became increasingly morose and depressed and his health failed rapidly. He died suddenly in December of 1876 at age thirty-eight.

Captain Myles Moylan continued to serve with the Seventh Cavalry and was awarded the Medal of Honor for gallantry in action at the battle of Bear Paw Mountain in December of 1877. He fought at the battle of Wounded Knee and retired as a major in 1892.

Lieutenant George D. "Nick" Wallace continued to serve with the Seventh Cavalry throughout the Indian Wars. He was promoted to captain and was in command of a company when he was killed in action at the battle of Wounded Knee in 1890 at age forty-one.

Lieutenant E. S. Godfrey continued to serve throughout the Indian Wars and fought at the battle of Wounded Knee. For the duration of his life he remained a staunch defender of Custer. He retired as a brigadier general in 1907.

Lieutenant Winfield Scott Edgerly served throughout the Indian Wars and fought at the battle of Wounded Knee. He later served in the Spanish-American War and retired as a brigadier general in 1909. He returned to active service for a brief period during World War I.

Orderly Trumpeter John Martin (Giovanni Martini) did not leave the Army as he had planned. Instead, he remained on active service for most of his adult life. He even named one of his two sons after Lieutenant Colonel Custer. After thirty years of service Martin retired as a sergeant in 1904 and found a job as a ticket agent for the New York subway system. He died on Christmas Eve of 1924, at his home in Brooklyn.

Private Gustave Korn decided that he too would remain in the Army and continued to serve with the Seventh Cavalry for the rest of his career. He became a superb blacksmith and assumed an additional duty as the permanent caretaker of Captain Myles Keogh's horse Comanche. Sergeant Korn was killed in action at the battle of Wounded Knee in 1890.

Comanche, Captain Keogh's claybank gelding, became a sort of regimental icon for the Seventh Cavalry. Officially retired from active service, he was trotted out only for special ceremonies, allowed to live out his life in ease and comfort, a pampered and much-loved pet of the Seventh Cavalry. He was allowed to scavenge through the garbage and was even fed beer by the enlisted mess. When his caretaker and friend Gustave Korn was killed in action, Comanche refused to eat, grew morose, and soon died. The regimental blacksmith noted in his diary, ". . . in memory of the old veteran horse who died at one thirty o'clock with the colic in his stall while I had my hand on his pulse and looking him in the eye—this night to be long remembered."

Two Moon (Ishi' eyo Nissi), Cheyenne, and his people followed Crazy Horse's band of Oglalas until they surrendered in May of 1877. Two Moon soon realized that continued resistance was futile and surrendered to General Nelson Miles at Fort Keogh, Dakota Territory. He and his friend Wooden Leg later became scouts for the U.S. Army and helped to subdue the remaining hostile Sioux. He served with distinction in the campaign against the Nez Percé. His distinguished profile would later appear on the famous buffalo nickel. He died quietly at home in 1917.

Little Wolf (Okom Kakit), Cheyenne, whose band finally reached the village on the Little Bighorn on the evening of 25 June 1876, helped in the fight against Reno and Benteen. After the battle he joined the Cheyenne chief Dull Knife and his band, and eluded the Army until Dull Knife was finally killed. In 1877, Little Wolf surrendered to his old friend Two Moon and followed him to Fort Keogh, where he signed on as a scout for the U.S. Army. When his daughter was abused by another Cheyenne, he killed the man and went into voluntary exile on the Powder River. He died, still an exile, in 1904.

Crazy Horse (Tashunka Witko), Oglala, following the battle of the Little Bighorn, split off from Sitting Bull to lead the Oglalas and Cheyennes in a running fight against the pursuing General Nelson Miles. But the war soon exhausted the remaining warriors, and on 6 May 1877 he and his followers surrendered at Fort Robinson, Nebraska. Some rival chiefs felt that Crazy Horse was receiving favored treatment, and discord was sown among the agency Sioux. Arrested for a minor infraction of agency rules on 5 September 1877, Crazy Horse resisted and was killed by a bayonet thrust while his arms were held by his cousin and former friend, Little-Big-Man.

Sitting Bull (Tatanka Iyotanka), Hunkpapa, spent several years in Canadian exile, but the disappearance of the buffalo soon threatened his people with starvation. Competing for scarce resources, the native tribes of Canada became increasingly hostile toward the Sioux, and in desperation Sitting Bull returned to the United States to surrender himself at Fort Buford on 20 July 1881. He was imprisoned for a time and then sent to the Standing Rock Agency in 1883. For a brief period in 1885 he and his friend Rain-in-the-Face toured with W. F. "Buffalo Bill" Cody's Wild West Show but soon returned to the reservation. In December of 1890 the Sioux experienced a surge of interest in a new religious movement called the Ghost Dance, which promised the raising of the dead and the return of the great buffalo herds. This movement became a focus of resistance to further encroachment by the *wasichus*. Some whites suspected that Sitting Bull would use the Ghost Dance to foment another Indian war. At the Standing Rock Indian Reservation, Agent J. F. McLaughlin, fearful of Sitting Bull's influence, and urged on by rival chiefs, sent a squad of Sioux Indian Police under the command of Lieutenant Bull Head and Sergeant Red Tomahawk to arrest the old man at his cabin. A gunfight broke out, and Sitting Bull and his fourteen-year-old son Crow Foot were killed. Lieutenant Bull Head, who was killed while trying to make the arrest, had fought alongside Sitting Bull at the Little Bighorn.

Not long before his death, and as the reality of his captivity began to sink in, Sitting Bull composed a song that expressed his growing sense of despair. It seems an appropriate epitaph for the Plains Indians:

> *A warrior*
> *I have been*
> *Now*
> *It is all over*
> *A hard time*
> *I have.*